Wolfsbane
CRAIG THOMAS

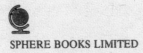

SPHERE BOOKS LIMITED

First published in Great Britain by
Michael Joseph Ltd 1978
Copyright © Craig Thomas 1978
Published by Sphere Books Ltd 1979
27 Wright's Lane, London W8 5SW
Reprinted 1979 (three times), 1980, 1981, 1983 (three times),
1984 (twice), 1985, 1986

Publisher's Note

This novel is a work of fiction. Names, characters, places and
incidents are either the product of the author's imagination
or are used fictitiously, and any resemblance to actual persons,
living or dead, events, or locales is entirely coincidental.

TRADE
MARK

Set in Monotype Times

Printed and bound in Great Britain by
Collins, Glasgow

For
Ada and Wilf

ACKNOWLEDGEMENTS

My thanks to T.R.J. for procuring the documents in the case.
My thanks also to Peter Payne, who arranged a boating incident.

Grateful acknowledgement is made for permission to quote from the following
'Old Friends' © Paul Simon, used with permission.
'Burnt Norton', 'Little Gidding' and 'The Dry Salvages' in *Four Quartets* by T. S. Eliot © 1943 by T. S. Eliot, renewed 1971 by Esme Valerie Eliot. Reprinted by permission of Harcourt Brace Jovanovich Inc,

It was
A time of innocence,
A time of confidences.
Long ago . . . it must be . . .
I have a photograph.
Preserve your memories;
They're all that's left you.

Paul Simon

CONTENTS

PART ONE

TIME OF INNOCENCE

'Time present and time past
Are both perhaps present in time future,
And time future contained in time past.
If all time is eternally present
All time is unredeemable.'

                – T. S. Eliot; 'Burnt Norton', I

CHAPTER ONE

A LA RECHERCHE DU TEMPS PERDU
AUGUST 1944

Richard Gardiner had expected to be briefed by someone from F (French) Section, Aubrey himself, or Hilary Latymer, who had picked him up at the small Kent airfield the previous day. Certainly, the appearance in Aubrey's office of Michael Stanhope Constant, a career intelligence officer from MI 6 confused him, and made him somehow resentful.

Latymer, observing him in the moments before the meeting started, sensed his discomfiture. Between him and Gardiner there had always existed an easy intimacy, and he now sympathised with Gardiner's dislike of the stranger. Yet at the same time, he was aware that a recent distance had sprung up between them. He had seen Gardiner only twice since the Normandy landings, and on both occasions he had observed what he could only describe as a cold place growing in the man, so that he was more abrupt, less inclined to conversation, less comfortable with easy camaraderie.

Latymer supposed it had to do with the destructive overdrive into which Resistance groups like Gardiner's in Rouen, the 'Ilium' group, had been pushed since the invasion.

Latymer had been Kenneth Aubrey's deputy at Baker Street in F Section of the SOE almost as long as Gardiner had been leader of the Rouen Resistance group. He was more used to the discomfort of the relationship between MI 6 and the SOE. Yet he too, sensed more vividly the habitual contempt in which SOE was held by Constant as he studied from his vantage point against the wall, elbow propped on the mantelpiece, the tall, ascetic individual, formal in black coat and striped trousers, which complemented his cover as a civil servant in the Ministry of Food, and which Latymer knew he always was careful to wear in uniformed company.

Aubrey, dapper in the uniform of a Major in the R.A.O.C., had claimed his own seat behind his desk after Constant had elected to perch himself in disdain on the edge. Constant, Latymer realised, was upsetting Aubrey too. The man had the ability to chill the room which Aubrey was always at pains to make warm, comfortable, suggesting the illusion of a common room from before the war. It was a bright hot day beyond the window, but somehow Constant had the trick of darkening the room.

Latymer shook off the idle speculation. Instead, he studied the man from MI 6 carefully, as an intrusive, possibly destructive, species. Aubrey, he could see, though in MI 6 himself until the outbreak of war, disliked him. From firsthand knowledge, Latymer assumed.

Constant was in his mid-thirties, but appeared older, especially in the green eyes, which habitually expressed a watchful assurance. His chalky, narrow features were unlined, aristocratic in their moulding and the hook of the nose; it was as if he were without experiences that aged him, or perhaps beyond such. Even the nasal drawl of his voice suggested to Latymer that they were transitory beings and that he, Constant, would continue forever. Yet, as the man unfolded his wares, leaning slightly towards Gardiner as the younger man sat stiffly upright in a hard chair, Latymer watched the voice catch Gardiner's attention, then his interest. The mission was important, it was obvious – less dangerous than important.

'The problem,' Constant elucidated carefully, 'is, of course, very difficult – though I've no doubt you chaps in the field can appreciate it. But let me lay out the background for you.' He smiled without pleasure or humour. 'It arises from that tiresome individual, Charles de Gaulle. He has an obsession that the Communists are planning to beat him to

Paris and install one of their number in the Elysée instead of himself – a changeling in his crib at Bethlehem. He really should be told that his triumphal return to the capital will fall a long way short, in sheer spectacle, of the Second Coming . . .'

'You haven't told him yourself, then?' Aubrey remarked maliciously, his mild blue eyes twinkling. Constant's thin nostrils flared for a moment, and then he continued, all irritation squeezed from his careful, studied tones.

'As you are no doubt aware, it is the Supreme Commander's strategy, and in this he is supported by the SHAEF Planning Committee, not to invade Paris. Too many divisions would be tied up, and the city might be destroyed in the fighting. The Wehrmacht will not give up Paris without a fight, because the Führer will not let them. Besides which, the V-1 and V-2 bases are SHAEF's first concern, and they are not in Paris.

'The Free French, and General Charles de Gaulle in particular, are mortally afraid of the Communists in Paris. There are, according to the latest estimates, at least twenty-five thousand Communists, well armed, in the Paris FFI. And most of the leadership is Communist, especially since the arrest of Lefaucheux in June by the Gestapo – and "Rol" may have turned him in for all we know.

'I don't need to expand on the danger these chaps represent to de Gaulle. What he is afraid of is an uprising of the Communists *before* he himself can march into the city at the head of the Free French.'

As Constant paused, Latymer lit a cigarette and glanced in Gardiner's direction. He caught his eye, and shrugged and smiled. He knew what Constant required of Gardiner, but would not by sign or gesture anticipate the revelation. The precursory remarks were necessary. Paris did seem to hang by a thread, together with the political colour of the post-war government of France.

Aubrey stared out of the window, as if he had heard it all before – which was true. He did not trust his features to remain smooth as the man's affected patronage extended minute by minute, causing him to boil slowly. Constant was an old adversary.

'You wonder, of course, what this has to do with you,' Constant proceeded. 'And, naturally, you are suspicious of my frankness. There is no need for you to be so. Let me explain. We are certain there will be an uprising in Paris this month. De Gaulle forbade any further arms drops in the Paris area on June the fourteenth to forestall it. But whatever de Gaulle wants or does not want, he will be unable to prevent it.

'If that fact occurs, then it is in SHAEF's interest to ensure that the uprising has a chance of limited success. The Supreme Commander does not want to enter Paris before the end of September. We must see to it, therefore, that the Paris FFI, Communist or not, has sufficient arms and ammunition to hold out – to *weaken* the Wehrmacht without involving Allied forces. You begin to understand, I hope?'

'You mean some kind of second front in France?' Gardiner said. Latymer, knowing him, sensed the effort he was using to keep excitement from his voice. The significance of the mission was reaching down into him, feeding the ego. Now he would not ask even about the risks.

'Precisely!' Constant said, ironic applause in his voice. Gardiner wrinkled his nose. It was evident to Latymer from Constant's tone that it was his own idea – whatever was to be told Gardiner – and that he had probably taken it very near Eisenhower himself before having to pass it on to someone who would introduce it to the Supreme Commander.

'Indeed a second front,' he proceeded. 'If the uprising was sufficiently strong, then the taking of the V-1 and V-2 bases would become something more of a formality – and we might even be across the Rhine before the end of the year. As long as the uprising is not crushed in its infancy.'

'Could I ask,' Gardiner began, 'could the Communists

take over Paris before de Gaulle gets there? Is it a real threat?'

Constant shook his head and studied his fingernails.

'We evaluate that risk as not very real. The Nazis will not let Paris go – Hitler will not let it go. They will fight to keep it, even though they may destroy it in the process.' Constant again shook his head. 'A great pity if they did. Still, better statuary and stone than lives, gentlemen.' Latymer, rubbing his chin, was aware that Constant's humanitarianism was nothing more than a gesture. 'There has to be an uprising, and it has to be a real threat to the von Choltitz's garrison of twenty thousand Wehrmacht and SS troops. Your task –' he added suddenly, his eyes sharpening in focus, looking directly at Gardiner, 'will be to estimate what supplies, in what amounts, the Resistance will need if it is to pose a serious threat to the Paris garrison.'

Gardiner nodded. Latymer saw Constant suddenly as a skull on which the stretched skin smirked. He hated the ease with which he manipulated Gardiner. The significance of the job appealed to Gardiner's ego. It was the mythical single stroke which could shorten the war – and Richard Gardiner would be part of it.

Gardiner said, 'The uprising is inevitable?'

Constant nodded. 'I'm afraid so. The Communists won't wait. The cry of "*Aux barricades*" will be heard in Paris before the end of the month.' He smiled, and added, 'Which is why I have been unusually expansive in my briefing. You will go to Paris in the company of Alain Renaud, who is on "Rol's" staff in the FFI, and is a Communist himself. He will take you to "Rol's" secret headquarters, "Duroc". What we require from you is a realistic shopping-list from them, and a realistic estimate of their present numbers, resources, and strategy.' He leaned forward on the desk until Gardiner could smell the faint, expensive cologne. 'You understand the seriousness of your task?'

Gardiner nodded. 'Yes – quite clearly.'

Constant looked at his watch. Something in his tone had

made Aubrey turn from the window, swivelling in his chair. Constant, having succeeded so well in enlisting Gardiner, masked his irritation at the evident insult, smiling with an attempted warmth.

'Good,' he said. 'Major Aubrey has all the details, and your documentation. You have four days, no more. Then you will be collected, and we expect your little head to be full of the most interesting material.' He smiled again, sardonically, and then added: 'I'll leave you to the rest of your briefing, then. Major Aubrey will give you the nuts and bolts, so to speak . . .'

He bade each of them a good afternoon, and left. Almost immediately, Aubrey lit a cigar. He seemed released from his former mood which he disliked, but always indulged during meetings with Constant. He beamed as he blew out the first smoke, running his hand through his thinning, sandy hair. Latymer uncurled his tall frame from the mantelpiece, easing the cramp out of the arm on which he had been leaning, and offered Gardiner a cigarette.

Gardiner said, 'Am I to swallow all that, sir?'

Aubrey appeared surprised, puffed at his cigar, and said, 'I should jolly well hope so, Richard, my boy.'

'Constant's assessment of the Paris FFI is correct?'

'Undoubtedly – why?'

'Perhaps it's just my dislike of him . . .'

'I expect it is. You don't want to believe the man because he's such an evident shit. You were obviously under his spell five minutes ago,' he added mischievously. Aubrey was almost blithe and he blew smoke at the ceiling as he spoke. Latymer and Gardiner raised eyebrows to each other at Aubrey's unhabitual vulgarity.

Then Aubrey said, 'Will you get out the sherry and the necessaries, Hilary. I didn't offer Mr. Constant anything to drink. He may have gone to Oxford, but he drinks sherry like a navvy drinks beer! However even though I don't like him, let me give you two young 'uns a piece of advice. If you want to go anywhere in the post-war intelligence service, remember it's people like him who'll be running the show.'

Gardiner made a face at Latymer, who said, 'God forbid.'

Gardiner added, 'I don't want any more of this after the war. Just my articles, then the quiet life of a country solicitor. That'll suit me down to the ground.' Latymer studied Gardiner as he said it; an unexpected sentiment, but he perceived that Gardiner was sincere.

'Shall I call in Renaud, then?' Aubrey asked. 'If we've sufficiently recovered our sang-froid after that visitation from Whitehall.' He popped out of his chair, straightening his uniform blouse as he did so.

'In a minute, sir.' Gardiner said. 'What sort of mood is he in?'

'Who – Renaud?'

'Yes, sir.'

'Hilary – you brought him here. Tell the young man.'

'Belligerent, suspicious, impatient – all the things you might expect. You know him. He's risen high with "Colonel Rol" in the FFI. He expects our assistance by some kind of divine authority.' Latymer sipped his sherry, and added, 'Not a comfortable travelling companion. At best, you'll be a pedagogue marking his essay.'

Gardiner shrugged. 'It is important, isn't it, sir?'

Latymer perceived the eagerness, the bloom of ego, like the switching on of some inner light. 'Yes, it is.'

'Then let's have him in, and you can give us Mr. Constant's nuts and bolts.'

'*My* nuts and bolts, if you don't mind, Richard. Mr. Constant does not bother himself with mere details, you know.'

Etienne de Vaugrigard was unsettled as he waited for 'Wolf' and 'Wolverine'. He had arrived late in the afternoon, and had waited in a cool, uncarpeted corridor that smelled of dust, on the first floor of the tall empty narrow house that was part of a smoke-blackened terrace of a Bloomsbury square. He spent most of his time standing at a tall window,

MESSAGE FORM

PRECEDENCE ~~ACTION~~ ~~INFO~~ ~~DEFERRED~~	DATE-TIME GP 200943/12-30	CLASSIFICATION Top Secret	ORIGINATORS NUMBER G.7.

FROM   G.7. WAR ROOM.

TO   GRANTHAM   S.26

Info   ————————

(1) COMPLETE FINAL DETAILS 39-144-2 POL/FR. IMMEDIATELY

(2) OPERATION "WOLFGROUP" MUST BE AT 12 HRS READINESS
BY 13/4/42 AND 4 HRS BY 18/5/42

(3) AN "OPEN ORDER" BOOK IS AUTHORISED FROM WAR ROOM & SENIOR
PROCUREMENT OFFICER WILL COMPLY

(4) PRIORITY OBJECTIVES REVISED :—

    a) ELIMINATION OF COMMUNIST FACTIONS IN RESISTANCE AND THUS
     THEIR POLITICAL POWER BASE IN POST WAR FRANCE.

    b) HARASS AND DEPLOY ENEMY FORCES IN WHAT WOULD
     APPEAR TO BE A "DOMESTIC" SITUATION

    c) TO ESTABLISH POTENTIAL LEADERS IN POST WAR
     FRANCE WHO TAKE THE WESTERN VIEW.

(5) STAFF APPOINTMENTS "WOLF" AND "WOLVERINE" URGENT
FOR POLITICAL BRIEFING.

(6) INFO. ONLY. WHITE HOUSE HAS ADVISED PENTAGON TO
ASSIST IN ANY WAY AND TO ASK NO QUESTIONS.

PAGE 1 OF 1 PAGES	DRAFTERS NAME & OFFICE G7	
Encoded by G7	System LE3G	OPERATOR 371 BARNES
		DECODED BY GRANTHAM.

staring into the untidy, weed-filled garden. The man who had driven him to the house in an ordinary civilian car had left him, and he had let himself in. He had been to the house several times before, and the cool, musty emptiness was familiar to him.

There was a primitive kitchen, and he made himself several cups of strong coffee, yet he had always returned to the corridor on the first floor, where his occasional footsteps echoed, to stare out over the garden at the sunlit, dusty space full of straggly yellow flowers and brick rubble. Once, in the early days of his association with the house, there had been a street there. Now, after the bombs, there were only the sunlit clumps of straggling weeds, and the bricks heaped as if after child's play.

Etienne de Vaugrigard was Gardiner's second-in-command in the 'Ilium' group in Rouen. His code-name within the group was 'Hector'.

The two men for whom he waited arrived together, a little after six. De Vaugrigard heard them let themselves in, and the mutter of their voices washed up the stairs to the first floor like a small wave. Their footsteps were sharp in the empty, tiled hall, then he heard them ascend the stairs. When they came into view, he recognised the 'Wolf' and his American companion. With a familiar sickness, he experienced the first of the reactions that assailed him during these occasions – impotent anger at the fact that though he knew their names, he was never allowed to use them. Instead, he paid deference to their code-names. And he the heir to the Vaugrigard Armaments fortune, and the factories in St. Denis that now turned out war materials for the Germans.

'Ah,' the Englishman said. 'Sorry you've had such a long wait, Etienne.' He hated, too, the ease with which they bandied his first name as that of a subordinate. 'Pressure of business while we free your beloved France, eh? I'm sure you understand.'

'I understand,' de Vaugrigard replied in a murmur. His nerves grated together at the man's tone. Behind him, the

American smiled with a genuine, unmasked pleasure at the
discomfort of the young Frenchman. 'Wolverine' was a
man with a humourless face, chiselled crudely, a large prow
of a nose and a square unrelenting chin. His eyes were flinty,
dead to light. De Vaugrigard tried to calm himself, reminding himself that it was always the same in that house, with
those two. He must not become unsettled. He must try. . . .

He disliked them intensely, so intensely that if he was to
retain any self-respect during their meetings he had to
believe he was using them and not they him. He disliked
most of all the clarity with which they understood his need
of them.

The office which the Englishman unlocked was spartan
in its furnishings and was sufficiently unused for dust to
have settled on all its dark wooden surfaces. The Englishman wiped a long finger lightly along the edge of the desk,
inspected it, then sat down with his back to the tall window
that overlooked the garden. He motioned Etienne to a deep,
sagging armchair covered in a chintzy material of hectic
colours. The American leaned against the fireplace, his
strong fingers laced across his chest, his hard eyes adopting
a look of satisfied detachment.

'What do you want, "Wolf"?' de Vaugrigard blurted.
'What is it this time?'

'Shouldn't you ask *who*, dear boy – mm?'

'As you prefer.' He was sullen now.

'Not at all – as *you* prefer, surely?'

De Vaugrigard shrugged his shoulders and held back his
feelings from his features. Satisfied with that tiny moment
of self-control, like a victory. Nevertheless, in the early
evening light that fell from the window on his handsome
features 'Wolf' could observe the minute flaring of the
nostrils, the slightest flush to the pale features. Etienne was
angry, and ashamed. He was only able to goad him because
the young man's anti-Communist bigotry outran his dislike
of his two superiors.

Etienne hated, and feared, the Communist party of France

with the totality of his awareness, his background, and his
upbringing. A deep and fanatical intellectual hatred. To
him, they represented the gravest of dangers of postwar
France; together with his devotion to de Gaulle and his
cause, it made him perfect material for the 'Wolfgroup'.
Etienne understood that – and hated the perfection of his
usefulness to others, as if it robbed him of identity.

'What do you want this time?' he said, looking across
the desk from beneath heavy eyelids. He did the work the
'Wolf' offered him with an eager efficiency. All that he
disliked – so fiercely that he often felt a physical nausea when
he left the Bloomsbury house – was the fact that he was
entirely 'Wolf's' man, *his* executioner. He hated that sense
of being completely known; it was like some obscene and
continuing intimacy, a marriage between them.

The Englishman steepled his fingers and smiled benignly.
His face was planed smooth, with sharp edges at the jawline
and the high forehead. His colour was almost grey with the
light behind him.

'I want to offer you "Colonel Rol" on a plate, Etienne –
simply that.'

There was a sudden heavy silence in the room. De
Vaugrigard was ashamed of the dry hunger in his eyes,
seeing it reflected by the man across the table in a satisfied
twist of the lips.

Henry Tanguy – 'Colonel Rol' – had been head of the
Paris FFI since June, and the leading Communist in the
city. The man, de Vaugrigard knew, wanted political power
in post-war France; wanted no Gaullist government ever
in Paris. Yes, de Vaugrigard wanted him.

'And Gallois, his chief of staff – and the others,' the
Englishman whispered like a tempter. Etienne smiled cynic-
ally, adopting a posture of assurance he did not feel.

'What do I have to do for it?' he asked, his voice tight.
'Sell my soul?' Now, the forced lightness came a little more
easily.

'Not at all.' 'Wolf' smiled. 'Not at all, dear boy. All you

have to do is to betray a man – as usual. Make sure that he
falls into the hands of the Gestapo in Paris within the next
couple of days.'

'Which man?'

'You know Alain Renaud?'

'Yes. He worked with our group in Rouen for some time.'

'He is in London at present, and returns to France tomorrow night. He must fall into the hands of the Gestapo
as soon after that as possible.'

'Why?'

The American spoke before 'Wolf' could reply. He was
still standing behind Etienne, leaning against the empty
fireplace. His voice was harsh with contempt and confidence.
He, like de Vaugrigard, seemed impatient with the feline
tactics of the Englishman, but for a different reason. His
contempt sprang from his obscure sense of de Vaugrigard
as some kind of traitor, however useful. 'Wolverine' hated
Communists, but he disliked and mistrusted Europeans also.
He bullied and bulled his way through every such meeting
at the Bloomsbury house.

'Because there's going to be an uprising in Paris before
the end of the month which, if it succeeded, would put a
Commie in the Elysée when the war's over.'

'This month?'

'That's what I said, friend.'

'How – do you know?' De Vaugrigard felt himself
choking.

'We *know*. Never mind how. We know.'

'You see,' 'Wolf' began, 'why we need Renaud captive
to the Gestapo. He will break under torture – even *you* know
enough about him to be reasonably certain of that.' Etienne
nodded slowly. He was swallowing compulsively from a dry
mouth. He felt himself in some light, anaesthetised trance.
'So – Renaud will tell the Gestapo where to find "Duroc",
and the names of the sector organisers, the arms dumps –
everything.'

Etienne was suddenly cold, as if some bag of iced water in

him had burst, flooding his body. He felt his hands quivering on his thighs.

He was afraid of the moment – *the* moment of his life. It was what he had waited for, ever since the shadowy 'Wolfgroup' had recruited him, as a prominent anti-Communist, in 1941. He had done his work, whatever they had asked of him, all the time silencing his vestigial conscience with the promise of the one stroke – the deed that would affect the war, affect the world after the war.

He had been responsible for the destruction of forty-three men in three years; he had no idea of how many other agents were employed by the 'Wolfgroup'. He had only a shadowy idea of its aims and purposes. He did not care. A self-assumed sophisticate before the war, he now lived an immature life, seeking daring and boldness as signposts of his experience or fulfilment.

In a moment of flickering, compound time, he saw faces, names – people dead because of him, every one of them a dangerous fanatic working only for the ruination of his country and his hero, de Gaulle. He knew how much the General feared the kind of uprising the American had spoken of. All those other deaths, then, had been in the nature of a prelude. This was his cataclysm.

He felt warmth in his loins, like a sexual arousal. He looked upon 'Wolf' almost as an ally. And the 'Wolf' saw the electricity of heroism, of self-posturing, alter the shape of the young man's body in the chair. His shoulders were subtly squarer, the head thrown slightly back, the half-profile presented. There was for the Englishman a cold pleasure, the prerogative of the manipulator, at the back of his mind. De Vaugrigard was now shaped as he wished him.

He said, softly and insinuatingly, 'There is one other matter, before we get down to the brassier tacks of this little operation – which we have called "Quick Red Fox", by the way. Renaud will be accompanied by an English agent when he returns to Paris. The betrayal of that man is also required in case the Gestapo begin to suspect that Allied Intelligence

is behind the whole thing, and don't for that reason do what
we wish . . .' De Vaugrigard nodded without real surprise.
'It is unfortunate, of course, but verisimilitude is of the
essence here.' He lowered his voice and said without a trace
of inflection, 'The man is your group leader – Richard
Gardiner is the man you must also betray to the Gestapo.'

Gardiner was arrested with Renaud at the Café Tabac in
the Left Bank's Rue de la Montagne while they waited for
the Paris FFI to contact them. He drank gassy beer and
watched the Parisians drift in and out of the dark café – and
the chain of betrayal achieved its final link.

There was no possibility of escape. He had seen that from
the moment the men in the stylised black raincoats had
blocked the light from the doorway and the noise of splintering wood was evident behind him as the rear entrance
was kicked in and three more men spilled into the café's
interior. Renaud was frightened; Gardiner had seen that
in the first moment of surprise. There was no moment of
shock; he passed directly from passivity to fear. Gardiner
dismissed him, weighed his own chances – and found them
hopeless.

There was one moment as they were bundled out into the
lancing sunlight of the Rue de Montagne, a narrow street
that ran twistingly down from the Pantheon towards the
Rue des Ecoles. Gardiner knew the Left Bank well enough
to understand its capabilities as a refuge of safe, blind
warrens. He squinted against the sudden light of the noon
street, then acted. He feinted a slip, lurched against the
guard on his left, freeing his right hand by the sudden
innocuousness of the movement. Then he jabbed for the
eyes with stiff fingers. The unbalanced man screamed, high
and terrible like a wired rabbit, and fell back into the doorway of the café. With a second swift blow, Gardiner struck
the other escort's genitals, feeling his fist drive into the soft
mass. He wasted no time in hitting him again.

He began to run, down the slope of the street, hearing a

voice calling after him. Then two shots puckered dust and
stone chips from the wall near his head. He skidded on a
patch of wet from a street-cleaning truck, and his cheek
dragged painfully against rough stone, his hands clutching
the wall for support. Then he pushed away from the wall,
accelerating again, surprised faces turning to him, bodies
making a passage for him, dressed as he was in French
clothes, fleeing from the Gestapo. The blood drummed in
his ears, the inward decibels rioting, and his chest heaved
as if it threatened the ribcage.

There had been others, of course, posted at either end
of the Rue de la Montagne. Even as he cannoned into the
smooth material of the big man's leather coat, felt the knee
drive for his groin even though the man was off balance, he
sensed that this was no chance arrest. The whole thing was
much too expensive in Gestapo manpower.

Which meant Renaud. They wanted Alain Renaud, a
man with secrets to tell them. A gun-butt struck him. He
keeled towards the pavement.

The man whose eyes he had ruined had to be taken to
hospital. The man he had punched in the groin had recovered
sufficiently to walk down the street to where he lay on the
floor and kick him three times, each action accompanied
with a grunt of effort and pleasure.

Gardiner was barely conscious when they bundled him
into the waiting car. As they drove to the Avenue Foch, he
kept passing out and briefly regaining consciousness. Each
time he opened his eyes, he seemed to see, foggily, the
frightened face of Alain Renaud, unmarked by violence,
and to understand that the man would talk, would tell the
torturers in the cellar everything they wished to know.

Before the car stopped and he was dragged out, he had
slipped into a steadier unconsciousness, as if seeking some
fugitive ease before the Gestapo began their work.

During the days in Fresnes Prison, as his body attempted
to forget pain and his nail-less fingers in the dirty bandages

seemed less clumsy as they grappled with cutlery and the chipped mug in which they served the vile *ersatz* coffee of the place, he became aware that the endless, mindless four days in the cellars of the Avenue Foch might conceivably have been worse. Much worse.

It had become apparent, perhaps on the second day, that Renaud had told them sufficient for them to believe that Gardiner's mission was of some significance but of no direct threat to the German garrison in the city. He believed that Renaud had told them something close to the truth. Therefore, their treatment of Gardiner, as newly-arrived and ignorant, might have been a secondary concern while they concentrated on Renaud.

As 'Wolf' had anticipated, the Gestapo realised who they held, and wanted to make sure they extracted everything held by the screaming mind that slowly retreated from them. They suspected an uprising by the FFI, and the opportunity offered them by the betrayal of Renaud made them greedy, and forgetful of Gardiner. His identity as 'Achilles', the leader of the Rouen group, was either unknown to them or of more long term interest. Nevertheless, with the efficient sadism that distinguished them from the more casual brutalities of the SS or the SD, they tortured Gardiner, wrung the sponge for any moisture it might hold.

It might have been on the third day, some time during August the seventh or eighth, that Renaud died under torture. Gardiner was never told, directly; but the body's agonised response to the intensified suffering inflicted upon it, informed him that Renaud was dead and that he had not told them all they wished to know.

It was perhaps another thirty-six hours before his torturers understood with reluctant fury that he could not give them the answers and that Renaud had been his only contact with the Paris Resistance. He craved death by that time, wanted the Gestapo to end their interrogation with a bullet in the brain. Instead, he was transferred to Fresnes, sensing, in the small bouts of consciousness as he bobbed

like a cork on the surging pain, the recriminatory fury of
the men who had learned nothing from Renaud before
he died. Gardiner presumed the body had been buried,
with all the others since 1940, in the cellars of the Avenue
Foch.

The womb-like, silent darkness of the cell in Fresnes was
welcome after the hard light and the rational moments of
eyes close to his, the smell of food stale in mouths whispering
against his face – sharper than the smell of his own vomit
and urine. He retreated from what had been done to him.
In the darkness he slowly healed. He touched the wounded
places of his body but kept clear of the wounded places in
his mind, and the memory of pain. There was no amnesia
to be gratefully embraced, but he was able to still memory
by an effort of will, separate mind and body so that each
painful movement on the narrow, filthy cot did not remind
him of the last few horrific days.

It was the morning of August the eleventh. Outside, it was
not yet light, and he wondered for a moment, what had
woken him. He craved sleep, and turned on the cot, digging
his head into the pillow which smelled of hair oil and sweat
and fear and hopelessness. Then, far below him, three or
perhaps four floors of the prison, he heard the slamming
open of cell doors and an unidentifiable metallic screech, as
of some alien bird. He shuddered. It might have been one
of his own screams as they pulled out his fingernails. The
bandaged hands throbbed by an act of memory, and he
gritted his teeth.

A pattern emerged even though he tried to ignore it. A
door would open and then the metallic screeching would be
heard. Then a silence, and then another door and the
screeching noise. He even began to be able to detect the
small increases in volume as the sounds approached. He
concentrated on ignoring them, considering instead the
fitful illuminations of his reason.

He had been betrayed, and by someone who knew of

Renaud's arrival in Paris – knew also the time and place of the rendezvous with the Resistance; knew who he was, and the importance of his companion. Now, it was only by channelling the pain into the narrow perspective of revenge, however distant and however hopeless, that he could ease the terror and agony of what had happened to him.

When the door of his cell banged open, and the metallic screech stopped, he was surprised. He had been drifting into sleep again, clutching revenge to him like a child's comforter, a night light to keep back the dark. He turned his head, puzzled and saw the SS guard in the doorway, his face wrinkled in a sneer. He realised that he was huddled on the bed, hands protecting his genitals, fear on his face, his lips automatically moving in a wordless plea. There was another figure behind the guard, fat and not in uniform, leaning over a coffee trolley. He heard, distinctly, the noise of the hot liquid filling the mug.

The guard, stepping to him, prodded him with his gun and said, 'Get up.' His English was adequate, snarled and confident. 'Coffee. For your journey, Englishman.' There was a smile on his face, and something that seemed eager for the shock of realisation by Gardiner.

'W-what is it?'

'Coffee – you understand? You don't like coffee?' He turned, as if to leave the cell, and Gardiner clutched the grey sleeve of his uniform. The SS man shrugged the wounded hand away, and it fluttered back to rest on the edge of the cot.

'Where am I going?'

'You want to know that? Better not to ask!' the German said, moving to one side to let the fat man pass the chipped mug of black bitter coffee to Gardiner. 'Drink!' the guard ordered.

Gardiner coughed as the liquid scalded his throat, then he said:

'Is everyone leaving?' He had now to explain the noises he had tried to ignore. It seemed important. He brushed one bandaged hand across his hair, as if to smarten his appearance before this proposed journey.

'More than two thousand.'

'Two – thousand?'

He had heard the rumours, naturally, in Rouen, passed from group to group like a message of defeat or an incitement to action. The trains – leaving for Auschwitz and Buchenwald and Bergen-Belsen and the other places. He shivered with knowledge and the hot coffee spilled into his lap, scalding him through the thin trousers. He looked down stupidly, as if he had urinated – perhaps afraid that he had done, like a frightened child or animal.

The guard said, 'You know, then?'

Gardiner nodded. From the two prisons, Fresnes and Romainville, thousands of men and women of the Resistance had been taken to the freight station at Pantin, just behind the Paris stockyards, to the cattle-trucks and the last journey to Germany.

'Christ . . . Christ . . . Christ . . .' he heard himself saying again and again.

The guard said, 'Get up!'

He sat there. It was only when the guard slapped him across the face, repeatedly, that he realised that he was listening to the cry of his own voice, something rusty and unused and frightened as it mounted and became a thin scream. He was dragged from the bed, the thin stuff of his shirt ripping in the guard's grip. He smelt the guard's breakfast still on his breath, and the hair oil he used. Then he was leaning against the door of the cell, and men were filing past him down the corridor. As if from a great distance, he heard the cup break on the floor of the cell. He looked round stupidly, mouth open, to see where it had smashed. The guard pushed him out into the corridor, into the stream of men and he fumbled one foot before the other to retain his balance. He heard someone swear in French, and by some instinct looked down. He had urinated, the spreading stain, with fear. He could smell himself.

By the time he got out into the prison yard, the women prisoners who were to travel that day had already been herded into buses and taken to Pantin. It was a little after sunrise. The sky was heavy with grey cloud, and there was a chill in the air – at least it seemed chill to Gardiner as he stood in his torn shirt and wet trousers, waiting to be herded onto one of the green and yellow buses.

There were a great many SS guards in the yard, and hundreds of prisoners. The place was crowded, yet almost silent. There was little tangible sense of fear, only a pause, a sense of release from the grey walls around them. The sense of the future was absent, the emotional temperature low. Only the present existed, and they were outside and the sun was coming up and trying to struggle through the cloud. It was as if they had learned the same trick of the mind at the same moment. Even Gardiner was able to forget why they had been herded there. He stretched his face to the air, a plant seeking the sun.

Someone spoke to him in French, but he did not answer. It was as if he had forgotten the language. There was only the grey sky above him, the distant sharp barking of names and commands harmless as the calls of foxes, and tee shuffling noises as feet pressed towards the buses.

An SS man roughly moved him in the direction of one of the vehicles. He stumbled, then drifted with the tide of men. His face was blank – pain, suffering, hunger, thirst, recrimination: all had been erased.

Once inside the bus, he continued to stare out of the window, upwards at the sky. It was through his nostrils that awareness returned. He could begin to smell the bodies around him, smell the prison smells and the new odour of fear, as the gears grated and the vehicle began to move. He kept his eyes on the thinning cloud all the way to Pantin, but his other senses allowed reality to seep into him again like an ague until the vacant stare was nothing more than an escape.

He felt the rough cloth of a man's jacket against his arm,

heard the muttered fear of other men behind him, smelt the unwashed bodies and the waves of terror – smelt his own drying urine on his trousers. His wounds caused him pain, especially his hands and back.

He stumbled out of the bus, and the cinders of the freight station crunched beneath their feet. A guard pushed him into line, and he lumbered forward with little more volition or intent than that of the shove in the back. Other men obeyed the same blind stutter towards the cattle cars coupled together in the siding. It was a walk of perhaps two hundred yards from the bus, yet it seemed to drain him of the little energy he possessed. Reluctantly, he summoned last reserves, the use of which would leave him spent. Even so, he lurched with weariness against the man in front of him.

The man displayed no anger, and no pity. It was a collision of air against his skin, a fleshy wind which had nothing to do with him.

Before they boarded the train, there was the final indignity of being searched. Gardiner, through fogged awareness, sweat in his eyes now that the sun was beating down on them from a sky being dried to a washed, pale blue, admired with irony the thoroughness of the SS. Even though the file of men had come straight from Fresnes and Romainville, and possessed nothing of any value, still they were searched efficiently and with the maximum humiliation.

Gardiner was forced to strip – he heard a muttered comment on the wounds across his back, the burns and bruises and the cuts – and stand naked while an SS Oberleutnant with a narrow dark face and thick eyebrows studied the heap of clothes. He grimaced at their filthiness, perhaps especially as his gloved hand touched the stained, fouled trousers, then looked up and smiled as he saw the humiliation in Gardiner's face.

'Put on your trousers – little boy,' the German said. Then he pointed to the shirt and an unteroffizier removed it to a huge pile of clothing heaped near the waiting train. Gardiner watched his torn and filthy shirt in disbelief, thrown onto the dump. He had heard that the SS collected everything, even old clothes – that they computed the value of rags, hair, bone . . .

He wanted to laugh. It was insane. The world's rag-pickers, the terrible SS . . . Just men with dirty carts crying out for rags. The oberleutnant slapped his face when the laughter was no more than a lolling grin, and he was pushed half-naked into the black interior of a cattle-truck. It was like being shoved into an oven. He remembered immediately one brilliantly hot summer before the war, hiding in a corrugated iron chicken-shed from his brother, and the choking heat which had finally driven him out. He had been thankful, almost, to be ducked in the river for stealing Stephen's best fountain pen and filling it with blackcurrant juice . . .

He looked up as other bodies, slippery with sweat, pressed against him, forcing him to the back of the truck. The roof was rusty sheet iron. His first breath inside the truck seared his throat. He was suddenly aware of the repulsiveness of sweaty contact. He could see, over cropped heads like a broken skyline, the top of the door, and other heads bobbing up into the doorway. The world outside was a ragged bar of blinding light.

He was slowly pressed against the far wall so that the rough, splintery wood tugged and scratched at his wounded back. He winced with the pain, winced too at the stifling pressure of bodies. Within a minute, it was almost impossible to breathe. His head lifted to the rusty, boiling roof and he sucked in the foetid air greedily. When the SS decided that the truck could hold no more, the door was slammed across the head-broken line of light, and they were in cooler darkness, a coolness that at once became hot and stifling as the mind's illusion slipped from them.

There was little noise, little movement. It was that which struck him most forcibly as the dead, endless time passed. It was as if he and the others had accepted the animal roles suggested by the truck. Gardiner understood the final and absolute condition of hopelessness; to stand like a beast, empty-minded, merely breathing.

Silence. The occasional slither of sweat-covered bodies, the shuffling of feet, the punctuation of streams of urine into the tin bucket in one corner. When they moved, to let someone use the bucket, his back was pressed against the wood, sharply and agonisingly. And then again the silence.

They waited for perhaps the whole day. One or two of them noticed, as if with a supreme effort, that the light had faded and it was night outside. There was a drop in temperature inside the blind truck – but they hardly registered it, so dizzy and lightheaded were they by that time, so parched of even the memory of water or cold. Many of them, including Gardiner, refreshed themselves by licking the sweat from their own and each other's bodies.

They refused to believe, at first, that they could hear a locomotive, cautiously approaching. Then Gardiner's back was rubbed across the side of the truck, and he heard through his renewed pain the grinding of buffers, the grate and clank of couplings. There was a pause, as if each of the hundred men in the stifling dark held his breath. Then the truck lurched, and the train began to move out of Pantin freight station. Though they could not know it, it was almost midnight on the eleventh of August, and the train, carrying two and a half thousand captured members of the Resistance had begun its journey to Metz and the German border.

When they moved, Gardiner was shaken by the pain and by a sense of relief from a light-headed dream in which the figures in the truck had become the drifting mariners of a great painting, struck in the attitudes of hopelessness. They were the survivors from the wreck of the *Medusa*; he had begun to believe they might descend to cannibalism, so potent was the delirium of the dream.

Then he heard it, as other men heard it – sad, ridiculous and defiant. Despair gave power to their parched throats. The rise in temperature had subsided. Now they seemed

cooled by movement. The night air reached them in puffs
and draughts from the rotten woodwork of the truck.

It was the *Marseillaise*. One or two voices picked it up,
then suddenly they were all singing. Men were smiling and
crying, leaning against each other now in a comradeship
each had before shunned. Now the weariness and wetness
of bodies no longer mattered. The din inside the truck was
incredible. Gardiner cried as he sang.

It was dawn before the train halted, a mere forty miles
from Paris, in a smoke-filled tunnel on the main line to
Nancy, at Nanteuil-Saacy. Unknown to the prisoners, the
track had been dynamited for a length of sixty-five yards
by an FFI commando unit. A message had been rushed
from Paris by bicycle before the train's departure, and it
had arrived in time.

Because of the risk of attack, the SS backed the train into
the tunnel. The initial surge of ecstasy that followed the
whispered inspiration that the track had been blown soon
subsided, and the blind, coughing men in Gardiner's truck
realised that the presumed attack on the train was not
about to happen. They understood that the FFI commando
unit must be waiting for reinforcements.

For two hours, the SS kept the locomotive pouring black
smoke into the tunnel, so that men began to think they were
intended to suffocate. They were sick over the floor and
each other, and the mood in the truck began to mount,
emotional mercury, towards panic. Gardiner, through a
smoke-clogged consciousness, through waves of nausea,
began to calculate.

There was one chance and only one. The men around
him clung to the fading hope that the Resistance would
attack the train and free them. Gardiner understood that
it would take only three to four men to dynamite the track,
but unless a great many more arrived to attack the train,
the track would be repaired, or . . .

His one chance was that the SS would find another train

and transfer the prisoners. In the tunnel, if the SS opened
the doors, or in the open, he would make his attempt.
Resolved, he began to breathe more shallowly, and to fight
down the nausea. He would have only seconds, and he
would have to run as never before. He prepared himself,
closing his senses to the urine and vomit and bodies and
fear. He had to live. Buchenwald and the other camps
had retreated in his imagination; all that was left was
revenge.

The train lurched forward, and daylight showed through
the cracks in the truck's walls. Then he heard the shouted
orders, and the doors of other trucks slid back. Gardiner
tensed himself, and the light and sweet air suddenly flooded
the truck. Men's lungs grabbed it as they stumbled, retching
and coughing, into the sunlight. They looked round them,
expecting death or perhaps hoping for rescue. None of them
seemed to possess the instinct to run. It was a pity. Had
many of them broken from the column that was forming,
he might have had cover for his own escape. The comradeship of the song and the night was broken for him, and there
was only himself to consider now.

He fell into line, attending to the scene around him. He
knew the area south and west of Paris well enough to know
roughly where they were, saw the loop of the river Marne
below him, the high sides of the cutting where the track had
been blown, and the trees dropping away to the river. On
the other side of the track were open fields white with daisies.
It would have to be the trees.

The guards were spread out every fifteen to twenty yards
on both sides of the track. He could see, ahead, the rear of
the train the SS had found – another cattle-train. He sensed
the returning hopelessness of the men in front and behind
him, but less vividly than the touch of the cool morning air
on his skin. He avoided looking at the sky and the sun.
They reached the stretch of exploded track, and part of his
mind admired the efficiency of the operation.

But the reinforcements had not arrived. Wherever the

commando was hidden, probably across the Marne, they must be watching hopelessly as the prisoners were transferred.

Suddenly, there was shooting, and he saw a man fall not ten yards from the truck. His was the dash of panic, of mindless fear. Gardiner was opposite one of the guards as his eyes flickered away from the line of prisoners towards the intruding noise. The scene had been so ordered, so like a herd of animals moving . . .

Gardiner leapt at him, striking him across the throat, beneath the chinstrap of his helmet. The SS tabs on the collar bulged in his vision, and then the man began to fall away. Gardiner wrenched the machine-pistol from the loosening grip and leapt over the body as it sagged to the tracks.

There were shots, whining over his head as he stumbled down the slope. There was no hesitation now, no awareness of danger coming through the spine or the shoulder-blades to stiffen or slow him. He was beyond being killed as blood pumped in his ears and his heart strained in great heaves.

Faintly, he heard whistles and shouted orders, and more shots. He understood that he had reached cover only because a bullet gouged a white patch in a trunk as he slithered against it then drove on into the shadows beneath the trees. He could not stop, even though he felt a fit of coughing beginning in his chest, and his legs threatening to give out, betray him. He drove on, head back, arms pumping, almost dropping the encumbering machine-pistol, its strap slapping at his arm and side.

Bullets whined through the trees and birds cried and flew up through the branches. He glimpsed something scuttling from his path, and then the ground lightened and the poplar trees vanished on either side of him. There was only the river ahead.

He paused for a moment, dragging in lungfuls of air, trying to still the exhausted shaking of his body. The SS would spare only a few men from the guard detail, at least

until the prisoners were safely installed in their new cattle-
trucks. He had perhaps a few minutes.

He listened like an animal, forcing his mind into his ears,
squeezing the other senses flat and dead. Faint shouts, and
already the slamming of doors. Five hundred yards away.
He looked back behind him. There was no flicker of unusual
shadow within the trees, but he could not be certain. Sunlight only emphasised the darkness beneath the leaves.

He looked at the river. Despite the narrowness of the
valley at that point, the current of the river seemed sluggish,
insufficient to carry him at any speed north-west, away
from the cutting and the train and the SS.

No alternative. He slid down the steep bank, and the cool
water lapped around his thighs. He walked out into the
current, feeling it stronger than he had assumed, grateful.
His feet lifted from the river bottom, and he rolled onto his
back, kicking wearily with his tired legs. He began to drift,
slowly it seemed, but pleasantly after so much effort, with
the sky and the fringe of the leaves and the sides of the
cutting which he could just see drifting slowly – a figure in a
punt, drifting on the sluggish Cam. The memory came back
softly, dreamily, so that he wanted to close his eyes, anticipate the flicker of light and shade from the branches above
him.

He snapped awake. He was drifting too far out into the
river. With a few strokes, he guided his body back towards
the shore. Checking, he saw that he had drifted only a
couple of hundred yards. Anyone coming onto the bank
from the trees would see him immediately. He trod water,
shook it from his ears, and listened.

Nothing. No doors slamming. The crowd of men and
women had been loaded aboard the new train. He trod water
awkwardly, as if weed clasped his limbs, and felt the desire
of the present moment overwhelm him, and tears prick at
his eyelids – he would wait until they came . . .

He had thought of moving in one line only, down-river.
He looked across at the opposite bank. He had to make it.

He fumbled the gun over his shoulder, but it slipped away into the water as soon as he began swimming. He let it go. He came out of the shadow of the trees into the sunlight, and his strokes became more positive, swifter. He had to cross the river before he was seen. He ground his teeth together, his head swinging from side to side as he breathed, his tired arms pumping feebly at the restraining water.

He lost track of time and distance. All his awareness had retreated to his arms and legs, trying to move the dead lump of the torso through the resisting water. Four limbs and a labouring chest was what he was, heaving through the water, feeling the tired current drag at him. He dared not look at the opposite bank – it might even have been slipping away from him.

A tired leg dropped in the water, sinking like a dead weight. His foot touched the gravel of the river bed. He tried to stand, and fell forward into the waist-deep water, coughing and spluttering. He tried to roll onto his back, but the water closed over his face. He splashed at the water, but it would not go away. It closed like the doors of the cattle-truck, final and solid like wood or steel. He could no longer struggle against . . .

Something grabbed at his arm and pulled. He felt the shoulder muscles protest, tried to shake the grip of the thing away. His chest and thighs scraped briefly on the gravel, then someone was holding him upright.

'Come, *mon ami* – we have no time to waste!' the Frenchman said.

Gardiner pushed, but his legs buckled. He felt himself dragged for a few yards before he blacked out.

He rested in a safe house in Nanteuil-sur-Marne until he was sufficiently recovered to be smuggled down the line of Resistance groups to Meaux, then Senlis, Neuilly, Beauvais, Gournay, and Rouen.

There had been five of them, the original commando who had blown the railway line to Nancy and who had then had to watch, helpless and desperate, as the prisoners were transferred, on the other side of the Marne, to the new train; and their reinforcements had failed to come.

They took him to a farmhouse outside Nanteuil, where he was hidden in a hayloft from German patrols, fed and clothed and his wounds treated. His wounds won him their respect and sympathy, yet without ever closing the distance between them. The distance that existed because, despite their belief that he was 'Achilles', leader of the Rouen group, he was an Englishman and two thousand and more French men and women had been on the train they had tried to stop. Not one of them had escaped.

Also, he was himself withdrawn. Though he listened to the broadcasts from London and began to understand the general progress of the Allied campaign, it was a war of which he was no longer a real part. There was a distance like thick soundless glass between history and himself, between himself and others.

After a week, he allowed himself to be ferried down the line like a parcel to be collected and opened on his arrival in Rouen. He felt his days of running and hiding, eating, sleeping, the faces of strangers and the steady scent of hope, pass him by in a dream of which he was no real part.

There was only one reality, a narrow pinprick of confusing light. He had been betrayed, and he wanted revenge. He had no idea of the origin of the betrayal – probably inside Paris, and perhaps intended only to net Renaud . . . many people in Paris must have known the date and time of contact.

He knew that he was likely to be recalled as soon as he made contact with his group, shipped back to London, at least behind the Allied lines. There, he could begin the task of retracing the path of his betrayal. Therefore, until that opportunity arose, he allowed himself the patience of something inanimate.

The Allied armies were close to Rouen by August the

twenty-sixth. It was a dull day, the afternoon sky oppressive with summer storm, the air rough and tangible against the skin. There was little trouble in getting into Rouen itself, to the suburb of Sotteville. He drove with a local farmer in an antiquated van, chickens clucking loudly in the rear, the whole vehicle smelling of droppings and dusty feathers and vegetables. He was relaxed, though aware. Tension had returned the previous night with the knowledge that he was so close to safety, but he had stilled it during the morning and now he functioned with professional competence.

He was dropped in the centre of the suburb, in a quiet backstreet, much of it reduced to the level of the cobblestones. Warily, he began to trace his steps from the dropping-point to the safe house. It was less than half a mile away.

The German garrison in Rouen was preparing to pull out, that much was evident. They paid him no attention, and he knew the Gestapo and the SS would have no time for arrests and interrogation. He was just a Frenchman, shabbily-dressed, part of a scene through which they passed. He was not stopped once.

He came into a quiet square with a small church. The safe house was two streets away. He began to cross the road and heard the engine of a small Renault fire. Casually he inspected it. It was not Gestapo, and he ignored it, his hands thrust into his pockets to hide the plasters over the fingers, his gait shuffling, purposeless, head bent as he seemed to stare at the cobbles across which he walked.

The noise of the engine leapt at his awareness, suddenly loud and near. When he looked up, the car was almost on top of him, and he saw quite clearly through the windscreen, the faces of two men he knew. Their code-names gleamed in his thoughts – 'Nestor' and 'Patroclus', two of his own group. Danger stuttered to attract his attention even as he instinctively raised his hand to greet them . . .

The eyes of both were intent, riveted. He sensed hands on the wheel of the car, determined. He tried to back away, and saw the car's nose swing with him.

Then he was flung through the air, and the body screamed at the impact, screamed again as it struck the cobbles, and he was hurled into a black pit. For a moment, the two faces with riveted eyes haunted him, looking down on him from the edge of the pit. Then they were gone.

FILE TITLE INVESTIGATION "HERETIQUE".

O.R.S. ACTIVITIES IN PARIS AREA

DOSSIER Nº 14 QTM 66

SUBJECT DE VADERKAGO, ETIENNE, JEAN-MARIE. ARMS MFR. SUPPLY OF FUNDS/ARMS — METROPOLITAN FRANCE

Initiated by HEAD OF SECTION U.P.9.

ALL ENTRIES MUST BE DATED ON THIS COVER AND INITIAL NOTED BY THE INITIATING OFFICER, BEFORE TRANSFER TO CENTRAL FILING PARIS.

Note 1. ANY OTHER ACTION ONLY APPROVED BY A VARIATION CERTIFICATE (VG12) SIGNED BY THE MINISTER.

		1	2	3	4	5	6	7	8	9
A	BIOGRAPHICAL									
B	FINANCIAL									
C	POLITICAL									
D	SUMMARY OF EVIDENCE AND INDICATIONS									
E	RECOMMENDED ACTION									
F	ACTION TAKEN									
G	RESULTS.									

NOTE

ALL DOCUMENTS, TRANSCRIPTS, PHOTOGRAPHS, ETC, PLACED IN THIS COVER MUST BE MICRO-FILMED AND STORED WITH TAPED MATERIAL UNDER RETRIEVAL CODE EJMDV 14 QTM 66

The Minister of the Interior   14.9.62

M. le Minister,

Ref: O.A.S.File 149TM 66

1.   I draw your attention to the enclosed section of transcript
from the above File.

2.   We shall have no problem in convicting the man de Vaugrigard
on the O.A.S. charges pending. However, I recommend postponement
of all proceedings against him.

3. De Vaugrigard's wartime connection with the WOLFGROUP, until
this time unknown to any section of the SDECE , is of crucial
importance, since the leaders of that Group between 1942 & 1945
(names deleted from the transcript and filed under a 333 CODE
  ref: 333-12/62B to which I request you make reference) have
a vital connection with the NATO Joint Intelligence Committee
'Utmost Security' breaches we know to have taken place during
the past two years.

4.   I recommend opening a file on Richard Gardiner, the man
betrayed by de Vaugrigard, with a view to his employment as an
agent of the Security Service, without his knowledge or consent.

5.   I further request an urgent meeting to discuss a possible
scenario.

                               Your Obedient Servant,Sir,

                               Head of Security UP/9

No immediate action other than :—

1. AXE FILE to be opened on Richard Gardiner.

2. Six month time limit on feasibility study
    of all possible scenarios

                               E.M.R.
                               21/9/62

Time Mark		
	INT	I assure you of that. You are in the corner, after all, Monsier. And you have brought yourself there.
	SUB	I am loyal - I have been loyal for ten, twenty years - since the war.
	INT	We were all loyal then Monsieur.
	SUB	Not as I was -you- yes, I shall tell you. This fabricated material you have here - it cannot outweigh the services I have rendered France in the past - I was a member of the 'Wolfgroup'. You have heard of it I imagine ?
◇31.15	INT	Perhaps. Is it relevant here?
	SUB	You know that it was partly because of the Wolfgroup that the General was able to succeed in France after the war -
	INT	Ancient history, Monsieur. It cannot be admissible -
	SUB	It has to be - it has to be - I betrayed Frenchmen on behalf of De Gaulle and London - you understand - on behalf of two men in London, I betrayed Frenchmen - on behalf of the General.
	INT	The names of these two men ?
	SUB	▇▇▇▇▇ ▇▇ ▇▇▇▇ ▇▇▇▇ COMPROMISE RISK - NAMES DELETED - FILED UNDER 3JJ DOSSIER (REF: 3JJ/12/K₂) UNDER DISCONTINUED PREFIXES WOLF AND WOLFGANG
	INT	I see. Proof would not be forthcoming of that particular operation, I am afraid. It is not of any importance.
	SUB	It has to be. I even betrayed my group leader, the man Gardiner - he was part of the betrayal. And I tried to kill him later, when he escaped from the Gestapo. I betrayed a friend for General de Gaulle. What more do you want as evidence of my loyalty ?
◇32.03	INT	Most of this is now unimportant, Monsieur. However, perhaps you had better tell me about it. Confession is good for the soul, so they say.

MINISTRY OF THE INTERIOR

M. Le Ministre,

I enclose the completed AXE File 1360982/45
on RICHARD GARDINER, which gives as complete an account
as is possible of the man's post-war life and career.

It has taken a great deal of time and work as you
will see from the choicer pieces I have placed at the
front of the File.

1. Since the identities of WOLF & WOLVERINE are known to
us, they provide us with targets we have known in
another context for a long time.

2. Our Subject would need to be brought to France -
the Tourist Office could send leaflets ,etc.unsolicited.

3. A complete scenario for the Operation, codenamed -
WOLFSBANE -could be with you next week.

H—

HoS UP/9

Action approved — open File : "OPERATION WOLFSBANE",
to commence when subject placed in proximity
to Dupuy, and triggered.   E.M.R.
28·4·63.

W.—C

CENTRAL RECORDS (Medical)   SUMMARY ~~ACTIONS~~
                                          ~~RESIGNATION~~

NAME *Chidwell, Richard*   RANK *Cpl.*   NUMBER *26413*   DATE *27 March 1946*

Whilst still 11 lbs. underweight, he has made a remarkable recovery
from his ordeal. Strength and stamina good, certainly above average.
Vision & hearing unimpaired, tactile sensitivity of hands & feet
improving and appear virtually normal.

Mentally, there may be difficulties. In layman's·terms, he appears
to have erased his recent experiences, and cannot be induced to 'bring
them into the open' by the usual therapies. His nightmares, etc., are
however now more rare.

There is a small risk of some sort of breakdown but the probability
seems less with the passage of time. His strong personality and
ability to identify with and relate to changing circumstances allows
him, it is felt, to suppress his feelings and responses to a remarkable
degree, in a deliberate and controlled manner. This would partially
explain the rate of recovery.

DISABILITY PENSION NEITHER REQUESTED NOR AWARDED

Signed *J. Hardie* Rank *M/Lt.*

DORSET POLICE

BRIDPORT Station

FULL NAME RICHARD GARDINER DoB 30-7-21 OCCUPATION SOLICITOR

ADDRESS THE OLD SMITHY BECKET LANE NORTH MILTON DORSET

Place of Arrest GARTH FORD Arresting Officer 761 Pc WILLIAMS Date Time 21/4/1627

FINGER PRINTED No   PHOTOGRAPHED No

PARTICULARS OF CHARGE

THE ALLEGED OFFENCE WAS COMMITTED SUBSEQUENT TO A MINOR COLLISION INVOLVING VEHICLE RFO 195, THE PROPERTY OF RICHARD GARDINER, WHEREUPON HE DID IN A PUBLIC PLACE VIZ. GARTH FORD USE THREATENING AND ABUSIVE WORDS AND BEHAVIOUR, WHEREBY A BREACH OF THE PEACE WAS LIKELY TO BE OCCASIONED CONTRARY TO SECT 5. OF THE PUBLIC ORDER ACT OF 1936.

Reported in answer to Bail (38(2) and advised by Chief Constable — in writing — No FURTHER Action DPHQ/337/6 dated 20/4/57 Refer. 143 P.C. Jobling

Person Charging 761 Pc WILLIAMS   Stn. Officer 138 Sgt Lawson.

Bailed in the Sum of £ 25 to BRIDPORT COURT/POLICE STATION

I, RICHARD GARDINER of THE OLD SMITHY NORTH MILTON DORSET acknowledge to owe our Sovereign Lady The Queen, the sum of £ 25 upon condition that I, RICHARD GARDINER shall personally appear at BRIDPORT COURT/Police Station on 30th APRIL 1957 to answer the Charge under SECT 38(2) of M.C.A. 1952

Richard Gardiner Signed

138 Sgt Lawson Stn. Officer

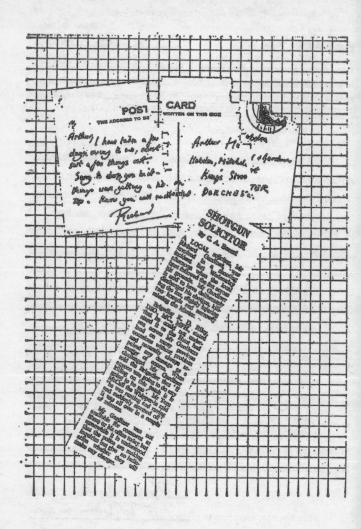

IN PLAIN
ADDRESSETB/R 6178 HOS UP3.
989513 X DST FOREIGN VISITORS SECTION
SERIAL 23,456. TIME 1437
HOLIDAY BOOKING IN NAME RICHARD GARDINER MADE 2 MAY 1963 STOP
CAR TOURING HOLIDAY STOP VISITING BRITTANY AND DORDOGNE STOP
FULL ITINERARY TO FOLLOW STOP
IS THIS WHAT YOU WANTED STOP

MINISTRY OF THE INTERIOR

HEAD OF SECURITY UP/9

TO : "WOLFSBANE TEAM"

a. Operation "Wolfsbane" is now 'go'.
b. Gardiner's arrival at LA BAULE confirmed for AUGUST 12th.
c. Dupuy installed through de Vaugirard as temporary waiter
   at HOTEL BOULEVARD DE L'OCEAN.
d. GREEN ALERT EFFECTIVE IMMEDIATE. Surveillance teams to be
   established with immediate effect.

HoS UP/9

FINAL OPERATION ORDER FOLLOWS WITHIN 6 HRS.

CHAPTER TWO

A FAMILY HOLIDAY
AUGUST 1963

Already there were figures moving on the beach, erecting huge sunshades or deck-chairs, or spreading towels; there were one or two pre-breakfast bathers. Sunlight splintered off the wrinkled sea, and the gleam of sand hurt the eyes. There was only the mildest of breezes. Richard Courteney Gardiner, on the terrace of the Hotel Boulevard de l'Ocean, left his newspaper unopened and watched La Baule slide effortlessly into the business of another hot August day. For a few moments, the oppressive presence of his wife and the attentions of his two sons were absent, and he enjoyed the luxury of an empty awareness, the merely sensuous registration of movement, figures, sound. A waiter hovered briefly, and he shook his head, indicating the empty chairs at the table. He began to feel that his motoring holiday in Brittany might exceed his slim expectations.

He knew that he had wanted a holiday away from his family, but he had been reluctant to suggest it. He had compromised – a touring holiday, a succession of good hotels with swimming pools or beaches to satisfy his wife and the boys, and for himself the hours behind the wheel, the absence of conversation as his wife dozed or read and the boys hesitantly taught each other chess in the back of the Rover; and the daughter of friends, Sarah, brought with them in the role of *au pair* to the boys, contented herself with the glamour of her first French holiday.

His wife and the girl joined him, and reluctantly, and with irritation, he pressed his attention to the present. He felt a sharp and irrational anger at the scraping of her chair, at the cigarette she was already smoking – even at the bodice of her low-cut beach outfit and the evident sensuality of her figure. Sarah's small breasts and slim hips were still girlish in the bikini she wore beneath the beach-coat. She hovered for a moment, then sat down silently, hands clasped between her thighs, eyes regarding the table-cloth. He did not look at either of them as he said:

'What would you like?'

'Just fruit juice – and coffee,' Jane Gardiner replied. Gardiner looked at the girl, who nodded in agreement.

His eyes remained expressionless, masked by the sun-glasses, as he summoned the waiter. He saw his two sons, both serious and intent, coming towards them, the travelling chess-set held between them like some precious burden. He ruffled the dark hair of each absently, smiled formally, and then looked up at the waiter.

He was a man in his late thirties. He was standing between Gardiner and the view, the sun at his back, and his head was haloed with light. The polaroid lenses of Gardiner's glasses showed him the man's features in shadow. He saw the man's nerves, the tic of an eyelid, and he saw the smudges of ingrained dirt on the man's collar. He had been out of work, or was habitually careless about his appearance. His face was thin, dark yet sallow, the eyes narrow, the mouth petulant, full-lipped. He appeared old in experience of the unsuccessful, even the sordid.

Because Gardiner felt so detached, he ignored a sudden pluck of subconscious recognition and dismissed the man's evident nervousness, ordered breakfast and proceeded to read his paper. The waiter scuttled away. Gardiner, once only, told himself that he did not know him, the cool appreciation of the man's appearance fading. He turned to the cricket scoreboard.

When they had eaten, and Jane was smoking another cigarette and drinking a second cup of coffee, he said:

'Well, you two – want to go sailing this morning?' There was a forced enthusiasm in his voice that seemed to communicate itself to Timothy and Giles. They watched him out of dark eyes as if judging whether they should indulge him or not. There was a long silence. He had not bothered to consult the girl.

Eventually Timothy, the elder, said, 'Can we finish this game first, Daddy? I've almost beaten him.'

'You haven't!' Giles snorted.

'O.K. Finish each other off, then we'll pop down to the yacht harbour and see what's for hire. You'll come too, Sarah?' The girl, startled from the crumbs of her croissant, looked up, and then nodded silently. Gardiner looked at his wife, saw the sense of satisfaction brought about by the general lack of enthusiasm for his idea, and added: 'What plans have you this lovely day, my dear?'

He studied the beautiful, chiselled features as small emotions chased and flickered like camera shutters. Then the face became smooth, a melting into self-assurance that began at the green eyes. She brushed a lazy hand through her blonde hair and said:

'The beach, I should think – unless you'd like me to come sailing with you . . .?'

'I'm sure you'd be bored.'

'I'm certain of it.'

'Darling . . .' His eyes indicated Sarah.

She smiled. 'Of course.' She stubbed out her cigarette, and stood up. 'I'll get ready for the beach.' She bent her face to the table, and Timothy and Giles bestowed small pecks at her cheek; then she was gone. Gardiner watched her move across the terrace, registering her body, noted the head held challengingly high, and recalled the time when he had desired her so greatly that the feeling was palpable, choking like smoke in the throat . . .

He dismissed her, watched his sons as hands hovered for the mate, the childish kill, and then returned his attention to his English newspaper.

The waiter, whose name was Alfred Dupuy, registered the departure of Jane Gardiner with scant attention. His

eyes, and his awareness, were concentrated on her husband.
The bent heads of his two children were dark blobs beneath
the umbrella's shadow, and the slim body of the girl, which
another time he might have studied with satisfaction,
required no concentration. But the man . . .

Impossible.

Alfred Dupuy could feel himself sweating even as he
watched the oblivious Englishman reading his newspaper.
It was the obliviousness that disturbed him, rubbing his
shallow self-possession raw. He could not bear the tension
of the apparent lack of recognition, not when he had been
so certain, and almost at once. The indifference, it had to be
assumed . . .

It was as if Richard Gardiner did not recognise him at all.
He had prayed for that ever since he had learned that he
and Perrier had failed to kill 'Achilles' when they ran him
down in the quiet square in Rouen, as he crossed the street –
had prayed for it intermittently for nineteen years, prayed
the previous night, awake and sweating, after seeing the
English family across the hotel dining room. Then, he had
not been able to believe it, though it was the first scene in
that waking nightmare that had never left him for nineteen
years.

He and Perrier – what they had done to Gardiner – why
had Gardiner never come back for them after the war? He
had seen the man's face through the fly-specked windscreen
of the van, had seen the shock of recognition in Gardiner's
eyes, the moment of hatred and fury that had surfaced
through the fear – he *knew*.

Borrowed time – always borrowed from somewhere, from
someone. Gardiner would come back. He had known that
for him, a situation had never been finished, never irrever-
sible – Gardiner never let go of things.

He's come for me, he must have . . . He formed the words
precisely, as if solemn and spoken aloud, and they orbited
in his thoughts. There was no other way that he could understand, or consider. He was unable to believe in chance, and

while each hour of the previous night had creaked past like an endless, marching column of haggard moments, he had come to what he thought was an understanding of the situation.

Cat-and-mouse. Gardiner's old game, the way he had seen him play before. Contempt for weakness, ruthless, arbitrary in his decisions – that was him. Dupuy knew him, only too well – knew what he would do, given the slightest chance.

He shuddered. Standing at the table from where he served the breakfasters with coffee and tea, he watched the man pretending to read the English newspaper, his eyes hidden behind his sunglasses. Dupuy could read the expression, even though he couldn't see the eyes. He had come there because he knew that 'Patroclus' was working there . . .

The Englishman was taunting him now, playing with him . . .

He had to act . . .

He felt cold with the thought.

When Gardiner left his table, the form of the waiter who suddenly turned his back flickered at the corner of his eyesight. He looked across at Dupuy, and a vague recognition muttered like distant thunder. Then he forgot it, and passed into the cool of the hotel foyer. Sarah and the two boys trailed reluctantly after him.

Soon after he completed his duties at breakfast, Dupuy made a telephone call to Paris, from a tiny, almost-bare room in the attic of the hotel. It was hot and airless up there, even with the window open. He sat on a hard chair, the telephone strained on its lead to the small coffee table with the marks of rested cigarettes around its edges. It took him several minutes to obtain the extension he wanted, and when he did he was nervous of the voice at the other end of the line. A blind panic had prompted him to make the call, and at once he began to despise the impulse.

Etienne de Vaugrigard, to whom he had gone seeking work, had found him only this menial summer employment in La Baule. The lever he had sought to apply, that of their mutual past and perhaps their mutual guilt, had functioned inadequately. De Vaugrigard seemed unsurprised, though contemptuous and aloof, as Dupuy explained the reasons for his call.

' "Achilles" is here,' he said, his voice breathless and quiet in the hot room, his free hand pressed down on the table to prevent its nervous palsy. 'He is staying as a guest at the hotel, with his family.'

'He recognised you?' the voice asked, its tone quickened by an interest that was disguised but not feigned.

'I – I am not sure.'

'Why have you rung me, Dupuy? All this was nineteen years ago, you recall? He never came back before. Of what interest is it to me now what our former ally is doing during his vacation?'

'You – you know why!' Dupuy blurted out.

'*I* know why?' the voice challenged him.

'The – orders. Orders . . .'

'Go on.'

Dupuy was silent. Then, cowed, he said, 'You – gave me this job. The only one, you said . . .'

'I did not request reports on your guests during the summer.'

'But him – in the whole world, he is *here*! You don't understand!'

'Understand what?'

De Vaugrigard had been 'Hector', second-in-command to 'Achilles' in Rouen. It was obvious. The orders, those he hardly now dared mention – orders that must have come from him. They both knew that – *knew* it!

'Why is he here? Why didn't he come back after the war? He saw me! Mother of God, I saw him looking into my *head* when we ran him down!' His voice sobbed, and for a while he was silent, oblivious of the man at the other end of the line, in his sumptuous Paris office. Then he asked, as if of the room, 'What shall I do?'

'Have you saved sufficient to be able to leave your employment?' Etienne de Vaugrigard asked sardonically.

'A little . . .'

'But you are greedy, in direct proportion to your laziness. Therefore, you will remain at your post.'

'But – I . . .' The confession was blurted, indistinct: 'He is a very frightening man.'

'*Was*. Remember that. You say he does not recognise you. Very well. Pray that it remains so, and keep out of his way. You believe that he saw you. You were mistaken. Not your only mistake during those years.'

Dupuy was suddenly angry. He had a quick, sudden image – a face bright with recognition, then pale with fear, then the wing of the Renault striking flesh, and the awful blackness for a moment when the body lurched up onto the bonnet and rolled across the roof . . .

'I saw his face – he knew it was me,' he said dully.

He had never been certain that de Vaugrigard had organised it. Perrier had forced him into it, and the implication had been that the word had come from Paris, from high up. Gardiner had been betrayed and knew it – now he had to be killed. He captured almost perfectly that moment, felt the prickle of tears he had felt then. They had to kill 'Achilles'.

'So?' the voice said, cold and brusque, as if there had been no implication on de Vaugrigard's part. 'I know what happened, and I know why you are afraid, perhaps.' There was little sympathy in the voice. 'But I saw Gardiner many times, in the army hospital, even after the war in England. He never spoke about it.' A sense of confidence entered the cool voice. 'I don't think he even thought that he had been betrayed in Paris, nor in Rouen. Do you understand what I'm saying?'

'Yes.'

'Good. If you are worried, keep out of his way!'

There was a click, and the receiver purred in his ear. He

took it from his cheek, stared at it, then replaced it. A fly
buzzed in the airless room, crossing vividly through a slant-
ing bar of sunlight.

He was on his own. The man at the other end of the line,
the millionaire de Vaugrigard, would do nothing. What had
he expected him to do? Nothing. He had not ordered
Gardiner's death, and he wasn't afraid.

Dupuy could see Gardiner's face again through the windscreen. He knew – at that moment, he *knew*.

And must still know.

Gardiner knew that his wife had embarked upon another
affair. She wanted to go shopping in La Baule that afternoon,
even though he had suggested that they all go to the beach
together. The excuses were feeble, and transparent. She had
met the man at the Casino the previous evening, and no
doubt on the beach that morning.

In itself, the circumstances of her infidelity did not disturb
him. It was the lack of concealment of her eagerness that
irritated. Not angered – that was too far in the past, and he
had achieved a shallow certitude that he was not to blame,
and that there was no recapturing the early days; he did not
question the relationship – or lack of it – any more. To have
done so would have courted a dangerous introspection
which had betrayed him more than once in the past. It was
her fault, all of it. Unbridled appetite.

When the boys showed reluctance to do anything except
assemble a model aeroplane kit they had brought from
Dorchester, he turned on them angrily, and turned also on
the girl, because, with her silent patience, she was little
more than part of the furniture of their holiday. They were
surprised at his anger, yet he felt that they sensed its cause,
and the nakedness their knowledge gave him injured his
ego, and he left them, the whole lot of them, grateful only
that in their still, hot bedroom Jane had made no display
of her body as she dressed for her assignation. She had done
that, in the past, and always it had incensed him, muddied

his feelings and tarnished his sense of detachment. At least
not that.

He took the Rover from the hotel car park, and headed
out of La Baule on the road to Vannes, heading north. He
did not notice Dupuy, still serving lunches, even though the
man's eyes were riveted upon him as he passed through the
foyer.

Once out of the town, he drove with little sense of direction, forcing the attention into the mechanical functions of
the body, into hands and feet, even into the hot leather of
his seat.

At Guerande he turned, on impulse, eastwards on a
minor road, heading for the Grande Brière, the fen country
crossed by drainage canals and margined and bracketed by
dykes lying north and east of La Baule. At first, the flatness
of the countryside, the white cottages and the slow cattle,
all dulled the awareness. It was perhaps an hour before he
realised he was becoming steadily more angry, that the car
journey was an irritation in itself, designed as it was as an
escape from the stifling hotel room and the proximity of his
wife. He could not escape his memory, his prognostications,
and these seeped back into the apparent and superficial
calm he had maintained.

Before long, the scenery along the D 47 as it skirted the
Grande Brière became unrelievedly flat, dull – reduced in
scale until it was a toy landscape, a painting done by someone with little taste and a cumbersome sentimentality. He
stopped the car, pulling into the side of the road, and got out.

He leaned on a fence at the side of the road, and tried to
watch the slow progress of cattle across the pasture. His
eye and mind were distracted for a few moments by the sight
of a flat-bottomed punt moving gracefully along the canal
half a mile away. But the stooping, rhythmic figure with the
pole was too insect-like to demand attention. He turned his
back on the scene and studied the empty road, and his car.

The car was new, and such as he might be expected to
possess as a partner in the firm of Hebden, Mitchell and

Gardiner, solicitors. He was forty-two, successful within the somewhat narrow confines of the legal practice of a country town, and his wife had money of her own. The Rover was dusty and travel-stained, and its appearance seemed an apt comment on his life. Substantial, comfortable, with a hidden power – yet somehow made ordinary, dull.

He wanted to blame her, and usually he could. She was the first to be unfaithful. His lips twisted at the quaintness of the expression. She was the first. She had told him, in the days of their blind, hating quarrels, how cold he was, how indifferent to her. Incapable of loving, of tenderness.

He drove the thought away, flicked at it as his hand flicked away an insect near his ear. He had drifted, he admitted, into the brief, ungenerous affair with the girl Diane, as a mirror-image of his wife's infidelities. He had intended his holiday as a break that would see the end of that liaison. He had not had the courage to break cleanly, to dismiss the girl who was twenty years younger than himself. There was a young man, he believed, a travelling salesman of some kind.

With the images of his brief entanglement with the girl fading in his mind, the anger seemed also to die. The girl had driven out the wife at least, he thought. The day was hot, and behind him the lush grass gave out the murmur of insects. His back was hot, and against his sides there was a dampness beneath the arms of his cotton shirt. He rebelled against the situation suddenly, against the image of his futility it seemed to encapsulate. He got back into the car, switched on the ignition, and the tyres squealed on to the road as he let out the clutch.

He followed the signs on the D 47 to Herbignac, and then he left the hamlet on the N 774 leading back towards La Baule. There was something contemptible to him in the way he had lost his wife to other men; something now more contemptible in his running from the knowledge of infidelity. He had always been a man in a car, driving furiously away from the bed, the assignation.

He had no intention of vulgarly surprising his wife in the

arms of her lover, seeing the man's head looking over his shoulder at the sound of a door opening, looking along the ridiculous white perspective of the buttocks . . . Perhaps she was astride him, the dominant position she often indulged . . .

He gripped the wheel of the car fiercely, and pressed down hard on the accelerator. Hatred, envious loathing, helped to emphasise her culpability, the completeness of her responsibility for their situation, the collapse of their lives. She was to blame even for the pettiness of his sufferings, which disappointed him.

The car's speed crept up satisfyingly. Fifty, sixty, sixty-three, sixty-eight . . . The traffic was heavy, though moving freely. Tourist traffic, a few heavier vehicles. He ticked off the cars he overtook, beginning to envisage the faces that glanced at him, oncoming or sliding past the window, as a sequence of defeated opponents.

He understood what he was doing. He had not invited it, or willed it, yet he understood it. He escaped into the present moment, utterly – entirely unconcerned at his progress, its consequences, the hot cry of the tyres on the tar of the road . . .

He did not kill anyone. Afterwards, even soon afterwards, when they strapped his wrist and saw to the knee in the hospital in La Baule, he was grateful for that, that the people in the oncoming Mercedes had been shocked but uninjured. That satisfaction remained with him.

The grey Mercedes came at him, leaping to occupy the gap of road he had entered as he overtook a slow Renault van just north of Guerande. He squeezed the brakes, hands suddenly wet on the wheel and the tremor of reaction beginning in his leg – he thought he might slow in time. The driver of the van, comically bereted and wearing a striped jersey, had been irritated at the foreigner's imperious use of the French road, and had accelerated. Gardiner could not regain his own side of the road, and the Rover's offside wing crunched along the flank of the Mercedes as its driver heaved the wheel desperately to take him onto the narrow strip of dusty grass at the side of the road. Gardiner was sandwiched for a moment as the impact threw him back against the van, then the wheel escaped his slippery palms, and the big saloon lurched for the far verge of the N 774, thrusting its blunt nose down into the ditch. By the time the front wheels began to revolve over emptiness, the engine squealing like a hurt pig, his hands were in in front of his face. His forehead struck the windscreen, which did not shatter, and he felt his neck heated by the wrench on his muscles before he passed out.

Afterwards, he could not decide whether he was conscious or not when the disorientation began. He was hurt, but out of the car now, and there were voices coming from an impossible distance, and hands fluttered out of his sight like glancing wings. He could see only the hot blue of the sky directly above him.

There was the expectancy of more pain. A strange dislocation of the awareness. His head hammered, but the pain was dying to a mutter now, and his knee hurt, and when he lifted his left arm there was a stab of pain in his wrist. It did not seem sufficient. He did not understand. He felt that the hands inspecting him were fumbling not with the blue cotton shirt but with the rough material of a jacket. He smelt the acrid, rich scent of a foreign cigarette. He expected the hardness of cobblestones beneath his shoulders, along his legs.

He heard the siren of an ambulance, sliding nearer. There was a redness obscuring his vision and he assumed that it must be blood from a cut on his forehead or face. A shadow bent towards him, wiped at the redness with something, and a voice asked him questions. A French voice. He saw the Mercedes coming towards him again, and he mentally braked. Yet the angle of vision of the memory was higher; he was standing upright, walking across a space of cobblestones as the car came towards him. He saw two faces through the windscreen, vague, pencilled sketches rather than human faces, and he saw the intent, staring eyes of each.

Another place, another accident.

Cobblestones.

Rouen.

'Oh Christ!' he cried out in protest as they lifted him towards the ambulance. Someone apologised, assuming they had hurt him.

He was being forced to regurgitate the past, the past he had buried so successfully for so many years.

He knew who the waiter was.

Etienne de Vaugrigard, as a consequence of Dupuy's call, made a telephone call of his own that afternoon, soon after returning from a heavy business lunch. The prospective purchasers, the government of an emergent African nation, had toured the St. Denis factories the previous day; a lucrative arms deal seemed sealed. Yet the euphoria of business success – he always liked to attend to major contracts himself, during their closing stages – was dispelled even as he dialled the Paris number he had been given and whose owner he could not trace. The capacious office, thick-carpeted, highlighted with ornaments, rich with decoration, was solid, comfortable – now suddenly possessing an insubstantial modernity of tubular steel and glass, a thing he had tried to avoid when choosing the furnishings.

He got through almost at once.

'He hasn't made any kind of move,' he said bluntly, feeling the tongue thick in his mouth, a dull instrument incapable now of the assured, sauve pleasantries that littered his lunchtime conversation. He was hot despite the air-conditioning.

The man at the other end of the line spoke French. He said, 'We expected that, Etienne.' De Vaugrigard winced at the use of his first name, usage which seemed to strip away the padding of deference with which his life had become surrounded. 'I have my own sources, Etienne, and I know that Gardiner has done nothing – that he took no notice of Dupuy. However, it would seem likely that Dupuy will force himself upon the Englishman very soon. As we anticipated.'

'Why do you always include *me*?' It was intended as rejection, yet it seemed like a plea.

'You are involved, Etienne.' The voice was inhuman. Etienne found the man incomprehensible; the one who called himself 'L'Etranger'. Ridiculous – and – yes, sinister.

'It won't work!'

'No?'

'I told you – it was nineteen years ago. He's buried it all deep down in his mind by now. Got on with life.' He was sweating and he realised he had balled his silk handkerchief into a damp little lump in his fist. He dropped it on the desk in revulsion. 'I've seen him since then. He had no suspicion . . .'

'That is not what you told me previously, Etienne. Nor is it true. Dupuy will bring the tiger out from beneath the sheepskin. I am certain of that. I, too, have been studying M'sieur Gardiner. If he is threatened – then . . .'

'Yes.' Something in de Vaugrigard had collapsed like a weakened cliff, sliding into the water. His voice was older than his fifty years. 'You are sure it – will work?' He had wanted to ask after his own safety, could not stoop, not so far.

'The price of failure is higher for you than for me, Etienne. We must both – pray for success.' There was not even contemptuous laughter in the voice.

'Yes.'

As if reading his mind, the voice said; 'I have promised you will be safe, Etienne. So shall you be. Goodbye.'

The phone clicked, then purred in de Vaugrigard's ear. Slowly, as if it were heavy, he replaced the receiver, then resisted the temptation to pick up the crumpled handkerchief and mop his brow, as he caught sight of his reddened, strained features in a mirror. Instead, he slumped back in his leather chair and stared at the ceiling.

There was little doubt that 'L'Etranger', as he wished to call himself, was SDECE – French Intelligence. And that he was playing some especially murky game which somehow involved Gardiner. De Vaugrigard could not feel culpability

at that involvement, just as he had dismissed guilt for
Gardiner's treatment at the hands of the Gestapo years
before. Feelings rarely lingered with him; as he admitted,
only the gratification of controlling De Vaugrigard Armaments had lasted down the years.

'L'Etranger' had come to see him concerning certain funds
that had reached the OAS, together with small arms un-
accounted for in the records of his companies. And, terrified
by the consequences of his actions, he had babbled the whole
story of the 'Wolfgroup', his loyalty to de Gaulle even to
the betrayal of his friend, Gardiner. And he had named the
'Wolf'. And sprung, it seemed instantly, his own trap.

He stared at the portrait of his wife, Geneviéve, next to
the carriage clock on the desk. His face wrinkled in dislike,
as if she were in some obscure way to blame for his predica-
ment.

He had been betrayed by de Gaulle, as had the army in
Algeria – he had helped, yes. But this? This kind of –
humiliation of terror?

Unsettled and dispirited in self-esteem, he visited the
Faubourg St. Honoré flat of his young mistress, parking his
large black Citroën near the Madeleine, before he returned
to his family house on the Avenue de Madrid. When he
reached home, late in the evening, his wife had already
retired. He took a bottle of cognac into the library, and sat
staring at the solid rows of gold-lettered volumes that had
belonged to his father.

Dupuy stared at the gun. His right hand was clenched
around the butt, the left curled tightly upon the barrel. It
was an old Luger, a prize of war. He had kept it as little more
than a memento of the past. He had cleaned it occasionall ,
and there was a full clip of ammunition on the coffee table in
front of him. He sat in a hunched, almost reverential
attitude.

Why he had decided to kill Richard Gardiner was clear
to him; it was something he must do. An imperative.

Through the rest of the morning, and the afternoon, he had sat in the airless room, the clouds of cigarette-smoke reluctant to diminish, the battered tin ashtray full of crumpled stubs yawning in his staring eyes as if it threatened to swallow him.

Gardiner would kill him. He knew that, with utter certainly. It was only a matter of time before he was recognised. *Kill or be killed*. He liked the narrowness of it, the definition it gave to the surrounding objects of his life.

Bigger, with the gun. Yes – he admitted it. Comforting blued steel, as he caressed it. Sharp feelings from the old time; he was younger again, and his head was clear. He did not blame Gardiner for having come to La Baule, stayed at that hotel. Not now. Now he would kill him.

The young policeman who interviewed him while they stitched his knee and strapped the wrist was hostile, arrogant. Evidently, he disliked tourists, especially English tourists who drove recklessly on French roads. Perhaps, Gardiner reflected with some small unencumbered part of his mind, it was only because the people he had almost killed were Germans that he was not arrested and charged. As it was, he was warned not to leave La Baule, and that he would undoubtedly be hearing from the police the following day when a fuller investigation had been carried out.

When he left, it was immediately as if he had never been in the chill little room where they gave him a cup of coffee, his trousers torn from turn-up to thigh, and pinned, his shirt-sleeves rolled up, and his head thudding. Two stitches in the cut, and a patch of wadded plaster covering the left side of his forehead.

He tried to grasp a minute of peace in the empty room, as if sensing that he could no longer open the door on the same world he had left on entering the room. He hated the French driver in the beret and the jersey; his revulsion at the immediacy of his own past required an object of focus.

He had been in a military hospital for eight months after

they tried to kill him in Rouen. He left it, to convalesce at his mother's home in Devon, a month before the war in Europe came to an end. When he was sufficiently well, he resumed his studies at Cambridge. Qualified, and under-standing precisely the motives behind his actions, he had joined the firm of solicitors in Dorset, married a wealthy young woman of rigidly conventional county stock, bred two children – and buried the past, and his former self.

He clenched the one good hand – the wrist of the other pained him as he attempted it – in fury that the mental equilibrium of years had been shifted like so much ballast by one single occurrence. He hated his past. Grateful it had not killed him, or permanently crippled him, he had lost all interest in it, all desire to revenge himself on whoever had betrayed him – even upon the mechanics, Perrier and Dupuy, who had driven the car to orders.

Dupuy. The waiter with the dirty collar and the rough hands that had seen too much menial work. 'Patroclus'. He squeezed the past out of his mind, his teeth grinding loudly in the silence of the room. His strength, over the years, had been measured in the success with which he was able to forget and ignore.

A lurch of his stomach like nausea. The image of the Renault van. He lifted his head as if to bay at the ceiling, his eyes tight shut, his mouth working, his breath coming like that of an exhausted runner.

Which he was, he recognised. Always running.

Now, having to run again. Get away from Dupuy, before he brought back the dreams. Dreams of fingers' ends, and fists and clubs. A white light and the questions. Urine-soaked trousers, and thirst. And pain everywhere, in his back, and legs, and head. Cobblestones, and Rouen.

The room stifled him. He tugged his jacket – no, someone else's, slung across his shoulders as he walked limping between the ambulance men into the hospital. To warm him, he supposed. He put the jacket untidily back over the chair, and let himself out of the room.

Someone gave him a number to ring, and he called a taxi. When he was dropped at the Hotel Boulevard de l'Ocean, he went quickly to his room, afraid he might confront Dupuy if he lingered in the foyer or went into the bar.

Jane Gardiner returned in sufficient time to change for dinner. When he explained what had happened – he was still dressed in the torn trousers and the bloodstained shirt – she was initially shocked. However, she seemed grateful for the reluctance of his explanation, and the aura of introspection with which he seemed to have surrounded himself since lunch. She ordered his dinner sent up to the room and took Sarah and the boys down to the dining room. When she had gone, the memory of her being in the room was as insubstantial as the last of her perfume on the still air. Alone again, he breathed calmly, attempting to relax, aware that there was still tension in his frame, as if braced to resist some shock.

Soon after his meal was delivered, the telephone rang, startling him. He picked up the receiver with a sudden dart of his hand, and gave his room number; a voice he did not recognise, speaking good English, said:

'M'sieur Gardiner. I – have some information concerning your wife . . .'

'Who is this?' He was aware of the blurted words, wishing to recall their frightened tone.

There was a brief silence, as if the speaker were taking stock of his mood, then: 'A friend. I have information concerning your wife's – *affaire* with a certain member of La Baule society . . .'

At first, Gardiner could not answer.

'What – are you talking about? What is my wife to do with you?'

After a pause, the voice said, 'You have no interest that your wife is unfaithful to you, M'sieur?' The tone was leeringly confidential.

'I don't care to hear it from you,' Gardiner said tiredly.

He assumed that the caller was a putative blackmailer. Ridiculous.

Yet he realised he would have to meet the man. Otherwise, there might be trouble, scandal that drew attention to him, or some means of forcing him to stay in La Baule – even Dupuy's attention . . . He had already resolved to leave La Baule as soon as the Rover was repaired.

He said, 'Very well. We must meet – but not at my hotel. Where?'

'That is more sensible, M'sieur. I would have had to mention the photographs soon . . .'

'Very well!' Gardiner said urgently. It seemed clear to him at that moment that he had to recover the photographs, had to pay off the blackmailer, whoever he was. He suspended examination of his motives. It had something to do with safety, he knew. Like the pattern of his life since the war. *Safety*. He said, 'Where? When?'

'Tonight,' came the reply. 'In La Baule les Pins, near the Parc des Dryades. There is an empty villa, set back a little from the street. Turn off the Avenue de L'Etoile at the squash club, into the Rue des Epinettes. The house is number forty-six. You have that?'

'Yes.' Gardiner's voice was a whisper in the empty room.

'Good. Until tonight. Shall we say eleven o'clock?' The telephone clicked, and Gardiner instantly put down the receiver. He slumped back in the chair, and his eye caught the crumpled edge of the bedspread where his wife had sat to roll on her stockings, the headscarf in blotched bright colours draped over the back of a chair, a cigarette-end smudged with pink lipstick stubbed into a crested ashtray.

He hated her for being caught out, for placing him in the hands of a blackmailer. She was making him behave stupidly, weakly. But the blackmailer threatened his anonymity. He had to see him, settle it. Get the pictures, hand over whatever was demanded.

He seemed to be sinking into a morass of weakness, and was unable to help himself. It was simply that he had to escape Dupuy, and his past. He couldn't bear the dreams again, the choking rages that had tormented him in the military hospital. Not again.

At ten forty-five he turned the hired Peugeot into the Rue des Epinettes. It was difficult to drive the car, even with an automatic gearbox. Yet he persevered with the pain in his wrist because he had to keep his appointment.

His wife had gone to the Casino, presumably to meet her lover, soon after dinner. The fact that she was, in his estimation, not worth one moment of the weak, fearful agitation in which he had picked at his dinner and then arranged to hire a car did not weigh with him. The completion of some deal with the blackmailer had assumed a symbolic proportion in his mind. It would be like closing the lid upon his past, on the box that had spilled out his world's evils.

The villa was half-hidden behind a dejected tall hedge, holed like dark lacework and unkempt. The tyres crunched on dusty gravel, and he pulled the car round to park it behind the hedge, opposite the porch. He got out stiffly, rubbing his knee gingerly to relieve the stitched discomfort. Straightening, he surveyed the façade of the villa. It had obviously been built in the heyday of La Baule as a new seaside resort, towards the end of the previous century. It was pale in the bright moon, ghostly rather than solid, ornate and decayed. It had evidently not been lived in for many years. Windows were boarded up on the ground floor – some of them, at least – and in the corners of the porch were still some of last autumn's leaves. Heavy old trees leaned towards the house, giving it a Gothic unreality.

He climbed the three steps to the porch, and touched the front door. It swung stiffly open. His first footsteps echoed in the hall, and the boards creaked. He called out, and the sound of his voice died somewhere away at the rear of the villa. He wondered, fearfully, if the man might not come.

There was a door open, and the light from a passing car

glanced across the portion of the wall he could see. Ugly blotches of an old wallpaper. It was a drawing-room, it seemed, overlooking the front of the house. He looked at his watch, seeing he was early.

He pushed open the door and stepped into the room.

There was a shadow by the window. He was relieved rather than afraid, then he saw, in the light flung by the headlights of another car passing along the Rue des Epinettes, the face of the blackmailer.

Dupuy. The waiter with the dirty collar. The face behind the windscreen.

' "Patroclus"!'

A moment's silence, then the flat crack that magnified in the room to a roar, and the spit of orange flame as the man fired the gun he held at his waist.

CHAPTER THREE

AN OLD GAME

Gardiner stumbled as he turned instinctively, and pain shot through the stitched knee – the wrist hurt as he braced his body against the door. He was deaf for a moment after the shot, and he moved as if in an alien element through into the hall, grabbing for the banister at the foot of the wide staircase. He heard the boards creak under his weight as sound returned, and his breath rushed in his ears. He went up the bare flight of stairs, dragging his injured leg behind him, adrenalin surging in his blood, his heart labouring with shock and fear.

Yet already it was as if something moved more slowly in him, something emerging from a chrysalis. Dupuy was the blackmailer, and he wanted to kill him – *kill him*. It was as if he had been hit by the wildly-fired bullet, the pain of fear was so tangible.

He flung open the blank door to a bare room, and ducked behind it. His back was pressed against the peeling wallpaper. The moonlight was coming dustily through the single tall window.

The man downstairs had not fired again. He pressed his damp palms against the wallpaper, feeling it clammy already, inhaling the musty, dead air of the room, trying to calm the body's clamour.

The face of Dupuy returned again and again, flickering like imitation movements from a flicked series of still pictures. In the passenger seat of the Renault, downstairs, and younger still, up at the farm near Rouen.

Dupuy had been precipitate – something told him that,

and he wondered why. Dupuy had not meant to fire at that moment. Yet the old code-name had startled him, and the sudden movement by Gardiner.

He wanted to cry out to Dupuy, to protest his harmlessness. He wanted to take hold of the last nineteen years like clothing, and wrap himself in them; they seemed unsubstantial, as if the pale moonlight had affected them. His breath sobbed in his throat, though his breathing had become calm.

He felt the acute physical symptoms of drunkenness or delirium, a wrenching pain in chest and stomach, the sense of leaning out over some dark gap . . .

And then he laughed, an explosive noise which seemed to expel not only breath, but the sense of nausea. He felt thinner, almost skeletal. He began to shiver in the returned silence, ears strained to listen; reaction, but he sensed it as transformation, hideous and sudden. When his body was still, he sensed that it was different, changed to something other than himself. A cold rage; a pure iciness of understanding.

Dupuy was afraid of him, afraid of the revenge he must have thought would come in 1944. Kill, or be killed, the law he had blindly obeyed.

Dupuy was already dead, even before he began to ascend the staircase. He shuddered with the resolve.

The fact that 'Patroclus' had a gun pleased him, absurdly. He would kill him with his bare hands. He began to laugh loudly, the sound chilling through the empty house. He called out:

'Dupuy – you bloody fool! Yesterday, I didn't even recognise you! I've spent nineteen years forgetting you! I would have run away – yesterday! Now you're a dead man – unless you can kill me first!'

A weight paused on a stair that creaked. Gardiner's ears, concentrating the moment he choked off the final word, heard it. Then he heard the shuffle as the man moved off the betraying wood. He laughed again, a sharp barking noise. He tested his knee, then grimaced as if at weakness he could not pity. Tensing himself, he moved from behind the door. He passed down the wide corridor, opening door after door on either side with as much noise as he could.

'Come and play!' he called. 'Come and find me!' He laughed again, and remembered his brother and he playing hide-and-seek as children, in the big old rectory. A high boyish laugh seemed to answer him, and he shook his head as if to clear it of muzziness. The memory was hampering now. It did not belong either to the war, or to the years after. He recalled instead the sunlit square, and the agony as they tried to lift him; the pain cleansed him. It drove him to extract recompense.

Dupuy fired a shot. Gardiner doubted whether he had even reached the head of the staircase. It was whistling in the dark house.

Gardiner ducked into a bedroom. Here there was the smell of empty linen drawers and lavender, fossilised. There was the shape of a bed, old, four-posted, and of huge dark-wood wardrobes. Perhaps the last refuge of some ancient female who had inhabited the house. He waited behind the door, and listened. Another stair creaked, and then nothing. He wondered how well Dupuy was relearning the old lessons. Had he removed his shoes yet?

Gardiner bent down and unlaced his suede shoes, took them off and slid them away from him. Then he tested the sprained wrist, grimacing as he tried to clench his hand. He cursed the weakness, then bent down and felt for the shoes. Swiftly, he removed the lace of one and tested it, snapping it taut again and again. He knotted it in the middle, and tied one end of the lace around his forefinger, in case the grip failed. Then he froze the sprained hand into a fist so that it clenched one end of the lace. He gripped the other end, raised his hands over his head until they touched the wall above him, and waited.

Silence. Then a door, banged back on its hinges, to

surprise him. Silence again, trembling with relief and the
spasm of fear.

Four bullets, perhaps six or seven. He did not know the
type of gun. It was unlikely that Dupuy would use any
more of them. Gardiner realised that he had repossessed
his former identity, redeeming 'Achilles' from burial in his
own mind and his post-war persona. It had been as simple
as peeling an onion, and without tears.

Now was *then*, a house in France and a man with a gun.
The skeleton of a world, the mere bones of a human
experience.

The footsteps had established a pattern now – mouse-
shuffles towards each succeeding door, then the banging of
the door as it opened, then silence. After long minutes,
Gardiner was able to pick out the explosions of breath,
muffled though they were, after each new empty room. Soon,
the noises became louder, more routine. Gardiner had
opened all the rooms along the corridor. Dupuy was being
lulled into a routine that would dull his awareness, finally
betray him.

Mouse-steps, then the slow creak of a door. Gardiner
relaxed slightly.

He waited.

Air moved against his cheek, and he heard the tiny noise
of a woollen sock in contact with rough floorboards. He
did not move. The door began to open very slowly. Gardiner
waited, aware only of the lace stretched taut between the
clenched hands. Dupuy's head appeared.

One further step. Gardiner saw moonlight glint on the
old Luger, and waited. Uncountable seconds later, Dupuy
moved. In the moment of less sure balance as he stepped
forward, Gardiner heaved the door against him, squashing
the man against the wall. There was a cry of pain and then
the mute struggle as the lace tightened across the throat with
its bobbing adam's apple.

By a desperate effort of will, Dupuy managed to drag
Gardiner across the room behind him. But the lace did not

slacken for a moment, and he felt consciousness slipping from him. He scrabbled at the lace, already buried in the folds of flesh of his neck. scratching his skin into bleeding lines. The moonlit square of window wobbled in his vision, and he lurched towards it. The pain was looser in his throat, and he tried to drag in air. Then he tried, suddenly, to put out his hands, to stop the idiotic descent of the body even as his mind registered the crashing of the dirty glass, the cool air, and the pricks and stabs of the shreds of glass in his face and hands. He tried to scream in the moment he broke his neck on the flagstones at the back of the villa.

Gardiner looked down briefly at the lifeless body heaped on the terrace, as if in satisfaction, and turned to leave. His body remembered the next movements, his mind seemed to be impelled upon a familiar course. He bent to look for his shoes, and a fierce pain gripped him, paralysing him and making him cry out. His stomach was tied in knots, burning as if it was tarred rope set alight. He vomited, and when he was done he was shaking uncontrollably; as if some spell or drug had worn off.

He realised what he had done, and it terrified him. Panic welled, and he was afraid of being found, of the noise of breaking glass, of the police . . .

Afraid of himself, as if he had escaped some awful moral vacuum.

He shrugged on the shoes, not waiting to re-lace the left, shoving the lace in his pocket – he became irritated to frenzy with the difficult tight knot around his forefinger as he tried to free it. His wrist hurt now, and his knee threatened to collapse. He limped his way down the stairs.

The door banged behind him, and he slithered into the driver's seat of the Peugeot, the key fumbled into the ignition.

The engine fired at the third attempt, and he revved far too much, the gravel spurting from beneath the rear wheels. He pulled the car round in a tight circle and drove straight out into the Rue des Epinettes, headlights ablaze.

He drove as quickly as he could back to the hotel and the safety of his room.

He had to lie rigid on the bed, arms at his sides, legs stiff, until the fit of shaking deserted him. He lost sense of passing time, only dimly aware of the toilet flushing in the next room as one of his sons used it. The noise was hundreds of miles away, and in another world of experience.

He felt himself to be more than one person – at least two, but he could not be certain. There might be more figures, half-formed personae crowding into the dank little room of his brain. There was the self that had embarked upon that holiday, shivering with fear, sweating and chilled alternately. That person was not indivisibly the same as the one who was afraid of the police or the discovery of Dupuy's body and his tyre tracks and fingerprints; nor was that second dim sense of being the same as the person who was afraid because the past had come back and assailed him with a gun. That was a younger man, growing younger even as he sought to define him, all the way back to the broken young-old man in the succession of hospital beds and wheelchairs which squeaked out onto terraces when the days were warmer – the young-old man becoming reconciled to a restoration of manhood as he began to be able to feel the rough material of his pyjamas against the legs that had been dead of feeling for so long.

And there was the other one – the person who had leapt on his back in that house in the Rue des Epinettes, seemed to burst from his body as if from a useless chrysalis. Gardiner the killer, the leader. The man he had run from to Dorchester and the safe country practice and the dull friends and the pomposity and coldness of his middle years. His sense of himself as a multiple image went that far back.

The worst thing was that he was fascinated by what that Gardiner had done. It had been years later but, threatened, he had been able to kill, coldly, confidently. An unhealthy glamour seemed to crowd round that forgotten self, and he raised his hands often, staring at them in the moonlit bed-room, feeling the shoelace taut across the palms, the bite into the heels of his hands as it bit into Dupuy's neck.

The first gulp of the whisky he poured when he finally moved from the bed made him gag, and he put down the glass with a heavy sound. It was as if the earlier Gardiner, that he now accepted lurked somewhere in him like a virus or a cancer, had rejected that way of being put aside. Because he had used drink once before, in the effort to renounce . . .

He went to the window, and for a long time stood in silence. His skin became responsive to the external tempera-ture rather than to the heat of thought, and the beach across the promenade was silver in the moonlight. A thin white moustache of foam showed where the tide was turning. Yes, he thought, again and again, *it is like a cancer. It is eating me*.

He shivered, yet it was a milder spasm, and might be attributed to the cool air coming through the windows, idling the net curtains against him. He understood.

He turned suddenly, as if someone had come in. Looking at the bed, making out the line of the depression where his wife had sat, the patch of her scarf, her clothes over the back of a chair in one corner. It was as if those fragments were all that remained to him of nineteen years. Suddenly, he wanted her there, with the deep pain of a child requiring maternal comfort, an embrace that would exclude the rest of the world, even banish thought – but she was not there. She was with her lover.

The quick ease with which he invested the thought with malice caused him to breathe painfully. Then he turned back to the window. His hands were clenching and un-clenching; his body could feel Dupuy pressed against him in the violent pederasty of murder as he strangled him. The memory trembled through him – the quick last shudder of the bodies in the moment before they parted, and he heaved the dying man through the window he had struggled to reach.

He lit a cigarette with shaking hands. The smoke calmed

him surprisingly quickly, and he found his mind turning, naturally, to the contemplation of his future. He had to leave La Baule as soon as practicable. Self-preservation.

Rouen. A garish thought. He had to go to Rouen. Dupuy and Perrier had run him down, intending to kill him, in the cobblestoned square in Rouen. Someone else had ordered them to do it. And, before that, he had been betrayed in Paris. By the same person.

He welcomed the decisiveness of the moment, its momentousness. He exhaled noisily. A kind of reversal had been accomplished – then was now, now then. He did not try to understand it, but he did embrace it.

He would need a *carte d'identité*, and money. He had to disappear completely. Without trace. If he left his wife without money, then let her lover keep her until she was repatriated with his sons. Pleasure from the thought, as if he had drunk something potent.

Cancer.

He dismissed the idea. Inevitable, he admitted. He had adjusted, painfully, to the post-war world, to what they termed normal life, because he had almost died. But he knew himself. The violent outbursts of temper, the drinking, the coldness to his wife, the abrasive relationships with partners he seemed somehow to – frighten . . . ? Gardiner was 'Achilles'. He knew that.

He had seen others like himself during the war, and he had never considered his own nature in the light of theirs. He should have done.

He wanted revenge.

The key lay in Rouen, with the former members of the 'Ilium' group. Some of them must be there, sufficient to tell him where Perrier had gone after 1945. His pulse quickened. The girl would still be there. She lived in the area before the war, on a farm. She would know.

He stubbed out the cigarette-end, and undressed. He wanted to be able to pretend sleep when his wife returned. Naked, he slipped beneath the sheet, then ran his hands

over the body as if in the act of inspection. Running to the
fat of middle-age. But not badly. He wasn't old, thank God.

He lay, staring at the ceiling, remembering August 1944 –
each moment of each day. He was asleep when Jane
returned, drifting into it perhaps half-an-hour after lying
down, satisfied that he had recalled every incident, perhaps
every thought, of those past days.

Gardiner dismissed his wife and children from every calcu-
lation he was in the process of making. In the moments while
he waited for the police to interview him in his room, he
allowed the lurid images of her copulation, of the heavy,
sexual happiness he had seen in her eyes when she had
awoken, to die; he found that it no longer rankled. He had
been able to watch the parade of her naked body before the
mirror, when she thought he was not observing her, almost
with equanimity. And for that reason, too, he embraced his
new future.

'You were dreaming again last night,' she said as he
shaved. He had looked up into the mirror, seen her face
behind him in the doorway, and noticed the lines of worry
at the corners of her mouth and eyes. Some vestige of concern.

He shrugged it away, and said, equably, 'Was I? I hope I
didn't disturb you, darling?' The acid emphasis at the end
removed her from the doorway with a flick of her blonde
hair.

He knew he had been dreaming, and supposed that, too,
was a part of his transfiguration. He had been frightened
again, in a half-waking minute, but his body had still been
dry, and the sheet was hardly ruffled. He had been murmur-
ing obviously. Jane had long ago stopped asking about his
nightmares, long before the dreams themselves seemed to
have stopped.

A moment of recollection, he sobbing in her arms, against
her cool skin his face wet with perspiration – he dismissed
it. Part of a buried life.

The boys were excited by the arrival of the police in the hotel, during breakfast. He had sent them off with plenty of small change in the care of Sarah. Jane went to swim.

Gardiner sipping at his coffee, heard a knock at the door. 'Come in.'

A small man in a tan suit opened the door, bowed with a miniscule nod of his head, and closed the door behind him. He crossed the carpet, smiled, and sat himself opposite Gardiner in the chair Gardiner had arranged. They were framed by the dazzling whiteness of the net curtains at the window. A breeze from the balcony stirred the curtains.

'M'sieur Gardiner – it is kind of you to make yourself available for questioning. As I explained in the dining room, we are investigating the death of a waiter at this hotel, a man called Dupuy . . .' Gardiner nodded at the recital, and the little man snapped, 'You knew him, perhaps?'

'No – I don't think so,' Gardiner replied carefully, trying to still the little vein of excitement that seemed to have opened in his temple. He was studying the man, and he had to struggle to control the obviousness of his interest. 'I'm sorry – er . . .'

'Inspector Costain, of the Prefecture.' He took out a notebook, as if reminded by something in Gardiner's manner that it was an official enquiry.

Gardiner said, 'Perhaps I know him by sight, but not by name. Is there something unusual about his death?'

Costain nodded. His dark features were rough-skinned, heavy for such a small head. His eyes had a spaniel brownness, a watchful patience. He would make a determined opponent, and Gardiner realised that the time he possessed for complete freedom of action was short. The policeman was treading on eggshells at that moment, questioning holidaymakers about a murder.

'*Oui*. He was thrown out of a first-floor window last night – and he was choked almost to death before that.'

'I see.' Gardiner pulled a face. He could feel himself again as a multiple of himself, drawing the post-war self about him like a cloak, remembering its pomposity, its *ordinariness*. 'How do you think I can help you?' He smiled inwardly. He might have been speaking to a nervous client.

'This is routine, you understand, M'sieur. We are questioning all the guests in the hotel . . .' He paused for a moment, then added, 'Everyone who was out of the hotel last night, that is.'

'Oh. Was – did the man not die here, then?' Costain shook his head, and his eyes watched Gardiner's face carefully, as if seeing beneath the surface. Gardiner, unnerved, adapted his nervousness to surprise. 'Sorry. I naturally thought it took place here. I don't know why.'

'You can account for your movements, M'sieur? It seems perhaps strange that you should hire a car, having been injured a little in your own. You did not wish to rest last evening?' He looked down at Gardiner's knee. 'How is your leg?'

'Rather stiff, I'm afraid. Yes, I did hire a car. I just drove around, I'm afraid . . .'

'You were seen? You went into a bar, perhaps?'

Gardiner shook his head, then watched Costain scribble for a moment in his notebook. He said, as if dictating, careful of his tone, 'I'm afraid not.'

'Why drive at all? You were recovering your confidence, perhaps? Was that it? Your wife was not with you. We have spoken to Madame Gardiner, in the lobby . . .'

Gardiner saw the moment slipping from him, and he grasped it.

'I see. No, Inspector, my wife was not with me last evening. She went out – to meet someone . . .' His lips compressed, and his eyes became bleak. The little pulse of excitement still beat in his temple, and he was aware of some objective part of himself studying his performance. Carefully, he lowered his gaze, and shuffled one foot, irresolutely. He held his breath, waiting.

'I see. Yes, Madame Gardiner supplied us with a name, in confidence, of course.'

'I do not want to know it,' he said freezingly, catching perfectly a moment of past reaction from years before. Two spots of colour glowed on his cheeks, and he appeared to regret his confidence to Costain. 'To you it may not mean very much . . .' he began, then tailed off. He let one hand quiver slightly, then moved the other to still it.

'I – forgive me, M'sieur. I have to ask, however. Is there anyone who can say exactly where you were and what you were doing between eleven and twelve last night? You returned to the hotel at about twelve-fifteen. Correct?'

Gardiner shook his head slowly. It was as if he was absorbed by another subject. 'I suppose it was,' he said. Then, more firmly: 'Yes, it was about then. I'm fairly sure.'

There was a silence in which Gardiner's confidence seemed to begin crumbling, and the silence roared in his ears. He was unenlightened as to the effect of his story on Costain. Then the policeman stood up.

'My apologies, M'sieur Gardiner, for asking you all these questions. You are staying in La Baule for another three or four days, I believe?'

'Yes.'

'Good. We have some checking to do on this man Dupuy – we shall try not to trouble you again.'

He shook Gardiner's hand firmly, and then he was gone. Gardiner looked at the door for a moment or two, then stepped out onto the balcony. He remained there until his wife returned to the hotel for lunch, and came up to the room to change.

He stayed out on the balcony, watching her through the shimmer of the idling net curtains. She seemed grateful that he was silent, yet also disturbed by the possible state of his knowledge. Only once, as she stood at the mirror to brush her hair, did a former self feel a catch of breath. He turned to look out over the promenade and the beach, and the emotion died in him. He observed with pleasure this new control of feeling, and reflected on the quality of his performance for Costain. He was relearning old skills, as he had relearned an old aptitude in the house on the Rue des Epinettes.

He followed her and the children down to lunch. He ate his way through the Breton leg of mutton and white beans almost without conversation. Jane Gardiner, intent upon preserving the silence which betokened ignorance, and her composed image in the eyes of other guests, mentioned neither the policeman nor his questions.

After lunch, he forced Jane to take Sarah and the boys to the beach, promising to join them when he had checked up on repairs to the Rover. He had no intention of doing either. When they had gone, he sat in the hotel lobby for a while, behind his copy of the *Daily Telegraph*.

It was four o'clock when he finally drove to the yacht basin at the northern arm of the shallow bay. The journey took him twice as long as it need have done, because he went through the old, laborious work of checking for a tail. He was relieved but unsurprised to find that he was not being followed. Once at the basin, he made enquiries concerning a dinghy to be hired the following day, but made no actual booking. He wore his dark glasses all the time, and presented himself as a Frenchman with a casual interest in hiring a small boat. After establishing that persona, he wandered about the basin, studying the boats and the people working on them. Sunlight glittered off the still water, gleamed from the bright hulls and chromework.

It took him more than an hour to find what he required – three possible boats, each of them thirty-footers or larger, and each of them owned by individuals who had not used them recently. Two of them were berthed near boats whose owners were on board or who were in the town at that time. Only the third boat was berthed alongside other boats with absentee owners. The third boat received the greatest attention – he put his shoulder to the door, broke into the cabin and inspected its equipment and stores.

The thirty-footer carried a Bermuda rig that he could handle alone; its charts were up-to-date and covered the required areas of the Brittany coast; there was food in the cupboards and water in the tanks. The boat was fuelled and he assumed that the owner was expected in the immediate future. It was too tempting to resist, nevertheless. He paused only for a moment to wonder at the helplessness of committing himself to a journey by sea if his method were to be discovered, then he decided. At high tide that night, he would steal the yacht.

He replaced the broken lock as best he could, smearing grease over the white, newly-exposed wood. Then he wandered with apparent purposelessness back to his car.

Before the shops closed for the evening he bought a stout haversack at one store and an anorak and waterproof overtrousers from a sports goods shop. He regretted leaving such signposts, but there were no warm clothes or waterproofs aboard the yacht.

It was on the journey back to the hotel that he realised that he was being tailed. Someone in a fawn Renault had picked him up, probably in the street near the sports shop. It did not look like a police car, but he knew he had little time left, much less than he had hoped.

The tail had unsettled him, even though the Renault had driven past the hotel car park, on down the promenade. When he reached the safety of his room, he urgently wanted a pen and paper. He had to make a list of names, some kind of talisman for the next few days. Each member of the old group. His mind struggled to recollect every name. Occasionally he put a thick line through a name – the man or woman was dead before the betrayal. He noted the details beside each name – colour of eyes and hair, weight, the name of a street, occupation, distances . . .

What if the fawn Renault had been at the marina, seen him there, looking for a boat?

Another name – this time the height, the age clear.

What if . . . ?

Stupid romanticism, escaping to sea, like a boy in a book.

He had to go that night, and he needed funds; and a means of escape. Under pressure of certitude that he was being watched, the boat became a chimera, something not to be trusted. Yet he had no alternative solution.

He was standing at the window again, leaving the list for a moment to clear his head. Below him, a woman in a swim-suit crossed the road, and a fat lady on a bicycle wobbled to change direction, ringing the bell furiously. The idea that came to him was associated with cool summer nights and a blackened face, perhaps, or rough workman's clothes; riding through the countryside around Rouen, carrying messages, checking on components of an operation, or meeting a drop . . .

He was pleased, though instantly aware that it was only half a plan. *Was the boat now only a bluff, a discarded card?*

Then the sandwich-board in the foyer, that had given him the idea of the boat. It was the remainder of his scheme. He knew how he could murder himself.

One problem – Jane had to be out of the hotel, with her lover, when he left.

When she came in, he sensed a returned bravado. She must have met the man on the beach, even though her sons had been with her. She made no remark as to why he had not appeared. He saw in the way she undressed for a shower that she was confident again, flattered and wanted by the young Frenchman. It would not be difficult to engineer a quarrel. She simply needed to feel threatened.

As she soaped herself in the shower, drawing the curtain when he appeared in the bathroom, he took off his shirt and washed his face. Then he lathered it carefully, inspected the blade, and began methodically to shave, luxuriating in the steam that rose from the hot water, partially clouding the mirror. At every stroke of the razor, the water in the shower streamed in a soothing background. As he cleaned his chin of the lather, he said:

'The car will be ready tomorrow – we'll move on then. I want to get down into the Dordogne as quick as we can.

It'll mean a lot of driving. You won't mind that, will you?'

There was a silence, only the swish of water. He scraped carefully at his upper lip, not glancing towards the shower.

Then he heard the curtain rings chatter back, and she said, 'Why do we have to leave in such a rush?' There was the smallest hint of nervousness, of disappointment which she could not quite squeeze from her careful tone.

'I've had La Baule,' he said, careful with the cleft in his chin. 'You and the kids have had enough of the beach and lazing around. My turn for some enjoyment – eh?'

'I don't see why we have to leave tomorrow, that's all!' she snapped.

He waited for a moment, then said: 'What's the matter – not sad to leave your lover, are you?'

There was an audible intake of breath. Still he did not turn towards her. Gardiner had mentioned the unmentionable.

'What do you mean . . .?' she began.

'There you are, then,' he cut in, snapping his head round so that he looked at her for a moment, then went back to his shaving, the last few spots of lather. 'Nothing to keep us here.'

'What did you mean?' Her voice was stronger, recovered.

'About your lover? Why, haven't you had time to find one yet?'

'You bastard!' she replied. 'What the hell do you mean by that?'

'You know very well what I mean – it's just that, although I usually refrain from comment, it does seem reasonable to me that you should contrive not to indulge your libido while we're on a family holiday. Don't you?' He eased a false sweetness into his voice as he said, 'If only for the sake of Sarah and the boys.'

'Christ! They wouldn't notice if I was making love to someone on *their* bed, unless I rolled over and broke one of their precious models . . .!' She was angry at him, but there was something in her that still seemed to wish to avoid the blunt directness of the confrontation.

He said, 'Quite possibly you're right. However, with the exception of changing for dinner or the beach, I do wish you would manage to keep your knickers on for a fortnight at a time.'

She swept past him, towel around her almost virginally. As he glanced up in the mirror, he saw that her face was set and frightened. She was angry and bewildered too. She could not take him for granted at that moment, like a safely-extinct volcano, and the idea disturbed her. She was remembering, he knew, the old, jealous outbursts, and perhaps even before that, when he might have considered himself to blame. Physical violence – even that, before she had been able to consider that he no longer cared, no longer objected.

'You – have a mind like a sewer,' she breathed, pausing at the door of the bathroom. She was short of breath, as if after exertion.

'Quite. And you have the morality of a sewer-rat, my dear – we make a lovely couple . . .' Without turning to look at her, he picked up the thick white towel and began to wipe his cheeks. Then he let the water out of the basin, amusing himself with the analogy of his marriage and to the last nineteen years. Just water running away, leaving nothing but a grey scum. All the while he could sense her anger, her hatred. Then he turned to look at her, and she hitched the bath-towel more securely around her breasts, as if threatened. 'Well, my dear. Do what you want tonight, for tomorrow we drive. We're leaving in the morning!'

There was a long, tense silence as they glared at one another. Then she turned away, biting the full lower lip, chastened and degraded. He had no sympathy for her, only a pleasure in having engineered the situation successfully. Now, damaged in self-esteem, she would determine to spend this last night in La Baule with her French lover. He had spoken the unspeakable, and made her into nothing more than a tart; for that, she would make him suffer. When she returned that night, or the following morning, she would expect to fling her infidelity in his face, her ego restored, her sense of her desirability returned to her.

To ensure that she telephoned her lover and made the necessary arrangements, he took Sarah and the boys down to dinner early, where he was affable, even light-hearted, with the girl and the other guests at nearby tables. As if, he admitted, he were taking his leave of a party apologising in advance for his plan to rob them of their French currency. For he had solved his currency problem, also.

He ate wheat pancake, lobster Armoricaine, and Rennes pralinés, drank most of a bottle of Muscadet, and lingered over his coffee. When Jane joined them half-way through the main course, she was carefully made-up, stiff and silent in her seat. Already, he witnessed the return of sexual confidence. Her lover had been flattering, eager apparently.

She left a little before eight-thirty, kissing the boys briefly and ignoring Gardiner.

At two minutes after midnight he knocked on the door of the manager's suite on the hotel's first floor. There was a muffled sound from within, and he pushed open the door. The manager showed a slight surprise at his appearance, but got up from the sofa where he was listening to Charles Trenet from a record player, put down his drink and said in English:

'M'sieur Gardiner, is it not? What can I do for you?' He came towards Gardiner without suspicion. 'What is it – is something wrong?' Gardiner took the razor-edged cheese knife that he had pocketed at dinner from the pocket of the new anorak, and pressed it against the protruding stomach of the manager. The small man's eyes bulged, comically, yet he seemed to be aware principally of the tallness of the Englishman rather than of the knife.

Gardiner said, 'You wouldn't want to end up like a piece of the rather inferior Camembert you serve downstairs, would you, M'sieur?' He pressed the point of the knife against the stomach so that it pricked through the man's waistcoat, touched the flesh. The manager winced, closed his eyes, then opened them again. Gardiner saw that he was sufficiently afraid.

The manager said, 'What do you want?'

'Apart from a small float, I presume you keep the currency from the Bureau de Change here, in your safe?'

The manager was incapable of lying. He nodded. 'Yes,' he said.

'Good. Shall we?' He prodded the knife into the stomach, and the little manager swallowed. As he turned to lead Gardiner, he caught sight of himself in a full-length mirror on one wall. He looked fat, and frightened and ridiculous. Gardiner allowed him to bend before the safe, holding the knife at his throat where it was irritated into a rash by the stiff edge of his collar. A pudgy hand fiddled with the combination of the small safe built into the wall of the room but undisguised.

The door of the safe opened, creaking slightly, but not as loudly as the man's stifled breath creaked in the silence. And he could hear the clock on the mantelpiece quite distinctly. Then he was handing the bundles of francs out to the man with the knife, and beginning to feel the questions thrust upwards through the rush of panic and reaction he could begin to sense in his body. He handed Gardiner dollars by mistake, and the man put them back in his hand then snatched them again.

'All of it, then!' he snapped, as if angry with himself. 'Quickly!'

The manager fumbled the neatly-stacked bundles out of the safe, the small sharp knife never moving from the side of his neck, the man bundling the money into his anorak – dollars, sterling, marks, francs, lire. Then, quite suddenly, the safe was empty and the point of the knife was very sharp against his throat. He dared not turn his head. It was no more than a moment before the knife was gone and Gardiner hit the little man across the side of the head, just

behind the ear, with his flattened hand. Soundlessly, he slid
to the floor, curled in a foetal position like some small
hibernating animal.

Gardiner put the knife in his pocket, then took the
unconscious form by the armpits and dragged the manager
of the Hotel Boulevard de l'Ocean across the room. He back-
heeled open the bedroom door, and dragged the body to the
bed. Then he knelt down, and pushed the manager under the
bed. He tidied the bedspread, straightened his anorak, and
closed the door behind him. He locked it.

The hire car was in its place in the car park, an ancient
bicycle, the property of a desk-clerk on duty until the
morning, in its boot. He drove towards the yacht basin.
There was little traffic and the journey took him less than
ten minutes. He drove straight towards the outskirts of the
town and the Pointe de Penchateau.

The road which had bordered the beach curved round the
low, rocky point here. The retreating tide still covered most
of the rocks – no sand would be exposed before his time
expired. Across the water he could see the lights of La Baule,
glittering and unsubstantial now. He unlocked the boot of the
car and took out the bicycle. He carried it across the road
and down the worn steps onto the rocks. It was slightly
risky, leaving it there for perhaps more than an hour, but
there was no alternative. He placed it against the sea wall,
a mere ten feet high but sufficient to hide the bike from eyes
on the road. He waited while a car went noisily by, the din
of a car radio fading behind it before going back to his car
and taking the haversack from the back seat. Into this, on
top of his change of clothes, he had stuffed the money from
his anorak. Leaving it, too, was risky.

He searched for some minutes until he found a deep and
narrow crevice in the rocks. He thrust the haversack into it,
out of sight.

Standing up, he dusted himself off, feeling the wetness of
the newly uncovered rock on his knees. He went back to the
car, turned it in the road, and returned the way he had

come, until he was opposite the yacht basin. He parked, locked the car, and left it.

The yacht basin was unguarded, as far as he could tell. There was a fence and a locked gate. He climbed over the gate, dropping soundlessly on the other side. The drop was small, but seemed to take an age, as if something slowed on film, and his mind raced through a hundred memories, nosed a hundred scents of his past, before his feet touched the earth. He understood it only as a dossier the body collated in a microsecond. He went into a cushion crouch, and as he straightened up it was as if he saw himself differently. He looked across the glittering water at La Baule – a million miles away, perhaps. Then he made his way swiftly to the thirty-footer he had already selected.

The tide was ebbing quickly, and the boat, dark-coloured, low hulled, slopped ungracefully in the idle power of the tide. He climbed on board, and went straight to the stern. For his purposes, he had no need of the small auxiliary motor, or to rig the boat. The ebbing tide would take him out with it – short journey, and he had calculated it. He would use the motor if necessary, but he considered that he had time to position himself where he wished without it.

Muffled rock music from a café or dance hall. He cast off, and took the tiller after thrusting the boat away from its berth, sitting in the lee of the tiny cabin. The boat, one he would have liked to have been able to afford in his previous existence, was nothing more than a tool now. The lights of the town were behind him, as the current plucked at the boat. The sky was alive with stars as he turned his face out to sea. To starboard he could see the small lighthouse at the mouth of the river he had crossed on his way to the point. His single point of reference, as he gazed to starboard, was a clutch of lights, sliding behind the rocks of the point, seemingly suspended. He knew the course of the pleasure cruiser, had seen it traversing the bay, back and forth, the previous night – midnight dancing, food and wine. His mouth grimaced at the remembered notice in the hotel

foyer, and he wondered whether his wife and her lover
might be on board. He rather hoped they would.

The minutes passed, and he moved with the tide on his
appointed course. The lights slid from behind the rocks,
and the music from the band on board the cruiser could be
heard across the dark water. The chain of lights was a
blurred necklace at first, slowly enlarging to individual lamps
of many colours. The music became louder, and he recognised
the melody. An old waltz which might have belonged to the
period before the war, to his youth. The warmth of the
summer night became real to him for the first time, and a
part of his mind idled with the music even as he computed
the distances, and the point of convergence.

He saw that he was not exact, and fired the auxiliary
motor. The tune washed from his thoughts as the motor
coughed, then stilled. He fired it again – it coughed, asthma-
tic promise, then silence. The music louder and the churn of
the screws audible. The passage of the boat thrumming
through the hull of the yacht. He cursed, looking up at the
point of moonlit sea already glowing with light from the
cruiser, and then fired the motor again. It erupted, spluttered,
then settled to a steady note. He slumped back in the seat
with the sudden forward movement of the yacht, and then
clasped the tiller to him, steering the yacht towards the
intended point on the gleaming surface of the bay. Perhaps
only seventy or eighty yards.

He watched the cruiser carefully. He had to make it
appear accidental, and he feared the watchfulness of the
crew. Guests passed, heads and no more, along the rail on
the port side. The cruiser loomed – then he heard the mega-
phoned cry, even as the music stopped and something
harsher and more modern took its place. Then a cone of
silence beneath the bows, and he was sharply, deeply afraid
as the cruiser towered over the yacht. The ship's hooter
bellowed, and the music had stopped, and there was the
faint cry of a distorted human voice, inadequate as a bird's
call. The bow-wave of the cruiser seemed to slip away from

him, the dark knife-edge in the water rearing above him
seeming to bend aside . . .

He stood up in the boat, then dived into the water on
the side furthest from the great bow over him, pulling down
into the water even as the first shock of the collision jud-
dered the tiny yacht. He pulled down frantically, blood
rushing in his ears until drowned by the deafening sound of
the screw passing above him. He began to be buffeted by
the cruiser's passage. The great dark shape passed over him,
cancelling the gleam of moonlight. He noticed, oddly, the
sting of sea-water in his stiched knee, and then only the
threatening lungs as they seemed to swell beneath the ribcage. He had to get deep.

There was a precise, stark moment when he realised he
might die. The sound of the screw was a hideous din, and
the water plucked at him, pulling him upwards, tearing at
his limbs. He was unable to swim in the maelstrom – he had
miscalculated. Then he was fighting for his life, spun like
something without gravity at the mercy of a great wind,
whirling in the dark water which churned about him.

Then there was an absence of thought, a suspension of
time passing. Feebly, he struck out, heading for the surface,
but without volition or urgency. He had exhaled, and he
felt empty, light and buoyant.

His mind, some part of it, warned him, and he realised
that he had become disorientated beneath the water. He
was striking *down*. Nothing but darker water ahead of him,
and he rolled clumsily so that the faint starlight gleamed
ahead of him. He had no sense of up or down, but struck –
because now the blood cried for oxygen, and the limbs were
heavy and the brain beginning to spin and fumble – ahead,
towards the faint light, hoping that the increasing light was
not a mere illusion.

His head broke the surface, and he choked in great
lungfuls of air, swallowing sea-water at the same time. The
cruiser was already changing course, trying to retrace its
path. There was hardly any wreckage of the yacht in sight

on the disturbed water. He heard muffled shouts, the giving
of orders. There did not appear to be any music. He forced
himself to swallow for a last time, and to push his head
back beneath the alien water. He was drained and forced
himself to strike out, beneath the water, in the direction of
the point.

When his head broke surface again, the cruiser seemed
no further off. He dived again, understanding, only very
distantly, that the cruiser was following a reciprocal course,
and that he might be in danger of being overrun again. He
could do nothing about it, only bob up to the surface again,
his lungs crying for relief, his body weary of the strange,
difficult element into which he had led it. He was heavy on
the surface, as if maintaining a precarious hold on a ledge,
about to slide off into air and darkness. He could not be
sure whether or not he was in danger of losing consciousness. He remained on the surface for a long time, the
cruiser appearing to have stopped engines. He saw the
lighthouse again as he trod water.

With each stroke he felt the current of the ebbing tide
drag at him, as if pushing him back out to sea. Losing a
sense of time passing, he seemed engaged in a continuing,
frenzied beating of the water with his arms. Later, he knew
that he must have almost passed out, several times, and that
he had rested often – but always the swim to the rocks of
the point came back to him in the same way – arms beating
feebly, as if keeping an enemy at bay, body losing purchase
on the ledge of water. He struggled in two separate periods
of time. Aware of himself now, reminded by the lights of La
Baule and the sweep of the lighthouse beam, and aware of
himself also crossing the river, towards the bank and away
from the train. 1944. Two persons fought, and became sealed
in some strange way, fused together – the years between
vanished, squeezed by effort from the aching muscles and
forced from the frantic mind.

When he pulled himself onto the rocks, he was spent. He
vomited, sea-water and half-digested food spilling weakly

from his mouth as he lay with his head hanging down into a hollow, the water of a rock pool inches from his bleared eyes, his feet still in the retreating tide. He shivered with exhaustion and relief.

Much later, when the tide had left his feet, as if it had thrown him up onto the rocks at the full and he was some stranded aquatic creature, clumsy and slow-moving, he turned on his back and laughed. Weakly, wetly at first, then forcing the sound to express his defiance of survival. When his breathing returned to normal, and the wet clothes were uncomfortable to renewed senses, he undressed and dried himself with a towel. He dressed swiftly in the least English-looking suit he possessed, leaving the money in the bottom of the haversack, beneath the anorak and the other wet clothes. He looked out into the bay once. It must have taken him a long time to recover – there was no sign of the cruiser or any search for him.

He cycled, via the backstreets of La Baule and country roads, to the port of St. Nazaire. Here, he boarded the early morning train for Paris, having left the bicycle in the left-luggage office at the station.

FROM   Head of Intelligence
TO   Foreign Secretary
DATE   12th February 1962

MEMO   Series   62/DEF/134

DIGEST OF LATEST INFORMATION & INTERROGATION DOCUMENTS TO
REACH ME FROM OUR SOURCE 'ANATOLY' HAVE INCRIMINATED, WITHOUT
DOUBT, <u>GEORGE BLAKE   SIS AGENT</u>.

                IMMEDIATE ARREST FOLLOWS.

FROM   Head of Intelligence
TO   Foreign Secretary
DATE   3rd February 1963

MEMO   Series   63/DEF/ 89

REPORTS FROM HEAD OF STATION MOSCOW, CONFIRM ARRIVAL OF
<u>PHILBY</u> ON SOVIET SOIL 27/1/63 , FOUR DAYS AFTER LEAVING
BEIRUT.

Extracted for post-operational ref.
by Head of Intelligence
4th November 1963

the debate eventually ending at about 4.0 a.m. —
followed by a couple of hours sleep! —

15th June 1963 —
        Worked on papers most of the evening before
routine weekly meeting with P.M.
At 3:0 p.m. 'C' came to see me for my decision.
There appears to be a fourth 'Judas' in NATO and
'C' tells me that Washington "concur" via Bonn —
Franklin's —
        I do not like private police forces and Wigg
would have a field day. If my decision came out
— but if this is an inside' affair, the fewer people
that know the better — I gave 'C' the go ahead
and agreed the appointments of Roxbey and Labynee
to command S.O.1. —
        The funding of the operation had been troublesome
but the P.M. advises me to go ahead and write it
down under 'research'. His precept appears to be —
do it first — and explain to the Treasury later —
that is if they find out!
        Had dinner with members of the Overseas Trade
Mission but — after an all night sitting I must
have been a very dull guest and had it not been

CHAPTER FOUR

AFFAIRS OF STATE

The river was an oily sliding grey under low cloud, cloud that was flecked across the belly from the rising sun, heavy and swollen on the lip of the city downriver. It was very much like a winter morning, after the overnight rain. Hilary Latymer, not having slept for another night, had left the house in Cheyne Row and had traced his steps to the Chelsea Embankment. His features, too, were wintry like the day, raw and drained. Light from the lamps on the Embankment coloured his face garishly as he continued his unseeing patrol.

Behind him the elegantly-furnished eighteenth century house that they had bought with Victoria's money was cold and silent. He had thought about selling it, then immediately stamped on the thought as if it represented some kind of betrayal. He had sent the one servant that Victoria had employed for years, their cook-housekeeper, away to her relatives in the north. There was no dismissal, merely that for Mrs. Wetherby to be present with her silent sympathy and dog-like, pained eyes, would have been too much of an irritant. He preferred to eat at unusual hours, mostly cold scraps if he ate at home at all. Empty of other human beings, the house was bearable.

Coming down to the Embankment had not been a good idea, he decided. Yet he could not bear the house at all after a sleepless night – the silent rooms, the drawn curtains, the furniture that announced Victoria wherever he looked, until the daylight was strong in every room. The harsh flickering of the striplight in the kitchen scratched at his nerves.

Only once before, when his brother had died in Normandy in 1944, had he felt anything like his present appalling misery. Grief pressed down on him, limiting his horizons of feeling. He had thought of resigning his post, yet he held back, as if dimly aware of the utter emptiness of his days if he had no work to occupy at least part of the brain.

Hilary Latymer, at forty-six, was by inclination a placid man. He was unused to intense states of feeling. His detachment had made him a good intelligence officer, during and after the war. His brother's death had been learned, and suffered, at second-hand and in wartime. With Victoria, it was as if he were dying. Without the comfort of drugs, deadening the awareness; the sense of being a dead thing held somehow upright by pointless sinews.

He needed something, he realised, in order to escape from his own devils. Someone else's demons to pursue, perhaps; a cancer in the body politic, driving out thoughts of the vile, inoperable thing eating at his wife's brain. Mentally, he was trying to breathe very shallowly these days, as he waited for his wife to die. He was treading a thin crust of feeling.

On the Embankment, he turned, the trees bordering the grounds of the Royal Hospital above him, and began to retrace his steps towards the empty house in Cheyne Row.

He arrived at his office before eight. He had picked at a breakfast he had cooked himself, but had fled the house as soon as he decently could, taking the tube to the City. In Old Jewry, he entered a side door which led to anonymous offices above a small private bank, Gairstang's, and a uniformed porter checked his pass, then nodded him in. Above the bank, which handled some of the SIS's Banking Section funds, principally those for operations in Europe, were the offices of Latymer's new section of SIS.

He glanced into the duty room, and saw Biggar with his feet on the table, two empty beer bottles in the wastebin, and the air thick with bluish smoke. Biggar opened one eye

lazily, nodded but did not speak, and Latymer closed the
door behind him. He went slowly up to his own office, next
to Aubrey's, up three steps from the main renovated suite
of offices which had only a few weeks before become the
home of SO-4.

The office was cool and dark until he released the blind.
He had worked late the previous night and there were still
papers on the desk, a sloppiness in security that he now felt
he had committed to assuage some personal resentment. He
had felt himself bound to his work last night, and had tried
to blame it for what was happening to him. The attempt
had been unsuccessful, and he had been left finally with the
empty Chelsea house and the bottle of malt whisky which
he had half-heartedly endeavoured to finish. Then the huge
empty bed and the smooth sheets and the lack of sleep. He
had begun, eventually, to imagine that he could hear her
breathing next to him in bed – a harsh, rasping sound. A
recollection of the early weeks, before they had taken her
into the nursing home near Oxford. It was as if the bedroom was a recording device, and he had willed it to play
back.

He sat down at his desk, rubbing his hands down his
smooth cheeks, and stared at the photograph he had maintained on his desk by an effort of will – Victoria, smiling
but unposed, with mountains in the background. Norway,
only three years earlier. A tall woman with a good figure,
fine-boned in the face, a rather large nose, fine grey eyes . . .
He held his fingertips to his temples for a long moment, as
if containing his thoughts.

SO-4 had been established at the beginning of Victoria's
terminal illness. He had transferred to it under Aubrey from
the Joint Intelligence Liaison Department, having worked
with Aubrey ever since the war in one or another of SIS's
departments. Aubrey had pressured him into accepting this
last transfer; the comforting illusion was to be that new, and
more demanding and sensitive work would offer some sort
of palliative, a drug. It had not worked. Already, Latymer

knew that Aubrey was beginning to have to apologise for his performance, to reconsider his decision.

He stood up and went to the window, looking down through the tinted glass at Old Jewry, at the self-effacing façades of the building across the street. He wished it had been otherwise – there was a nagging disappointment that he was not as greatly esteemed within the service as formerly. He did not blame Victoria, or himself. It merely saddened him that he was not as – *efficient* as he once had been.

Because, after Philby and Blake – there was another. There always was, it seemed. After the resignations – and in one case the removal of a personage from the ranks of the SIS by means of a car accident – there was now a double within NATO, the wider sphere. A double undoubtedly British, and the evidence suggesting he was a member of the SIS. In the House, questions had been asked when Philby went over, questions that presupposed another man who had warned Philby as Philby had warned Burgess and MacLean. The Foreign Secretary had done his utmost to calm such rumours while at the same time causing the head of Intelligence, 'C', to stir the ant-heap with a stick, and witness who ran for cover or out into the sunlight. And then – step on them.

And, Latymer reflected, SO-4 was the stick, and the crushing foot, for this time there would be no trial, and no eventual exchange. The 'mole' would die. And SO-4, as watchdog of the SIS, had no other brief than to find that 'mole', whose sphere of operations was the NATO Senior Joint Intelligence Committee.

Latymer observed, with the detachment, or helplessness – he could not decide which – of an outsider, that time was running short. The Americans and the French were both clamourous that the leak be stopped. Leaks which had been confirmed only recently by a highly-placed double, code-name 'Franklin', inside Moscow Centre. 'Franklin' was anonymous, but evidently one of a handful of KGB officers turned while resident on service abroad. 'Franklin' confirmed the leaked material covered weapons re-equipment, dispositions of troops, attitudes within NATO – and, especially, the worsening relationship between de Gaulle's government and the rest of the NATO alliance. But 'Franklin' was unable to name the source.

Latymer, swiftly tired of the profitless regurgitation of data, sat down at his desk again, opened a drawer, and removed a bottle of whisky and a glass. He examined the bottle, and the clichéd act, considered the condition of his nerves, and the tiny pulse already beating in his temple – and poured a drink. He swallowed the liquor greedily, and with a shame that seemed to assail the nostrils like stale sweat or grime.

He put down the glass, and crossed to the mirror on the wall. A soberly-dressed individual stared out at him, still almost boyishly-slim, the full head of hair brushed back from the high forehead beginning to grey. Chiselled features, almost delicate, the curving nose, the blue eyes. Not sharp now; slightly fuzzy, marked with dark stains beneath. A hollow man looked out at him. He felt dirty in body, as his wife had confessed she did when she had first learned of the tumour.

He shook his head at his reflection, aware even as he did so that he was attempting to transmute guilt into rueful disapproval.

Before he could regain his desk, Aubrey opened the door, and his head, pinkly shiny above the two grey wings of hair, appeared. He seemed to take in the slope of Latymer's shoulders, the glass and bottle, even the photograph of Victoria, at one glance, then he said: 'In my office, if you would, Hilary. I want to arrange our story before Deputy gets here.'

The head disappeared, and Latymer felt he had been caught out in some shameful act. Shrugging, he followed Aubrey's rotund figure along the corridor and into the larger office of the department head of SO-4. Unlike Latymer's own office, which had become an arid, sterile place even in a few short weeks, this was warm with the personality of its occupant. Everything was impeccably tidy, but a spider plant trailed across the top and down the front of one tall grey filing cabinet. The curtains were heavy, richly-patterned in golds and browns, and on the desk two small pieces of jade – a horseman and a small Buddha, set at either of the front corners of the desk. They seemed to highlight the aesthetic and ascetic in Aubrey.

Aubrey was dressed in a black jacket and striped trousers like the archetypical civil servant he considered himself to be. Though Latymer entered almost immediately behind him, he was already looking out of the window, back to the room.

'Close the door, Hilary, would you?' he said, and Latymer, who would have done so, felt he was being treated like an errant schoolboy. Then the little man turned from the window, stared at Latymer quizzically and without apology, then said, 'You've not slept.' Latymer shook his head. 'You'll be precious little use to me – and no use at all to Victoria – unless you sleep . . .' Latymer knew that Aubrey was deeply distressed at his wife's illness, but he regarded his grief as irrelevant, even impertinent, and therefore hid it.

'I know,' Latymer observed, shrugging, an unhabitual gesture which Aubrey noticed with distaste. 'Not that my professional uselessness will be any new turn of events.'

Aubrey wrinkled his nose. 'I don't like self-pity, Hilary – don't bring it in with you again.'

'Sorry.'

Aubrey stood on the other side of his desk. He possessed, like many small men, the ability to appear belligerently bigger than he was. Latymer sensed him bristling, then Aubrey took his hands from his pockets, sat down at the desk, and smoothed the two wings of grey hair.

'Sit down, Hilary. I want to be clear on our scheme before Deputy gets here.'

'Quite.'

'These weekly tutorials are becoming rather a bind, don't you think? Have you your essay to hand?' Latymer smiled, conscious he was being charmed from his depression. 'It really is very naughty of the KGB to penetrate us quite so successfully – one feels quite raped!' Latymer laughed aloud at the image. 'Mm. What have we got?'

'Not very much, I'm afraid . . .' With a sharp, though momentary, regret, Latymer felt himself drawn effortlessly into the world of his peculiar profession. It was as if he were leaving Victoria alone in a dark room. He went on: 'I've been running over the timetables of committee meetings from which material has been provenly leaked. It gives us all four of our suspects, assuming the usual gossip in rooms and corridors, and the sub-committee which would have possessed a lot of the stuff. The sheer volume, and diversity, of the material confirms one of our four and no low-grade personnel – but not which one.'

Aubrey shook his head. In the sharp blue eyes there was a momentary pity, then he said: 'I see – not very encouraging, mm?' Aubrey was sympathetic, but disappointed – in Latymer.

'No.'

'Still, it can't be helped. If the CIA won't give us access to "Franklin", we can't do much more than work in the dark. And the fact that "Franklin" is a totally *anonymous* source as far as we're concerned is – most *irritating*.'

'They're not likely to tell us while our little friend the "mole" is still in business.'

'I agree. But the CIA won't use "Franklin" to obtain a complete breakdown of leaked material unless it passes across his desk. Heavens, the man, whoever he is, can't have more than two or three years before he's tumbled. What could he do that's more important than this – eh?' There was a silence for a moment, then Aubrey said, 'I have an idea, which we will broach with Deputy when he gets here.'

'Yes?'

'When is the next meeting of the full Committee in Paris?'

'Thursday.'

'Who is to attend?'

'All four of our men.'

'Mm. I thought so. Very well, we shall be more drastic. Questions will be asked of us soon, Hilary. We are the new blue whitener in the service, and we *have* to get rid of the stains! We shall prevent one, if not two, from attending, and concentrate our efforts on the other two. If it doesn't draw anything, then we go to work on the other two. Agreed?'

'Yes, of course.'

'It's a pity we can't do a nice little bit of spadework at this end, and – up pops our little "mole", blinking in the sunlight. I'd hand you the spade to beat him over the head. Now, instead, because we think it all happens in Paris, we shall have to run some sort of operation. What we want is something juicy fed to the Committee, which is bound to be reported back – then "Franklin" can keep his eye open for it. Who can we trust?'

Latymer, intrigued despite the sudden fits of indifference that seemed to come like the stuttering onset of narcosis, thought for a moment, then said, 'Jorgensen. The Norwegian. He's a full member of the Senior Committee, and he worked with SOE during the war. You recall he's worked for us since the war?'

'Yes. We'll use him, then. Something juicy – is there time to put it on the agenda?' Latymer nodded. 'We'll think about it, then. Something going on inside the Arctic Circle, I shouldn't wonder. Up near the Soviet border. Now declassified for NATO dissemination. Would that be in "Franklin's" area at all?'

'You know it would.'

'Mm. It *is* a pity! I do so hate operations – all the paraphernalia. The men, the nasty guns, the timing – ugh! It really puts us on the level of the CIA. But I see the necessity. Our little "mole" is eating up the ground beneath our feet.

Our whole NATO Intelligence credibility will be a myth if we don't stop him. And not to mention the French kicking up such a stink because they are thinking of pulling out of NATO – and then making an unholy fuss because our man is giving the Soviets first-hand accounts of the fuss they're making! Really, it is too ridiculous for words – especially since it is only a matter of a few years since the French were busy as bees being penetrated themselves. It really is most unsporting of them not to extend a little sympathy to fellow-sufferers. "Martel" made them put their house in order, and now they want to show the rest of NATO how pure they are by making a moral crusade against us.'

Latymer smiled. 'We'll get him, Aubrey.' He had projected himself, almost without decision, into his work, for the moment. It was much easier to take it all seriously when Aubrey was present. In dialogue, it had solidity, was in three dimensions.

'I do hope so,' Aubrey said. 'Otherwise we shall look such clots, shan't we?'

Latymer got up to go. Aubrey watched him, then seemed to recollect something. As Latymer pushed open the door, he said, 'Oh, by the way. I had a little note yesterday, via the usual channels. Richard Gardiner is dead.'

'What?'

'Yes. Some kind of accident, I believe. A great pity. He was on holiday, you know, in Brittany.' Aubrey shook his head. 'Only one thing mars the natural decencies. He's supposed to have killed a man!'

Latymer closed the door and came back into the room suddenly. His face was drained of the liveliness and health induced by Aubrey's *bonhomie*. He said, sitting down, 'Killed a man – who?'

'Ah. Now that is indeed an interesting item.' For a moment, before he looked up, Latymer suspected Aubrey of some bizarre lapse of taste. He was wrong. There was a slight smile on Aubrey's lips, but a bewildered pity in his eyes. Probably, his voice had imitated the manner in which he had received the news, which must have come from the department which, among its other tasks, monitored the world's newspapers.

Aubrey went on, 'During the past two days there has been a very apparent loss of newspaper interest in the case.'

'Blackout?'

'No more than second-degree – however, interesting, all the same.'

'We haven't asked for it?'

'Why should we? Gardiner is – *was* – a citizen of the United Kingdom, pursuing his lawful occasions. He hasn't worked for us since 1944.'

'Correct. Then why?'

'Don't ask why – ask who?'

'Who?'

'Whom did Cock Robin kill – "Achilles's" last victim?'

'Who?'

'A waiter at the hotel where he was staying. A certain M. Dupuy. Does that mean anything to you?'

'No. Does it to you?'

'Perhaps. There was an Alfred Dupuy in the "Ilium" group. His code-name was "Patroclus". Recall him?'

'The name, yes. I think so – but not the man. Is it the same man, do you think?'

'Name and age fit. I went down to the warehouse to look at the old records. Do you know, old Carstairs is *still* down there, pen poised to await the day he can write the full history of SOE.' Aubrey shook his head. 'He looks as dusty as the piles of bumph down there – I wonder if he feeds from the stock?'

'Don't mock those records, Aubrey. Our pasts are in there . . .' Latymer's face clouded, and he said quickly, 'Why did he kill him? They're certain of it – the French police?'

'I haven't checked. Thought I'd have a word with you first. Of course it's of no interest to us, professionally. But

I was very fond of Richard, and so were you. Did you keep in touch?'

'For some time – not recently, though. Victoria quarrelled with his wife.'

Aubrey clicked his tongue as if regretting the inevitable complications women introduced to human life. A bachelor himself, he was suddenly thankful he would not have to face the blank desertion that Latymer would encounter when his wife died.

'I see,' he said quietly.

'How did Dupuy die?'

'A cord around the throat, then a swift exit via an upstairs window. One of the tried and trusted methods. A shoelace, probably. Oh, there was a gun near the body, and Gardiner stole the contents of the hotel manager's safe, at knifepoint, before he disappeared.' There was the shadow of a smile on Aubrey's face; a schoolmaster hearing of a former pupil's success later in life, and allowing himself a modicum of self-congratulation for academic groundwork firmly laid.

'It was him, then,' Latymer said. 'But – why the hell . . . ?' Then an idea struck him, mentally winding him for a moment. He said: 'Then nineteen years of trying to forget all about it has come to nothing – just because he met Dupuy.' He paused, then added, 'Dupuy must have been the man who betrayed him. You realise that? The past must have caught up with both of them.'

'Poor devils.'

'How did Richard die?'

'Oh – making his escape by yacht. He was in collision with one of those dinner-and-dancing jolly-boats – midnight cruise across the bay.' Then Aubrey stared at the ceiling, his hands in his pockets. He ignored the cigarette-case held out by Latymer, who lit a cigarette. He heard the lighter grate, then the spurt of gas. He saw the bluish smoke drift into sight, rolling under the ceiling.

He said, 'What an awful, awful shame. You're quite right, of course. He must have identified Dupuy as one of the men.' He sat up suddenly, and stared at Latymer, whose eyes seemed to be considering the crease in his trouser-leg. He said: 'I saw him only the once, you know. After they transferred him to hospital over here. He wouldn't tell me anything about Paris, or Rouen. I couldn't even debrief him. It was – quite terrible, the way he seemed determined to forget. He was determined to blot it out. I always wondered what happened . . .'

'Not that it mattered to us,' Latymer observed drily. 'There was never any problem with the Rouen group, since it was abandoned as an operational force only a few days after he was run down.' His voice hardened. 'The little bastard! Why the hell should he run Richard down?'

Aubrey shook his head. 'I presume his wife is back in England.'

'You – think I ought to see her?' Latymer asked, understanding the duty of the moment, and experiencing an awkwardness which he disapproved.

'I think that would be a very good idea – do that, would you?' Then Aubrey shrugged, and added, 'Now, leave me to compose my thoughts, and I'll call you when Deputy arrives.' He waved his hand, dismissing Latymer.

Michael Stanhope Constant, as Deputy-C and effective second-in-command of the SIS, was less inclined than ever to conceal his arrogance of mind and temper; he was prepared to enjoy Aubrey's discomfiture and Latymer's sullen silence. The scheme that Aubrey began to propose – neat, logical, and face-saving – irritated him because of its very existence.

He arrived a little after ten, and Latymer was immediately summoned.

Constant was seated in Aubrey's chair, and Aubrey had placed narrow armchairs for himself and Latymer on the other side of the desk. On this occasion, Latymer noted, Aubrey had introduced the sherry bottle, despite the early hour.

Constant, despite an evident reluctance, was impressed
by the operation proposed. Unlike Aubrey, who was much
more apt to enjoy paperwork and committee-style espionage,
Constant relished the flair that a quick mind could bring to
a field operation. This piece of saturation surveillance
appealed to him, and he applied himself to the details with
an alacrity that Latymer had not expected.

'I can divert Lavender,' he offered, sipping cat-like at his
sherry. He was referring to his compatriot, Deputy-C1 whose
responsibility was for the oversight and analysis of inbound
intelligence, unlike Constant, who as Deputy-C2 was operations manager. 'It shouldn't be difficult. He and I should
have our monthly planning meeting the day before he goes to
Paris – I'll have to fall ill, but make the meeting urgent.
Then he'll have to stay home. What do you suggest, Aubrey
– a little gastritis?'

'I think that would do very nicely, sir,' Aubrey replied
blandly. Latymer watched him enjoying the encounter with
Constant.

'Good. Who else do you suggest?'

'I think – Allom. He's Head of Ciphers, and he only
attends the full Senior Committee meetings once or twice
a year. Even though he is on a couple of the smaller sub-
committees. He would have to work hardest to collect as
much as our "mole" seems able to pass.'

'Good,' Constant said, nodding and finishing his sherry.
He put down the crystal glass carefully, in the exact centre
of the green blotter. 'That leaves us with Lidbrooke and
Melluish. One of them is to attend the full Committee, the
other the Eastern Bloc Co-ordination of Intelligence Sub-
Committee. Yes. Anything juicy to offer them?'

Aubrey said, 'I think so – do you want all the details, sir?'

Constant shook his head. 'No, I shouldn't think so. Just
make it an "Eyes Only" memo, in retrospect.' He linked his
fingers behind his head, leaning back in the chair. Though
older, he was, remarkably to Latymer, still the man who had
unwittingly sent Gardiner to the cellars of the Avenue Foch

and to the square in Rouen. With a sudden flood of feeling, Latymer disliked Constant intensely at that moment.

Constant said, 'I'm sure that "C" is most afraid that it's Lavender. He has, of course the taste of thirties Cambridge, and he was well acquainted with Philby for years. Also, he's not a career intelligence officer. A former Foreign Office Special Adviser is a suspicious breed in itself.' He laughed, a short barking sound without humour. Aubrey smiled non-committally. He knew that Constant and Lavender were suspicious of one another, and that Constant would be pleased to discover that Lavender was the sought-after double. It would leave him in an unassailable position as inheritor of the office of 'C' when Sir Dick White retired.

'Quite,' Aubrey remarked. 'Very well, Deputy. We'll make it Lavender and Allom to sit this one out. Saturation surveillance on the other two while they're in Paris and after they get back. I take it you'll want to review the matter in . . . ?'

'Give it two weeks. If nothing happens, then we'll try something else for the other two.'

'I take it you'll sign the appropriate chitties for phone-taps and the like, Deputy?'

'Naturally,' Constant replied, his airy tone dissipated. He leaned forward on the desk, elbows resting, arms flat, fingers still linked. 'But there must be no slip-ups – no suspicion by any of the four that we are investigating them. I want this little mess cleared up before it begins to stink.'

'I understand, Deputy.'

'I hope you do, Aubrey. This is an emergency, as far as NATO Intelligence is concerned. The Americans are screaming for action – worse than that, ever since the French put their intelligence service to rights so ruthlessly in the last couple of years, they are quite unbearable!' He paused, then added: 'Besides which, we don't want SIS used as the whipping-boy if and when the General decides to leave NATO flat!'

When Constant had gone, Aubrey ordered coffee, and

appeared to relax visibly. 'Well, what do you think of that, Hilary?'

'Of Deputy?'

'Everything – down to the last flicker of his nostrils and the tiniest inflection of his voice. What a masterly performer – eh? He's absolutely wetting himself in the hope that our man is Lavender, who's far more astute than Constant in many ways and is blessedly without his overweening vanity – and might get the top job when "C" goes to pasture!' Aubrey laughed. 'I can see an image of myself in him,' he confided. 'As I was when I left SOE and came back into this show. You went off to Cambridge for a while. But I had everything worked out, especially an assessment of my own capabilities. Then I worked for eighteen months with Deputy in SO-1, the Action gang. By the time that was over, I found myself trying to be everything he was not. Consequently, I am very highly thought of, but very rarely promoted!'

Latymer smiled. There was no need to commiserate. Aubrey was a man who had learned contentment with his rank. He said, 'Who is your money on, Aubrey?'

Aubrey tucked his thumbs into the pockets of his waistcoat and leaned back in the chair he had recaptured after Constant's departure.

'Ah, my money? Melluish is the obvious bet – former Head of Moscow Station where he could be easily got at. But he's a very strict and upright man, is Mr. Melluish. A lot of the Scots non-conformist temperament about him. He might be unable to bear the burden of guilt which he would undoubtedly contract if he went over to the other side. And he isn't ambitious, nor uxorious, nor homosexual – what did the Russians do to him, then? He'd have to be persuaded he was doing *right*.' Aubrey shrugged his shoulders. 'Perhaps he has been?' He paused for a moment, then went on: 'Lidbrooke – a flashy character, reckless, one might say life-loving. He would think it an awfully good wheeze to work both ends against the middle. As Assistant

Head of SO-1, he would be a good capture – right up at the sharp end. Mm.

'And Mr. Allom, whose wife drinks and whose daughter married a Ghanaian up at Leeds University, having to go through the formalities to legitimise the fruit of forbidden passion. Poor Allom's life is a bloody mess, but he's brilliant and dedicated.'

'But he doesn't have the ideological commitment?'

'Do we? No, you can't demand of others loyalties we often wonder about ourselves. He does need money, but as Head of Ciphers he ought to be collecting sufficient. After all, I believe his wife drinks only an inferior sort of gin . . .'

'Then – Lavender?'

'Who can say? As Tungay says of David to Mr. Creakle – "nothing known against him – there's been no time"!' He laughed aloud, then said, 'All right, let's get this show on the road, as I believe they say at Langley. We'll want a number of Patterson's men for this one – most of the Beaters we've used before, I think. They'll be discreet, I'll order them – you get hold of a full schedule of the Committee and sub-committee meetings for Thursday.'

'What shall I do about Richard Gardiner's wife – widow?'

'What? Oh – get that out of the way as quickly as you can, would you? I'm sorry about Richard, but we have something more important on our plate at the moment.' He held the telephone in his hand, and looked up from dialling. 'I suppose there *is* a certain heady delight connected with action. I feel as if we've been sitting on our bums doing absolutely nothing for weeks!'

Latymer was still smiling as he reached his own office.

The man who had introduced himself to Etienne de Vaugrigard as 'L'Etranger' sat at his desk in a small office in the Quai d'Orsay, the French Foreign Ministry, dictating quietly into a tape-recorder. The office was one which he had acquired with his official rank in the French civil service.

He had another, more anonymous office in his role as a functionary of SDECE, French Intelligence.

The tape was intended as protection, yet even as he moved his lips he knew it all sounded just as if he were making a speech for the defence, or a plea for clemency before a court. Perhaps, he reflected, it was the only way the words would ever emerge. His masters in SDECE had sanctioned his bizarre maverick operation to employ Gardiner, to trigger him by using Dupuy, one of the men who had tried to kill him in 1944. They had not even objected when Dupuy had been killed . . .

They had agreed to postpone the investigation and undoubted arrest of Etienne de Vaugrigard until the operation was completed – or until it had manifestly failed.

'It was the most fortunate of accidents,' he said in the room innocent with mid-morning sunlight. The window was open – he could almost smell the river and the traffic across the great bridge was audible to him; certainly, the tang of August dust from the Paris streets was sharp in his nose. 'To be told about the "Wolf" and the "Wolverine" by a man afraid of his silly little games with the OAS now that they had been found out.'

He sighed. It sounded so – flat, unconvincing. Not at all like the leap of insight he had made, the daring scheme that had seemed fully-armed even as he formed its haziest outlines. When he spoke again, he said:

'Gardiner is now in Rouen, proceeding with his investigation, which will lead him to de Vaugrigard. Of course, de Vaugrigard has been promised protection . . .' He cursed. His mind was wandering. This was not a progress tape, but something else.

Insurance? Is that what he craved?

Frightened, then?

He needed the tape.

'The two men who are our operation targets are dangerous to France, much more dangerous than Etienne could ever have suspected. This operation has been approved despite the current governmental opposition to NATO – it is for the medium-term, even the long term, that their removal becomes important . . .'

Yes, he thought, *it is because of de Gaulle that I have to make the tape.* He shook his head, and the tape whirred on, recording the muffled traffic and the drumming of his absent fingers on the desk. *Because what I am doing is a kind of – potential treason?*

Stupid.

Etienne knows about treason, he thought savagely. *Twisted sense of loyalty, and Renaud goes to the Avenue Foch, and Gardiner with him – twist again, and he supplies the OAS with money and guns to fight back at de Gaulle, hero turned traitor . . .*

If France withdraws from NATO? He wondered whether he had voiced the thought, and made as if to rewind the tape, then relaxed in his chair, his face smiling.

'If France withdraws from NATO, and stays out – then this operation will be disapproved by my masters, even disowned. Which is why I am making you, little spool, bear such heavy and such unconnected thoughts.'

The tape picked up next the sound of his laughter. In the smaller outer office, an assistant looked up from a sheaf of papers, winked at another young man, and went back to his work.

Gardiner's house was a converted mill. Once inside, however, conversion left Latymer with no sense of its past occupation. A modern coolness, even sterility, possessed the long lounge on the first floor, its windows overlooking the Dorset countryside. He was assailed by an almost feminine intuition that it was a room in which Richard Gardiner had ceased to live a long time before.

Apple-green carpet, brown-covered suite, low tables; a room waiting for occasions. He felt almost as if he were attending Gardiner's funeral in a tasteless, bricked, modern funeral parlour, and half-expected piped hymns to issue from the walls or the hi-fi equipment on the uncluttered shelving.

Jane Gardiner was self-possessed about the meeting. She seemed indifferent to his initial murmurings, waving him to a seat. The view was suddenly behind him, and the room became more arctic than before. Jane sat opposite him, on the other side of a low table, smoothing her narrow dress over her knees. It was green, silk Latymer thought. She was dressed to advantage, and he disliked her for that.

'It – came as such a shock,' he asserted diffidently, possessed by awkwardness.

'Yes,' she said. 'Would you like coffee?'

He was about to refuse, when he wanted to be rid of her for a moment, while his preconceptions adjusted, or were buried. He nodded.

'Thank you.'

She was little more than a few minutes. He stood up, looked out of the window, despising her, but having the innate justice to sense that he had prescribed a role for her which she could not have supported – even had she appeared as the tearful and repentant wife, he would have suspected the honesty of the portrait. He slouched before the picture window, hands in pockets, as if asserting some role within himself.

Jane Gardiner wasn't a likeable woman. Victoria had said that and, imperious as she was, she was warm towards people at first. One had to rebuff or rebuke Victoria to earn her poor opinion.

He did not want to think about his wife; not even her opinions, and shrugged her away, concentrating on the carpet and white walls, their history smoothed out by plasterers, until his hostess came back with the coffee.

Almost the instant she was seated, he with his cup to his lips, she said, 'Why have you come here, Hilary?'

He looked up at her, putting down the cup. Coffee tickled in his nose from the little splutter of surprise. Her face was raw with challenge, the eyes alight. So she must have faced Gardiner often, he thought.

'I – wanted to pay my respects – no, that sounds too pompous. I wanted to know whether you were all right.'

'Thank you for that.'

'I'm sorry. I sense I'm intruding.'

'Perhaps. I don't suppose you mean to. Not many people have called, you know. Richard's stuffy partners, one or two of his boating acquaintances – they probably came for the drink, or a description of how he went down with colours flying while the band played . . .'

She seemed to cut herself off with an effort. She looked self-betrayed. Latymer was surprised at the intensity of his dislike.

'I see.'

'Do you? You're one of his friends, of course. I'm wearing my armour visibly this year. You know, of course, that I was having another of my interminable, incessant affairs at the very moment he died. Yes?' Latymer shook his head. 'You don't seem very well informed, Hilary. I'm surprised. But I won't bore you with the details. I don't suppose it will surprise you, any more than it would surprise Richard's other friends. Some of whom would welcome the opportunity of replacing him between his sheets . . .'

It was said without arrogance or self-compliment. Latymer stared at her, his coffee growing a skin, as if willing her to reveal a weakness in the hard mask, some gleam of emotion behind the self-possession. Perhaps so that he could sympathise with her.

'I – knew, of course, that Richard and you were not happy together . . .'

'Not quite true. We enjoyed some of our quarrels. However, Hilary, that isn't your concern.'

'No.'

'What is?'

'Just – making the gesture, I suppose.'

'Ah,' She seemed pleased by his honesty, as if a schoolmistress whose pupil has recited something well-learned.

W.–P

'That's about it, isn't it?' he said suddenly. 'You and I, not really giving much of a damn.'

'Perhaps.'

'Can I be of practical help, then, in his affairs, money, the boys . . . ?'

'Arthur Hebden, the senior partner – he's taking care of the business side of things. The boys are with my mother, in Cheltenham. They'll be going back to school early this term; there's an arrangement in cases like mine – no, I don't think there is much for you to do, Hilary.'

'You'll stay on here?'

'It's mine now. And Richard was heavily insured.'

She seemed determined to present nothing of softness, nothing he might catch hold of, regard as *proper*. He wondered how hard she really was, what had attracted Richard Gardiner in the first place – he knew. She might well be that hard, that withdrawn. He could be like that; like to like?

'You'll be comfortable, then?'

'Thank you, yes.'

He no longer wanted the coffee, which had cooled. She seemed pleased at his confusion. He said, because he could not get up and leave at that moment, having made such little impression on her: 'What exactly happened? Can you tell me?'

'Professional interest?'

'I don't know, to be honest. What about the man he is supposed to have killed?'

'I never knew anything of that. The French police asked me about him – I could tell them nothing. They told me that he was a wartime acquaintance. Something to do with that part of Richard's life.'

'This was Dupuy?'

'I think that was the name – yes.'

'You know that Richard was betrayed – tortured. Then someone apparently tried to have him removed altogether . . .'

'Something of it. He never talked about it. He dreamed

about it sometimes – but he'd never talk about it in the mornings. I stopped enquiring a long time ago.'

'Yes. This man was a waiter at the hotel?'

'Apparently.'

'Why did Richard go to meet him?'

'I've no idea. Auld lang syne?'

'Perhaps.'

Latymer was soothed by being obliquely in control of the conversation now; it was a professional enquiry, mere routine. Broken bones of emotion and hostility no longer stuck up through lacerated skin. Smooth. Like the walls, behind which the rough mill still existed.

'He robbed the safe, and stole a boat. Was he a good sailor?'

'Yes – at least, he should have been. He spent enough time in the last four or five years with the boat he bought. Which I shall now be selling, naturally.'

'What was the weather like that night?' He asked the question because his mind had suited itself to familiar grooves. A logical progression, in one way.

For a moment, recollected pleasure. But unshared with Gardiner.

'Fine – a lovely summer night.'

'Where were you at the time?' He felt himself being distracted; something else, he had meant to ask something else. But she created emotions in him that got in the way. With her lover . . .

'I was on board. Isn't that rich. I wonder the French police didn't suggest I bribed the captain –' The eyes challenged him, daring him to condemn her.

'No, not that – say what you said again. A fine summer night, was that it?'

'Yes.'

'The boat? Was your boat illuminated?'

'Of course. A pleasure cruise . . .' She smiled, almost to taunt. *Pleasure* . . .

'Was there a wind?'

'None. We – were on deck. A calm night.' She seemed
seized by something that would reassert control, shock him.
'I didn't even see his boat, didn't hear anything until it was
all over. Just a light tremor in the deck . . . And it was over.'

Reactions flooded Latymer's awareness, but he rejected
the mess of information. 'He was a good sailor. You said . . .
Did he want to die?'

'I – hadn't thought of that.' She considered. 'Perhaps. He
had killed a man. He was strange, that evening, as if drawn
up tight in himself . . . I don't know.'

Latymer wanted to get out, then. Quickly. The woman
confused him. He saw, in a moment, that it was all an act;
the hardness, the glinting armour of unfeeling – nothing like
the truth. But he did not have time to spare on her now.

He said, getting up, 'If there's anything I can do – at any
time . . .'

She stood up. 'Of course.'

They knew that they would not meet again. She smoothed
her dress over her hips, formalities over.

He went down the stairs, and she let him out. She took his
proffered hand, lightly and without meaning, and then the
door was closed behind him. He got into his car, sat for a
moment, excitement welling in him. Then he started the car,
and drove off. Unaware that she was watching him from
the picture window, his cold coffee grey in the delicate cup
she held in her hands.

Latymer rang Aubrey from a public call box outside
Dorchester. When he was put through, the excitement in his
voice was evident.

'I've just spoken to Jane Gardiner. Richard is supposed
to have collided with a cruise yacht illuminated like a
Christmas tree on a fine night in a calm sea. Do you realise
what this means, Aubrey? Richard's still alive. He just wants
everyone to think he's dead. I'll stake my life on it!'

PART TWO

THE ANGER OF ACHILLES

'We shall not cease from exploration
And the end of our exploring
Will be to arrive where we started
And know the place for the first time.'

T. S. Eliot: 'Little Gidding', V

'THUS the highborn son of Priam pleaded for mercy with Achilles. But there was no mercy in the voice that answered him. "You fool," he heard Achilles say, "do not talk to me of ransom: I wish to hear no more speeches. Before Patroclus met his end, I was not disinclined to spare the Trojans ... But now not a single man whom God brings into my hands ... is going to live; and that holds good for every Trojan who lives ... Yes, my friend, you too must die. Why make such a song about it? Even Patroclus died, who was a better man than you by far".'

Homer: *The Iliad*, *Bk.* 21
(trans. E. V. Rieu)

CHAPTER FIVE

FRENCH CONNECTIONS

'L'ETRANGER' picked up the secure telephone on his desk, in response to his secretary's instruction, and listened to the code identification at the other end.

'I see. Your men are in place? You have briefed the Grodin woman – what was her reaction?'

'Truculent – bloody-minded. But she'll do as she's told.'

'Can she act the part well enough?'

'Tough as nails. She'll do. I wouldn't like to have met her on a dark night around 1942 – at least, not wearing field-grey.' There was a chuckle at the other end of the line.

'Where is Gardiner?'

'Hotel de St. Ouen – one of the shadows is booked in there, just in case.'

'Good. I've spoken to the local inspector. No questions to be asked. I must admit, I'm pleased with the way in which Gardiner dealt with his identity, and his disappearance from La Baule.'

'Clever bastard, isn't he?'

'He is. I'm beginning to respect him more and more. As soon as he's been to see Grodin, you check back with her, then get to Paris as soon as you can – take over here.'

'Sure, Chief. See you.'

'L'Etranger' put down the telephone, and opened a drawer in his desk. Time to commit a little more to tape. He smiled. Gardiner was a man one could easily admire – in doing so, he was aware of admiring his own brilliance of mind.

He pressed the record button.

The Hotel de St. Ouen in Rouen in the Rue de l'Hôpital

was situated on the right bank of the Seine. Richard Gardiner stood looking from the tall narrow window of his third-floor room, obliquely along the street towards the cold, uninspiring façade of the church of St. Ouen, a nineteenth-century addition that appeared to him as the work of some clumsy plasterer, hiding a mosaic or a frieze. He was smoking a cigarette after eating breakfast in the dining-room, and preparing himself for his visit to Vivienne Grodin, still living at the farm in the Seine valley west of the town, one of the wartime headquarters of the 'Ilium' group. As her father's only child, she was now the owner. The old man had been dead for many years and Gardiner was glad of it. The old man was strangely sacrosanct in memory.

He had driven out to the fruit farm in the car he had hired in the name of Jacques Remy, whose face stared muzzily back at him from the *carte d'identité* he was currently using. Remy was a fictitious character, but his face was the face of a man he had seen on the Paris metro and whose wallet he had stolen in the rush-hour crowds. It was a simple matter to alter the typed details so that they applied to his alias, but he was unable to alter the photograph with its embossed stamp crossing one corner. Therefore, all the men whose *cartes* he had acquired appeared much as he did himself. For Remy, he had grown a moustache which altered the shape of the mouth; and his hair was a little darker. He had found on those occasions when he had used the *carte* that close scrutiny was entirely absent. The man in the car-hire office had had to be pressed to more than glance at the khaki fold of paste-board in Gardiner's hand.

Gardiner thought about Vivienne Grodin. She had once been the mistress of Renaud, who had died in the Avenue Foch; once Gardiner had been her perfunctory lover. Yet she had relatives in the group. He was uncertain of her reaction to any request for information. He recalled her as a girl of twenty-two; she had been tough with the slow, definite toughness of her peasant background. She had taken orders, chosen the men she slept with, and developed a capacity for independent thought and action. It was that last quality that threatened the smooth progress of his plans. She was capable of proving an ally, or an opponent.

During the days in the scruffy *pension* on the Left Bank, after his hours of haunting the metro for faces that resembled his own – a grotesque, nightmarish journey it had seemed at times – he had begun to limit the horizons of his revenge. A crazed capacity and desire for violence had come to him in the aftermath of Dupuy's death – he understood how easy it would have been to kill the little hotel manager, or anyone who might have challenged him at the St. Nazaire station; now that had abated, and burned with a colder, more regulated flame. He wanted Perrier now, the other man in the Renault that had broken his body like matchwood, and the man who had given the order for his death. They would suffice.

It had to be justified revenge, and the sense of something left unfinished. In these terms, he disguised his nature from himself.

The cigarette burned his fingers, and he smelt the coffee-smell from a shop across the street as his senses reawoke. He would accept the risk. He had to talk to Vivienne Grodin, and he did not think she would know about Dupuy.

'Au 'voir, M'sieur Remy.' He passed the clerk and was smiling by the time he stepped onto the pavement outside the hotel. The smell of coffee was stronger – he could see the roaster rotating in the window of the shop-cum-café. There was a pleasing atmosphere of unhurried tourism in the street. The traffic was light, and in the shadows on that side of the Rue de l'Hôpital there was retained the illusion of early morning freshness. The water from the cleansing cart was still evident in the damp patches on the pavement.

He drove out of the town, following the D 51 as it threaded its path through the industrial suburbs along the right bank of the Seine. Then scrubbed residential developments, hotter it seemed than the old town, dry and dusty with use. Traffic increased. Factory chimneys thrust into a sky already becoming hazy and colourless, and his attention was retained only by his recognition of change. It was somehow unpleasant, the admission that something loved had changed; a body, known and explored, changed by some accident, broken and put together differently. There was no sense of the irony of his part in the destruction. It was Allied bombers that had done the damage.

He passed through Croisset, then Val-de-la-Haye, where Napoleon's body had rested on its journey from St. Helena to Paris. He recalled members of the group who had begun by hardly noticing the place, especially the column to commemorate the event, but whose need for such a tangible evidence of their country's credibility had deepened through 1941 and '42 until the village had come to possess an almost talismanic effect upon them.

The slopes on which the fruit trees clung were right against the road as it followed the Seine, on the edge of the Forêt de Roumare, in a clasping loop of the river. He turned off the main road, and climbed towards the farm – whitewashed, red-roofed, tiny above the valley slope, enlarging to human dimensions as the car ascended the rutted, dusty farm track. He inspected his feelings, and sensed the ruts of the road beneath his feet or through the jolts of a bicycle saddle. He smiled.

It was no homecoming, but the farm still possessed some of its elemental power suggestive of rest and safety; even of the quick, necessary encounters with Vivienne in the hayloft. He nor any others of the group had ever brought outsiders to the farm. He had lived for several months in the house itself; he could visualise it, knowing that it would not have changed significantly. It had become his headquarters in February 1943, a season of iron ruts in the road and thick rime on posts and fences and pasture – bare trees. He had moved into Rouen itself in 1944. Yet it had always continued to function as an important staging-post for drops and later for the small, single-engined, high-winged Lysanders to land, or as a hide-out for members of the group when the Rouen

Gestapo made one of their periodic, ritual acts of cleansing in the old town.

He parked the car outside the gate. Through the heavy, laden greenness of fruit trees he could see the farmhouse. He passed through the gate and thought about Dupuy, but only now in his identity as 'Patroclus', the boy who had hero-worshipped 'Achilles'. There was a sudden sadness as he remembered a conversation with the boy as he tried to explain what had happened to his father and mother.

It was not that Gardiner would have turned back at that point. In fact, he pressed the thoughts down, expunging the memory which had been evoked as he crossed the orchard, the grass rustling round his shoes, the pink rump of a pig disappearing behind a tree; they had chased a pig once, he and the boy and even Perrier, and dressed it in a captured German uniform as much as they could. Then they had tied it to an apple-tree, and marched past it, arms outstretched in the Nazi salute. The boy had tried to paint a swastika on the pig's rump . . .

He shunned his memories, sensing their power, the freedom with which they moved here in their own element. His shoes scuffed on the dusty track. He knocked on the door.

For a moment, he did not recognise her. She had never been beautiful; thin-faced, dark-eyed, a long nose. She had put on weight now, ample breasts swelling beneath the black dress. She dressed in an almost-forgotten style. She might even be married, though her name was still her father's name, so they had said in the village. She greeted him, and the voice still belonged to Vivienne.

He said, 'You don't remember, then?'

A slow recognition, dismissed. She said, 'Can I help you, M'sieur?'

Gardiner watched the mouth open into a round hole, and the eyes fill with something akin to fear. There was a delay of recognition. She had to see beyond the new moustache, then adjust to the past to provide his proper context.

'Vivienne,' he said warmly, preparing his role carefully.

He smiled as he might have done had he really been only a
visitor, his object mere nostalgia.

' "Achilles" . . . ?'

He nodded. He watched her face intently. It seemed for a
moment as if she had expected him, but not at that moment,
then she held out her arms and took his hands firmly. He dismissed the idea as a mistake. He laughed – there was,
surprisingly, a genuine pleasure, something come back out
of the past that was not unclean or violent. It was not love,
but something like, the camaraderie of the past, of living
together at the extremes of experience. It was good to see
her.

'Vivienne!' He kissed her cheek, tasting the face-powder
as something strange that he did not associate with her,
feeling the roughness of the skin.

'What are you doing here – Richard?' She struggled with
his name. 'Richard.'

'I'm on holiday!' he said with conviction. The role was
easy to play; he wished to play it. He would count the cost
of using her, making her betray confidences and men's lives,
later. This had to be done in this way, as if to compensate
for spending the last year of the war in hospitals and for not
having come back before this. He added: 'Touring! I left
my wife and children in Rouen, and came out to see you.'

She was still holding his right hand, and he felt a tremor
run through her which he assumed was shock, or relief. She
led him into the big living-room of the farmhouse.

It was as he remembered it. The old furniture, heavy and
graceless, and highly-polished, the deal table scarred with
work, the stone floor partially covered with dark faded rugs
and pieces of carpet.

She said, 'It – it has been so long!' She motioned him to
a chair at the table. 'Sit down – coffee?' He nodded, taking
in the room still. Its contours re-established their old
familiarity. It *was* pleasant; as long as he continued to behave
as he had, it would not be awkward, or dirty.

He watched her move towards the kitchen with the slight

sway of a big woman, the economical slither of someone used to labour that continued from birth to death.

He called out, looking at his soft hands, 'You're not married, then?'

'No!' she called back. A moment's hesitation, then she laughed. It was as if she, too, were relearning an old role. 'Who would have me? All the men in this area know I used to kill Germans for a living – who would not be frightened?'

He laughed.

When she brought in the coffee, and sat down, her face was more open, the sharp eyes softer, more humoured. They talked – only moments of awkwardness while she enquired tentatively after his injuries in '44, then recollection achieved its own momentum. They talked through the remainder of the morning, until she prepared a lunch of bread and cheese. There was a bottle of young, strong wine, and he understood that it, too, was in tribute to the past. Only one part of his mind stayed alive to his purpose, and he was satisfied that she had had nothing to do with his betrayal. Then he relaxed. There was no need to point the conversation; it would arrive at the necessary destination, given time.

The bread was fresh and warm, sticking to his palate so that it had to be washed down with the wine. He watched her, just as she watched him. She spoke of her sister, Marie, who had married Georges from the café in Hautot-sur-Seine, a couple of kilometres away – Georges he remembered, surely? He nodded, smiling and raised his glass – it had been tin or enamel mugs before.

Sunlight spilled into the room through the small windows. The shadow of a man flickered in his mind for a moment, looking out across the orchard from beside one of these windows. As if it reminded him, he settled to the less pleasant work of memory.

'What about the others?' he prompted. 'How many of them still live near here?'

'You want to see them?' she said quickly. He shook his head.

'No, just idle curiosity. What about "Patroclus", or "Nestor" – how are they? Do you hear from them?' He asked the question lightly, looking at the last of the wine in his glass, swilling it idly round.

'No . . .' One eye had watched her face. Dupuy's code-name had caused a tightening of the skin around the mouth, but nothing in the eyes.

'Not "Nestor" – I suppose he went back to Paris?'

There was a moment of silence, then she said with a mechanical lack of inflection: 'Yes – we heard from him, Marie and me, once or twice. He had begun a small business, fruit I think, because he said it had been the farm that had given him the idea.'

He nodded. 'My family and I are thinking of ending our holiday in Paris – you wouldn't have an address for him, I suppose?'

'I don't think so . . . I can't really remember. Perhaps it was on the Left Bank, and he was very proud of the shop because it had his name above it. There was a photograph of him standing outside, showing the sign. François was very pleased with himself, and already putting on weight . . . !' The laughter was not quite real. He nodded.

The moment was past now, and he concentrated on disguising any tracks he might have made towards the information. They talked for perhaps another hour before he left, and both of them seemed more relaxed. When they parted, he kissed her on both cheeks and she returned the light pecks firmly. They had never spoken of their relationship, a part of their mutual past that had slipped over memory's horizon. He waved to her through the trees as he reached the gate.

When he was gone and she could no longer hear the car, she collapsed in her chair and laid her head on the table, her cheek quivering against the rough wood. Her mouth worked in an hysterical, silent relief, and her eyes were wide as if she were witnessing some horror.

She had performed the task appointed to her. She did not

know how well, but she had done it. And she knew, without doubt, she had sentenced François Perrier to death.

The man who had come to see her a month ago had told her everything. She did not know him, and he did not give his name – but there was the insidious, insistent recognition that he was French Intelligence. She could not be sure, of course, because she had seen no papers; but she knew. The task he had given, and the understanding that she had no real alternative, had made everything simple and naked. Only in a moral sense was it appalling.

Perrier had betrayed Gardiner. Gardiner would come, looking for Perrier. She was to point Gardiner towards Paris, and Perrier's shop. She had been horrified, even twenty years after, at the bald narrative of duplicity and betrayal. When Gardiner had indeed come, she had inhabited a little room of fear inside her own room until he had asked, and she had told. Then she wanted him gone, because he appeared just as he had done, her leader from the old days softened a little by time and affluence.

Even now, with her head against the rough, comforting wood, she thought with pain of the memories he had brought back; as if he knew she was betraying him.

It was a long time before she went slowly back to her tasks, and the two men, father and son, who worked for her went unnoticed until they finished their day's work. She tried to learn the art of forgetfulness – but his face was still vivid to her when the man came to speak to her in the evening. It was not the same man who had rehearsed her in what to say. This man, paunchy and with vivid eyes closed in lines of fat, asked her about her conversation with Gardiner and seemed satisfied with her replies. When he had gone, she realised she could begin to forget.

Later that evening, she went to visit her married sister. She did not mention 'Achilles'.

Aubrey had set up his Paris headquarters in an apartment leased by the Embassy in the Rue de Castellane which lay

between the Madeleine and the Boulevard Haussmann. He
went no nearer the Embassy than that, though it was close,
in the Faubourg St. Honoré. Both Lidbrooke and Melluish
would use the Embassy facilities during their stay in Paris,
and he had no wish to meet them by accident in a corridor
of the building. By the same token, he intended avoiding
the NATO building.

Latymer had brought with him the files he had drawn
from the warehouse in London and which related to the
'Ilium' group.

Now, sitting in the apartment, he had made his decisions.
Aubrey could run Operation Guesswork, and he would try
to trace Gardiner. Both he and Aubrey owed sufficient to
Richard to try to stop him from what Latymer knew he
must be planning. In Latymer, there was a puritanical streak,
narrow but evident. He was a civilised man, and he believed
in the wrongness of Gardiner's actions; Dupuy might have
been self-defence, and Gardiner was still not over the edge
of the flat moral earth. Latymer might yet save him.

He did not consider his motives too deeply. He left them
at the bottom of his consciousness. They were confused, and
muddy, and he decided, though normally fastidious in self-
analysis, to let them be.

When Aubrey returned from his initial briefing of the
Beaters, stationed in an empty warehouse near Les Halles
and owned by the Embassy through an extended lease –
Latymer never remembered the address – Latymer said to
him with an assumed blandness – realising as he did so the
imperative nagging at his stomach:

'I want you to give me a certain freedom of action for a
few days, Aubrey.'

Aubrey, helping himself to a mid-day sherry, inspected
the label on the bottle, recognised the firm with the current
F.O. contract for 'Embassy Victualling, Wines and Spirits',
and seemed satisfied. Then turned his head and smiled
quizzically. 'Yes?' he said. 'I thought you were keen to come
in on this affair?'

'I was. But not to see it through.'

Aubrey sat down opposite Latymer, silently raised his glass and said: 'Oh. Don't tell me you only came for the night life. I shall be disappointed.'

Latymer shook his head. The nerves seemed to be tapping at his stomach like cold fingers. 'I want to look for Richard Gardiner.'

Aubrey seemed unsurprised, and his head wobbled like that of a small bird eating, and as if in some kind of compact with Latymer. Nevertheless, Latymer uncomfortably sensed that he understood something about him that he had not wished revealed.

Aubrey said, 'I don't quite see things with your moral squint, Hilary. But I suppose there *is* an obligation ...' He sipped at the sherry. 'We sent him to Paris in the first place.' He appeared to be talking to the ceiling. 'I don't understand it after all this time – Richard is a reasonable man!' He was almost pleading.

'But we can both deduce what he's planning,' Latymer said heavily. The flutter in his stomach had hardened into a ball. It was as if he had been frightened that Aubrey would forbid him. Now, that did not seem likely.

'Yes.' The sunlight from the long window, spilled on the shoulder of Aubrey's grey suit as he moved in his chair, focusing his attention on Latymer. Once again the sharp, appraising stare, the tiny nod of acceptance, then: 'Yes, I suppose we do owe it to him, to try and stop it.' Then he burst out, the patch of sunlight sliding across his chest as he moved: 'But it was nineteen years ago ... ! Damn it, why can't he forget?'

'He's been forced to remember it all again. Nineteen years wiped out for him. He can't forgive that.'

Aubrey looked sharply, and nodded. 'We both know what kind of man he is.'

Latymer could not suppress a shudder. 'Richard was not a – *kind* man ...' The phrase was hopelessly inadequate.

As if embarrassed, Aubrey said, 'Do you think that the

last nineteen years have been a kind of fiction for him, then ?'

'I don't know. I don't think so. He was trying to adjust. Did it. But something's come back from the dead now, and it isn't interested in being a county town solicitor any longer!'

'I suppose you're right. Where will you begin?'

'Rouen, I think. Then here in Paris, with Etienne de Vaugrigard – he might perhaps know where the rest of the group is now.'

'Very well. I'll run Guesswork from here. Everything's staked out, and you're not really needed. I wonder whether I'm not letting you go on this thing just to spite Constant? But I can't spare you any help.'

'I understand.' Latymer's eyes suddenly blazed. 'I can understand it, you know, Aubrey! I can understand, dimly, the power of the past over Richard Gardiner. It has the satisfying element of mystery, and it's tied up with the people we once were. It's an escape, you know. For him and me.'

'Mm. Do you think he *prefers* being the man he was?'

'Perhaps he does. He – amounted to something then.'

'Yes. But what hope have you of finding who was responsible for what happened to him?'

'I don't know. But Richard doesn't know, either, perhaps. Not yet. If I can get to him first. He'll have gone to Rouen, or to de Vaugrigard, I think. I'll try both.' His hand rubbed his thigh. 'I just don't know *who* . . . He was one of the most successful leaders we ever imposed upon a group. He wasn't material for betrayal.'

'I wish you luck. Sincere good fortune.' Aubrey looked at his watch. 'I should think the first session of the Senior Joint Intelligence Committee has adjourned for lunch by now, and I suggest we do the same. Jorgensen will bring up 'Snowshoe' this afternoon.' He smiled. 'There'll be opportunity for our man to bring the subject up this evening. There's an informal cocktail party for the chairman. He's being posted back to Washington.'

'Van Lederer's done a good job,' Latymer remarked idly, standing up and putting on his jacket. 'Whither General Eugene van Lederer? Saigon?'

'I shouldn't be at all surprised. Come, let's eat, Hilary. I have reserved a table at a little place I know.'

Latymer smiled, content in some strange way, and allowed himself to be ushered out of the apartment.

Lt. Colonel Nils Jorgensen of Norwegian Army Intelligence ate his salad lunch slowly. He was not partial to the heavy, oily dressing, but it was not the food alone that failed to please. It was the memory of that house in Fulham and the little man he had known in wartime Intelligence, Aubrey, that robbed him of appetite. It had been two days ago when they had concocted 'Exercise Snowshoe', a fake term for a fake operation in the Finnmark the previous winter, around Vadso and the Veranger Fjord. The details were sketchy, but even the summary which would be all expected of him that afternoon, was explosive. 'Snowshoe' was the name supposedly given to the training of British SAS officers and men in Arctic conditions, including secret night landings from nuclear submarine and sabotage of radar and naval installations. The exercise was supposed to have prepared a small force for long-range penetration down the Finnish border, even into the Kola Peninsula as far as Murmansk – in time of war. The training had taken place inside the agreed limit between Norway and the Soviet Union forbidden to foreign troops.

In his general report to the Committee, Jorgensen would introduce this bombshell. Since the operation did not exist, the Russians could not know of it. And if there was a 'mole' on the Committee, then it was too fat and tempting a grub not to be digested, stored, and regurgitated for the information and use of Moscow Centre. With reluctant admiration, Jorgensen admitted that Aubrey had provided a very tempting meal.

Which did not make the whole thing any more palatable.

It merely made Jorgensen, who had spent most of the war
in the Norwegian mountains as a member of the Resistance,
long for past simplicities and an enemy as declared as the
invading Nazis.

He ate slowly, and his conversation with those around
him in the fourth-floor dining-room of the NATO building
was desultory. As a normally reticent man whom they
respected, his behaviour was neither misinterpreted nor
condemned.

He was glad not to be sitting near either Lidbrooke or
Melluish.

Latymer, though surprised at the lack of hesitation in
Aubrey's acquiescence, suffered the small waiting time with
impatience. A sequence of routine procedures resulted in a
telephone call to Etienne de Vaugrigard, whom he had
known with some little intimacy during the war and had
met some three times since. He was invited to dinner. The
family had just returned from their holiday at Deauville,
where Etienne owned a small villa. They would be delighted
to see him – eight o'clock, black tie. Latymer smiled at the
continuation of Etienne's stiff formality. He had never been
able to *like* de Vaugrigard; even as a young man he had
possessed an arrogant, unyielding temper and a stiffness of
bearing. Like the General he had idolised. Growing older,
and the phenomenal success of his business, had not softened
him.

He provided himself next with a telephone directory of
the Rouen area. He checked with the local police that the
Vivienne Grodin shown in it was the woman he remembered,
and decided that if de Vaugrigard was unable to help him,
he would take a train or hire car to Rouen the following
day.

In mid-afternoon, Hawthorne from the Embassy called
in at the apartment, bringing a report from the London end
of Guesswork. It stated that none of the likely contacts for
the 'mole' had left the city. A close surveillance of the Soviet

and other likely East European embassies was being maintained. It was much as Aubrey had anticipated. The contact was in Paris.

While he waited for Aubrey to return from the warehouse in Les Halles, Latymer worked his way through the Paris telephone directory, attempting to match names with people in the files of the 'Ilium' group – and regretting that from the faded text of the files the past had risen like smoke. A fire was burning, and its name was Gardiner.

From time to time he remembered Aubrey's words about the 'mole' and they seemed to apply equally to Gardiner. He had said: 'This one, if he feels threatened or cut off, then he'll do the maximum damage possible before we catch up with him and put him down. He'll know that we won't arrest him, or make his treason public ... He could do anything – anything at all!'

The cocktail party began early. Most of the afternoon session had been taken up by Jorgensen and 'Snowshoe'. Its announcement had been greeted with shocked silence, then vivid and vocal disbelief. It was a hardline exercise, so many of the security delegates said. The Committee was baffled as to its usefulness, troubled by its anti-Soviet blatancy, and intrigued to know more. Jorgensen felt more and more that Aubrey had placed him in a most unfavourable light, and regretted the involvement of his country, through himself, in such ridiculous deception. If the Russians made a formal complaint, or took some kind of covert action ... ?

He defended his position in as tight-lipped a manner as was possible, implicating the UK as Aubrey desired, and then squeezing his lips into a bloodless line and folding his arms, he refused to say more.

The smaller groups at the cocktail party were obviously still considering the implications of a military exercise by British troops in the north of Norway as Jorgensen waited for someone to approach him on the subject more directly.

If Aubrey's 'mole' was present, he could not afford to pass up the opportunity.

There was general *bonhomie* to which each man responded as the drinks flowed – they were saying farewell to a chairman each of them respected, US Army Intelligence General van Lederer; a big man with heavy features, a straightforward lack of tact and nicety that made him an efficient chairman of committee, and a blunt respect for the men who had served with him.

When he spoke to Jorgensen during his circulation of the groups in the room, a large bourbon in his hand, he was intrigued, and the grey eyes gleamed – but he seemed intrigued by Jorgensen's reticence as much as by the information he had imparted.

He said, 'Hell – I don't know what the British are up to with that crazy sort of provocation. What if the Russians found out?' He swallowed at his drink, smacked his lips, and added, 'Hell, they ought to get rid of this post-facto clause in the rules of this committee. We ought've cleared something like "Snowshoe" before it got off the ground, or sat on it. Who cleared it, I wonder? Our two British friends don't know about it, not by the staring faces they put on this afternoon!'

'Quite,' Jorgensen murmured as the General passed on to another group. 'I knew nothing of it myself until recently,' he added with a sour attempt at a smile.

Jean-Jacques Haussman, the senior SDECE member of the full Committee, watched Colonel Jorgensen carefully for perhaps ten minutes after he had finished his conversation with van Lederer. He thought he understood what was happening. For that reason, he watched the two Englishmen carefully, without appearing to distract himself from the conversation with Helvigsson, the Icelander, and Protti of Italian Military Intelligence. He considered Jorgensen's performance as having the slightest air of unreality, especially now that he appeared to avoid conversation, as if waiting for a chosen partner. Lidbrooke or Melluish, Haussman thought. And that meant a British 'ferret' operation; 'Snowshoe' was a blind, concocted probably by Aubrey to smoke out the 'mole'. Which would explain why the other two, Lavender and Allom, were not present. Two at a time.

He was certain that Lidbrooke and Melluish, like the rest of the committee, had been taken in. It was only because he had spent most of his post-war career in the counter-intelligence section of the SDECE and was trained to a pitch of concentration on human beings, that he suspected anything. Having interrogated perhaps thousands of men and women, he knew the signs of a lie.

It was perhaps an hour later when Lidbrooke approached Jorgensen. It was the moment the Norwegian had been waiting for; yet when it came it was a surprise and he experienced a watery feeling of nausea in his stomach, and a vague, infinite regret. He had to concentrate very carefully on the tone of his voice and the stance of his body to avoid giving himself away.

Lidbrooke, after the introductory pleasantries, said, 'God, Nils – that was a bloody bombshell you dropped this afternoon! I almost wet myself at the idea!'

Jorgensen managed a small, weak smile and rubbed his forehead, mumbling something about feeling hot and perhaps opening the windows a little wider.

Lidbrooke, smiling sympathetically, adopted a conspiratorial look. 'You know, they're not supposed to do things like that?'

'Who?' Jorgensen said abruptly.

'The SAS – and my masters. I'm supposed to know about things like that – you know my position, Nils. Don't you think I ought to have been told about this lunatic thing?' Jorgensen nodded. 'Who sanctioned it, Nils? Have you any idea who thought it up?'

Jorgensen shook his head, and said: 'I don't, Derek. I was given a summary of the material, all names removed, and told to pass it on to the full Committee. It had just been downgraded for dissemination by our security chiefs.'

Jorgensen had found himself suddenly calm. He was playing a role he had practised, and that had a certain narcotic effect. Also, he was beginning to enjoy the bating of Lidbrooke, was able to think of him as a discovered double-agent. He studied the green eyes, the fair hair which curled over the collar of the suit; the slightly-flashy clothes included a wide-striped shirt, and a yellow tie.

He knew that Lidbrooke was a flamboyant operator – a very successful field-agent. Jorgensen knew his power as assistant Head of SO-1. The slight smile on his face seemed to further incense Lidbrooke's curiosity, and he said, 'You can't tell me anything, Nils – just between ourselves?'

Jorgensen could sense the urgency of the man, but could not be certain of its cause, anger or treachery. He shook his head.

Lidbrooke added, 'Well, I'm going to make a right bloody stink about this when I get back to London. I'll take it to the top, if necessary. Bloody fools, living in the romantic after-shave of imperialism! Who the hell are we to go pissing about up in the Finnmark with SAS men and a nuclear sub? Christ! What a mess it could have been! Do we know whether or not the Russians know?' Again, Jorgensen shook his head. 'Bloody fools!' Lidbrooke snapped again, downing the remainder of his drink in a single gulp.

When he wandered away, Jorgensen saw him in earnest conversation with Melluish, who seemed to be on the end of a verbal outburst similar to the one he had borne. He shook his head and wished Aubrey luck. Lidbrooke's interest might be professional, or sprung from a dented ego.

Jean-Jacques Haussman watched the exchange between Jorgensen and Lidbrooke with interest. He too, privately wished Aubrey luck – and looming behind his private wishes was the growing anger, self-righteous and even unreasonable, of the Quai d'Orsay, the SDECE, and even the Elysée, at the reports reaching the Russians from the centre of NATO. Lidbrooke, he concluded, had taken the bait, hook and all.

Etienne de Vaugrigard had always regarded his mistress's apartment in the Faubourg St. Honoré with a certain clandestine excitement. It was not so much that it contained the secret sexual part of his life, the young woman elevated from the offices of Air France on the Champs Elysée; rather, it was the fact that he had come to use the place for that other secret part of his existence – the OAS and his financial connection with it.

Two men sat with him now in the apartment. It was almost seven, and he expected to be back at the Avenue de Madrid house in time to welcome Hilary Latymer at eight. At the moment, however, another Englishman occupied his thoughts.

François Perrier sat with his cousin, Henri Janvier – 'Plastique', a Congo mercenary, a former member of the Foreign Legion who had operated in Indo-China, and who was now on occasion a sabotage expert for the secret forces of the OAS in the Paris area. Perrier, the member of the 'Ilium' group who had driven the van which ran 'Achilles' down, was a fortuitous accident since he connected de Vaugrigard with the man he needed – 'Plastique'.

Perrier had been part of the OAS for years, a low-importance errand-boy and occasional driver, depending on which was required. He had prospered in his fruit business, sold it and moved into the wholesale side of his trade. Yet, de Vaugrigard suspected, there was something left over from a former life, as with himself, though he did not make the comparison readily, something that chose to coalesce round the symbol of de Gaulle's betrayal of France and the army in Algeria. Perrier, like himself, had funded the OAS, but in a lesser fashion, and involved himself personally with low-risk enterprises – recapturing the feeling of Rouen and its times, perhaps.

Janvier was different. He was tied to the OAS by the money it paid him, and by nothing more. After Dien Bien Phu, and his march to safety through the jungle with the other pitiable units that remained uncaptured or wiped out,

he had turned away from all idealism, all appeals to any
better nature he might have. The Congo had allowed him
to practise his facility with explosives, and the OAS campaign
in metropolitan France was simply another backcloth against
which to play a mercenary role. If anyone could kill Richard
Gardiner for him, it was Janvier.

For that is what de Vaugrigard had decided to do. The
idea had come to him simply, and entire. In the bed in the
next room, waking from a stupidly-crazed, sweating dream,
and after the girl had turned over and resumed her sleep,
he had known what he must do. The distrust of 'L'Etranger'
had suddenly thrust itself like a cold plant through the earth,
telling him his own life was in danger, that the man from
SDECE would not protect him from Gardiner.

And the solution had been simple. A convincingly violent
OAS outrage in which Gardiner just *happened* to die. It
would not be traced back to him. Of the consequences of
his known association with the OAS – he refused to think
about it, enclosing himself instead in this chill passion to
rid himself of the Englishman.

De Vaugrigard knew he could frighten Perrier into helping
him; the man would be afraid of his own skin, just as – de
Vaugrigard admitted once more, with distaste in his mouth
like drunken sleep, vile and bitter – the similarity between
himself and the fatter, more vulgar Perrier. But it was
'Plastique' he needed, and that meant money.

He said, 'We agree, then? One hundred thousand francs.
Not a small sum for the death of one man, eh?' He smiled
at Janvier. It was an unreturned gesture. He watched the
lined, moustached face, unmoved, though the eyes flickered
slightly at the sum mentioned.

'He is a very dangerous man, then?'

'Perhaps. I want him dead, and it must look like an OAS
thing – you understand? He dies by apparent accident.
Which is why I need you.' He looked as if in apology at
Perrier, and added, 'Perhaps you could impress upon your
cousin what this man is like, mm?'

Perrier, apparently pleased to be making some contribution, said, 'Henri, – this man is a good killer. As Etienne ...' He looked swiftly at de Vaugrigard, who smiled to encourage the use of his first name, resenting it only secretly. 'As Etienne says, if he wants revenge now, and he has already killed one of our Rouen comrades – then it's him or us.'

'Not me,' Janvier observed. 'He doesn't know I'm alive.' He sounded blunt, uninterested, but de Vaugrigard understood it as a minor exercise of power. Perrier's face fell. Then Janvier added, 'However, if he is worth the price, then he is a dead man.'

'Good,' de Vaugrigard said. Perrier was evidently relieved. He had been almost perpetually afraid since de Vaugrigard had told him of the death of Dupuy. He was an image of de Vaugrigard's fear, enlarged. Etienne hated him for it, and was subtly gratified at the same time. 'Good. I will not ask for details – the money will be paid to you how and when you wish.' Janvier nodded. 'Half this evening. But there is very little time. The man must be in Paris by now. I want him dead within the next forty-eight hours – understand?'

CHAPTER SIX

THE LADY OF SITUATIONS

AUBREY was still up when Latymer returned from the de
Vaugrigard house. The little man had removed his collar,
and the shirt was open at the throat. In his scarlet braces,
he looked peculiarly untidy, even vulnerable. His slippered
feet were up on a stool. He was sipping meditatively at
a whisky and soda, and a heap of discarded sheets of
flimsy lay near him on the sofa. He looked tired and
frustrated.

'Did you have a pleasant time?' he asked with an acidic
edge to his voice.

'Very pleasant, thank you. The de Vaugrigard family have
a very good cook at present.' Latymer slipped off his dinner
jacket, loosened the bow tie, then poured himself a whisky.
The ice clinked loudly in the tumbler, intruding on the
expectant silence.

'I'm *so* glad!'

'What's the trouble, Aubrey – drawn a blank?'

'Indeed we have. I begin to wish I'd assigned you to over-
see Guesswork and given myself the task of saving Richard
Gardiner from his own worst excesses ...' He swallowed
some whisky, and added: 'It would seem that Lidbrooke
and Melluish have developed an infatuation for one another's
company, or their sense of insularity is much greater than
usual.'

'How come?'

'They haven't left each other's sight all night! After the
party at NATO, they went to a restaurant, then to a night-
club – all on SIS expenses, of course – and then they went
to bed!'

'Together?' Latymer, sitting in an armchair and stretching his long legs, could not resist the remark.

'Not according to my sources. However, they may be being very discreet about that.'

'No drop?'

'Not so much as a toffee-paper. No – Lidbrooke isn't clever enough to fool the Beaters. The drop must be in London, even though Paris is more likely.'

'What about the Russians?'

'Nothing. Nor the Czechs or the East Germans or the Poles. Everyone being impeccably innocent. You'd think there wasn't a Centre man in Paris, it's so quiet.' He looked at Latymer. 'What did you find out?'

Latymer shook his head. 'Not a great deal.' Aubrey appeared disappointed. 'Etienne de Vaugrigard doesn't like the General, he's self-satisfied, smug, over-wealthy and a prig, and I'm sure he has a young mistress stowed somewhere Geneviève won't find her – but he doesn't know a thing about Richard. He's had no word from him, nothing. He didn't even know about Dupuy, which I suppose is not surprising.' He picked at cigarette ash that had fallen on his trousers.

Aubrey, as if reminded, lit a cigarette himself and pulled an onyx ashtray to his side. 'I see. And you don't like Etienne very much, either – eh?'

'True. The son seems much in the same mould, and Geneviève is the classic aristocrat who married money, feels grubby because of it, and really ought to have been handed over to Citizen Robespierre years ago!' He smiled at Aubrey's smug expression. 'Yes, I'm frustrated, too. I shall have to go to Rouen tomorrow to talk to the woman, Vivienne Grodin.'

'Oh dear. These moral crusades *do* run out of steam very quickly, don't they?'

Latymer raised his glass, acknowledging the hit. Then he said, 'The daughter was different – Françoise. Beauty among the Beasts, rather.'

'Ah.'

'She's nineteen,' Latymer observed. 'And has taken to calling me "Uncle Hilary", if you must know.' His face darkened as if with memory for a moment.

Aubrey, aware of the direction of his thoughts – Oxford – said quickly, 'I see. But there's nothing, then?'

'No. Except confirmation that Richard won't stop now until he's evened the score. Etienne talked about him during the war. Not a pleasant picture, or a man a young lady would take home to meet Mummy. But we know that very well for ourselves – mm?'

'Quite.' Aubrey mused for a moment, then looked at Latymer with a strange, intent expression. 'You do want to follow this up, don't you?' Latymer opened his hands, shrugged. 'Do you or don't you?' He seemed to be willing Latymer to answer in the affirmative.

Latymer nodded. 'Yes,' he said. 'I think I must. Richard will kill himself over this. He can't get away with it – and I must stop him trying.'

'Good. In that case, you may continue with your enquiries. Alone, of course. Personally, I don't think you have a hope in hell of stopping what was begun in La Baule, or even in the Avenue Foch. It has the smell of a certain unpleasant kind of destiny about it.' He shook his head.

'I shall talk to Jean-Jacques Haussman, I think. Tomorrow, after I've seen the woman. He might be able to help – unofficially.'

'Able – but willing?'

'"I think so. Well, perhaps. He belongs to the same period, to liaison with SOE and all the rest of it. One of yesterday's spies, like ourselves. And we keep in touch. I think he might help, yes.'

'Good.'

'What of you? One of the other two, is it?'

'I'm not sure. Lidbrooke went for Jorgensen like a ferret down a hole – after our "ferret", as it were. But it could have been hot air, or righteous indignation. "Snowshoe" should have reached his ears in the normal way.' Aubrey plucked at his lower lip, shifted his feet on the stool. 'I just don't know. He *could* have been turned and we wouldn't necessarily have known. Keep him asleep for years, bring him out when the time is ripe. Who knows?'

'Post-Philby?'

'I should think so. Post his original resignation, anyway. After all, dear, charming, urbane Kim was their prize, their star.' He smiled, sadly. 'And when he went super-nova, it was too good an idea not to have someone else very close to the top, perhaps in line of succession.'

'Mm. But why use him at all?'

'Proof of usefulness. There are always doubters in the Centre set-up, you know that. Prove your double is capable of the sort of thing you claim or we won't authorise these ridiculously high payments he's demanding. That sort of thing. Or just the utilitarian approach that also characterises the Centre. We have a double, so he must be employed. It's part and parcel of dear Kim's reasons for failure. He had to carry on spying on his way to the top. That and the gross ineptitude of some of the people who inhabit those plush little offices in Queen Anne's Gate.'

Aubrey finished his drink and stood up.

'Are you retiring?' Latymer asked.

'I think so. My job has a certain urgency, dictated by others. Otherwise I would stay up and listen with you to the music you undoubtedly intend to play ...' He moved to the door of his bedroom, and added, 'Don't have the volume too far up the scale, will you?' I haven't brought my earplugs.'

When the small noises in bathroom and bedroom had stilled, Latymer idly inspected the collection of gramophone records in the teak cabinet against one wall. Most of them were not to his taste, but he found two records of excerpts from Bach cantatas, and sat listening, the volume low, for more than an hour. It was one-thirty when he finally went to bed – the sombre passages running in his head uncomfortably. Bach, he sensed, had taken him closer to the real, the oppressive, and he was sorry he had not drunk more or less.

Aubrey had switched the telephone through to the extension in his bedroom, and its noise awoke him, but not Latymer. Aubrey's blue eyes blinked in the sudden light of the bedside lamp like those of a child. He rubbed at his thinning, tousled hair, and looked at the travelling clock. After three.

'Yes?'

It was Rushton, one of the Beaters, on night surveillance of Lidbrooke.

'Mr. Aubrey? We've just followed Lidbrooke from his hotel to an apartment house on the Left Bank. Rue Soufflot, behind the Sorbonne, near the Pantheon?'

'Yes. Go on.' Aubrey had come fully awake, as if a strong scent, animal and pungent, had come to him.

'He took care that he wasn't followed, but we managed to use the two-car dodge to keep on his tail.'

'Yes!' Aubrey snapped. 'Whose apartment?'

'We don't know, sir. There are six of them in the building, and we haven't approached the concierge yet.'

'Good. Leave it. I'll be right down.'

Aubrey put down the receiver, dressed swiftly, and went down to the ground floor. The door opened onto a small courtyard blank with drawn curtains at the windows. He had not bothered to wake and inform Latymer.

He started the car, and rolled it quietly through the archway into the Rue de Castellane. The street was deserted, the orange glow of street-lamps making pools of shadow. He wound down the window, and the cool night air flowed into the car. Pleasantly.

He drove past the huge, oppressive bulk of the Madeleine which housed a sombre and affecting interior which always impressed him, and down the Rue Royale, past Maxim's, to the Place de la Concorde. Even at three in the morning red lights glowed as cars braked and minced across the vast expanse. He eased his way across the square, turning left into the Quai des Tuileries.

He crossed the Seine via the Boulevard du Palais, to the Left Bank. It took him only another five minutes to locate the Rue Soufflot.

There were a number of cars parked in the street, but he picked out two shadows in a parked Renault, and parked as close as he could. Rushton got out and came towards his car. Aubrey opened the passenger door, and the heavy man slid into the vacant seat.

'Which one?' Aubrey asked.

'Over there – number twenty-six.' Aubrey followed Rushton's pointing finger. A blank, light-stoned façade, many windows open, the shutters folded back against the brick. No lights. Anonymous. It appeared promising, and Aubrey nodded to himself as if to confirm the thought.

'What have you done?'

'Names from the board, checking now with the Embassy night-staff – and kept our eyes open.'

'No one else has arrived?' Rushton shook his head. 'No lights on. How long before they went off?'

'Maybe half-an-hour – no more.'

'Mm.' Aubrey retreated suddenly into a concentrated abstraction. To Rushton, he seemed a great distance away; he had worked for Aubrey on previous occasions, and settled to wait for the little man's emergence from his mood. Then Aubrey said, 'What papers have you on you?'

'Police Judiciaire, Vice Squad – SDECE, Customs – the usual range.'

'What's your French like?'

'Not bad if I play stooge.'

'Good. Then I think that sometime soon we'll be having a word with the occupant of that apartment. Which one, by the way?'

'We think it's the front one, top floor. The pattern of lights agrees with someone arriving when Lidbrooke did . . .'

He paused, and then removed the mask of professional detachment for a moment. 'Do you think it's him, sir – Mr. Lidbrooke?'

Aubrey looked at Rushton solemnly, and said, 'I don't know – I just don't know. This doesn't look good anyway, whatever his explanation.' He waved his hand at the street outside the car, the sodium lamps flaring in the soft darkness, the blank, unlit wall of the apartment building.

'I suppose it's got to be someone . . .' Rushton murmured.

'It doesn't *have* to be anyone!' Aubrey snapped. 'It happens because they choose treason.'

'Yes, sir.'

Aubrey looked at Rushton again. Like most of the Beaters employed by the SIS, often paralleling the functions of the Directorate of Security (MI 5), he was a closed personality. A complete and entire functionary, without power of decision, without the expansion of personality of those who constructed policy or who enacted field operations. It was almost strange to hear him express a human reaction.

Aubrey said, 'With SO-4, more and more of your work is going to be like this, you know.'

Rushton nodded. 'Great,' he said tiredly.

'Mm. Now, when Lidbrooke leaves, we'll go in and see the concierge. Vice Squad, I think. That always has a nice ring to it. Then we'll have a word with our mysterious occupant. Man or woman, by the way?'

'We think it's a woman – but there are probably two flats on the top floor and we don't know which is which. One's a man, the other's a woman.'

The conversation subsided. It had become to Aubrey rather like sitting next to a statue, and he wished he had woken Latymer and brought him in the car. It would have been easier on the temper to have discussed music, or even Lidbrooke. He did not know what Rushton thought of either subject – he suspected, however, that Lidbrooke was admired by the Beaters in general because most of them were field-agents of one kind or another, and Lidbrooke ran the action department, SO-1, under the urbane and in-effectual Kennedy-Shaw – Head of SO-1 only so long as Lidbrooke carried him.

Lidbrooke left at six-thirty, after it was light but while the Rue Soufflot was still deserted. The gutters flowed with the cleaning stream of water, and the air was still fresh. The sky was pale, the bellies of the few small high clouds lit with pink. It promised another fine day.

Rushton roused Aubrey from a waking doze in which he was examining Lidbrooke's career in the SIS, and finding very little that was suspicious and few occasions when the man might have been turned. He watched, his body slumped as far down in the seat as possible, as Lidbrooke walked down the street to where Rushton explained he had parked his car. As he turned the corner, Rushton signalled the black Renault and the engine fired almost immediately. Aubrey saw Horton's face briefly as the car passed them, then it turned the corner into the Rue Paillet, the brake lights flickering for a moment, then vanishing.

Aubrey nodded, and they got out of the car and crossed the street. As he glanced to the left, the Pantheon, forbidding and grandiose, loomed at the top of the Rue Soufflot. The street, and the Place du Pantheon, in daylight possessed a flinty appearance, as if there was nothing in their com-position but stone. It was the absence of trees, Aubrey supposed.

The concierge was in her booth inside the green-painted door. Aubrey, who had taken a police ID card from Rushton, knocked on the glass, and the old woman with a squat, unsmiling face looked sullenly out at him. A black cat nestled on her aproned lap, and she wore thick stockings and dirty carpet-slippers.

'What?' she asked, opening the door of the booth, having delayed to stoke the small fire she kept going even in August. A waft of heavy, stale air seemed to creep over her shoulder and assail Aubrey's nostrils.

'Police,' he said swiftly. 'Vice Squad.' His French was hurried, slurred, colloquial, and Parisian in accent. 'We want to interview one of your tenants.'

'What for?' The woman's eyes had narrowed craftily, a peasant cunning in her face.

'None of your business!' Aubrey snapped. 'Just stay out of the way – but don't disappear. I may want to ask *you* a few questions!'

The woman's attention to his unFrench clothes vanished as she felt herself threatened. 'It's none of my business!' she almost whined.

'The man who left here – who was he?'

'I don't know, M'sieur!' Now she was whining, her body adopting a suppliant posture, her hands clasping one another across the heaving bosom of her apron.

'Why didn't you ask him?' Aubrey snapped again, a look of contempt on his face, his blue eyes uncharacteristically cold and shallow. 'Are you getting a rake-off from what goes on here?'

The woman started to snivel and to protest her innocence. She said, 'I tell them the rules, I warn them about the police ...'

It was obvious to Aubrey that there was at least one prostitute in the apartment house. He hoped it was not the woman in the top-floor flat. He dismissed the concierge with a stony glance and headed up the stairs, narrow and uncarpeted, his feet and the heavy step of Rushton echoing coldly. The building seemed to possess a dampness, a musty smell, now that they were inside. He heard the noises of waking, and a toilet somewhere in the building being flushed. A man's voice flared briefly, admonishing a child. The sound of slapped skin and a tiny cry. There was the smell of coffee, and the stale smell of meals from the previous night. Aubrey wrinkled his nose.

On the top floor two dark-brown, blank doors confronted him. He knocked peremptorily at the flat which overlooked the Rue Soufflot.

A woman neither young nor pretty, but evidently French, answered the door, Aubrey held out the ID card, and said, 'Vice Squad. May we come in, Madame?' He saw the ring on her finger, which she clutched at his form of address, as if reminding herself of it.

'What do you want?' she asked, backing away slightly. She was perhaps five feet eight, an inch taller than Aubrey. Yet she appeared at a loss, and frightened, as if she did have something to hide.

Aubrey came through the door and Rushton followed, closing it behind him. The thing that struck Aubrey forcibly, even with his first glance at the room, was its transitory nature. No one lived there, which appeared promising; a drop, or a safe house. It had the smell of such a place, the dry, stale mustiness not erased by the very temporary presence of two human beings. It still clung to the walls, to the closed and grimy windows, and to the few scraps of furniture.

'Who was the man who left you ten minutes ago, Madame? Your husband?' There was a contemptuous twist of disbelief to Aubrey's mouth; he enjoyed his portrayal of a man of less sensitivity and intelligence than himself; a kind of histrionic slumming for the ego was how he always regarded such impersonations.

'Y - yes,' the woman said. 'Why?'

'We know he is not your husband, Madame - he is English, and he is in Paris for a few days only. Please do not lie to us. What is your relationship with him?'

From the evidence of her eyes, their rapid movements like dreaming with raised lids, the woman was thinking furiously. Then she said, 'You're not French - those clothes you're wearing, they're not French either!' There was something challenging about her voice that intrigued Aubrey. And she seemed to welcome having settled something about him that had previously puzzled her. She was a professional, or something very akin.

'You are an expert on the fashion sense of the Paris police,

Madame?' he asked with a smile intended as sardonic. Then he said to Rushton, 'Rostand – search the place.'

Rushton opened the door to the tiny, cramped kitchen, then to the bathroom, and the one bedroom. Aubrey had a glimpse of sheets pulled back and rumpled. It possessed no necessary significance. He returned his attention to the woman. He did not know her – it was unlikely he would – but there was a nagging sense about her that she had expected him, or someone like him, though not perhaps at that precise moment. He picked her handbag from the table and spilled its contents onto the stained tablecloth. Then he sifted through the items. Nothing – but on this occasion all she would possess would be a verbal report from Lidbrooke for Moscow Centre.

He looked at her *carte d'identité*. He thought he knew the name.

'Madame Rollin. The same name as the journalist who writes such powerful articles against the American involvement in Vietnam – eh? You are not related, Madame?'

The woman hesitated just long enough for him to understand that she was lying, then she shook her head and said, 'No, I have nothing to do with that Catherine Rollin. May I have my *carte*, please?' She held out her hand, and Aubrey reluctantly returned it. Then she said, 'Why do you come here? What do you want? I am not a whore, and you have no right invading my privacy like this!' Aubrey registered a sense of making up for lost time and lost impressions. She was over-reacting now, but it was just a fraction too late. She had been too cool at the beginning.

He said, 'You do live here, Madame?' She nodded. 'We can check, of course.'

She hesitated, and with apparent nervousness she bit her lower lip. It was a sensual mouth, and arrogant, and it did not lend itself readily to indecision or fear. Nor did the dark eyes. And there was a confidence about the slant of her body. He could not quite believe in her. He suspected that Latymer, though more susceptible than himself to this kind

of powerful, dominating woman, would have the same
reservations.

She said, 'I – have the lease. I use this place from time to
time.' She hesitated, then it blurted out, the supposed truth.
Aubrey considered it quite a reasonable performance. 'I –
you know that I am married. I cannot meet – someone – at
any place my husband might use. I use this place, to entertain
a friend . . .'

'And he is the man who just left?'

'Yes,' she said in a small voice, and then she looked up
at him, her eyes brighter with tears, but her mouth adopting
a defiant pout. She was not ashamed, it told him.

He said, leading her with a sense of amusement, 'And your
husband is unfaithful to you, and he no longer loves you.
And this other man – he loves you?' She nodded. 'He is
English. How often do you meet?'

'Whenever he is in Paris – perhaps once a month . . .'

'Here, like this? Every time?' Aubrey commented with a
sense of using a knife on the woman, whose arrogance was
beginning to irritate him. His performance was better than
hers, and that also irritated him. It was not such a good
and satisfying game, after all. He waved his hand in the
direction of the dirty tablecloth, and the poor scraps of
furniture – a pair of decaying armchairs, a bare sofa, two
upright chairs for the table.

'The rent is cheap,' she said. 'Now – what do you want
here? In *my* flat?'

He looked at Rushton, standing behind her, and the big
man shook his head.

Aubrey said, 'I may need to talk to you again, Madame.
I have your address now. Your real address that is.'

'My husband?' she said quickly.

'You will have to trust me to be discreet, Madame. *Au
'voir* until we meet again. Rostand – come!' He nodded to
her, and left the room, Rushton looming behind him. He
heard the door of the apartment close, and saw the fright-

ened face of the concierge as they reached the ground floor;
a prisoner in a glass cage. He glared at her.

'You did not tell me that Madame entertained her lover
here!' It was as if he had been embarrassed.

The old woman cowered. 'But, M'sieur –' Nothing was her
fault.

'You fool! I want no trouble from women like her – they
can always cause trouble, you understand? How long has
she had the lease, eh?'

'I – perhaps a year or more.'

'How long has that man been coming here?'

'What man?'

'Don't be more stupid than you have to be, you old cow –
tell me!'

The woman's craftiness dissolved in fear, and she said,
'Almost from the beginning, perhaps once a month, sometimes more. He does not stay during the day, and he lets
himself in with a key, late at night. I do not know who he is.
Madame is married . . .' The latter was a bonus, offered by
way of conciliation.

Aubrey sneered. 'You are the *Madame*! If I can get you
on a vice charge, I will! I'll be back with more questions –
understand?'

She nodded her head, and he turned on his heel and went
out into the fresher air of the Rue Soufflot. There was a
smell of coffee and breakfast and rubbish out there, too,
but not so insistent.

As they crossed the street, he said to Rushton, 'We'll take
both cars, since she may have seen both. You wait round
the corner, and I'll send a relief as soon as I can. But nothing
on this street at the moment. She's Catherine Rollin all
right – and Lidbrooke is mixed up with her. What the hell
he thinks he's doing – if he's doing anything other than
being a traitor – I can't imagine. A bloody, bloody shame!'
He did not look into Rushton's face but walked straight to
his own car.

Aubrey was slumped on the sofa when Latymer returned to the apartment from Rouen. The name of François Perrier had been supplied to him by Vivienne Grodin, just as she had been instructed to do if enquiries were made by any Englishman concerning Gardiner. Aubrey's face was grey with fatigue, and the blue eyes were dimmed with concentration. He looked ill, or drunk; certainly troubled in thought.

Latymer poured himself a drink and was about to recount his day when Aubrey said, 'Sit down, Hilary – I've got to talk to you, or I shall burst!'

Latymer poured two sherries, handed one like a solicitous doctor to Aubrey, stared for a moment at the numbed, sacklike posture of the man, then said, 'What's up? You look as if the whole thing has blown up in your face.'

'It's Lidbrooke – has to be.' He pulled a mournful face.

Latymer understood the expression. It was not that Aubrey held any special brief for Lidbrooke as an individual. The man had a certain flair, but he was far from irreplaceable. It was merely the confirmation of the fact that there was a 'mole'.

'Why him?'

'He's mixed up with Catherine Rollin ...'

'The journalist? Fearless fighter for the oppressed and the Left – always supposing there's no difference? God, that's a little obvious, isn't it, using her as his contact?'

Aubrey's face darkened, and he snapped: 'What the hell do you mean, it's *obvious*? It's bloody devious, Hilary! Bloody devious.'

'I suppose so.'

'You suppose so? The only thing that's odd is the fact that we haven't seen him in her company before!'

'She was downgraded to category D as a suspected foreign courier months ago! Deputy-C himself agreed to it. So we weren't watching her. She's not serious, Aubrey – *wasn't* serious. How long has this – association been going on?'

'A year. Damn it, more than a year! And if he's innocent

of treason, what could he be doing having a sordid little affair with *this* woman? Good God, aren't there sufficient women in Paris for him – women in whom we have had no interest whatsoever?'

Latymer ignored the testiness of Aubrey's reactions, the formality of his description of Lidbrooke's supposed crime. He considered the information, and could only discern a strangeness that it should be Lidbrooke. He said, '*Is* he entangled with her in any other way?'

'I saw bedclothes pulled back, but that could mean something or nothing. He visits this poky, sordid little flat every time he's in Paris. And no doubt makes the drop, or simply relates events, every time. Whether he does it while hunched over the lady's nakedness or while they merely sit in arm chairs toasting the Politburo with Russian vodka really would not appear to matter a great deal!'

'How did he meet her – is there any cover at all?'

'I don't know. I haven't asked him. I'm waiting on investigations into her movements, as from now. She guessed we weren't Vice Squad ...' Latymer laughed at the improbability, but Aubrey merely glowered and added, 'So she may tell him, she may not. In any case, she may well run for cover. She's being watched, and it may be a long business.' He looked up at Latymer. 'One of these self-possessed, cold madams, the kind that always make me feel uncomfortable.' He stared into his memory, scrutinising her image, and added 'She wasn't a very good actress, Hilary. I think that annoyed me as much as anything.'

'You're still watching Lidbrooke?'

'Naturally.'

'What moves has she made so far?'

'Gone back to her flat in the Rue George V – a very nice little place, according to Evans who's parked along the street. And since then she's stayed in. We can't know what calls she's made, but if she comes out, then we follow her. Her husband is a businessman – advertising, I think. I believe London cleared him of any involvement with

Madame Rollin's suspected activities. So we shall be hanging on here until there's confirmation of some kind. That should please you?'

Latymer nodded.

'I am rather pleased. I know the intended victim's name ...'

Aubrey, with surprising venom, said, 'God, I wish I was playing around with yesterday like you, Hilary! The present has the smell of decay about it!'

Latymer, relying heavily on wartime acquaintance as well as more recent favours, was able to persuade Jean-Jacques Haussman to assist him. He was able to convince him that Gardiner would kill, and kill again, unless he was stopped. Haussman, checking discreetly with La Baule, assured himself that the likelihood of self-defence existed in the death of Dupuy. Therefore, he assigned some of the men under his control to trace François Perrier. They found his former shop, then the wholesale business, before Perrier left his office for home.

He was dragooned by their presence, and his own fear, into assisting them. A guard was placed inside the house, and surveillance teams set up around his home in the suburb of St. Germain-en-Laye, in a street of pretentious new houses that had come within his pocket only a couple of years earlier. His wife, who seemed to belong to a past era of his life, and to have been left behind like a quiet fossil, was shallowly frightened by the presence of the SDECE men. Then the wait began.

When the telephone rang, Aubrey was sitting alone in the apartment, reading, by the light of a single standard lamp, papers that Hawthorne had brought from the Embassy. The papers contained little beyond a rather haphazard account of surveillance on the Rollin woman over the past two and a half years.

Catherine Rollin had, at the beginning of that time, made

an extensive tour of Eastern Bloc countries. She had therefore been the subject of a routine alert and handled by the
SFC (Suspect Foreign Citizens) section of the Beaters. She
had written a syndicated series of articles on her experiences,
and then had travelled in Cuba and Latin America, and
still later in north and south Vietnam. There was no proof
of any enlistment by Moscow Centre or any East European
intelligence service. She had been marked as a 'Potential',
awaiting further proof.

As the telephone shrilled in his thoughts, Aubrey looked
at his watch. Eleven.

'Yes?' There was no sense of tiredness in his voice, only
a consuming impatience.

It was Rushton again, back on duty and leading the night-
shift team watching Catherine Rollin.

'She's running, Mr. Aubrey.' His voice was without
inflection.

'Where?' Aubrey's voice was small in the room which
seemed suddenly to have expanded, fuller with dusky
shadows thrown by the standard lamp.

'Right into the Czech Embassy, sir. She was admitted five
minutes ago.'

Aubrey sat with the receiver held limply against his cheek,
tugging the flesh out of shape. His eyes were dull, his lips
set. Lidbrooke was a dead man.

CHAPTER SEVEN

CONCORDE

RICHARD GARDINER had been watching the house for most of the day. It had not been difficult to find, which pleased him since he could begin almost at once to study the behaviour of its occupants. He had very deliberately conceived the death of François Perrier as a species of hunt. He had not considered the method of execution; he knew only that he wanted the man to be afraid. He did not want him to suffer the quick kind of death of Dupuy, whose culpability had receded in death. For Perrier, who had driven the van, there had to be terror.

It was not obvious that there was at least one other man watching the house until the minutes just before darkness, when the long day and the anticipation of relief betrayed another man. More than one, he confirmed half an hour after sunset; and perhaps more inside the house.

Perrier had come home alone a little after six, driving the big black Citroen straight into the garage. Gardiner had been intrigued by the bald, stocky man in the expensive suit as by a stranger – then Perrier had fumbled for his keys in his trouser pocket, and the slump of the shoulders leapt nineteen years. It was 'Nestor'. He watched him enter the house.

A girl came out of the house a little after seven, collected at the pavement by a youth on a motor-scooter, his hair long and fair. The girl, in a red mini-skirt, sat side-saddle on the scooter, which imitated a much larger machine until its noise died round a corner. Other than that, there was no sign of life about the house set back behind a sloping sheet of lawn and a dwarf hedge, except for the routine gleam of lights in various rooms.

Except for one room – on the ground floor, perhaps a study, overlooking the wide, tree-lined street; a room into which people went, but never switched on the light. He could see the pale flicker of light as from a door opening, and an occasional shadow moving in the room.

It had to be a watcher, or a guard.

There was a thrill of excitement, almost corrupt, at each confirmation – two watchers in the street, and at least one man in the house. In some way, Perrier was forewarned. It did not matter.

He took the field-glasses from his eyes. There was no light left, no need for more confirmation. The eye-pieces were rimed with sweat and his eyes ached with the pressure of them. He rubbed his neck where it ached.

It had been fortunate that the neighbours who lived directly opposite the Perriers had taken their summer vacation rather late in August. Apparently, M. Armand Selincourt was a barrister.

Gardiner was seated in an armchair dragged to the window of the first floor room which he took to be their son's bedroom. The boy had to be in his teens; there were large posters of the Beatles, and rugby players cut from the pages of *Miroir du Rugby*, most of them French, one or two in scarlet. There was a daughter. French pop stars and Paul Newman had looked down at him from the walls of her room. The Selincourt family, according to the diary he had found in a locked desk, would not be returning from their touring holiday of Austria and Switzerland for another week. It was ideal for Gardiner. He had eaten from the fridge, consumed orange juice, and stolen a bottle of milk from another doorstep to make himself coffee.

He was grateful, having discovered the other watchers, for the audacity that had made him choose the house rather than a parked car as his base.

He freshened his mouth with orange-juice from the fridge, then stood in the darkened kitchen, swigging at the wide-necked bottle. Then he went back upstairs. Though he had smoked during the day, he did not light a cigarette in the now dark room. Instead, he settled his cramped limbs back into the chair, and leaned back into it, eyes remote.

He could not now afford to warn Perrier; he felt the irritation intensely. Someone had spoiled the corrupt, pleasurable game of terror he had intended playing. Yet he had to take Perrier away from the house, and from his new protectors – without arousing their suspicions. He had to talk to Perrier, to know who had given the order for his death; the man who had assumed the mythic proportions now invested in him during the last days, the days of silence and hiding, and preparation. He had been as a man on a retreat, but it was a darkening rather than a cleansing of himself. Judas. The man who had betrayed him twice. Perrier knew the name.

He existed now in an intellectual and emotional limbo. He related to no one; his horizons had shrunk until there was nothing outside himself against which to measure what he had become. The skeletal landscape contained only himself, and Perrier, and, like a distant mountain or safe place, the unknown man who had given the orders.

It was a self-induced vision, a shallow imitation of life. He clung to it as reality, seduced by its obscene glamour – the charm of the power of life and death. He felt that he was fulfilling something from his past; his real self.

The talking and the killing must have but the one location – he would take Perrier at his work. Minutes only – that would be all he would need. Unpoetic, it would have to be violent in the extreme to satisfy the state of feeling that had been generated towards Perrier in the past few days.

It was almost midnight when the police car stopped outside the Perrier house. Gardiner put the glasses to his eyes without excitement. He watched the downstairs light come on, and saw the rumpled, pyjama-ed figure of Perrier open the door. He swung the door wide after an indecisive moment, and the two detectives went inside. A light flickered on in the lounge, and shapes moved behind the curtains.

Gardiner got up from the chair. His car was two streets away, parked in the drive of another empty house and hidden from the road by a tall hedge. If Perrier were taken away by the police, into protective custody – his throat was suddenly hot and full with rage, so that he wanted to scream to clear it.

He did not stop to remove the evidence of his occupation of the Selincourt house, but let himself into the rear garden by the kitchen door. There, he paused by the double garage, then walked nonchalantly down the path to the street. He knew where the surveillance car was parked, and turned in the opposite direction, his gait suggestive of a late-evening stroller, slightly intoxicated.

The hire-car was still where he had left it. He got in, started the engine, then turned out of the concealed drive. He drove slowly and quietly across the intersection of the Avenue Charles de Gaulle, on which stood the Perrier house. He saw the police car still parked outside.

He got out of the car and walked back to the corner. Then he waited. Ten minutes later Perrier, accompanied by the two detectives, came down the path and got into the car. Gardiner waited beyond the pool of light from a street lamp until the car turned the corner of the avenue and headed east. The surveillance car remained stationary.

He ran back to his car, and turned it full circle in the road. The tail-lights of the police Citroën were specks in the distance, then they turned a corner and were gone. He moved smoothly past the intersection, and then accelerated.

The Citroën remained, apparently, unaware of its tail throughout the journey to the centre of Paris. Gardiner, content to remain well behind it, as if already sensing its destination, considered dispassionately the reasons why Perrier was being taken into custody. The surveillance team did not belong to the police; that mystified him. Their identity confused things . . .

He clenched his mind against the vague doubts, pushing

like tired fingers against his determination. It would do no good to consider them. He had to keep his attention and concern rigidly focused on Perrier. A growing sense of being cheated possessed him; he was being robbed of the revenge and the information he wanted from Perrier.

The police car turned into the courtyard of the Préfecture de Police in the Quai des Orfevres at twelve-forty. Gardiner parked his car almost challengingly in the Place du Parvis Notre Dame, near the Hospital and the Préfecture, and settled to wait.

'For God's sake, Hilary! Don't adopt that hangdog look of spaniel sympathy with me!'

Aubrey was angry, with himself primarily but also with London, and even, obscurely, with Lidbrooke. Perhaps most powerfully with him.

Catherine Rollin had been incarcerated in the Czech Embassy all that day. Evidently, she was not an unwelcome guest. Aubrey instructed the Beaters to stay on watch and to miss no movement on her part – though he did not know why he had iterated and reiterated that order. She had given them all the necessary proof. It was speculation of the most unproductive kind to hope that Rollin would walk back out and explain everything away.

Aubrey wondered why she had fled – that was the word that came to mind. Had it been simple fright at his appearance in the Rue Soufflot? Did she understand, however dimly, that shades of night were falling about her protested lover? The game, as far as she saw it, was evidently up. Yet – and this was the strangest aspect of the affair for Aubrey – her supposed paramour, and an agent of irreplaceable status, had not been warned. Lidbrooke had attended that day's session of a senior sub-committee, and was now in his hotel room. The courier had sniffed a nasty smell, but the agent had not been warned.

Latymer grinned at Aubrey's sudden outburst, and angered the little man even more.

'Don't lose the poor remainder of your hair, Aubrey,' he observed good-naturedly. He had himself just received Haussman's call to tell him that Perrier was in the Préfecture, and that Gardiner had followed him there. Though nervous, even afraid, of his forthcoming encounter with Gardiner, he was pleased with the efficacy of his scheme to flush Gardiner.

'Thank you!' Aubrey snapped. He walked once more the line he had trodden across the fitted carpet, from bedroom to kitchen door, for the best part of the evening. 'I did wonderfully well on this operation without your assistance, and I certainly don't require your gratuitous advice at this stage!'

'Calm down, Aubrey!'

The little man turned on Latymer, waving a sheet of yellow flimsy in his direction. 'You know what this is, don't you – yellow sheet. Message from Deputy-C. We're going to dispatch poor bloody Lidbrooke tomorrow! The executioner's arriving on the morning flight from Heathrow. Can we please meet him! God, do they want us to carry his gun, or something?'

'Why is it annoying you so much?'

'Because it's so bloody precipitate, that's why! An unseemly rush into the house of death, and no mistake. It's very, very distasteful, this whole idea of not arresting him, not even talking to him, draining him, even turning him again ...' Aubrey paused opposite Latymer. He looked down at the younger man's face, at the clear eyes, the smooth skin. Latymer, he saw, had forgotten Victoria in the imbroglio of the Gardiner affair. One good thing, at the least.

'No,' he continued. 'I am not at all happy at this new policy, which seems to be of Constant's devising. I can't forgive "C" for agreeing to it. If Lidbrooke is our "mole", then we know nothing about him, nothing at all. And we're not going to find out!'

He flopped down on the sofa, into the impression he had

earlier left, before he had begun his prowling. His face was irritable; one of those faces, Latymer observed, whose most violent expression is a petulant crossness. It was hard to take his anger seriously; everything else about the man, but not that. Yet he was deeply angry.

'But they've had enough, Aubrey – Blake and Philby, and before them Burgess and MacLean. And every spy the DS catches gets exchanged for a businessman being used by SO-1. It's Voltairean espionage – *'pour encourager les autres'*, as it were.'

'It's all very well you taking that detached, urbane view, Hilary – but Lidbrooke is going to be executed on my say-so – and I don't know whether I'm right!'

'What about Rollin?'

'Why not ask Lidbrooke? But oh no – we've to meet dear, sweet Mr. Napier at the airport tomorrow morning. That nasty little psychopath they kicked out of the SAS! God! It's more than flesh and blood can stand – death at the hands of Napier! I preferred the old method – give a chap a service revolver, and tell him to blow his own brains out!'

'Mm. Perhaps – I hold no brief for Napier and his kind myself. And they are a little more prominent at our place of work than formerly. It must be a sign of the times.' He rubbed his chin. 'Haussman may want something in exchange for all this help he's been giving me. What can I tell him about Lidbrooke?'

'What? You're cleaning up a mess on his doorstep, aren't you?' Aubrey was evidently sulking. 'Oh,' he added 'tell him we have a suspect, and are awaiting confirmation.' He raised his hands in the air, then slapped them down at his sides; two puffs of dust rose from the sofa, curling in the light of the lamp. 'The bloody impossible French! Them and their defector they bought who came bearing news of a top-level source inside NATO working for Moscow Centre. Damn them! Until it was confirmed by "Franklin", I was prepared to discount the whole thing. The usual Gallic delight in troublemaking!'

'I'll be on my way, then.'

'What? Oh, yes.'

Aubrey sat alone for a long time after Latymer had left.
He seemed not to notice the passage of time, or the discomfort of not moving his position. A frown of thought
creased his bland features, and his expression did not alter
except to deepen in concentration. From time to time he
would shake his head slowly, as if discarding an idea.

It was almost three-thirty when the telephone rang again.

'Rushton, Mr. Aubrey. She's on the move.'

'What?'

'Rollin has just left the Embassy, in an official car. Three
men accompanying, and a tail-car. Wilde is after them with
Evans. He's got radio. What do you want us to do?'

'Collect me here. What cover have you got?'

'The same range as before, sir.'

'SDECE?'

'Yes.'

'Good. You'll need those. The others have the same?'

'Yes.'

'Then get moving. Pick me up – but don't lose that Czech
car.'

It was Orly of course. Aeroflot to Warsaw, leaving at
seven. Aubrey got hurriedly out of the car, brisk, plump in
the morning wind that had sprung up, and which plucked
at his coat and flurried dust from the concrete outside the
main terminal building. The sky was already light, greyish
and dull but with the promise of another hot, cloudless day.

Evans was waiting for them in front of the glass doors into
the terminal.

'They're in the Diplomatic Lounge, Mr. Aubrey. All nice
and cosy with the early edition of the papers and fresh
coffee.' Evans, a short, stocky individual running to fat,
smiled encouragingly, as if to indicate his readiness for
anything, especially something with the glamour of risk and
a slender chance of success; he seemed to look upon this

excursion, Aubrey thought, as a possible reward for two
days of surveillance.

'Where's Wilde?'

'Keeping an eye on the door of the lounge from a convenient seat. He's hiding behind the *Paris-Soir* ...' Evans's
cheerfulness was infectious, and Aubrey permitted himself
a small smile. Swiftly, he told Evans what he had told
Horton and Rushton in the car. The small man nodded
sagely and tried not to smile as the scheme was unfolded to
him.

When Aubrey had finished, he said, 'You're the only
one whose Frog is good enough for this, sir. We'll have to
stand around and mutter throaty noises like they do in the
films.'

'Very well. But, for Heaven's sake, don't keep smiling
while I'm trying to extract Madame Rollin from the
Czechs!'

'Sir,' Evans snapped, keeping his features under control.

'Good. Now, Horton, you go and join Wilde, and we'll
be along in a couple of minutes. I'll barge straight in and
take it from there.' Horton nodded, and wandered into the
terminal. A gust of warmed air sighed from the glass doors
as they closed behind him.

'Now, you two. Just play the heavies, will you? You know
what these Czech boys will expect to see ... smoke French
cigarettes, there's a cover-story in every one!' He looked at
his watch, avoiding Evans's grin. 'No one leaves that room
to get to a telephone before I've finished – understand?'
They nodded. 'I'll bluff us past the policeman on the door.
Right. Let us begin.'

The Diplomatic Lounge was on the first floor of the
building, a spacious room set aside for the comfort and
convenience of diplomatic passengers passing through Orly.
It was a small neighbour to the VIP lounge used for more
public arrivals and departures.

The lounge was walled with glass, slightly tinted. There
was a wooden door, and a French policeman standing guard

with a sten-gun. Aubrey passed the black PVC bench on which Wilde and Horton were seated, and nodded to them. Then the policeman began to witness a small pantomime for his benefit; Evans was stationed on the bench, and Rushton and Horton instructed to accompany Aubrey. They saluted ostentatiously. Wilde was ignored completely, as Aubrey's undeclared cover. Both Horton and Rushton lit cigarettes, and Aubrey bustled up to the policeman, a small, round little man with a fierce downturn of the mouth and narrowed brows.

He flashed his ID card at the policeman, and was immediately confiding as far as the occupants of the lounge were concerned, requesting details of their arrival and making pointed references to the woman. The policeman was impressed. Obviously the SDECE man in front of him carried a lot of weight. He held open the door, then adopted a fierce pose before it, the safety-catch on the gun thrown to 'Off'. Evans nodded to him, the nod of a superior being to an ordinary policeman.

The crew of the tail-car had returned to the Embassy. There were just two men with Catherine Rollin, Czech or Russian it did not matter – both of them were operatives of Moscow Centre. They stood up when Aubrey entered the room, and he saw the surprise on the woman's face as she recognised him. He bowed to her, then to the two men. In his hand, he held out for inspection the ID card in its plastic wallet, putting it away as one of the two men tried to take hold of it.

'May I have your names? Madame Rollin I already know.' He smiled briefly. She was confused, and perhaps afraid.

One of the two said, in atrocious French, 'We are members of the Embassy staff of the Czechoslovakian Socialist Republic.' It was a threat. 'What do you want?'

'You have a French citizen in your company – I wish to speak to her.'

'This room has diplomatic immunity from French authorities,' the taller of the two men grunted. He was stolid, unimaginative, hedged round with the protection his police office gave him in his own society.

'Immunity for you, perhaps. However, Madame Rollin has no diplomatic status – as you must realise. She is a French citizen on French soil.' He was silent for a moment while he let the significance of his words sink in. 'If you will excuse us, I wish to talk to Madame Rollin.' He bowed again.

The two Czechs looked at one another, clearly at a loss. They were evidently impressed by the scant regard to their official status, perhaps more than by the ID card. One of them said, 'I must telephone, please.'

'Why?' Aubrey asked. 'I do not know why Madame Rollin wishes to leave France in your company – that is her business. But you have no need to telephone in this matter. I wish to question her on a French matter.' He looked at Catherine Rollin closely, for the first time. She was perturbed by the turn of events; but he considered her convinced by the act. She had solved his former mysteriousness.

'I must protest!' the taller Czech said, his shoulders moving in a threatening manner.

Behind Aubrey and on cue, Rushton took a step forward. Aubrey waved him back. 'You may, of course, protest later. Now, Madame Rollin – would you accompany me, please?'

'Where?' She looked like a woken sleeper. The eyes were sharp, but shallow with forced attention.

'Hopefully, just a little way out of this room.' He indicated with a gesture that the two Czechs had no business to be present. 'Do not worry, Madame – we will not be leaving Orly at the moment.' It was evident that she did not believe him. He saw the two men look at her, and realised that her authority was greater than theirs; an acceptance like deference in their faces.

Outside the door, he took her to the bench and gestured to her to sit. Wilde looked up and moved away, while Evans remained. Catherine Rollin looked around her, as if for a means of escape, then settled back, the black plastic of the bench squeaking like leather. She lit a cigarette. When she exhaled, she had recaptured her usual pugnacious self-control.

'Well, M'sieur. What can I do for you?'

'Why are you going to Warsaw – and in that company?'

'Is that any of your business – SDECE?' She asked the question with a sneer. 'The pigs?'

He smiled, humourlessly. 'We know your opinion of Western security services, Madame. Your uncovering of CIA plots in Vietnam does you great credit.' He removed the false smile. 'However, what I have to say concerns France, and it also concerns my colleagues in British Intelligence ...' He paused, then snapped, 'What is your relationship with Derek Lidbrooke?'

Her hand covered her mouth, and she appeared shocked. 'How did you find out?'

Aubrey shrugged in what he considered a Gallic manner.

'Madame – we have known about you and him for a long time. What you do in that sordid little flat does not concern us – except that you are a suspected person and you are now with two men who are evidently policemen!'

She ran a hand through her hair, pulling it back from her forehead. Aubrey sensed the sexual appeal the woman might have to someone like Lidbrooke, and winced inwardly at the obviousness of the manner in which Lidbrooke might have been trapped – no, he thought. The erotic element of their relationship would have to be subordinate, and successive. He glanced at the two Czechs through the glass. Their mood was now anxious. Soon they would demand to contact their Embassy, and Aubrey could not afford to provoke an incident.

Then Catherine Rollin said, 'This is nonsense! What do you accuse me of – spying? I am a journalist with Left-wing views. Are you pigs interrogating me for that?'

'Madame! I could arrest you now – at this moment!'

'Why don't you?' There seemed a secret source of amusement in the question; certainly a challenge.

'I wish to avoid a scandal. I am pursuing the matter in

my own way, and you are perhaps an unimportant part. But your relationship with the man Lidbrooke places him under suspicion. I want that suspicion confirmed or removed. Well?'

She was silent for a moment, then she shrugged. 'We are lovers – *were*. There is nothing more to tell. I shall not be seeing him again. I did not know he was a *pig*, like you. Now that I know, I shall not see him again. Anyway, the day you called, we had quarrelled.'

It was too easy, too simply stated. *A pig like you.* Aubrey assumed that any innocent affair between them would not have led to any revelation of Lidbrooke's status as a member of the SIS. He would have been a minor diplomat, if he had revealed that much. Yet the emphasis had been clear, the indiscretion of anger. He watched her face.

'And is that all? How did you know that Lidbrooke was a member of a foreign security service? Did he tell you?'

She appeared shocked. Right hand over her mouth again, as if to summon back the words. 'No – I didn't know. You made me angry, that's why I said that. Is he such a man?'

Sense of betrayal, perhaps? Aubrey could not be certain.

'How long will you be away from France, Madame? You do intend to return?'

She smiled. 'Those men are not policemen. I am being escorted by two cultural officials from Czechoslovakia. I shall be in Warsaw for three days, then Prague for perhaps a week. Why? Am I not to be allowed to go?'

'Madame, I have no reason to detain you. I am not prepared to do so on behalf of another country's security service. You may go.'

He stood up and bowed stiffly. She smirked contemptuously and turned away. Horton and Rushton came through the door, and Evans and Wilde joined him. They watched him in anticipation. Aubrey stared into each face, and then through the glass at the relieved Czechs and the woman now at her ease.

'Damn that woman! She's just killed Lidbrooke. Handed him over to that little psychopath Napier – damn it to hell!'

Latymer put his hand on the door-handle of the car, and said, 'Hello, Richard – I've come for a little chat.'

He found himself looking into the neat round hole of the barrel of a Browning 9mm. Gardiner had found himself a gun.

It was seven-thirty. Latymer had left Gardiner alone in the car parked under the trees near the hospital until the man was tired, perhaps off his guard, perhaps at his most isolated and vulnerable.

They had kept Perrier in a small, first-floor room of the Préfecture de Police, with a single narrow window looking out over the river to the Left Bank and the Quai St. Michel. The remaining hours of the night had been spent in questioning him. Latymer undertook the task himself while Haussman, only peripherally interested in the matter, it seemed, thrust his head occasionally round the door.

During the hours of their enforced companionship, it was as if the Frenchman had visibly diminished. A result, it almost appeared, of the sweat that seeped through the blue shirt, staining the armpits in two widening circles that threatened to meet across his chest. The man smelt, too; a sharp, rank, fox-like smell of fear and captivity.

He had told Latymer nothing – except to confirm, after being bullied, that he and Dupuy had driven the car which had knocked down Gardiner in Rouen. He would give no motive for the act, and would not name the man who had given the order. His balding head shone in the light, less greasily than his forehead, thickly bright with sweat. He kept wiping at it with a handkerchief that became a wrinkled grey ball in his fist. He was afraid, righteously indignant, and fawning in turn – but silent a great deal of the time and never to the purpose in his words.

Eventually, Latymer left a policeman guarding Perrier, and

told Haussman what he intended. The Frenchman was gruffly solicitous.

'Watch yourself. You have no idea of the mood your friend might be in. He may not be the civilized Englishman you remember.' There was a curious, ironical light in his eyes. 'What about Perrier?'

'What do you suggest? Keep him out of Gardiner's way?'

'Hopefully. But I can't hold him here if he wishes to leave. Soon he will have to see his lawyer, if he asks.'

Latymer went out, and the sky seemed cold. He moved to turn up the collar of his coat, and then dismissed the gesture. A detective pointed out the location of the car from the archway of the Préfecture, and he moved towards it.

His hand was still on the door-handle. His smile was frozen on his face. There was a long silence, and then Gardiner said, 'What in hell are you doing here?' He grimaced, as if he perceived some weakness in himself, perhaps observed the true inadequacy of what he had said.

'As I said, Richard – I've come to talk.' As if awakening from a trance, Gardiner swung his body in the seat and craned his head to see in a full circle round the car. 'It's all right,' Latymer added solicitously. 'The police know where you are. I'm alone, and unarmed.'

He held open his coat to demonstrate the fact, and Gardiner nodded and unlocked the passenger door. Latymer walked round the car and climbed in, his tall frame suddenly bunched in the narrow seat.

'You never were a gunman anyway,' Gardiner observed with a brief smile. 'You had too much grey matter for that.'

'Many thanks.'

'What do you want, Hilary?'

'A talk.'

'What about?'

'Cabbages and kings, and bodies in La Baule, and *self-defence*.' Latymer replied, lightly and carefully. The gun was still pointed at him, close to him now so there was no conceivable chance of his not being hit if it were fired. It was inches from his ribcage.

'What about all that?' Gardiner seemed to resent the words, as if they detracted from him. 'I suppose he's still in there, is he?'

'Who – Perrier?'

Gardiner nodded, staring straight ahead of him. The traffic was beginning to build up, and he appeared worried by it.

'Are you keeping me here while he makes an exit via the back door?'

'No. He's in protective custody at the moment.'

'What has he told you?' There was a barely hidden hunger in the voice.

'Nothing of any interest or value. I think he knows – but he's not telling.'

There was contempt in Gardiner's comment as he said: 'What did you do to him, Hilary? Ask searching questions – *shout* at him? You don't know the first thing!'

'Was it bad in the Avenue Foch?' Latymer asked insinuatingly. The gun dug him viciously in the ribs, and he winced.

'To hell with you, Hilary! Forget that!'

'Why? You evidently haven't. Look, Richard – I understand, but it's no good going on with this crazy scheme. I think I can persuade the authorities to allow a plea of self-defence in Dupuy's case ...'

Gardiner turned to stare at him. Latymer saw, with misgiving, that a younger man stared out at him. Gardiner *was* younger; Latymer had a presentiment that he had lost him, that his words already had a hollow ring. They were the arguments of a civilised man speaking to something alien.

'You don't understand! You don't understand any of it!' Gardiner cried. 'That's why you can't make me change my mind.' The gun jabbed again painfully in Latymer's ribs. 'That's why I'll kill you if you try to stop me, Hilary.'

Latymer saw him as a man trying to sever bonds and

codes he no longer believed or recognised. *To kill Latymer . . .*
The break would be sudden, and complete. Latymer was
afraid.

'I – I do. I know what you went through. It happened to
a lot of other people too. And you did nothing about it, for
so long . . .' The unvoiced camaraderie of suffering groped
for Gardiner, trying to diminish him in his own eyes; like
the nineteen fat, useless years of being smaller, *less* than he
was now.

'No. Not like me, Hilary. I want Perrier, but more, I want
the man who gave the order. I'll go to the end of the world
for him.' He smiled as if in mockery of his sudden rhetoric.
'I don't want anything else. You see, it is as if it was only
yesterday, and I've been asleep since. It's because I tried to
forget . . .' His eyes closed for a moment. 'But they made me
remember it. Dupuy tried to kill me as soon as he recognised
me. *I* tried to forget – but no one else had done, not for a
bloody minute!'

'It's not like that, Richard! Dupuy was just a fool, and
gutless. You frightened him, being there. That was *guilt*.
Everyone else has forgotten . . .'

'But I've remembered.'

Latymer knew it was no good. Gardiner had caught sight
of himself in a strange mirror which reflected a younger self.
Perhaps he was the kind of man he seemed to have become.
He had never really known him, he decided.

He could not hand him over to the police. That would be
another betrayal.

And he could not take him – he was certain of that.

'What – will you do?' he asked. 'They won't let you get
close to Perrier now.'

'I'll find a way – don't worry.'

'You may get away from here – but they'll hunt you
down.'

'You don't have the first idea, Hilary.' Latymer saw,
oblivious of the gun, the power of the man, the unbelievable
power within the skeletal limits of life and death, hunt and

be hunted. He saw 'Achilles', and perhaps fully for the first time.

It was ludicrous and pathetic, the attempt he had made. Whispering across a chasm of civilisation and decency and morality – when he should have yelled.

'I'm very sorry, Richard – very sorry indeed.'

'Mm. Are you? Perhaps I am, too. But it's my malaria, the thing that hangs on from the war's jungle. I don't think I ever got rid of it. It just was waiting there for a re-infection ...'

Suddenly, Latymer said, employing a new perspective, 'But you might have lost him even here. Four archways out of the courtyard. You can only possibly see two of them. He might have left and you couldn't have known! Doesn't that make it all rather hopeless?'

'No. It wouldn't have mattered. I would have found the trail again.' There was a resignation and a certainty about him that was more chilling than any other aspect of Gardiner's changed self.

'Why – why did you stay here, then?'

'Stupid, wasn't it?' Gardiner smiled. In it there was the glamour that the young man had always possessed; and something else, something only glimpsed in Baker Street or when they dined together, and buried since the war. Menace.

'Yes.'

'Perhaps I guessed you would come, or someone like you.' His face was grave, as if thought pressed him urgently. 'No, not that. Perhaps just the satisfaction of having run the quarry to earth. Or testing the nerve – setting between the cathedral and the Préfecture. The moral absolutes and the danger of arrest.' He smiled, enjoying the sudden rhetoric of associations.

He turned his gaze ahead. There was more traffic passing the entrance to the Préfecture. Morning, and the crowd. He had begun to consider how to rid himself of Latymer when he felt the man stiffen in his seat, and then his attention was caught by movement beneath the archway. He realised that

Latymer's eye and brain had been quicker than his own. A sandy-coloured suit, the slope of the shoulders, balding head – Perrier was standing next to a bored-looking detective and a taxi was sliding from its parking rank towards them.

'God,' Latymer breathed, unable to stifle his reaction.

'Not God, just Perrier!' Gardiner snapped, and the gun came up and pressed against Latymer's jugular. 'Out!' The voice was harsh.

Latymer stared ahead, and wondered why, if Haussman had been forced to let Perrier go, he had not concealed his departure. It was criminal folly. He did not move from the seat.

'You – what do you intend?'

Perrier climbed into the taxi and it moved away from the kerb, turning into the Rue de Lutece. The gun quivered in Gardiner's hand, then pressed even more firmly against Latymer's neck.

'Get out, Hilary – or I'll blow your head away!'

Latymer opened the door. It was an instinctive reaction, something he had decided against but which he could not help. He knew that Gardiner would kill him, just as he intended to kill Perrier. He had looked in vain for a tailing police car, but there hadn't been one. Perhaps in the Rue de Lutece, coming out of another archway . . . ?

Then Gardiner hit him across the shoulder with the barrel of the gun, and heaved against his body. The pain ran through him, making him sick, then he tumbled into the gutter. As his long legs came from the car, the door slammed shut and the engine fired. He rolled away and had a crazy, inverted view of the façade of Notre Dame, grey and looming. Then he pushed himself to his feet, the effort making him grab at his damaged shoulder. He hobbled after the car as it turned into the Rue de la Cité and then the Rue de Lutece.

It passed out of his sight. He ran past the surprised guard, into the courtyard, looking for Haussman.

The taxi was six cars ahead of Gardiner as he turned out

of the Rue de Lutèce into the Boulevard du Palais, opposite
the Palais de Justice. A flash of gold on high black gates,
then the stream of traffic over the Pont du Change. It was
eight-ten, and he was in the surge of the rush-hour. The
traffic streamed over the bridge in both directions and there
was no way in which he could get closer to the taxi. He
caught only occasional glimpses of it, and of the shadowy
head of its passenger through the rear window.

He rounded the Napoleon monument in the Place du
Chatelet, and saw the taxi clearly as it swung broadside to
him into the Rue de Rivoli. He was still six vehicles behind,
and locked into the traffic flow. Perrier was an impossible
distance from him. He could not feel confidence, or relaxa-
tion.

He saw Perrier's face for a moment, looking around him
as if blinking in unfamiliar sunlight or afraid of pursuit. He
could not know that Gardiner was behind him. The thought
of his lack of suspicion, of any focus for his fear, held a
grim satisfaction for Gardiner. He thought, momentarily,
of Latymer's rigid surprise that Perrier had been released,
and considered the possibility of some kind of trap. But the
release *had* surprised Latymer – either the man had been
double-crossed by the French, or there was no trap.

He sensed a seed of disappointment, but the ego swelled
round it, and he lost sense of anything beyond the pursuit,
willing some of it from his mind, the rest dropping away
into darkness.

The brakes screeched as he stamped on them, and the car
lurched sideways as the wheels locked. The face of the
young woman with the pram – why was she out so early
with a baby, he thought – was ashen and then hateful as she
glared from windscreen to pram and back, her head beginning to wobble like a puppet. There was a pedestrian crossing, and a red light against him, and other people, some of
them glancing at him, others angry already with the woman
for blocking their path, were passing across his gaze.

He realised his hands were shaking – with reaction, he

thought, until he sensed the mounting anger at the young woman as the light changed to green and she was still blocking him, and someone hooted – he slewed the car around her, and she had the baby in her arms as if to demonstrate to him the possibilities of collision, or wave a banner of normality. But he was round her now, and into the Rue de Rivoli proper, the great morning artery from the Place de la Bastille to the Place de la Concorde, one-way, thick with traffic that congealed at each set of lights.

Perrier was safe, he realised. A microbe flowing down this sluice of the city's body. There was insufficient time for him to get out of the car, and get to the taxi at each of the sets of lights.

Traffic lights at the corner of the Louvre. Sandy stone, and the bare lawn and gravel that fronted the building. The traffic lurched forward again, and he could see the taxi ahead of him; Perrier was still aboard, unaware.

The stream flowed turgidly past the Economic Ministry, and the Place du Palais Royale; then they stopped again at the Place des Pyramides, and traffic flowed across in front of them. He became increasingly aware of the danger of the traffic lights. He was still six cars behind the taxi, and at any intersection he could be left stranded by a change of lights. He kept glancing around at the traffic on either side. Four lanes, all closely bunched, yet moving between the sets of lights as a rapid surge, a lava-like suddenness.

No reaction over the incident with the pram and the white-faced, dark-haired woman – except an instant in which contempt of her short skirt, the skimpy clothes, the untidy, unwashed hair, ridicule at her thin voice piping at him from in front of the car, fear at the sense of the thing she held up in her arms – then nothing. Mind clamped down on the bubbling, pathetic stuff.

There were lights for pedestrian crossings at the Place des Pyramides and the Rue de Castiglione which led to the Place Vendome. Between those two points, he had to improve his position relative to the taxi.

Green. He let out the clutch, twisted the wheel so that the car crossed the next lane of traffic, the howl of three separate car horns behind him. Five cars, and his lane moving with perhaps more speed. Four cars. Yes, it was. An elderly man in the line he had been following, one ahead of the taxi and moving at a sedate pace.

Past, on his left, the Jardin de Carousel and then the high railings through which he darkly glimpsed the dusty trees and flowerbeds of the Tuileries. He marked off the narrower streets to his right – Rue de St. Roche, Rue 29 Juillet, Rue d'Alger . . .

An impatient driver tried to pull out from the Rue d'Alger into the stream – an eddy of suddenly halted traffic blared at him, and settled on springs – the image of a Citroën settling back like a matron – and then his line of traffic continuing; three cars, two . . .

The taxi began to pick up speed again, and then slowed almost immediately as the lights at the Rue de Castiglione halted the traffic, glaring red. Gardiner realised he was sweating, that his hands gripped the wheel fiercely. He did not allow himself to relax. He was one car behind. Only one now.

Perrier's head, frizzed hair, balding, and the collar of the sandy suit, and the thick shoulders. It was close, pleasingly so; no fierce urge to hurt or kill, but a subtler, more corrupt sense of terror unguessed, the infinite superiority of waiting in a darkened room for an unsuspecting victim. Close, the still air, the oppressive, choking sense of omnipotence.

Perrier turned in his seat. Perhaps he wondered about a police car following him – perhaps his neck was stiff. He saw Gardiner – and then after a long moment he recognised him. The recognition invaded the face, pulling at the mouth until it fell open. 'Achilles'.

The lights changed, and the traffic surged forward. Gardiner could see, almost level with the taxi, Perrier lean forward and speak to the driver. He was terrified. The gratification was an almost sexual release. Rue Rouget de

L'Isle, and the English bookshop under the arches and the taxi was speeding up with three or four other cars ahead of it before the lights at the Place de la Concorde.

Gardiner kept the car almost level with the taxi, judging the lights ahead. Amber. Perrier was shouting at the driver. Red. The taxi was across the lights, but the driver refused to encounter the currents of the square and screeched to a halt. Gardiner was one car back, in the next lane. He moved swiftly.

He almost vaulted the bonnet of the hire car, and closed on the terrified face of Perrier as it stared from the taxi. He pulled open the door, and the atmosphere was heavy with body odour and rank fear. Perrier's mouth opened to say something, but nothing but air was expelled. It was as if his tongue had stuck to the roof of his mouth. Gardiner pulled at the lapels of the suit, dragging the man backwards, and the Frenchman's legs scuffed at the road. His body had collapsed in terror. His face, close to Gardiner's, was map-like in the detail of impressions and emotions.

'Tell me!' Gardiner ordered, his face pressed against that of Perrier in some kind of parody of love and loving. He straightened the limp form, pressing it against the solidity of the taxi as if trying to make a doll assume a human posture. Perrier shook his head, and Gardiner hit him once so that blood spilled immediately from his nose and split lip. He wanted to hit him again, all reason, all coldness gone – but more he wanted the name, the cryptogram.

'Tell me! Who gave the order? Who?'

A hand fell on his shoulder, and he drove back against the man who must be there – the taxi-driver, a pedestrian, elbow driving into something soft. Concussion of breath, but Perrier was pulling suddenly away from his grip, a feeble fist waved close to his face, then Perrier was doubling round the bulk of the taxi. Gardiner heard, distinctly, as if in prelude to the concert of horns as the lights changed, someone laugh. He was involved in some sordid comic little domestic quarrel. He ran after Perrier, taking the wrong direction because he expected Perrier to head for the Rue St. Florentin.

He was heading for the Place de la Concorde.

Perrier was going to get himself killed. Perrier ran, head down, dodging the amused pedestrians, hearing the first scream of brakes as the six lanes of traffic coming from the left around the outer circle of the Place moved in the direction of the Rue Royale, encountering Perrier.

Gardiner felt sick.

Perrier handed off a car that slid to a halt, the movement of a rugby player in grotesque. The impact made him wring his hand, and overbalance. Other cars swerved to avoid him, and Gardiner began to gain on him because the traffic was already still.

It was the experience of watching the world changed – the noise of brakes, tyres, horns, the certainty that he could smell the rubber, the swift-moving lines of jockeying cars and lorries suddenly bunched, distorted, broken.

And the man still moving across the face of the traffic, a desperate shuffling figure fleeing for its life.

A car struck him a glancing blow, then careered into a truck that had stamped on its air brakes. Another car ran into the back of it. Other figures now, climbing like dreamers or submariners from their cars, mouths opening slowly like snails to shout words that could not be heard. There was an element of farce in the thing.

Perrier staggered, his trouser-leg ripped and the flesh red beneath it. He was twenty-five yards from the lights at the top of the Rue de Rivoli, and dying like a hunted animal. It was as if the cars were dogs, and they had been afraid, yapping and nipping round their quarry. Now, they saw blood and closed in.

Perrier was blind to each succeeding line of traffic, as they were to him.

Suddenly, with Gardiner still ten yards from him, his body was flung in the air like something small and furred worried by a dog, flipped so that its neck broke. The sandy suit, the inverted, twisted face, the clumsy, ugly loop of the body over the bonnet of a black car. Then he went down, and Gardiner could not see him. But he saw another car rear up, then settle, having run over the inert body.

Gardiner felt the nausea rising in his throat. Perrier was dead. He began to run, blindly himself now, towards the Rue Royale, away from Concorde.

CHAPTER EIGHT

PROFESSIONAL EXPERTISE

NAPIER arrived on the morning flight from Heathrow. Aubrey, tired and unshaven as if in calculated insult, had not left Orly since his interview with Catherine Rollin. He had watched the Aeroflot Tupolev take off for Warsaw, climbing into what was already a dazzling clean sky. Then he had drunk coffee with Evans and Rushton in the main lounge while Horton and Wilde returned to tailing Lidbrooke, who would spend most of the morning and early part of the afternoon in sessions of a sub-committee.

Aubrey felt wretched. The imminence of Lidbrooke's death was like a heavy stone on his chest making the act of breathing painful. There was a kind of moral nausea attached to it, of course, but more insistently, the depression of a dedicated but civilised man forced once more to confront the stark, final, unambiguous realities of his strange profession. It unnerved him, as if the firm ground had unaccountably shifted or become sandy beneath his feet. He liked to think well of the work in which he engaged, and the execution of Lidbrooke was not a good thought.

Napier looked very young, his hair cropped as if he had just left the army, his skin unlined and boyish. He was wearing a grey suit with narrow lapels and manufactured in some shiny mohair material. It looked cheap, like the pointed shoes that curled at the toes. He carried a single bag as luggage, though Aubrey knew it contained very little. Napier would be back in London that evening. His eyes were grey, and sullen. There was something slightly unfinished, certainly unpolished, about Napier.

When he spoke to Aubrey, his tone was intended to be

respectful, though he was at no great pains to disguise the aristocracy of his function. He held out his hand, and the grip was soft, girlish.

'Good morning, Mr. Aubrey.'

'Morning,' Aubrey replied abruptly.

'Deputy asked me to convey his congratulations, Mr. Aubrey. He's very pleased.' There was a slightly mocking light in his eyes. It was apparent to Aubrey that Napier was totally unconcerned at the prospect of executing his own assistant head of section, and there was something hideous in the lack of concern.

'You have your orders from Deputy, I presume?' Aubrey said.

Napier nodded, and Aubrey confirmed, in his own mind, the growing influence of Constant within the SIS, an influence which far outweighed that of Lavender, the other Deputy-C. The control of SIS was slipping into the hands of a career professional, away from the kind of watchdog HM Opposition desired.

Aubrey understood the power of Constant, the decisiveness that had led from his own report directly to the arrival of Napier. Napier had not taken his orders from the Head of SO-1, who might have protested, but from the overall operations director, Constant, who was establishing a precedent, a mode of internal operation which Aubrey detested, and against which he was impotent.

They took Napier to the car, and drove back to the city. The traffic was thinner now that the rush hour was over. Aubrey's hair prickled at the back of his neck as he remained continually aware of the occupant of the back seat. He felt actual physical discomfort throughout the journey.

'What is his programme for today?' Napier asked as they crossed the motorway ring. It seemed an age since their pursuit of Rollin. *An age has passed*, Aubrey thought. Napier spoke with complete detachment.

'NATO HQ this a.m.,' Aubrey replied, the tone of his voice turning Evans's head quizzically towards him. 'Then, after lunch, he has a plenary session of the sub-committee, then home . . .' He let the words fall away, sensing the thin smile on Napier's lips.

'He'll have to leave the building, Mr. Aubrey.' It was not a request.

'And how do you intend to dispose of the body?' Aubrey's lips were compressed, his voice impotently angry.

'A hit-and-run.' Aubrey wondered again about Napier's origins. There was a Northern flatness in the voice, overlaid with the nasal whine of an urban area. Liverpool, perhaps.

'Constant's idea, I presume?'

'Yes, sir. It's the least fussy way. I'll use one of the pool cars from the Embassy, with changed plates.' Again, it was an order, Constant using Napier as a ventriloquist's dummy. 'You'll arrange for him to leave the building, Mr. Aubrey.' Aubrey thought of Constant again, hearing him in the voice. He shook his head to clear it of the hateful, clogging images.

The car rolled into the courtyard in the Rue de Castellane, and Aubrey climbed wearily out. He was tired now, and he had begun to anticipate returning to London. Evans and Rushton took away the car, and Aubrey preceded Napier to the first-floor apartment.

Latymer was unsurprised by the appearance of Napier behind Aubrey. He, too, appeared tired and he was nursing his shoulder and a large Scotch, despite the early hour. There were heavy shadows beneath his fine eyes, and his skin was pale and drawn. For a moment, Aubrey wondered whether Victoria had died and he had just received news, then he saw irritation on his lips and knew that Latymer had in some way lost Gardiner.

'What happened?' he said, indicating a chair to Napier, who nodded to Latymer and sat down. Immediately, he appeared to retreat into some comfortable, abstracted state; a piece of machinery switched off.

'I spoke to him. Then Haussman released Perrier right in front of Richard's eyes, and he went after him like a dog after a hare.' The image was light, but the voice sombre.

'Perrier tried to escape – some lunatic dash across the Place de la Concorde. He was knocked down!'

Aubrey's eyes flashed involuntarily to Napier's face. It was impassive. Then he said, 'What about Gardiner?'

'Vanished from the face of the earth.' Latymer shrugged, and Scotch slopped from the glass onto his trousers. With an almost fierce concentration, he rubbed at the wet stain. Then he looked up. 'Richard still doesn't know the name he wants . . . God, it's a bloody mess, Aubrey!'

'I agree,' Aubrey replied softly. 'What did Richard have to say?'

'Very little. He's changed, Aubrey.' Latymer looked up again, and there was a strange and desperate expression on his face. Aubrey was reminded of the occasion on which he had informed him of Victoria's illness. Latymer had perceived some terminal disease in Richard Gardiner. 'I don't understand it. Perhaps it needs a psychiatrist to unravel it. I think he will go on now until the end of the world, until he finds his betrayer and kills him. Something – *legendary*, I suppose is the only word. Something out of a myth.'

'Don't grant him that kind of status. He's just a little more mad than the rest of us. Life is simple for him as it is.' He glanced at Napier and added, 'Catherine Rollin nailed down the coffin when I spoke to her this morning!'

Latymer appeared barely interested. Instead of replying, he swallowed at his Scotch, choking on the liquor.

'Derek – may I wish you a fond farewell, my boy!' Eugene van Lederer held out his hand, gripping Lidbrooke's long, delicate fingers in his own huge hand. Grey hairs sprouted from the knuckles.

Lidbrooke looked into the eyes, and smiled. 'Thank you, General – and may I wish you the same, and good hunting, wherever the hunting is to be.'

Van Lederer smiled. He was in full uniform, and had just attended to last pieces of unimportant business before flying back to Washington. He anticipated a couple more days in

Paris, but on a strictly unofficial basis and devoted to pleasure.

His business as Chairman was over, but he was a man who appreciated those who contributed positively to the work of the Senior Committee, and meeting Lidbrooke by chance in the corridor, he had spontaneously greeted him, taken his hand.

Lidbrooke had never been anti-American in his spoken or unspoken attitudes, unlike so many of his colleagues in the SIS. He had always admired their budget for Intelligence, their thoroughness, their gadgetry and their temperament. He was a man who wore his own emotions and opinions openly, and this made him warm to a man like van Lederer. A professional, yet with his humanity close to the surface.

'Take care, Derek – always take care!' van Lederer said with a smile. 'Be seeing you.'

'Thank you, sir. And you – stay around for the pension from the Pentagon!'

Van Lederer laughed aloud, and waved his hand as he moved off down the corridor. Watching him go, Lidbrooke shook his head affectionately. Then the tannoy spoke over his head.

'Telephone call for Derek Lidbrooke.'

'Damn!' He was irritated suddenly. He wanted his lunch. He made his way to the nearest telephone, and requested the call be put through. It was Kenneth Aubrey.

'Derek – glad to have caught you before you left. Can we have a spot of lunch together? One or two things I'd like to discuss with you, away from the hubbub of the office.'

'You're in Paris, Kenneth?' And Lidbrooke was suddenly aware that Aubrey was head of the new section, SO-4, the watchdog on internal security in the service. And he felt afraid. 'What – what is it?' he asked, silently damning the throat that was suddenly clogged with phlegm. 'I – I haven't a lot of time, you know.'

'It'll take no more than half-an-hour, I promise. Can that much time be spared from your busy schedule?' The voice was sudden with asperity, and Lidbrooke felt prepared for some unpleasantness.

'Oh, very well,' he said as off-handedly as he could. 'Where shall we meet?'

'Pick me up at the Rue de Castellane apartment. Can do?'

'Yes. I'll get a taxi.'

The dialling tone purred irritatingly in Lidbrooke's ear. As he replaced the receiver, he saw that it was damp, and rubbed at his ear, which seemed hot and burning. He was suspicious now, because there was a cause for suspicion.

Aubrey, the watchdog.

What the devil did he want?

He walked out of the foyer of the NATO building, past the bright-buttoned marines on guard, white puttees and slim rifles, eyes expressionless, but less significant than the men behind armoured glass of the reception booth who had recognised him and not impeded his exit.

He was worried, and the thoughts tumbled into his head like childish fears. As if he had stolen from his mother's purse, or cheated in an exam and been discovered – lurid images of disgrace, embarrassment, failure flickered in his head.

Catherine Rollin. Of course he had known of the suspicions, had known, too, when she was cleared and downgraded. Not that it had mattered. By then, he was involved with her. It hadn't mattered. She was his mistress, and the suspicions, even the possible dangers to his career, had all seemed to add some piquant *necessity* to his relationship with her.

Now what could he say? *I am libidinous, forgive me. Mea culpa. The sins of the flesh, and she is very good in bed and I could not resist the sense of danger accompanying every bout beneath the sheets … Surely I received your permission when she was downgraded?*

Aubrey would not believe it, any of it, nor pity. His blue eyes would *glitter, and he would go for the throat.*

He walked past a fountain, feathers of spray from the

peacock tail of water light on his face, as if trying to cool what he knew must be a burning blush. He would have to explain. Aubrey, his subtle and complex mind – he could never bluff it out as a weakness of the flesh.

He looked swiftly in each direction as he crossed the boulevard towards the taxi-rank on the other side. But, distracted in thought, he did not hear the anonymous black saloon with the reinforced fenders, the damage-proof head-lights and the scratch-proof bumper as it pulled out from the kerb. It was a classic kill.

Napier's view was of the white face, the slow stain of fear spreading on it lividly, like fungus, then the arched leap of the body as it was flung onto the bonnet, then the slide of the distorted cheek down the windscreen – usually, they did not obscure the windscreen, except for a moment – the mouth plucked open absurdly by the wiper so that the lip pulled like the mouth of a fish on a hook ...

Then the body was behind the car, and Napier knew that Lidbrooke was dead. He glanced in the mirror to satisfy himself finally, and then accelerated away from the activity that was beginning to cluster round the body – a marine running as if through thick amber, a taxi-driver crossing the road through the same glutinous reality ...

Henri Janvier knew of his cousin's death. He knew that Perrier had been taken to the Judiciaire, later released, and then got himself killed in the Place de la Concorde, with the man Gardiner in pursuit. Gardiner had since disappeared.

He sat outside a café, apparently idling away time watching the passers-by in the Rue de Medicis near the Luxembourg; in fact, he was watching the entrance to Gardiner's hotel, two doors away. At that moment Gardiner was in his room.

To Janvier, who had found Gardiner's hiding-place the previous day, his cousin's death meant nothing; nothing emotional. Naturally, he had been in touch with Etienne de Vaugrigard, and the man had, with an air of reluctance now that Perrier's death seemed to make him safe, renewed the offer. Because Janvier reminded him that he, too, now possessed the information Gardiner sought.

Janvier's slow mind was marked by its avarice. He did nothing except for money, a lot of money. His prices were high, and he was especially deaf to the appeals the OAS made to his patriotism when it was bereft of funds.

He poured himself another glass of rough red wine, and swallowed a mouthful. It bit the back of his throat, and he could almost feel it coating his teeth. He drew on his cigarette. As he sat at the table, he was anonymously French, attracting no attention, a check shirt and loose, old trousers. His jacket, in which he carried the gun, was over the back of a chair, close to his hand.

He was not a stupid man, though slow. His sense of self-preservation was enormous. At thirty, at forty, even at forty-five, he had enjoyed the handwriting of his own violence, the signature of 'Plastique' on everything he successfully attempted. The notoriety pleased him, easing by its assertion of identity a loneliness that he was hardly aware of most of his conscious life. Now, over fifty, that flirtation had died, and the narrower, more insistent grabbing of an ageing man had overtaken him. Now, imitations of his handiwork irritated, even frightened, him.

He had not worked for some months. His prices were unrealistic. It was obvious that he was asking higher prices because he wanted to retire – caring a little too much about the security of his future.

Whatever de Vaugrigard said, it would stretch credibility to assume that Gardiner's death would be construed as that of an innocent victim of the OAS.

So Henri Julien Janvier had got himself a gun. An old service revolver, heavy calibre, something he had stashed behind the skirting in the damp, cheap, apartment he rented under another name in the Rue de Bievre, a narrow, twisting alley that ran down to the Seine from the Boulevard St. Germain. It was something he had intended, in brave for-

gotten days, for that final shoot-out when the police came
for him. The early days of big money and the newspapers
clamouring for his arrest, and the secrecy of the Rue de
Bievre. Now the street was designated for rebuilding, and
the apartment would be swept away, together with the smell
of damp that never left it, and the narrow courtyard full of
rubbish and dogs who relieved themselves against the door-
posts.

It would be a simple robbery with violence. A burglar who,
disturbed during his work by the occupant of the hotel room,
would have killed in blind panic.

Janvier was nervous; he could not disguise that in tobacco
and wine and memories. He was a good shot, but he was
out of practice. And Gardiner had killed Dupuy, and
Dupuy had had the gun. It was why he had drunk most of
the wine, though it was barely midday. The only solution
was to give himself the advantage of complete surprise.
When Gardiner was out, he had to occupy the room in the
Hôtel Fleur de Lys, a tourist trap of ordinary rooms and
high summer prices, and wait for him to return. He would
suitably arrange the corpse later.

His hand jumped on the table, and the dregs in his glass
stained the check cloth. Gardiner had walked out of the
hotel entrance, and past him to the Place Edmond Rostand.
Janvier did not look at him, hid his face as the man passed,
dressed in a summerweight suit of French cut, sandals, and
open-neck yellow shirt, and a cravat. He was wearing dark
glasses, and carried a camera. Tourist.

When he had gone, Janvier turned to follow him. He saw
him go into the Luxembourg, and changed his mind. He was
in some danger of being picked out as a tail, and that he
did not want. He turned back in his seat, and attended with
a fierce concentration to the wet rings of dull red wine
on the tablecloth. In a moment, he would enter the hotel,
and force his way into Gardiner's room. It would be
simple.

He found, not really to his surprise, that his hand was

sweating. The knowledge disturbed him. He wiped his hand
angrily on his trouser-leg.

The sunlight in the Luxembourg was blinding, splintering
off the huge ornamental pool in front of the palace and
whitening the strips of dusty, gravelled path. The grass caused
the eyes to ache, a painted colour, unnatural.

Gardiner had stilled the shaking of his body by an effort
of will. For perhaps an hour after he had returned to the
hotel from the Place de la Concorde, he had not been able
to still the racing images, like those of a drunken half-sleep,
as they flashed upon the mind; minor explosions in a moral
war. He squinted behind his polaroid sunglasses against the
light and against his own disappointment. He felt cast
adrift, having exchanged the tillers of morality and custom
for one of will, or desire. The death of Perrier had snapped
cables, torn off a rudder he thought was there.

He began once more to perceive the changes that the
death of Dupuy had worked in his personality – changes, or
reaffirmations, he could not be certain, and would not
enquire closely. Now, cold moral sense vied with hot anger
and frustration for possession of him.

He sat down on a bench, and watched children playing –
bright blobs of colour, focused spots of bright sound. He
tried to think of his own sons, the sombre old children now
probably returning to their boarding school. There was no
call to him from their direction – they were faces held up,
like the white bundle in the woman's hands on the pedestrian
crossing, which he did not acknowledge.

A chequered plastic ball trickled to his feet. He watched
the dark-faced child approach without nervousness, picked
up the ball in one hand and threw it to her. It was as if he
did not wish her to come any closer; the carrier of some
virulent disease.

He began to think in some sort of sequence.

There were others, perhaps, members of the old group,
still alive. Perhaps Vivienne Grodin had not told him every-

thing? He began to imagine the conspiracy against him, exorcising lingering traces of loyalty, evidences of admiration and respect. The faces flickered, and each one of them acquired a patina of guilt. His anger against them grew, out of a need to avoid the recent past, which had threatened to come back, and to reforge links with the age of monoliths - 1944. He had to go back to work, to seek out, discover.

It did not occur to him to question what was happening. He merely wanted to go on because anything else seemed more painful or empty or complex. If he had to kill them all, he would find out. There was the refreshment of a close shave or a long drink, in that blinding sunlight, to be drawn from such a simplification of reality. He was able soon to get up, to walk back to the hotel with purpose. His steps were swifter, positive.

There was a letter waiting for him at the desk. Gardiner took it from the clerk and glanced at it on his way up in the lift, a gilded cage from a film set or a more grandiose establishment.

The letter bore a Paris postmark, dated that morning. He wondered at it, staring at the anonymous type. Then he ripped open the envelope, pulling out the single sheet, his fingers nerveless with the shock that someone knew his pseudonym. The loose bars of the cage rattled as the lift jerked away from the second floor where it had stopped. There was no one waiting for it.

It was a confession, in handwriting; he did not believe it, but his blood pumped in confirmation. The flimsy sheet of cheap paper quivered in his grip.

The lift stopped. He moved jerkily out into the corridor, robotic and stiff. It was signed by Perrier - a handwriting and signature he could not certify. It was brief, and complete. It was what he would have beaten from Perrier, blown off the kneecaps and electrocuted the testicles to find out. The name of the man. Perrier had known, even before the police had come for him, known he would give in. The will had collapsed. He had written the letter to save himself.

Etienne de Vaugrigard.

He felt nauseated. It was a tangible blow to the stomach. Etienne de Vaugrigard.

He paused at the door of his room, pushed it open and found himself looking into the face of a stranger and down the barrel of an old service revolver. It was pointed at Gardiner's stomach.

After a long moment of silence in which Gardiner kept glancing from the letter to the gun, the man said, 'What does your letter contain, M'sieur? It seems to distract you even from the gun. That is very strange.'

Gardiner looked up from the letter, irritated by the intrusion of the man's voice. He had almost forgotten about him as his attention was drawn insistently back to the name at the bottom of the letter. *Etienne* ... He did not know this man's name. The gun moved a little in dramatic emphasis of the voice.

'Who are you? What do you want?'

'I am here to take care of you, M'sieur. My name does not matter.'

The big man smiled. The body was awkward, Gardiner thought, but the eyes were coldly professional. Someone else who had learned his trade by practising on the Nazis in Occupied France. And perhaps Foreign Legion, even OAS.

He was sitting with his back to the window so that the light was not in his eyes.

'Are you anything to do with Perrier?' The man's eyes did not flicker. 'What about Etienne de Vaugrigard?' The flicker then. Gardiner held out the flimsy sheet of paper. 'It's in here, you know. Your man Perrier – he wrote a full confession ...'

The man was startled. 'A gross forgery,' he suggested.

'You're sure of that?'

'I do not know of Perrier, or this other man.'

'Why deny it? It doesn't matter, since you're going to kill me anyway.'

'The latter is most certainly true, M'sieur.' The gun steadied again on his stomach.

'Then tell me.'

'Knowledge might make you desperate. I don't want a struggle.' The man shrugged, as if in sympathetic understanding.

The conversation had awoken Gardiner. Now, his brain raced to solve the simple problem of survival. Knowledge defined itself as distances, reaction times, the quality of the light, the accuracy of the French-made service revolver. It was an amusing irony, he was capable of thinking. To be killed by one of the guns made in the factories of Etienne's grandfather for the Great War. Ridiculous.

'I understand,' he said. 'I simply hope that you were well paid for this job. Better paid than the bastards who ran me over in Rouen!' He was sweating now, a forced raising of the emotional temperature. He had to look frightened, even cowed. Janvier nodded, and smiled. Gardiner saw the assumption of superiority given him by the gun now increased by the fear in the victim's eyes. That sense of comforting superiority would delay the execution, perhaps for minutes.

'A shame, M'sieur. I am sorry for you.' Expansive talk, the adoption of mannerisms from the cinema. It was the first time, or nearly so. He should have understood that from the old revolver. This man killed at a distance, or had done so for many years; explosives, probably. He was unused to this kind of confrontation, and was unable to control the mounting satisfaction that the gun gave him. Gardiner had to wait, to prolong the moments.

'For God's sake, I'll give you more than he did, whoever he is!'

'I am sorry, M'sieur, but it cannot be done. I have accepted the contract, and I cannot go back on it.' The luxurious delight was still there.

Gardiner said, 'Think about it. For God's sake, think about it!'

Again, the big man shook his head. 'I was told you would not beg, M'sieur. That you would be a difficult man to kill. You do not impress me, however.'

Gardiner was winning. He realised that this man was afraid, that he had been anxious of using the gun, of facing his victim. There had been one like him in the old group. Death at second hand, and they could stomach the slaughter, even delight in it. But they did not like blood on things, or the twitch of the body, the wild faces of death.

He said, 'For God's sake, don't you have any human feelings? I don't want to end here, blown to pieces by that cannon in your hand. I'll *pay* you!'

Gardiner saw the avarice for a moment in the narrowed eyes, the smell of temptation. And he saw the sense of the binding contract, and the satisfaction at his present helplessness. The big man could not be bought; he would have to kill him.

They were three yards apart. He had managed that much from pure instinct, the prompting of old reflexes. He was sitting on the newly-made bed, and the big man was in the chair. There was little purchase in the soft springing of the bed. He could feel them yielding under his hands now. He had one chance, and only one. One shot from the old revolver, at that range, would be accurate. It was hopeless.

'M'sieur – why not accept things as they are? You are going to die.'

'Oh, Christ ... !' Gardiner's mouth trembled. He concentrated fear and pleading into his facial muscles, and the rest of his body learned the necessary tension. He would have to close his eyes, and his ears. Noise, and the flash of the gun, close enough to stun him.

The big man in his confidence brought out a packet of cigarettes. He had reached a state of incaution towards the snivelling wretch at the other end of the gun. He could afford this last gesture. He tossed the packet, and a box of matches, into Gardiner's lap.

'Smoke, M'sieur. It might help you.' His big face twisted

into a sardonic grin. Gardiner lit the cigarette and held the packet in his hand. He offered to throw it back, then did so. Just a foot or so wide of the big man's lap, low down.

The smoke was still in Gardiner's mouth, expelled with the same kind of force that explodes a ski-jumper out into space; his hands dug into the bed, finding the limits of the springing's resistance, and then his body uncoiled. Janvier moved instinctively to catch the cigarette packet. The gun moved aside, momentarily.

Then Gardiner was on top of him, the chair forced backwards, over-turning, the big man's body stretched under Gardiner. The gun exploded, and its smoke was in Gardiner's nostrils. He opened his eyes and saw the big man's face beneath his own, then grabbed the wrist of the right hand, forcing the barrel of the gun up and away from him. The chair bucked under them as it hit the floor.

He worked in a deaf universe, grappling with the big man. The gun had done that. He felt the fat hand reaching up for his chin, to force it back, and he went for the eyes – the soft squelch of the jelly, the shudder that he felt and the scream that he could not hear. Then he leaned back, still holding the right wrist, and chopped across the white throat, exposed to him with its stubble from poor shaving. The wrist in his grip went slack, began to fall. The big gun hit the floor, and he heard the distant sound.

He stood up, shaking with relief and the excitement of the kill. He did not look into the big man's eyes, nor at the head hanging slackly to one side, a dribble of blood combining with the spittle round the full lips. He kicked the gun savagely under the bed, as if in an expression of anger.

It took him only a few minutes to clean the cupboards and the drawers of everything he required. He abandoned most of the clothing, but took the money and the *cartes d' identités* he might require. Then he straightened his clothing, washed his face in cold water, and left the room. He had the letter from Perrier folded inside his wallet.

'Gardiner has left the hotel – but Janvier hasn't come out.' The voice from the telephone was cool, matter-of-fact.

'L'Etranger', who had sent the letter purporting to be from Perrier, was angry, yet relieved. 'Use your official identity, and go in and find out what has happened. If 'Plastique' is dead, then do what you have to. But give Gardiner time to act against de Vaugrigard.'

'Very well. You think he's dead, then?'

'Of course. He was a fool, trying to take Gardiner with a gun. He should have stuck to his speciality.' The tone was gruff, business-like. There was no place for pity; only a certain satisfaction that he had chosen well, that Gardiner was living up to a forgotten reputation. 'Get on with it.'

'Shall I report back to you straight away?'

'Naturally. I'll wait for your call. There is someone on Gardiner, I presume?'

'Fouquier and Matisse. They won't lose him.'

'Good. It will take Gardiner approximately ten minutes to discover where de Vaugrigard lives. I want to make sure he talks to him first, not kills him straight away. That's why the confession from Perrier had to contain a reference to someone else giving the order.'

'Clever,' was the dry comment from the receiver.

'Find out what has happened.'

He sat at his desk for a few moments, his strong fingers drumming on the surface, next to the square blotter. Then he picked up the telephone again, and dialled. When a woman answered, he asked for Etienne de Vaugrigard.

'Etienne,' he said when he heard the quick breathing at the other end, 'you have been a very naughty child! You have tried to protect yourself, not believing that I would do that for you.' There was a mocking remonstrance, and a world-weariness in the tone.

'What – do you mean?'

'To think that you believed I would not know that "Plastique" is Perrier's cousin. And that you employed them both. And now they are both dead.'

'What?' A small choking sound at the end of the line.

'Gardiner has just left his hotel. He won't be back. Henri Julien Janvier was waiting for him inside. He has not appeared. I'm afraid he is dead. In the newspaper tonight you will no doubt read the popular headline "*Plastique*" *est mort!*' He laughed without humour.

'Oh my God ...'

'Don't worry. He's on his way to see you now, I shouldn't wonder.'

'Don't worry ... ?'

'We will keep an eye on him. He knows who he's looking for and he will want to talk to you – if not kill you. However, he has been informed that you possess valuable information about the real betrayer. He *will* want to talk first. I'll arrange for you to be protected. You won't be in any real danger.'

'Told him? How?' De Vaugrigard was dangerously near the death of all courage.

'L'Etranger' said, 'No worry of yours. Just expect a visit, that's all.'

He replaced the receiver delicately, and sat back in his chair. It was proceeding according to plan. Gardiner, fresh from another death, was eager for knowledge. When he gained it, he would be unstoppable. The 'Wolf' and the 'Wolverine' were finally in real danger. It had been a wise choice, that of Gardiner. Solution to his problem by a single stroke. Two strokes, he corrected himself.

And the 'Wolverine' was in Paris at that moment. Perhaps it might be as well to inform Gardiner, as soon as he had spoken to de Vaugrigard.

A beautiful plan. And the 'Wolf' and the 'Wolverine' having climbed so high as to be virtually unassailable. No ordinary method of removing them would have sufficed. But a rogue agent, from the war – doors would open, because he would not know they were there. And who would ever suspect him?

He laughed aloud, and his secretary looked up in the next room.

He shuffled the papers on his desk, as if mimicking the act of completion, of tidying – and a thought struck him. His mind lurched on its calm pinnacle for a moment, then felt embroiled in another consciousness, as if Gardiner's personality had somehow found entry to his mind.

He dialled the number of the phone-tap room his team were using, and waited impatiently for the receiver to be picked up. Strong fingers drumming on the blotter.

'Yes? Challot? Listen. I want to be informed of any telephone calls that de Vaugrigard makes in the next minutes – any meetings he arranges, any name he uses – understand? It's urgent.'

He put down the telephone. If Etienne moved, he would be tailed. But he would arrange to meet – who? 'L'Etranger' had an idea, though uncertain. Etienne would run – that had been the purpose of his call.

But – what would Gardiner do? The man had just killed again, frenzy of adrenalin, of ego. Broiling in him. Would he stop to ask questions of Etienne?

'L'Etranger' knew a moment of acute fear, heard at the back of his mind the crumbling of great and solid-seeming edifices. It could, even now, all come to nothing, if Gardiner killed before he asked. Gun before conversation.

'*Merde,*' he muttered, then over and over: '*Merde.*'

Too clever by half – people aren't robots, you can't predict everything – the ideas ran in his head, clichés which assumed a new power.

The telephone rang.

'Yes?' Hand jerking like that of a puppet, snatching the receiver.

'Tap-room, Chief.'

'Yes?'

'He called the Englishman, Latymer – arranged to meet him straight away.'

'Where?'

'The Avenue de Madrid house – suggested an afternoon horse ride, then asked him to come at once.'

'Right.'

He put down the telephone, considered for a moment, received an image of a man riding a horse in the field of vision of a telescopic sight, clear as celluloid entertainment, luridly coloured, then snapped on the intercom and summoned a senior assistant from the outer room.

CHAPTER NINE

MOVEMENT AND REST

ÉTIENNE DE VAUGRIGARD kept a clutch of horses for himself and his family at the stables of the Société d'Equitation de Paris in the Bois de Boulogne. His house on the Avenue de Madrid was almost directly opposite one of the entrances to the Bois.

Latymer felt oddly defenceless and at the same time ridiculously ill-garbed for his meeting with de Vaugrigard. Bright yellow sweater, jodphurs, riding boots that creaked with good leather and desuetude. All the while they changed, and walked to the Bois, watched while the horses were saddled and led out, Etienne said nothing, seeming pleased that Latymer had assented to the change of costume.

Latymer knew that Etienne was frightened; yet he retained his own silence until they had trotted across the tarmac of the Route de la Muette and into one of the *allées des cavalières* that threaded through the Bois. Then:

'What is it, Etienne? What's troubling you, that we need this pretence of normality?' He gestured with riding-crop and reins. De Vaugrigard seemed as if physically struck. Sunlight split down through the heavy trees, and he acted as if it caught him naked. He urged his horse to a canter, leaving Latymer behind.

Latymer drew alongside after perhaps a hundred yards. Suddenly, Etienne de Vaugrigard angered him, and he raised his voice.

'Etienne – I asked you what the matter was? This pretence is getting us nowhere!' The horses gathered speed, Latymer this time anticipating the surge. 'What the devil is it? If I can help, I will!'

His voice seemed to calm Etienne for a moment. The man reined in abruptly, so that Latymer was made to turn awkwardly on the docile mare, nudging her close to de Vaugrigard. Looking into the face of the Frenchman, he saw patterns of confusion chase across his features, as if years passed across the face.

'I have to talk to you about it, Hilary – about Richard Gardiner.'

'What – about Richard?'

'I lied to you before!'

It was hysterical, almost womanish. They had stopped in a clearing. Sunlight spilled down through the broken roof of branches, sheets of yellow-white. The two horses began to nuzzle each other, and the grass. Two middle-aged men, out for an afternoon ride – lucky to have the time and income. Latymer nudged aside the sudden deception of stillness.

'What is it?'

A door had opened; Gardiner's name was talismanic.

'I – I am the one he is looking for, Hilary!' Blurted out, like a child owning up as a circle of parental enquiries closed round him – intense experience, whole years compressed into tense, clipped words.

'You? What do you mean, you're the one he's looking for?'

'He wants to kill me! Can I make it any clearer than that?' It was one of the most pressingly real encounters Latymer had ever experienced. Some cone of silence enveloped the two of them. Waves of anger, fear, shame broke against the wool of his bright sweater, emanating from de Vaugrigard.

'Why?'

'I betrayed him – I was the one!'

'You?'

Excuse, justification, imperatives – rushing now after confession. Putting back the torn mask. 'I – had to hand Renaud over to the Gestapo, and Gardiner was to be the proof that it wasn't a set-up – for *verisimilitude*!' He spat out the last word.

'Oh my God ...' Latymer breathed, then felt the contempt surge through him like an icy wave. 'Why did you do it?'

'The group – orders ... I was a member of the "Wolf-group", Hilary. Does that mean anything to you? The "Wolfgroup" – you know what it was for?'

Latymer nodded, his face screwed up like a child remembering some difficult lesson – the algebra of secret betrayals.

'Yes – anti-Communist, wasn't it? Just rumours ...' Then, seized by the intimacy of revelation: 'You were recruited into it?'

'Yes, yes. I – betrayed many Communists to the Gestapo. It was my function. Renaud was supposed to give away the location of "Duroc" to the Gestapo, prevent the uprising in Paris – that's why I did it. I didn't have any choice!'

Latymer said without trace of sympathy: 'Who gave the orders, Etienne? Who?'

De Vaugrigard's face closed with craft. No longer two middle-aged men. One of them had shrunk, an ancient creature in a bag of skin.

'Not until you promise to help me.'

'What help?'

'Protection.'

'God, Etienne – do you know what happened to Richard in the cellars of the Avenue Foch – what happened to all the others you helped send there?' Latymer felt the moral temperature rising, the condemnation choking him. 'You want me to help save your miserable skin?' He paused. 'No,' he said as if to himself. 'Not that. What help can I give you? I don't even know where Richard is.'

'You must help me – there's more to it. Something from now, not from the past ...' De Vaugrigard was cunning, the horse edged closer, conspiratorial against the flanks of Latymer's mare.

'More?'

And he caught a shadow of movement at the edge of the clearing.

'Yes, more. But, promise me . . .'

'I – '

A shirt or sweater, caught by a sheet of sunlight. The slight movement of a bush. Suddenly, another image, the one that had to do with nakedness, of the target he made in the bright colour; he wondered, for an instant, whether de Vaugrigard had made him the better target, his own sweater an olive drab.

He had to come out of the bushes – that was part of it, the bravado of execution, not the slinking murder. Richard. Latymer gasped, and there was a pain at the side of his head, as if he had been struck by the gun Gardiner held stiffly out from his body. Execution.

De Vaugrigard, seeing something in his face, turned to follow his gaze. Saw Gardiner.

'You . . .' he whispered, and seemed to accuse Latymer.

'Richard! Listen now – listen to me!'

There was all the time in the world. Latymer could see the thought in Gardiner's smile from thirty yards away. He could see the words forming as the man decided that talk was profitable postponement.

'Hilary – stop shuffling your horse to shield him. I'll kill you both, if necessary.' The words were spoken almost softly. Authority, certitude, carried them across the still clearing. Loudly, around the mare's head, a fly buzzed. Latymer, watching the steady aim, was careful not to brush it away as it spun round his ears. A bead of sweat ran down the side of de Vaugrigard's smooth face to the heavy jowl. He, too, seemed incapable of movement, or careful of it.

'Richard – we must talk. You have to understand this –'

'Understand? I understand. You want to keep it nice and civilised. Don't worry. The equivalent of the parks department won't let him lie here for long. Bad for tourists!'

'Wait – !' De Vaugrigard, a strangled cry.

'Ah. I think he wishes to add something to the conversation. Yes, Etienne?'

'I – had orders – orders, from above, do you understand? I can give you names!'

'Names?' Did your orders include trying to kill me in Rouen, on top of everything else?'

Latymer listened to the boom of the voice, heard the words bounce off some wall in his mind; rise in volume and import. Gardiner was moving closer to the kill with every moment.

The horse snickered, stamped beneath him, releasing the tension it felt through his thighs.

'No, Richard – you have to listen to him – you have to.'

The impotence he had felt in the Place du Parvis, staring at Notre Dame, assailed him again. He would be nothing more than a spectator at this ritual.

Then de Vaugrigard moved, something snapping inside him so that all that was left was panic flight. The horse bucked, surged away, flowing into a gallop. The first bullet whined audibly past Latymer as he spurred towards Gardiner, throwing his shadow between gunman and target. The second and third, loosed off, seemed to miss de Vaugrigard as he gained the trees away to Latymer's right. Then Gardiner was twenty feet or so ahead of him, and he spurred the horse forward, possessed by some madness of relief. He watched the gun come up, level with the gaudy yellow sweater – then suddenly drop, and spurt flame, twice.

The horse reeled under him, let out a whinnied scream. Flailing legs and hooves, as he spilled out of the saddle, forward and away from the thrashing horse. His shoulder and head struck the ground. Winded, blinded by sudden darkness. The cries of the horse becoming suddenly fainter, yet more insistent even as the pain in his head increased, the struggle to regain his lost breath.

A shot, and silence from the horse. A shadow between his closed lids and the fierce light. Then he expelled the fought-for-breath, and dropped into the dark that was waiting for him.

Richard Gardiner shuddered still with the cries of the horse. He had had to silence it, that inhuman screaming, stop the great arch of blood coming from the chest, splashing Latymer's riding boots and sweater. He looked down briefly at Latymer, felt a momentary hatred of frustration, then turned on his heel. In the silence after the shots, he could faintly hear the retreating hoofbeats of de Vaugrigard's horse.

He began to run, breath or emotion sobbing in his throat, ramming shells into the Browning as he went. He was angry that he had been going to kill de Vaugrigard, in that beautifully arranged innocence of the sunlit clearing, prompted by the sight of the man's face, the prosperous body, richness of clothes, the palpable fear.

Without asking him a single question – even when he knew that Etienne knew of others, always others, behind and behind, retreating like shadows or ghosts ...

He shook his head to clear it, and stopped to listen. Nothing. No hoofbeats. He glanced wildly around him, as if he sensed hostile bodies closing in. Which direction? What would he do now?

Stables, house, car – run, run, run ...

Logic of survival. Had to be.

Gardiner began to run, back the way he had come, towards the exit from the Bois into the Avenue de Madrid.

'What's happening?'

Challot's voice crackled over the car radio.

'We were just about to move in – he had de Vaugrigard and the Englishman cold. But Etienne bolted, and Gardiner missed with his only good shot.'

'Where are you now?' 'L'Etranger' looked through his own windscreen at the cars passing across the Carrefour des Sablons, perhaps half-a-mile from where Gardiner had tried to kill his target. The windscreen was opaque – and he realised that, even though the day was dry and warm, his own tension had become a steam in the car. His driver leaned unconcerned against the bonnet, smoking, watching pedestrians as if practising the arts of surveillance or lechery.

'Avenue Madrid house in sight, Chief. He went in about ten minutes ago.'

'Have you located Gardiner's car?'

'No.'

'Where is he?'

'On his way here – Spotter Three called in a minute ago. He's worked it out.'

'If you have to, stop him. He mustn't get to de Vaugrigard until he's more rational. What about the Englishman?'

'Still lying where he fell. But he's all right. One of the Spotters checked him over. Just concussed, no bones broken.'

'O.K., he's out of it. Let me know when Etienne leaves. If Gardiner doesn't interfere, tail them, but let it run.'

'Understood.'

'Channel left open.'

'L'Etranger' felt calmer. He had managed to avoid the consequences of the confrontation. Gardiner had not killed Etienne, and now Etienne would run either to his mistress, or to his château. Either way, Gardiner would follow him. He did not now believe that Gardiner would kill Etienne out of hand – but every minute that ticked away calmed the Englishman, made him more rational. He waited. The open channel made a buzz of static, fly-like, in the car. He found himself looking repeatedly at the microphone lying on the transmission tunnel.

His own confidence, massive as it was – he admitted it now – had been shaken by Gardiner. Yes, shaken . . .

The amount of blood from the dead horse had made one of the spotters sick, according to Challot. Somehow, the image of the breached animal adequately expressed Gardiner. A tremor passed through 'L'Etranger's' hand.

'Chief? He's on the move – daughter's sports car, by the look of it – taking the Boulevard Maurice Barres towards the city. Running for cover.'

'Tail him – where's Gardiner?'

'No sign of him.'

'All units – I want a report immediately – whereabouts of Gardiner ...'

'Wait – Chief!' Challot. 'That's him, just turning out in front of us. He must have been parked near the house, in the Rue du Bois.'

'Are you certain, Challot?'

'Yes, Chief. It's him.'

'All units – two cars, description to follow, on Boulevard Maurice Barres, do not intercept, but do not lose. Challot, give them the descriptions.'

He put down the microphone as Challot described the two cars – grey Simca, blue Ferrari, can't miss that one – and knocked impatiently on the windscreen. His driver flicked away a cigarette, and heaved himself into the car.

Hilary Latymer painfully dragged himself across the clearing, after he had vomited, and hauled himself to his feet with the aid of the cool, rough bark of a tree trunk. He pressed his quivering cheeks against the bark, almost rubbing the skin as if to rid himself of it. The regularity of the movement, its insistence, cleansed him of the image of the horse's carcass, and the hideous, magnified clamour of the cloud of flies feasting on the blood. It cleared his head, also, of something of the hammering pain of the concussion.

He wanted to do nothing. There was an element of fear in his resignation. Gardiner, gun aimed, squeezing off those shots, had frightened him. The impact with the dry, hard earth had knocked something out of him, expelled resolution with breath. He didn't want to get in the way.

He stared at the bloodied sweater, and the soiled boots and jodphurs, and knew that he remained involved. Blood had been spilled *on* him, making him a member of the unholy fraternity that embraced Etienne and Richard Gardiner. He had no easy way out.

People he passed as he made his way towards the Avenue de Madrid exit stared at him, but made no effort to stop him. The blood might have been his own, and they sensed the urgency with which he weaved and stumbled.

A car hooted, then another, and he almost giggled at the spectacle he must present, at the drunkenness of his passage across the Avenue de Madrid. Then, somehow, ages later or only moments since he had woken on the ground, he was banging on the front door of the imposing white house and, though he seemed to hear his unfamiliar voice through a roaring sea, he was yelling at the top of his voice:

'Etienne! Geneviève! For God's sake, let me in! Etienne! Geneviève!'

He was leaning so hard, banging so furiously, that he almost fell into the hall when a frightened maid opened the door. He stumbled, capered to retain balance, and brought down a vase of flowers on a delicate table. A rug slid from beneath his boots, and he sprawled. He almost giggled again, as if experiencing the drunken analogy that came to mind. He looked up to see Geneviève standing half-way down the main staircase, her face a tight, disapproving mask. He blinked, stared, and the mask became entrenched lines of fear, panic, ignorance, shock. She came down the rest of the steps, knelt by him.

'You're hurt!'

'No, no – your horse, I'm afraid. Dead.'

She blurted: 'He wouldn't tell me what had happened – to you.' It was as if they had acquired an intimacy that excluded her husband.

'He did come back here?'

'Yes, yes. Panicked by something–what happened, Hilary? He wouldn't tell me!'

'Someone tried to kill him. Help me up, I seem to have gone light-headed ...'

The two women bent to him, raised him so that he leaned

against the wallpaper, probably soiling it. He was aware of
that, confronted by Geneviève. He shook his head, which
threatened to inflate, or explode, or dissipate – he could not
decide which.

'Thanks. Where has he gone?'

He wasn't sure she knew, for a moment. Struggle in her,
freezing hauteur overcome by sudden panic, by perhaps the
sight of the dried blood – perhaps the memory of her husband's face when he returned. She was making herself admit
to something she normally chose to ignore, buried from
herself – now admitted, even in front of the maid.

'Perhaps I can save him,' Latymer urged. 'Tell me where
he might be.'

'The – Faubourg St. Honoré. An apartment there. He
will have gone there. It is his – *secret address*!' The hauteur,
the inability to admit, returned suddenly, and closed her
mouth, dried the face of feeling.

'The number?' he said, breathless with urgency. She gave
it to him. He turned to the door.

'I may be in time – if I hurry. Don't – don't tell the police
for the moment. Understand. It's *not* a police matter.'

She nodded. She was frozen again, forgetting the admission. The mistress was unimportant, did not exist. Latymer,
for a moment, felt sorry for her. Then he opened the door,
and let himself out.

The afternoon traffic was heavy, and it was more than
thirty minutes before he reached the Faubourg St. Honoré,
another ten before he turned into the courtyard of the
apartment building behind a couturier's. Something seemed
to slide inside him, as if it had been balanced on his chest,
and now tumbled to the pit of his stomach – a block of ice –
as he saw that there were no cars, other than one Citroën,
parked in the courtyard.

The wooden door he had to take was open, showing the
foot of the staircase to Etienne's mistress's apartment. He
unlocked the glove compartment, felt for the gun, found

nothing, remembered, with thick-headed difficulty, that he
had drawn no gun from the Embassy. Cursing he got out
of the car, steadied himself and crossed the courtyard.

He paused at the bottom of the wooden stairs. Clumsily,
with ridiculous effort, he removed the riding boots. Then
he began to climb the steps, pausing after each movement.
The apartment house seemed still, unnaturally silent, and
he was seized by a momentary physical nausea that only
gradually became related to anticipatory fears.

The door to the apartment was open. He squinted through
the gap, shadowy as if the doors were closed within or
curtains drawn – then he pushed the door wide, very slowly.
A short carpeted corridor, solid varnished doors, all closed
except one – a room in which curtains were drawn. He moved
very slowly, stockinged feet soundless on the thick carpet.

It was the bedroom. He waited for what seemed an
interminable time, then pushed back the door.

Fortunately, the girl seemed more frightened than hurt.
It took him five minutes to find her, having looked in the
other rooms before returning to the bedroom. She was in a
fitted wardrobe with louvred doors, and she rolled out at
his feet, tied hand and foot as she was, and her wide eyes
stared up at him in terror as he loomed over her. He bent
down – her skin seemed to retreat in revulsion from his
gentle touch – then he undid the knots, and took off the
gag, smiling.

'There, there,' he said, over and over as if to a small dog
or baby. 'It's all right now – it's all right.' An imperative
slammed him in the back, palpable as an assailant, but he
knew he could not panic or bully the girl. Gardiner had
evidently done that already, to find out what he wanted to
know.

He went to fetch her a cognac, and found himself looking
for blood-spots as he moved through the apartment, while
something else in him measured the money that had been
spent to furnish the place.

The girl gagged on the cognac, but hugged the glass to her

breast. There was some bruising on the high cheekbones, and on her bare arms. She was wearing only a thin sleeveless dress. Reaction was beginning to make her shiver in the hot, airless, darkened bedroom.

Latymer sat in impatient silence, until he said, 'Don't tell me what happened, Ma'moiselle. Tell me where Etienne went – just tell me that.' Somehow, he could not ease the urgency entirely from his voice, and she looked frightened. Gardiner had asked much the same question, and his hand had struck her. The girl seemed to be watching his hands, clasped on his lap as he sat on the bed. He kept them very still.

'He was followed here – but where did he go ... ? Where did the other man make you tell – where was it?'

He saw the guilt, and the pressing fear. As if someone had pulled down the walls, vandalised the apartment. She was defenceless.

'No,' was all she said.

'Yes,' he insisted. 'Tell me where Etienne went.'

He knew he might have to hit her, and was appalled at the idea. Repetition of what Gardiner had done, and she would tell again. He began to steel himself, as the urgency came back to him, reducing her helplessness to stubborn refusal.

Then she said, 'His château – he went there.'

'Where is that?' he asked as her eyes cast about for some tangible sign of security, safety.

She got up, jerkily, surprising him, spilling the cognac on the fawn carpet, and rummaged in a drawer. She held out a photograph to him, silently. He looked at the snapshot, turned it in his hand. Azay-le-Rideau. He looked up at her, but she offered no information, sensing that only silence was safe for her. Even the date of purchase was emblazoned on the back of the snapshot. Probably, the girl had never been there, but Etienne had boasted to her, as perhaps to everyone else.

He left the room quickly, and picked up the telephone in

the lounge. He dialled the Embassy, staring at the print as he waited for the reply.

'Hawthorne? Put McNeil on.' He waited again. 'McNeil – I want a trace put on a small château belonging to Etienne de Vaugrigard – probably in the Loire Valley. Yes, at once. Where? I see. And, McNeil – I shall want a gun. Revolver, not automatic. Sign the forms and bring it to the apartment in the Rue de Castellane, as quick as you can.'

He put down the telephone. Twenty-five kilometres from Tours, on the Indre, McNeil had supplied at once. The rest would be ready for him by the time he changed his clothes. Together with the gun.

He went back to look at the girl. She was seated, crouched, on the bed, clutching what he finally realised was an evening dress. Pink, elegant, crumpled now but a couturier's model. He wondered how many occasions she had had to wear her comforter. She did not look up at him, and he left her, closing the door behind him.

Richard Gardiner had parked his car some distance from the château. It had been easy to find, the information ridiculously easy to obtain from the girl, with a few casual blows. Even though she had never been there, she swore, she knew its location, could have described it in even more detail had he required.

He had watched the apartment until Etienne de Vaugrigard left it, driving hurriedly off down the Faubourg St. Honoré. Only then had he gone in, confident again, convinced that he had not lost the man, wanting the man to believe he was making an escape, was ahead in the game. The young mistress was as he predicted, and was able to supply the information he required. He had hit her because he was in a hurry, and because suddenly there flared up in him something of the madness of the Bois de Boulogne. He was damaging something that belonged to his betrayer. That the girl had passed out had probably saved her a worse beating.

Now he was a man holding himself in harsh ropes. He

desired, more than anything, to go down from his outlook
on a tree-tufted outcrop overlooking the château and confront the man. Kill him – perhaps make him beg; humiliate,
hurt, terrify ... The words of power circled in his mind,
hypnotic pendulums which his inward gaze followed until
their outlines blurred, until the words drummed like blood
in the darkness behind his squeezed eyelids.

Yet one thing kept him where he was, looking down on
the toy house and the tiny toy car parked in front of it –
the thought that inside the house there was a frightened man.

He fed on de Vaugrigard's imagined fear. He was alone,
except perhaps for a housekeeper. And the afternoon was
waning, the shadow of the outcrop creeping across the lawns
in front of the house as if to swallow it. The perch he had
obtained, its detachment and sense of power, was what he
enjoyed.

He did not think of anything except his destruction of de
Vaugrigard. His vision had tunnelled so that he could see
no moral perspective, until there were no questions that he
asked himself and no sense of what de Vaugrigard's motive
migh t have been. There had been times in the past days when
he had tossed on his bed, unable to sleep because images of
his past, and the stench of the present, came at him out of
the dark like intruders or succubi. But not at that moment.
There was nothing to think of except the death of the man
in the toy house below him – once darkness had come.

And from his perch up there, up above the toy house, it
would be an easy, easy thing to squash the toy man under
his foot, like an insect.

Latymer crossed the motorway ring around the city and
picked up the stretch of wide road towards Orly, before he
needed to branch south-west towards Chartres and the A10.
Already, there was the sense of driving through a dream
landscape. There was an insufficient reality to the road, even
when he passed two cars piled into a ditch, and the anonymous grey blankets that covered shapeless forms at the side

of the road. There was no *colour*, he decided, about the scenes through which he moved, as if all that mattered to him was the collision of past and present that he feared would occur at Azay before he could get there. His headache was receding, as if he had willed it to disperse, or become distracted from it.

And Richard would lose something more of himself if he killed Etienne.

An aircraft lifted into the pale sky to his left, from Orly. A silver cigar, a further silver wink like an early star. He sensed that they were moving towards places he might have known, or might have inhabited with comfort. Not this lunatic chase, the Smith and Wesson heavy and refusing to warm against his thigh.

He passed along the grey outskirts of Palaiseau, and then he was out of the Paris conurbation, or so it seemed to him. It was as if the centre of Paris was some kind of cleansed, spacious, distilled crystallisation, and the deposits and impurities clustered round that centre in a thick, sombre, smoke-belching ring. Then pasture-land, suddenly.

And the villages. Detached from him as he sped down a narrow strip of the world, as if the road had been ripped up and accelerated into another dimension.

The Forêt de Dourdan, with more than half the journey to Chartres done; the dappling of sunlight through low branches or sliced into glowing bands as he passed in the Peugeot. He stopped at none of the frequent lay-bys, but pressed on as the evening began to gather, south towards Châteaudun and Tours. His bruised shoulder ached as he sat rigid in the seat. His head thumped. The traffic thinned as the holiday-makers or the French villagers deserted the roads in favour of hotels and inns, or their homes.

He turned the lights on while he was still north of Tours, sudden beams springing out from the car making the road a glinting ribbon of tar and the trees, tall and slim, sentries of his passage.

He passed the airport at Tours, and a shape he could

distinguish as that of an old Dakota lumbered skywards, lights winking. There was something poignant about the slightly sweptback wings and the stubby fuselage, as if he were watching some other aircraft from a previous time climb towards the night sky, carrying agents he had briefed from airfields in the south of England. He turned to watch it, slowing the car, until it was only a black shape, lights under its belly, against the stars.

The aircraft betrayed him to the past, which rushed at him like the beams of cars travelling north. The plane had been a clean image, for a moment, something that survived intact and unchanged from the war; unlike, and like, Richard. Then the past came back, and the filthiness of it, and the squalid, violent present.

Richard was a killer, Etienne was a traitor – men were dead because of them.

The centre of Tours was busy, and he concentrated grimly, thankful to escape his own oppressive thoughts. He crossed the dark, sliding river by the Pont Wilson, and then headed down the Rue Nationale until he picked up the D 7 which would take him to Villandry and Azay.

Soon, the town was behind him and he drove faster now, as if something pressed at his spine, urging him. He swept in the comet's tail of the headlights through the dark country-side. Hedges disguised the land. Villandry was quiet; and the empty streets seemed ominous, as if reverberations of an event ahead of him had driven the people to shelter. He was certain that Richard Gardiner would have got to Azay by now. He began to study every car, and their shadowed occupants, as they passed him on the road.

A dog squeezed past the wing of the car on the outskirts of the village, sudden and large and terrified in the headlights, eyes glowing in an unearthly way.

Azay was funereally quiet. He turned off the road and began to climb a tree-covered rise, some sterner outcrop of rock above the river. Trees closed around the road and then the Peugeot passed through open gates bearing some unidentifiable heraldry in stained design. He suddenly became cautious, and the car slowed as his senses braked. He pulled into the trees and switched off the engine. He wound down the window, and it was suddenly quiet, his ears ringing with the unaccustomed silence.

He checked the revolver, rolling the chamber in a series of loud clicks. Five bullets. He had a sense that he might need them, and he shivered though it was a mild night. He got out of the car and walked through the trees silently. On the ground floor of the house, as he came out of the trees, he saw a light but no shadows thrown on the lawn. He skirted the ornamental lake, footsteps careful on the gravel, and came to the façade so that it loomed over him, washed lighter by the moon. He watched the square of muted gold quartered by the window-frames. Suddenly, he ducked along the wall of the house, moving as silently as he could, until he could raise his head to look into the lighted room.

The library. And he was too late. The posture of Gardiner's slumped body relaxed in the armchair, the glass of whisky raised to his lips, told him that. Only after he had registered the look of dumb aftermath on the face did he see the body of de Vaugrigard, arranged on a chaise-longue, arms folded across the breast, some kind of ritual that Gardiner had performed upon it. He could not see the bullet hole. There appeared to be no blood on the body. Etienne de Vaugriard's face, in profile, had set in the death mask. The long, curved nose raised to the ceiling, the lips pressed tightly together, the eyes closed. And the folded arms, the illusion of an untroubled end. It caused Latymer's stomach to heave.

He looked again at Gardiner. The man was ignoring the body, and seemed to be deep in thought. There was a frown on the face now, as if the features moved only slowly, subject to some great aquatic pressure distorting the features. There were no emotions, only the effects of gravity on the facial muscles. Latymer saw the Browning on a table, feet from Gardiner's hand.

He ducked down and crept back along the wall, conscious of every minute disturbance of the gravel and his own hoarse breathing. He reached the front door.

It was open. He pushed at it gently and it opened silently. He stepped into the huge, dark hall.

He made out, in the moonlight filtering through undraped windows, the huge central staircase and the gallery beyond it. There were rooms and corridors leading off the hall, and he took the one that would bring him to the library. It was carpeted, a thin, faded strip of carpet down the centre, the wooden floor gleaming darkly in the pale light from the tall windows at the end of the corridor. A thin line of light, barely escaping, indicated the door of the library.

He paused outside it. There was the chance that the door was locked, and that his hand on the knob would betray him to Gardiner. He held the door knob, having wiped his palm on the seat of his trousers. Then he turned it, with delicate patience, very slowly. The door opened a crack, and squeaked. He thrust it open, took in the figure of Gardiner already bending to the low table and the gun, and said, 'Leave it!'

Gardiner looked up, into the barrel of Latymer's revolver, stiffened as if weighing his chances, then smiled, waving his hands in innocent retreat.

'Come in, Hilary. I'm sure our host won't mind another guest ...'

Latymer did not glance towards the chaise-longue Gardiner had indicated with his eyes.

'I've already seen the body, Richard, through the window – thank you all the same.' Gardiner merely smiled.

Latymer crossed the room, took the heavy Browning and threw it into a corner. Then he sat down in another armchair, well away from the table and any leap from Gardiner, and then looked at the body.

'The arrangement is rather – *obscene*, wouldn't you say?'

'Sorry it offends you.' Gardiner looked at the body, swiftly, as if he were the one with the gun and dare not miss any sudden move by a treacherous Latymer. 'Yes. Beginning to seem that way to me, too. I thought it a good idea at the time.' He rubbed at his forehead, as if soothing away a pain. 'I don't know why I did it now.' He looked at Latymer, and pointed to his whisky. Latymer nodded. Gardiner swallowed at the drink, then sat back in his chair. He said. 'It's all right. I shan't throw the drink in your face and hope to leap on you while you're blinded. That sort of thing got a great many of our more amateur colleagues killed during the war.' Again, Latymer nodded.

'It's over, then,' he said.

Gardiner shook his head as if maddened by insects.

'No, it's not over!' There was a deep, flaring bitterness, almost a wail of anguish, and his whole being seemed to take its colour. Latymer was shocked. He had expected the beginnings of a new purposelessness in his quarry, the dejection in the aftermath of revenge. Even a new sense of self-preservation.

'What do you mean? He's dead now, isn't he? Or do you want to kill all the others?'

'It isn't him – wasn't, should I say?' There seemed an inward collapse of the structure of the face until it registered nothing more notable than sulkiness.

'Then why, for God's sake?' Latymer indicated the recumbent corpse.

'Oh, yes – he betrayed me. He told me that. But he wasn't the only one!' He laughed suddenly, a harsh, braying sound. His eyes were fierce.

'Who else?' Latymer was resigned, suddenly, to an endless debate, a psychopathic condition. Gardiner had rendered himself beyond help, beyond persuasion. 'What kind of thing have you become, Richard? What? You can't take your revenge on the whole world.'

Latymer realised he was leaning forward in his seat, his hands clenched together around the gun butt, the gun angled to the floor. He was overtaken by wariness once more. The old moral considerations, which no longer applied but which he couldn't rid himself of, had tricked him. He still wanted to help Gardiner. He had wanted a regenerate Gardiner, appalled by the fever of madness that had possessed him, not this unrepentant, malevolent presence with burning eyes.

'No, not the whole world, Hilary – just two men.' Latymer was chilled by the confidence, the authority of the voice. It was as if there were no gun, or that Gardiner held it. He seemed still unbeaten, uncaptured. Latymer looked at the gun, as if reassuring himself, at the five copper studs of the cartridges in the chamber.

'Just two *more*, is that what you're saying? Just another two, and then you'll stop?' His voice sounded thin and unconvincing.

'Yes.' Again the arrogance, the assurance.

'Christ, Richard! It's all dead and buried! Can't you see that, man?'

'No. Because it's not, Hilary. For you, yes – and for him.' His head nodded towards the body. 'But not for me. I was – *delayed*, by various things, which amount to nineteen years of my life. But I have arrived, to find the party not quite over.'

Latymer shook his head. 'My God, Richard, but something's happened to you . . .' It was ineffectual, like his sense of being able to help. He admitted now, that he might even have let Gardiner go – had he fulfilled certain moral requirements. It was ludicrous, pathetic – arrogant and blind, too.

Gardiner smiled. Latymer felt suddenly weary; weary of Gardiner, the pursuit that had accomplished nothing, and weary of the alienness of the life he felt going on in the man opposite.

Who were they? he thought. Some pathetic little men who had rebuilt their lives, now to have them pulled down? Growing protective scabs over the memory of what they had done to Gardiner?

'Don't you want to know, Hilary?' Gardiner asked

quietly. He was leaning forward in his chair, his eyes bright with longing.

Latymer shook his head. 'Not particularly.'

'The names are known to you – on a time,' was the reply. The voice was seductive with knowledge.

'Indeed?'

'Indeed. Perhaps you might like to try them on, to see if they fit the mind? What about Constant, for example, and van Lederer? Don't those names mean anything to you?'

Latymer was seized by the ridiculousness of it. 'Nonsense!'

'To hell with you! That's what he told me. I wasn't betrayed by a damn Frog, but by my own people! By that smooth individual from MI 6 who came to see us the day I left for France, and gave me all that crap about the importance of the mission – who *set me up*!' He saw the disbelief on Latymer's face, the stubborn refusal to believe. Suddenly, he wanted to convince the man with the gun, to make him understand. The desire unnerved him like a dim memory. He said, 'You must have heard of the "Wolfgroup", operating behind the scenes in France and other occupied countries, throughout the war?'

Latymer's face creased in thought, then he said in a quiet voice, 'Rumours, and rumours of rumours. Nothing tangible.'

'Etienne was a *member* of it. It was set up to affect the post-war governments of occupied countries. Wipe out as many prominent Communists in the Resistance movements as they possibly could. They wanted Renaud all the time, not me. Crazy, isn't it. I had to go to the wall, just to make it look good. And Constant and van Lederer *were* the group! He told me everything, to keep himself alive. It didn't help, of course . . .'

He sat back in his chair, and allowed Latymer time in which to absorb the information, just as he had required time. He recalled de Vaugrigard's frightened, mobile face, the collapse of the will behind it, the pleading – then the sudden and desperate revelations. At first, they had driven everything else from Gardiner's mind, but when he had finished, and confessed that he had finished, Gardiner shot him.

He glanced at the body once again. He felt no remorse. Instead, creeping back into him, was the sense of the futility of what he had set out to do. There was always someone else. And to take on van Lederer, who was now, according to de Vaugrigard, a senior NATO Intelligence officer, was a prospect which daunted him. Robbed of immediate freedom of thought and action by the inhibition of Latymer's gun, he did not feel equal to his task. He looked at the drapes, the lines of leather-bound volumes, and they, too, seemed to press on him with a weight of civilisation. He had killed a man in this room; now, he could not think of killing other men, not with the evident comfort, the evident *reasonableness* of Latymer and the room. Violent death had no place here. He shivered slightly.

'*Verisimilitude*,' Latymer said quietly without looking up.
'What?'

Latymer seemed to awaken from some mild trance. As he looked up, Gardiner was surprised to see the oppression that registered in his face.

'Just something someone said to me – a very frightened man.' He cleared his throat, which seemed clogged. 'You realise who these two men are? Van Lederer is retiring chairman of the NATO Senior Joint Intelligence Committee, and Constant is one of the two Deputies in the SIS. To contemplate killing them . . . ? You'd do too much *damage*, Richard! Can't you understand that? It isn't 1944, or '45. It's 1963. The world has changed around you!'

'You advise me to desist in my efforts, then?' Gardiner asked with a smile. 'You think the task beyond my puny resources?' He was willing a sense of dislike, even hatred, into his voice. He wished to avoid the lethargy that seemed to be creeping over him, the futility knocking at the front of his mind.

'No. I don't underestimate anything, Richard. I'm just

telling you that the thing can't be done. Not by you. I won't let you.'

'You'll turn me in, then?'

'I have to,' Latymer replied, trying to quell the flush of guilt he irrationally felt. In a moment of great intellectual clarity he saw that he had intended that in some way Gardiner should escape the consequences of his actions.

'Yes. I understand that, especially now. Since Constant is your boss, itself a neat irony, you have to protect him from someone like me.'

'Look, I don't like the idea of what he did any more than you do!'

'Of course not,' Gardiner said mockingly. 'You're just doing your duty. What every stupid man claims when the situation turns out not to be precisely what he hoped!'

'You don't even know whether any of this nonsense is true!'

'Men in his position don't tell lies – at least, not well-documented ones.'

There was a silence. Latymer appeared on the point of pursuing the argument, then gave it up and slumped back in his chair, reasserting the aim of the Smith and Wesson as he did so. Gardiner nodded at the adjustment, and smiled.

It was horrible, Latymer thought. So clinical for Richard, so lacking in any sense of the healing time was supposed to provide; its necessary compromises, its changes of loyalty. It was true, of course. He believed the dead man on the sofa, as much as if he had been given incontrovertible proof. It was a Constant style of operation from beginning to end.

Gardiner was the man he had been in 1944 – Latymer could no longer disguise that truth from himself, or see the younger Gardiner in the same diffused light of memory. A hard, sharp whiteness showed him the real being. Gardiner had been really born some time in 1941 or '42, in the war. Here he was now, unchanged.

It was Gardiner who heard the approaching helicopter first. Latymer saw him sit upright, alert like a hound.

'What is it, Richard?' It was as if the movement had surprised some part of the shared past. Then he heard the steady beat of rotors nearing, lowering from the brilliant night sky.

Gardiner said, 'The Seventh Cavalry, unless I'm very much mistaken.' He sat back in his chair, a stony expression on his face, his eyes riveted on the gun. He checked Latymer's eyes once, and despite the conflict of emotions he saw, he knew there was no chance of escape. The man would shoot him if he moved.

'You?' he asked.

Latymer nodded. 'Yes. I telephoned earlier, before setting out. Someone I know in SDECE. His housekeeper took the message. Evidently, he received it.'

'You knew I'd be here, then?'

'You had to be.'

Outside, the helicopter dropped onto the lawn, and the heady beat of the rotors died down through the scale. Latymer could see the red light at the tail winking, see the men in the cabin of the helicopter. He avoided thinking about Gardiner. He emptied his mind of past and present, and made of him an object of flesh and bone and blood that he was quite prepared to kill. He almost succeeded, and would have done but for the intrusive sense of something that had been lost, somewhere in their mutual past. It continued to make the situation a human one which he could not quite render into two simple dimensions.

The footsteps of men, now that the rotor had died, could be heard on the gravel outside. He saw Gardiner's face flicker, registering the approach of other captors. He saw the face momentarily livid in defeat and frustrated rage – then the stony indifference again.

The door of the library opened cautiously, and then Haussman, in a light overcoat, stepped into the room. His mane of grey hair was awry from the downdraught of the rotors; his face was red, and his sharp eyes flickered from Gardiner to the corpse and back again. He nodded to

Latymer, and went outside. Latymer could hear him talking to someone in the corridor. Then he re-entered.

He looked at Gardiner, nodded again as if in acknowledgement or recognition and then recited, in a flat, official voice: 'Richard Gardiner, you are under arrest. You will be charged with the murder of Etienne de Vaugrigard, and also with the murders of Henri Janvier and the man Dupuy. You do not need to say anything to me. However, is there anything you do wish to say before you are taken to Tours Police Préfecture, and then to Paris?'

Gardiner shook his head, and stood up, ready to leave. He looked at Latymer, and deliberately smiled in a confidential way. He intentionally brought their mutual past to mind. Latymer nodded, and then looked at the body, as if admitting other imperatives.

A moment later, Gardiner had gone with Haussman. Latymer got up, and poured himself a large brandy. He swallowed at it, shuddered slightly, and returned to his chair. He did not want to think. Haussman would watch Gardiner being taken away, and then he would return and they would have to talk. But not for the moment.

It was over, he admitted cautiously. Gardiner had destroyed himself. And he was wretched about it, so that the paucity of his own circumstances struck him with new force. *Victoria, dying.*

And he worked for a man who had betrayed Richard Gardiner.

The thoughts revolved with a slow frenzy as he sat sipping his drink. He lit a cigarette and then let it burn unnoticed between his fingers. The thoughts continued, depressing him further.

In France, they still employed the guillotine. Gardiner, with his head struck off . . .

PART THREE

THE NATURE OF
THE BEASTS

'We had the experience but missed the meaning,
And approach to the meaning restores the experience
In a different form, beyond any meaning
We can assign to happiness.'

> — T. S. Eliot: 'The Dry Salvages', II

CHAPTER TEN

CONTACT WITH 'FRANKLIN'

THE HOTEL BELVEDERE was situated on the Rue St. Antoine, near the Place de la Bastille. General Eugene van Lederer had booked a room on his arrival in Paris for the meeting of the Senior Intelligence Committee; he had lodged at the American Embassy until this particular night – particular because he had brought his mistress to the hotel.

Mme. Catherine Vigny was married to a senior official of the Quai d'Orsay, the French Foreign Ministry. They had met, and commenced their affair, when M. Vigny was an attaché at the French Embassy in Washington, a tour of duty which had ended twelve months earlier. Since then, van Lederer and his mistress had met only when he was in Paris. Always, they took the same room at the Belvedere, perhaps because it provided a degree of familiarity in their locationless relationship.

The pattern was simple – dinner, then love-making. Which was passionate, untender and assertive on his part, submissive on hers. It was, van Lederer had admitted to himself on more than one occasion, the youthfulness of his mistress, only a little over thirty, that attracted him and kept him attracted. And the convenience of not seeing her too frequently.

They had finished making love when the telephone rang. Van Lederer was idling into sleep, his mistress satisfied for the moment, her demands having been such as he could amply fulfil on this occasion, such as inflated his sexual vanity and increased his sense of well-being in the aftermath of the climaxes they had both reached. Then the unfamiliar foreign telephone, cutting into drowsiness, rousing the mind.

'Van Lederer,' he grunted into the telephone. The woman at his side, one breast free of the sheets as she turned in her half-sleep, moaned softly. He had, as he always did, left the number with the Embassy's security staff. But it had to be something of an emergency before they would presume to intrude upon the open secret of his nights with Mme. Vigny.

'Sorry, General . . .' There was a faint hint of amusement from the other end. 'We have a slight emergency on our hands. Source "Franklin" is arriving in Paris tomorrow – you're delegated to meet him. There are some broad hints that he's loaded for bear, and Langley won't trust my staff to handle it. They're afraid he wants out . . .'

Van Lederer sat straight up in the bed. The bedclothes slid from his mistress's back, baring the arch of the spine.

'You have to call me at *this* time, when we're worrying about tomorrow?' There was a rough humour in the voice, and a sense of shared secrets and actions more arcane, and more satisfying, than those which he indulged with the woman.

'Sorry, General. Langley sent us the message "Priority Blue", and that meant waking you up. Sorry.' There was a shared intimacy, a joke ebbing between the two men.

'O.K., Buckholz. I accept your apologies. But why me? They've got time to fly someone over here by tomorrow.' There was no irritation in the voice.

'You're the man, sir. You set up "Franklin" and you're still here in Paris.'

'And you can bet Langley knows *why* I'm still in Paris!' Van Lederer looked at the woman beside him, who had moved again in the bed so that the breasts, slightly flattened as she lay on her back, were exposed. There was an encouraged lust at the sight of the helpless, unconscious nakedness. Increased, perhaps, by the anticipation of the meeting with 'Franklin'.

'See you then, General.'

'What's his cover – how did he contact? I don't want to

walk into some KGB outfit trying to lift me or someone like me.'

'Normal channel. He's inspecting the Resident and his personnel at the Embassy in Paris. Slacking on the job, or something. Or maybe they suddenly don't like the idea that their boy Lidbrooke is dead . . . No sweat, General. It's all above board. Just watch the contact. He's too valuable to bring over unless it's necessary, and he's got good stuff – the best. He may just be a little windy. Oh – and there's confirmation from London about Lidbrooke's accident – Langley is sending flowers and a cable of congratulations.'

'Yeah, sure. Now will you let me get some sleep?' Again, the amused tone.

'Sleep, General? G'night.' The receiver purred in van Lederer's ear.

'Sure,' he murmured 'Why not sleep?' He put down the receiver, and lay back in the bed, his head against the quilted headboard, hands knotted behind his head.

'Franklin' was his baby, that much was true. Three years ago, in Washington, he had helped turn him into a double, working for the CIA. And 'Franklin' had the best motives, it appeared – fear and disillusionment. He went back to Moscow, promoted, known only to a handful of top advisers around the Director at Langley, and with contact with only one of the security staff at the US Embassy in Moscow. Van Lederer, almost as a reward, had got the chairmanship of the NATO Senior Intelligence Committee soon after 'Franklin' returned to a top job in the First Chief Directorate. 'Franklin' was a winner from the beginning – a beautiful, beautiful winner.

Van Lederer had had one other telephone call that day, to remind him of the existence of someone called Richard Gardiner. He had had to be reminded who the hell the man was. 1944. A hell of a long time ago, more than a world away. This guy coming back for revenge, like some ghost in a play. Looking not for him and Constant, not then, but for Etienne de Vaugrigard. Etienne, chicken Etienne, running for his life . . .

Van Lederer enjoyed his superiority over other men, as over women. He was not frightened by the idea of Gardiner, the man who had gone down to the cellars of the Avenue Foch with Renaud. It was crazy to be scared. Constant, in his infuriating cold voice, had supplied him with a timely reminder.

He shook his head and looked around the darkened bedroom. The illuminated face of his watch told him the time was three-thirty. Ridiculous. There was no reality in the idea of Gardiner, none at all. He proposed to take no action about it.

He stirred in the bed, and touched the woman on the breast. She muttered in her sleep. Suddenly aroused by the unconscious display of nakedness, he pulled back the sheets and browsed his lips against her skin, against the flat stomach, the pubic hair below it. He felt himself harden, and the woman's legs move. He moved his tongue against her skin, pushing it deeper until the thighs parted. It was piquant, irresistible, the fact that she was still asleep. Helpless nakedness. He thrust his tongue against the softness, felt the body tremble against him. He would not wake her, not yet . . .

Latymer picked up the telephone. Its noise had insisted until his dreams could no longer contain it, and he had woken. He pulled the instrument onto the pillow beside him, then clumsily fitted the receiver to his cheek, the action of a man relearning some part of his life. His watch-face informed him it was six. Faint outline of the window, curtains lightening.

'Yes?'

It was Haussman. Latymer came bolt awake as the voice's first words chilled him.

'Hilary – I am as angry at this as you will be. Richard Gardiner escaped from police custody two hours ago!'

'What?'

'I am afraid it is true. He got out through a toilet window in the Tours police headquarters – how he managed it . . . ? Of course, the police have been incredibly stupid. They did not realise quite what kind of a man he was . . .'

Latymer felt a strange thrill run through him. He said, 'Are they searching now?'

'Naturally. And I am drafting some of my men into the area . . .'

'Good. But they won't catch him, you know. Why weren't you there?'

'I was. I did not offer to accompany him to the lavatory, however.' There was a sense of irony not entirely divorced from humour in the voice.

'It means he'll be after van Lederer, doesn't it?'

'Yes. I shall warn the General, and offer him protection – if that will be of any use.'

'Perhaps. Very well, Jean-Jacques. I'll call on van Lederer myself, and put him in the picture with regard to Gardiner.'

'Thank you, Hilary. It would not be politic for someone like General van Lederer to be killed on French soil, especially by an Englishman.'

'I understand,' Latymer replied, suddenly frosty. 'It would not be politic in any way for another death to occur in this matter. I'll speak to him. Tell him I'm on my way when you call him. And will you screen him as from now?'

'Of course. I have given orders, though I do not expect Gardiner to have been able to make his way to Paris in so short a time . . . The General is staying at the Hotel Belvedere in the Rue St. Antoine. He is with a married lady, and I do not expect him to leave the hotel with any great speed.' There was a dry chuckle at the other end, then: 'Au 'voir, Hilary.'

'Goodbye.'

Latymer put down the receiver, and the impressions and reactions tumbled through his mind; transmitted, it appeared, to his hand, which began to tremble as soon as he released the receiver. He stirred himself, and sat up in bed.

His reactions were complex, diffuse, and difficult to comprehend clearly. He had grown accustomed to not examining his thoughts in the past months. Now, the only simplicity of the matter lay in the enormity that Gardiner, free, was a danger to US Army Intelligence, the NATO Intelligence hierarchy, and the SIS: a rogue element in their complex infrastructures, a loose piece rattling in their works.

To kill van Lederer, then Constant.

Unthinkable. They were far too valuable to their respective, and common, agencies to be sacrificed to any wild impulse towards a vague larger justice. Expediency demanded that Gardiner be stopped; at the same time a vague, infinite pity settled on Latymer, though he could not precisely define its object.

Gardiner would be killed, he acknowledged, as soon as Constant realised his danger. Because Gardiner had been good – was still good, amoral, clever, lethal. The morning seemed cold, though he knew quite certainly that it was close and hot, as the night had been. He admitted, as the tremor passed through his body, that there was no control he could exercise over Gardiner.

The telephone rang, startling him, even as he considered what calls he should make himself.

It was six-thirty.

'Yes – oh, what do you want, McNeil?'

'Sir, I have a message for you, priority, and direct from Deputy, timed at six-seventeen. Shall I read it out?'

'Yes.' There was a hollow feeling, like foreboding.

'It reads – "Imperative you return London immediate. No discussion possible on this" – that's it, sir. Nothing else.'

'Damn!'

'What was that, sir?'

'Nothing, McNeil. Thank you. When is the first London flight out of Orly?'

'Nine-thirty, sir.'

'Get me on it.'

'I already have, sir.'

'Thank you, McNeil.'

He put down the receiver absently, as if he had already forgotten its existence. *Why?* The question was absolute. Constant had ordered him back to London. What in the devil's name did he intend to *do* about Gardiner?

As he got out of bed, the thought was like a heavy weight of undigested matter in his stomach. Constant was consigning Gardiner to van Lederer. And the CIA. There could be little doubt of it. It was typical of Constant – have Gardiner finished off by someone like Napier, only with an American suit. There need be no unnecessary fuss in Whitehall. Latymer cursed as he began to shave. He felt separated by a strange, haunting gulf from Richard Gardiner.

It was ten before van Lederer arrived at the US Embassy. He went directly to the third-floor office, overlooking the avenues of trees bordering the Champs Elysées, which was normally set aside for him during his visit to Paris. Then he summoned Buckholz, the Embassy CIA Resident. As soon as the bullet-headed, square features appeared round his door, he threw up his hands, and said, 'Hell, Charley – what do we do?' There was no trace of nerves in his voice or behaviour, only an impatience as at some small part of a jigsaw working loose – threatening the whole design.

'What with "Franklin", you mean?'

'Yes, with "Franklin". I've got to talk to him, and I've got to be free to do it. We can't have saturation surveillance and a Screen when I meet with him. Moscow Centre is bound to be taking precautions, and they'll spot one of your guys if there're too many.' He rubbed his cheeks with his big, hairy hands. 'This guy could wreck it – understand?'

He looked into Buckholz's eyes, knowing his competence, knowing him destined for high rank at Langley, given time and a clean record. If he believed . . .

Van Lederer smeared the thought like wiping away a drop of spilt liquid. He would not admit that he was afraid, fearful because of the weight of the past, the sense of what must have been done to the Englishman who now threatened him. He was relieved when he saw Buckholz nod.

'I agree, General. We've got to look out for "Franklin". The whole operation could come unglued if this guy Gardiner gets onto you.' His pale eyes widened. 'Hell. Imagine if he got "Franklin" while trying to get you! The whole contact has just the sort of opportunity he would be looking for.'

'Right. So I want action on this, Charley – real action. I want this guy wiped, and quick!'

'O.K., General, it's your show. What about the French? They're covering you at the moment.'

'Yeah. I'll get that cleared, and your boys can take over. If "Franklin" comes in today and wants to meet, he'll have to wait until tomorrow. That gives you twenty-four hours. This guy doesn't know me, but he'll know who and what I am. So he may come here looking.' Van Lederer turned in his chair and waved his arm at the window, through which sunlight filtered, slatted by the blinds. 'He'll be out there, somewhere, waiting to pick me up. He'll have at least some description from de Vaugrigard, the guy he knocked off.' His voice suddenly became harsh, more violent as if he were attempting to diminish the threat that Gardiner posed. 'He wants me, and he wants me bad. But he's alone, got no help from anyone. You can get him for me, Charley – get him.'

'Sure, General.' Buckholz saw the General's body stiffen against the implicit comfort of his tone. 'We'll get him. Don't worry about it.'

'I only worry about "Franklin", Charley – remember that.' His eyes were hard, shallow grey surfaces in his expressionless face.

'Sure, General. But we could do with some shots of this guy. It would help. And we got to make sure the French keep their noses out. If you want this to be a kill, then we got to have a clear field of fire – real and diplomatic.'

'O.K., I'll get onto that. I'll talk to Constant in London, and then to the SDECE. Who's the man?'

'Haussman – you know him?'

'Yeah. He'll swallow an operation from us – until someone gets hurt, then he'll have his mob and the Sureté crawling all over us. He's typical French Intelligence. Wouldn't stop us, but couldn't pass up an opportunity to kick us in the balls, either.'

Buckholz smiled. 'O.K., General. I'll get the team together, and bring them back to you.'

When Buckholz had left, van Lederer wasted no time, instructing the secure switchboard to put through a call to Queen Anne's Gate, and Constant. The connection took seven minutes, and a number of code-names, to establish, then the American heard the familiar drawling of Constant's voice. He received, suddenly, an image of the Bloomsbury house, and he could see the back of Etienne de Vaugrigard's head and Constant's thin, ascetic face with its humourless smile and infinite superiority.

The two men spoke as if they still worked in the closest co-operation.

'So you want me to sweep the shit up from your doorstep, Michael?'

'Ah, Eugene – good morning. How are you, and how is the weather there? It's a cool but sunny day here.'

'Cut it, Michael!' van Lederer snapped with a fierce amusement. 'You know why I want to talk.'

'Ah, yes. Our common ghost.'

'Yes, that's him. Jesus, I never even met this guy – I don't know what he looks like, and I hardly remembered his name. Now he comes out from under some stone. Where's he been for the last nineteen years, for Christ's sake?' Van Lederer paused, then snapped, 'I'm meeting "Franklin" today or tomorrow–you know what that means. This guy could blow the whole damn thing sky-high – that's all that's wrong at this end! How are *you* feeling?' After a silence, Constant said, 'Of course, you'll have to silence him. He must be got out of the way, as soon as possible. How will you do it?'

'Jesus, you're a bastard! You pulled your guy out, because you knew it forced me to take care of this nut! And you wouldn't have to get your lily-white hands dirty! You're a bastard, man!'

'Sorry, Eugene. I didn't realise about "Franklin", which does rather complicate things. However, if that is the case, it's all to the good my man is out of the way – wouldn't you say? What can I do to help?'

'Photographs. And as much information as your man has, the one you upped and outed this morning.'

'Very well, I'll do that. By the way, did you have a word with Lidbrooke before his – demise?'

'Yeah. I wished him all the best. Nice touch, uh?'

'Quite. I'll get those things wireprinted to you as soon as possible. You might get the same sort of thing from the French ...'

'I'll try. Don't take any wooden nickels, Michael.' He put the receiver down.

Now that he had spoken to Constant, he had minimised the problem. The discussion with Buckholz, and the confidence of the Englishman, conspired to make Gardiner a puny enemy, impotent and incapable. The sexual imagery satisfied him. Like his control of women, he sensed he controlled this situation. He plucked at his nose with thumb and forefinger, his forehead creased with thought. Now that he considered it, he felt a certain satisfaction in having to confront a palpable enemy.

If that was the way Constant wanted it, then he would get Gardiner's head on a plate. He no longer resented Constant's implied challenge to his ability to survive – now, he welcomed it.

'This situation has got entirely out of hand,' Constant remarked to Aubrey and Latymer before motioning them to be seated. There was a long moment when they were made to feel like miscreant juniors brought to the house-master's study; then he had snapped out the single sentence.

'I understand your irritation, Deputy. But this was in no way an official enquiry by the department – or any department, come to that.' Aubrey was at his most bland and comfortable. The blue eyes were ingenuously wide, the features round in baby-like innocence. Constant refused to be humoured by the performance.

'I should have been informed what Latymer was doing in France – I don't like these *private* enquiries. They usually have the messy incompetence of the Irishmen who offer to tarmac one's drive – they are as likely to tarmac the lawn!' He glared frostily at each of them in turn. 'Even if you began in this cavalier manner, it should never have been allowed to reach this stage! This man has been wandering freely around France, doing what damage he will. You, Latymer, should have informed the French of everything you knew – *everything*! And you should have let them take care of him.'

Aubrey glanced at Latymer, and saw the cold blaze in his eyes, the pinching together of the nostrils; he shook his head in warning, but Latymer took no notice.

'Take care of him, Deputy?' The voice was superbly modulated, despite the anger which rubbed at its veneer like sandpaper. 'You had two attempts yourself, once upon a time. Gardiner appears to have survived those without too much trouble!'

Constant's eyes blazed. He had expected to chafe both men, but he had not expected either of them to strike at him.

'What do you mean by that remark, Latymer?'

'Simply this, Deputy. The "Wolfgroup" left Richard Gardiner for dead. It cannot be surprised that an agent of his dedication and calibre should come back from wherever he went and seek them out.' Latymer sat back in his chair and studied the wall to the left of Constant's head. Behind Constant, the bright morning filtered through the curtains and the sounds of the minimal traffic through Queen Anne's Gate were excluded by the soundproofing of the first-floor office. Constant had this office at the headquarters of the SIS, and another, more official, habitation at the Foreign Office.

'I see. And, no doubt, your misguided sense of fair play would like to give him a sporting chance – mm?' Constant was gratified by the sense of complex and contradictory feelings that he saw mirrored in Latymer's eyes.

Aubrey said, to mollify, 'What do we do, Deputy? Now that the situation is here, I think recriminations are futile. What is to be done about "Achilles"?'

Constant glared at Aubrey, suspecting some hidden significance in the use of the old code-name. 'Quite. There i no point whatsoever. I will explain my feelings on the matter Simply put, they are these. I think that Gardiner is being operated by someone else. Whether he knows it or not. No private revenge takes this long to work itself out. And be sides, he's been far too successful to be working alone.'

He allowed them time to digest the opinion.

'On what do you base your assumption, Deputy?' Aubrey asked.

'Suspicion, mostly. But other things. Such as the news blackout on the murder of Dupuy – we didn't request it. And his escape from the French police. Both points are most questionable.'

Latymer said, 'There's one other thing – the death of Perrier. He was released very conveniently for Gardiner. Though, as it turned out, he could have learned nothing from him.' Constant looked at Latymer, and accepted that the man's anger was past. He had given both Latymer and Aubrey a sufficient bone to occupy them.

'Then it has to be the French,' Aubrey said, unconvinced.

'Not necessarily. What motive would they have? Frenchmen may be involved, but that's something else. SDECE that most nymphomaniac of intelligence services, may have been penetrated yet again.' He permitted himself a wintry smile for a moment. Aubrey chuckled, genuinely amused.

'I agree,' Latymer added. 'The release of Perrier worried me. But, if Gardiner didn't learn anything from him, which he could hardly have done in the circumstances – then who told him about Etienne?' He stared at them both for a moment – then realised that he had admitted to himself, for perhaps the first time, the ramifications Constant had erected around his Samaritan task. The recognition silenced him.

'Well?' Constant said with a grimace of satisfaction. 'What are the results of your new deliberations? Enlighten us, Latymer, if you please.'

'There are – things that might support your contention, Deputy. Things I hadn't considered . . .' It was appalling, as if Gardiner were being betrayed all over again. 'But they don't make sense,' he added feebly.

Constant steepled his long fingers, and looked at them over the spire. He said, 'Let us use what minds we have to merely posit a likelihood. Revenge, if you like. Simple revenge. For Blake and Philby, perhaps. Or merely to – weaken the succession?' There was a slight pause. 'I do make a rather important, if not expansive, target, gentlemen. And Eugene van Lederer thrown in as a bonus when Lidbrooke or someone else finds out about the old "Wolf-group"?'

'You make it sound like a former pupils' organisation,' Latymer observed acidly. 'Was it? And how did the secret leak out?'

'I have no idea. But it could have. You must have known in SOE about the rumours – and there must have been people in the Abwehr and the Gestapo, as well as the SS, who understood what was going on. I don't know how your man got the names, but apparently he did. Then Gardiner is primed, by this unknown or by Moscow Centre, and away the thing goes. Running on castors.' He raised his hands in the air to signify an explosion.

Latymer, watching the imaginary cloud rise above the desk, said, 'Ingenious, Deputy. But why not the simple revenge of Gardiner for what you did to him? It makes a weird kind of sense. At least, it would to Gardiner – the Dupuy thing having triggered it all. Besides, how could anyone keep such close observation, predict his behaviour?'

'You're not surprised at it. Why should anyone be who had studied the subject?'

Aubrey said softly, 'Then we ought to take him alive, if possible.'

'Not necessarily. I don't think he knows anything.'

'Do we have to kill *everyone*, Deputy?' Aubrey asked in exasperation. He stared at Constant for a long time, then subsided into his seat again.

'It is, in this case, not up to me. I'm afraid that the CIA insist on taking the greatest care of General van Lederer, and I have no power to prevent any steps they may take to do so. They would hardly be likely to accept our unproven word for what is happening.' He smiled.

'But, if what you suppose turned out to be true, shouldn't you at least inform the French?'

'The SDECE can clean out its own place.'

Latymer, watching carefully, considered that Constant was masking a distinct self-preservation beneath his elaborate theory. It was all possible, he admitted – but less likely than the fact that Gardiner wanted revenge, even after all this time. After all, neither of the two men with him had actually *talked* to Gardiner as he had done. Gardiner was certainly in no doubts as to why he was doing things.

The telephone rang as Aubrey was about to speak. Constant picked up the receiver with irritation, listened, frowned and then put it down. He said, to Latymer, 'I'm afraid that was the hospital – your wife. They think you ought to be there as soon as possible. Naturally, you may leave at once.' He tried to appear concerned, but failed. Latymer felt the news like a blow to the stomach that he had prepared for, but which still surprised him. He muttered something to both of them, and excused himself. Aubrey signally avoided looking at Constant for a long time after Latymer had closed the door behind him.

He could not say, precisely, when she died. It was the final betrayal, the last moment of inattention in the sequence of indifferent moments that seemed to make up love. He noticed, though that seemed a work of protraction rather than a moment, that she had stopped breathing, that the white sheet, which cancelled her body, had stopped rising and falling. He had not been able to hear her quiet breathing. He felt obscurely cheated, as if she should have breathed raggedly loud, or death should have shaken her throat like a rattle. It was meaningless, the manner of her going. No climax at all, to anything.

They had made sure she would die in her drugged sleep. It was a mockery, ghastly.

In final mockery – after he had bent to her nostrils, wanting to feel the breath caress his cheek, and then had reseated himself – there appeared no change in her. Even the pallor of her skin retained the grey tinge he had come to associate with those last weeks. He could not bear, suddenly, to be in the room with the body. The woman, in company with all the dead, had wrested herself from him, given the lie to the life they had had together.

And there was nothing in him. He was bereft of emotion. The tearing pain had gone, as if she had released her grip. There was no flicker of light through leaves such as her pain, her dying, her ageing might have induced. Nothing.

He made the arrangements for the removal of the body, and resisted the specious comfort that was offered him. The day was bright still when he went outside, the early evening providing a sunset glow ridiculous and inappropriate.

It was fifteen minutes, and ten miles, from the hospital before he had to stop the car, and vomit into the thick, tufted grass beneath a dark hedge. It was not for a long time after that his body stopped shaking from the spasms, and he was able to drive on, in the direction of the empty

Chelsea house. By that time, his numb mind had returned to
life, and he could recall her clearly – so many painful
images.

Gardiner knew, at that point in time when the traffic began
to thin as the last of the rush-hour travellers deserted the
centre of the city, that however clever he had been, or however lucky, there was now no other step he could take. In
the Champs Elysées, he hated the sense of being alone, a
before he had cherished it, because isolation now mean
powerlessness. In trying to locate van Lederer, he dare no
reveal his interest to anyone. The stake-out of the US
Embassy was necessary, but grew more futile as the hour
dragged by.

He had reached Paris half-way through the morning
thumbing a lift for most of the way in a truck, once he had
got clear of the immediate area of Tours in a stolen car
The car he had crashed into the Loire.

He had hired another car in Paris, and it was parked a
the Rond Point, a distance away, but safe. To hire it, h
had used the last of the identities with which he had bee
furnished by stolen *cartes*. He was Armand Skrela, from
Toulouse. On holiday, without his family, in the wicked city
To accompany the *carte*, he wore a bright striped shirt, ligh
slacks, and sunglasses. Suspended from his neck by a leathe
strap was a camera to complete the disguise.

He began to pick out the surveillance activity as the hour
passed. It informed him that van Lederer was in the Embassy
and that he was expected. He wore the sunglasses, the
discarded them – left the camera in the car, wore a ligh
jacket, then discarded it again. He used the other side of th
Champs Elysées, and the metro tunnel to cross the Place de
la Concorde. He identified the pattern, and saw that as ye
they had no photographs of him and were hunting blind
He kept moving, always with apparent purposelessness, and
tried never to reappear in the same place in exactly th
same disguise. It was difficult, it stretched the nerves. But i

obviated the need to ponder his situation. Only the successive moments were real.

He made one telephone call, posing as a British journalist, to NATO headquarters, and was informed that General van Lederer was not in residence, but that he might like to try the US Embassy. And he had searched in the photo-library of *Paris Soir*, until he found an old photograph of the man. And that was all the pressure he could apply.

When he returned to the sandy-coloured Simca he had hired, to collect the camera again, he found a large buff envelope on the driver's seat, and no evidence that the car had been forced.

He sat in the seat, shaking. Clumsily he tore open the flap of the envelope and fished out a clutch of glossy prints. They were all of van Lederer, neatly labelled on the back in ink. He was shocked into stiffness, a paralysis of the will and muscles. Had the surveillance team found him then, they could have taken him. He could not even control the sweat breaking on his forehead, or the trickle of coldness on his sides. The car was stifling, and he wound down the window.

And the release of Perrrier, and Latymer's evident shock, as at some betrayal, and his escape from the police – so easy, with security so unexpectedly slack.

It was someone helping him – someone with influence. As he opened the parcel of his fears, clumsily and greedily, this was his conclusion. Not that the photographs were a trick. He was a cog, part of a larger design or pattern. It appalled him. Angered him too, in an extreme reaction to the loss of solitariness.

Why?

He was being given van Lederer – he remembered, with an effort, that the man was high in NATO Intelligence, a fact Latymer had confirmed – on a platter. Free, *gratis*, for nothing. Someone was concerned to make van Lederer his creature, his for the taking. Someone wanted van Lederer dead.

'*Why?*' This time the thought reached his voice, and he startled himself.

As if with the shock of cold water, the face of a passer-by, glancing at him momentarily because of his stifled cry, woke his will.

He had to think ...

Someone wanted van Lederer, perhaps Constant as well, out of the way. It had to be an intelligence operation. KGB, or some satellite service taking its orders from Moscow Centre. *Did he baulk at it on the grounds of patriotism?*

No.

Decisive. It *was* simple. Even as the implement of an enemy, he still *wanted* the thing that others seemed to want. *Yes, he wanted it.*

He saw, as if through a tiny gap in a door, the blank future that lay in front of him – and it turned the scales. He was committed, whether he wished it or no. Dupuy and Perrier and de Vaugrigard were dead, and he was now pursued for those murders. It did not matter who was operating him, even controlling him. Or why.

It was a bleak moment, so bleak that he thrust his head out of the window to suck in the dry air outside, redolent of petrol fumes and the dusty scent of trees and flowers in the middle of a city. It did not clear his head, or drive away the tunnel-like straightness of the path he found before him. There was no driving that away.

In the end, it was his stubborn narrowness of mind that rescued him. He would not open up the past or the present, but move across them as across treacherous, rotten ice.

He closed down the vision of the future, which winked out like a screen switched off. There was a very limited time-scale, and a double object. Two deaths, and completion of everything when the second man died. *Just think of that. Just that.*

His head was dizzy with effort when he got out of the car. All the time his mind had been in turmoil, he realised, he had been studying with some other part of his awareness the photographs of van Lederer. That pleased him, the functioning of the personality he most admired, the complete and utter man of action. He had begun to live in his own dream of himself. To do that was like living with an unsuspected amnesia. A surface, without depth.

It was a kind of freedom, that. At least, he clung to the idea that it was.

He knew they must have picked him up – at least, they were suspicious that he was out there, somewhere on the Champs Elysées – when he saw van Lederer leave in the open sports car. It was the evidently unsuitable car that gave him the answer. It was a dummy run, to draw him out. He stayed where he was, the single still point, it seemed, in the moving scene, until the second car left the gates ...

He picked out two other cars, parked, their drivers' faces oblique and anonymous inside them. They were waiting for him. He remained still, until the desire in him to move, to pursue, was as tangible as an itch. Van Lederer crossed the Place de la Concorde in the sports car; he saw the mane of grey hair above the civilian clothes as they blended with the thicker traffic, heading down towards the last set of lights in front of Les Invalides. Then he lost sight of him, and walked slowly back towards the Rond Point, watching two well-dressed children strolling with a nanny.

He walked on beyond the hire car, and did not return from his window-shopping until he had reasserted his tourist mask. He waited across the street until he was sure there was no one watching the car, then crossed to it, climbed in, and drove out into the Champs Elysées, heading up the avenue towards the Arc de Triomphe. It was time for him to find somewhere to stay, just for that night. Then he would come back.

As he drove, the envelope lay on the passenger seat, at the edge of eye-sight. He began to wonder about it, but without any questioning of his own direction.

'L'Etranger' lay on a comfortable sofa in the lounge of an

apartment on the Avenue de Wagram, one of the thorough-
fares running away from the whirlpool of the Arc de
Triomphe, as Gardiner's car passed beneath his third floor
window, unobserved.

One of his men had placed the buff envelope in the Simca,
just as another of his men had facilitated Gardiner's escape
the previous night.

That had been a desperate, hurried action. To learn that
the Englishman, Latymer, had cornered Gardiner in
Etienne's château at Azay was an unexpected shock, however close Latymer had always appeared to his quarry.
Latymer had always, he admitted, been a rogue element in
his calculations concerning Gardiner.

The man drew on his cigarette, and puffed the smoke
towards the high, ornate ceiling of the lounge. His stern face
was relaxed, but the muscles seemed habitually tight, the
expression of his determined will, whatever his superficial
mood. At present he possessed a certain sense of well-being,
but without absolute confidence. He had spent twenty-four
hours with the nuts and bolts of his complex operation, and
had almost lost sight of its larger design.

He had shown his hand in the photographs of van Lederer.
And he wondered whether Gardiner had opened the case
of his camera and found the pictures of Catherine Vigny,
the woman who might flush van Lederer out into Gardiner's
fire. Van Lederer was in her company in two of the shots,
and her address had been pencilled on the back of one of
them.

He was almost certain that he could predict Gardiner's
reaction. His whole operation had been based on a correct
reading of the man, and thus far, events had robed themselves as he wished and predicted. But, with his primary
targets alerted as they now were, he had had to declare his
hand. Gardiner worked best against the odds. In this case . . . ?

He got up, and crossed the carpet with a heavy tread. He
opened a delicate cabinet that seemed threatened by his
bulk as he stood before it, and took out a bottle and a glass.

Pernod. He poured himself a large measure, added water and then returned to the sofa, sipping thoughtfully. The sharp aniseed taste on his tongue pleased him, and he raised his glass silently in salute to someone not in the room – perhaps only to himself.

Naturally, when the operation was over, he would meet Gardiner. He relished the thought. He had wished it to come as a complete surprise, but perhaps it did not matter.

He sighed, a sound strangely loud in the empty room. The CIA might use the woman to bring Gardiner out. He would have to anticipate that. That might prove unfortunate.

Of course he had proof, and he might have done it another way. But proof could always be labelled forgery or fake, and he might have come under suspicion as its author. Gardiner was an opportunity heaven-sent. A human bomb, planted at the door of the two men he had to destroy.

At eight, Paris local time, KGB Colonel Innokenti Vassilyich Petrovich, source 'Franklin', stepped off the Aeroflot flight to Orly, dressed in civilian clothes but making no other concessions to secrecy or a low profile by his manner or bearing. It would have been evident to anyone watching with a trained eye that a high-ranking officer of the Committee for State Security had arrived. A note, together with a photographic record, was made by the SDECE team, and a CIA officer also recorded the arrival with a certain satisfaction and excitement.

Petrovich was greeted by two men from the Soviet Embassy, with whom he shook hands rather reluctantly, and on whose part there was a marked deference towards him. They walked quickly through the diplomatic lounge, where his official accreditation was accepted by the passport official. His single suitcase joined him there, and neither it nor his briefcase was subjected to inspection.

A black saloon, a Mercedes rather than a Zil, was waiting for him. Petrovich was installed in the rear seat, and the two men with a coarser-grained sense of self-importance slid into the front of the car, separated from Petrovich by thick glass.

While the car purred towards the city, Petrovich smoked the American cigarettes which he obtained cheaply at the official KGB shop across Dzerzhinsky Square from the Centre, and perused some papers. The papers referred to his supposed inspection of the Resident and his staff, and to a new initiative to penetrate the SDECE which he was intended to implement.

There was no nervousness in anticipation of the meeting with van Lederer; instead, a cautious self-congratulation, a pervasive, though subtle, sense of well-being.

CHAPTER ELEVEN

VENERY

HAVING slept well and shaved and bathed in a leisurely fashion, Petrovich visited the KGB Resident. He was dressed in a dark grey suit with white chalkstripe, and wore a striped shirt and bright tie. It was a conscious effort to rid himself of his Soviet trappings. Bukhov, the Resident, was dressed in his normal attire, the uniform of an Embassy chauffeur. He shared the same rank as Petrovich in the KGB, in common with most of the senior Residents, but in Paris a lieutenant-colonel fronted for him; he it was who strutted, ordered, was photographed and filed as the Resident, while Bukhov went about his real business.

Petrovich had let his hair grow longer, in a more Western and less military fashion. Bukhov's dark hair was clipped short and shaved over his ears, so that the skull there shone in grey, oiled bristles. His thick neck threatened the tight uniform collar. When Petrovich found him, he was seated in the small rest-room allocated to the chauffeurs, which also served as his office. It was in the underground garage, and was soundproofed.

'Well, Innokenti Vassilyich – you slept well, I hope?'

'Indeed, Sergei Kuzmich. I thank you. A very comfortable room.' There was the sense of the two men sparring, but only as a preliminary and superficial exercise, as if they were enjoying some course of fitness exercises for the intelligence.

'It is arranged – the contact with "Wolverine",' Bukhov said. 'The fourteenth choice of location, at lunchtime. The Luxembourg will be crowded at that time. I have had prepared a selection of sandwiches which will assist your cover ...' Bukhov smiled. 'Your Western persona is most impressive!'

'Too obvious, you mean?'

'No, not at all. Very French businessman, I should say. A good choice, though perhaps the suit is a little dark for the summer — carry the jacket, perhaps?'

Petrovich nodded.

'What of the Lidbrooke business? It *is* over now, is it not?'

'I am fairly certain that it is. It was handled most carefully, and there were no mistakes. Lidbrooke is, I am certain, accepted as our "mole". Swift action has a conviction of its own, an inertia which persuades ... ?' Bukhov smiled, showing strong teeth. He was a man still in the prime of years, though the short haircut and the thick nose gave him an older, more peasant-like appearance than was the truth. Like all the younger generation of foreign Residents, he was a graduate of the KGB training school and of the Lenin University.

Petrovich nodded, apparently satisfied. He had met Bukhov on each of his visits to Paris as source 'Franklin', and he liked and trusted the man. He was calm, efficient, and not hidebound like many of the older, more senior men at the Centre, Beria's survivors and those who had been trained in the NKVD and the MGB.

'I agree. It was a good choice of subject, and a better removal than might have been expected in such a hurry. You are to be congratulated on picking Lidbrooke as a possible scapegoat. When I supplied Rollin, who is *very* persuasive in bed, I gather, Lidbrooke jumped into the trap. He was a libidinous fool, as his dossier always suggested.' He paused, then, changing the subject, said, 'I have to provide the "Wolverine" with information that satisfies the suddenness of this meeting. I have prepared documents that suggest I may be under suspicion by the SID, and another set from the last three meetings of the Politburo Security Sub-Committee which suggest the introduction of sweeping changes in the structure and manning of our organisation. Though I will plead with the Americans to be got out,

Langley will be tempted by this great prize, and order me back. No doubt they will promise me the earth. Jam tomorrow is, I believe, the expression.'

Bukhov laughed. 'Will you ever go over, Innokenti Vassilyich?'

'It is not beyond the bounds of possibility.' He smiled sardonically. 'But only when the Centre can be certain that I have done enough to merit re-employment within the CIA. When that position is achieved, I shall scream to be got out!'

'Very loudly, I have no doubt.'

'What are the arrangements for this lunchtime contact?'

'The usual – very sparse. You will follow the prescribed pattern of movements from here, and the tail-car will break down at a predetermined point. You will not, of course, realise this, and the relief car we send out will not find you until after your meeting. I suggest you are especially careful in trying to lose the tail-car *after* the breakdown, to convince the Americans of your fear of our people.' Petrovich nodded. 'There will be at least one man in the gardens. He will be your emergency bell, should you need one ...'

Petrovich was already shaking his head, but he said, 'Of course. But the "Franklin" cover is intact, Sergei. It was not my danger that worried the Centre, but the establishment of the SO-4 department specifically to find our "mole".'

'Which reminds me – two of their men were in on the Lidbrooke thing – Aubrey, the small, fat one, and Latymer, his senior assistant. Both of them have now returned to London, I believe.'

'Good. All is arranged then. All we need now from my meeting with the "Wolverine" is a full report on the sessions of the NATO Senior Intelligence Committee, together with CIA reaction to the death of Lidbrooke.' He looked at his watch. 'Send for some coffee, Sergei – we have time for a cup.'

Van Lederer listened to the voice of Catherine Vigny, and

sensed how well she had been coached and controlled by
Gardiner before he allowed her to make the call. Obviously
she was fully aware of what she was doing, and by now she
was convinced that her own survival depended on the
quality of her performance. Had he not been warned about
Gardiner, he might have believed her.

The story she told concerned her husband, who had
written from Bonn in reference to certain rumours which
had reached him. He was threatening to expose van Lederer
to scandal. It was a very good performance, he admitted.
The girl was an accomplished actress. He looked across at
Buckholz, on the extension, and saw the frown of concentration he was employing to hide his sense of success. Van
Lederer himself felt a keen anticipation, a sense of the power
of the assassin in the dark room.

He let the woman continue, and was duly frightened,
and solicitous. Then he remarked at length that he was too
busy to come, and then, a further chord on the instrument
of Gardiner's belief, he argued that they had agreed he
should not be bothered by her in this way – he almost began
to quarrel with her.

Finally, he said, 'Catherine, it's damned inconvenient,
and probably damned stupid too, for me to come out there
to you. But, all right – give me half-an-hour, maybe an
hour . . .' He glanced at Buckholz, who nodded. 'I'll come,
so for God's sake get a grip on yourself!' He sounded
impatient, weary of her suddenly. 'Don't go to pieces. I'll
see you.'

He put down the telephone and exhaled loudly in unison
with Buckholz. It was as if neither man had breathed since
the call had been put through.

Then, staring at Buckholz, he said simply, 'Get him.'

Gardiner was suspicious, simply because the task he had
set the girl was an impossible one. She had been good and,
as he listened on the bedroom extension, watching her as
he did so in the long mirror on one wall as she sat in the

spacious lounge and made the call, he had to admit that
van Lederer sounded convinced. Yet . . .

It was the fact that van Lederer had to know about him,
that he would be cautious to a final, unguessable degree,
especially after the decoy run in the sports car had failed
to draw him out. He had not asked the girl to meet him on
some neutral ground – which had to indicate that he knew
Gardiner was there.

He put down the receiver and walked into the first-floor
lounge, its tall windows overlooking the Avenue Gabriel,
the heavy curtains pulled back and the sunlight pouring into
the room. He felt clean in that room, especially after the
night he had spent. He went to the window and looked out
at the Avenue Gabriel and its urbane affluence. He had
spent the night in a sordid, nameless hotel out among the
dirty sediment of workers' suburbs beyond the motorway
ring. He had found the snapshots of Catherine Vigny, and
her address scrawled on the back. He had felt the sense of
being the creature of another, and a communion with cold
shaving-water and grubby sheets. But he had come there,
and forced the woman to make her telephone call to the
'Wolverine'. He turned to the woman then, and saw that
she was exhausted, and suffering acute, if temporary,
remorse. He knew that the mood would pass, that before
long she would wish only to be absent when the act was
performed. She would feel nauseated at the prospect of
blood and violence, at the smell of fear, but not at her
betrayal of her lover. She might even worry about damage
to the carpet.

A little guilt might return later, before use and custom and
marital ordinariness made her secure. It was easy to despise
her, and perhaps he did so as an antidote to her undoubted
attractiveness. He felt, perhaps for the first time since the
end of his affair with the girl in Dorset, a sexual urge which
he disliked but could not ignore. She was still dressed in the
flimsy, clinging silk nightgown, with its narrow shoulder-
straps and low bodice. White, against the suntanned skin.

The shoulders were flawless, and he was reminded of his
wife. He decided to hate her as another cuckolder. Yet she
was immediately desirable. He did not know the other men
her body had been given to – except the 'Wolverine'.

'Well,' she said, and he could have sworn that she was
aware of the half-formed desires. 'I've done what you asked.
Now you can kill him – bastard!' The defiance was brittle,
temporary, and masked her own guilt.

'You have indeed, Madame – and very nicely too, if I
may say so.' He stood in front of her, and bowed ironically.
She curled her lip in contempt and fear, rubbing her arms
suddenly as if he had hurt her. In fact, he had not touched
her.

'What do we do now, eh?' she asked, seeming to taunt
him. 'Do we just sit here and wait for him to come?'

He sat down next to her on the low sofa, the cushions
seeming to climb round his limbs as if to hold and detain.

'I think we will,' he said. The gun was in the pocket of
his jacket now, as if to increase the ordinariness of the
morning now that the call had been made.

She said, 'Who are you? What is he to you?'

He shook his head, and was silent. She plucked at the
stuff of her nightgown absently but intently. She had aroused
her own curiosity now, and wished it satisfied. And she
seemed conscious of his proximity in a more evidently
sexual manner. It was an awareness she did not enjoy, he
could see. Yet it pressed her, perhaps now because her
sexuality seemed a way of ensuring her safety. He saw the
pout of her full lower lip, the slightest closing of the eyes.

He said, 'What about some coffee, Madame – would you
make me some?'

Catherine Vigny shrugged, stood up and moved out of
the room. She crossed a bar of sunlight, the motes leaping
around her like stars, the silk nightgown rustling. He followed her to the kitchen, where she seemed relieved seeing
the old housekeeper he had surprised when he made his entry
via the courtyard door, tied to a chair, wide-eyed but un-

harmed. Then she took little more notice of her. She filled a percolator and carried it back upstairs.

The percolator plopped rapidly in the silence of the room and the red light went on with a sigh. She poured coffee into a delicate cup and handed it to him. Her hand trembled very slightly.

She lit a cigarette. He sensed the suspension of thought, or perhaps the decision she had made. She was frightened because she knew nothing about him, therefore could not be certain of her own fate. She had decided to use her sexuality. She was displaying like some exotic bird. And he was, despite himself, increasingly sexually aware of her. His mood of anticipation at the possible meeting with van Lederer had become a desire to touch her.

He put down the empty, toy-like cup and reached across to her and cupped her breast in his hand. He felt the nipple harden involuntarily, and he squeezed the breast, flattened and pushed upwards gently. He watched her eyes – satisfaction, and perhaps pleasure. There was something of appetite in her, some ability to suspend awareness of her situation in favour of immediate desire. Her eyes were suddenly wide with challenge; she seemed to welcome his admission of desire, as if it contained him at her level, removed any lingering sense of his superiority or danger.

He said, 'Madame – I only wish I had the time – truly, I do.' Then he stood up, and smiled at her. He had decided the moment before that he would hurt her, insult her in order to reassert his superiority. He had not done so. It would have cheapened what he intended, the ritual of the slaughter, even further. The hand which had clasped her breast was hot, somehow soiled.

He added, 'I shall have to tie you up, Madame.' Her eyes were wide with a new fear. 'No, I shan't hurt you. But I think the General, your lover, suspects something ... No, I'm not blaming you, Madame. It is merely the nature of the beast. Now, if you would like to put on some sort of wrap,

in case of feeling cold . . .' She had become indifferent again,
sensing she was in no danger.

He tied her with cord from the curtains. There was no
need to hurt her, and he tied the knots expertly so that she
was incapable of freeing herself.

'It doesn't hurt?' he asked solicitously, and she shook her
head vaguely. 'Very good. Now I'll have to gag you, but I
sha'n't bruise your mouth. It won't be too uncomfortable . . .'
He used a silk scarf from a bedroom drawer. Her eyes
watched him with a resignation he was forced to admire, but
which he could not be certain was not stupidity or a total absence of imagination.

He crossed to the door, turned and nodded to her as she
sat trussed on the sofa, and then closed the door behind him.
He went downstairs, and checked the old woman's bonds.
She still seemed to resent him for the indignity she had under-
gone when he had removed her dentures before gagging her.
He let himself out and walked through the courtyard to the
front of the house. Only ten minutes since the call – hardly
time for them to stage anything.

The Simca was parked in the Avenue Matignon, around
the corner and two hundred yards away. Unsuspicious outside a restaurant. He walked to it, then he began studying
the Avenue Matignon, assessing it for his purposes.

He could not stay in the car. It was the first thing they
would be looking for, a man in a parked car – and he knew
it would be *they*, the unavoidable plural. He would be taking
on the resident CIA staff at the Embassy. A small, skilled
team – though perhaps not containing any top men who
had served tours of duty in East European embassies. They
would be young men learning the job, or second-rate older
men. He would have left then, but for the chance that van
Lederer, with such cover, might come himself, just to
observe.

There was nothing that would serve as an unobtrusive
vantage point. The avenue contained private apartments, a
few couturiers, art galleries, restaurants. It was busier now,

with shoppers and window-shoppers, delivery vans, and some through traffic between the Faubourg St. Honoré and the Champs Elysées. It would have to be a moving surveillance. He took the camera from the back seat, and hung it round his neck. Then he walked back to the Avenue Gabriel.

It was ten-fifteen when the first car arrived, parking well down the avenue from the Vigny house. Gardiner had strolled to the corner of the avenue, gazing into the plate-glass of the few shops in the Avenue Matignon. Casually, he came level with the car, and saw that van Lederer was not one of its three occupants. He knew then, with a sharp sense of disappointment, that he would be unlikely to show. This was the observation car, and he would have been in it had he intended a personal appearance.

He watched the other two cars arrive, and checked their occupants, then watched their approach to the house. He picked out the team's leader, and guessed that van Lederer had sent the Resident himself. He evaluated correctly the danger to himself.

Gardiner walked slowly back down the street into the Avenue Matignon until he reached the Simca. When he opened the door, he saw the buff envelope on the passenger seat. It shocked him, yet somehow he had expected it, even relied on it when he knew that van Lederer would not show. He turned the key in the ignition, and turned the car out behind a small van, then into the Avenue Gabriel. He passed the Vigny house, and saw two men in lightweight suits standing in the courtyard – glimpsed through the archway. One of them was smoking.

Through his disappointment, relief leaked like an odourless gas, exciting the nerves, pressing out drops of sweat on palms and forehead.

The buff envelope burned at the corner of his vision.

Van Lederer was in place in the gardens of the Luxembourg before eleven-thirty. He received a report from Buckholz that Catherine Vigny and her housekeeper were unharmed, and both of them had identified Gardiner as their intruder. The CIA team had scoured the avenue as soon as they discovered he was gone, but they found no trace of him. Then he had left the Embassy for his meeting with 'Franklin', a meeting which soon drove all thought of Gardiner from his mind.

'Franklin' was his control, and his contact, the KGB agent to whom he made his reports on the workings and decisions of the NATO Intelligence Committee. And this was to be his final report.

He parked his car in the Rue Gay Lussac and walked across the busy Place Edmond Rostand to the gardens. A CIA man followed him, and a second member of Buckholz's staff front-tailed him. He could see the man fifty yards ahead of him. It did not matter; they assumed he was going to an appointment with a Russian double. As the piquancy of the double-bluff he was operating reached down into him, he knew that Gardiner was a nobody, a loser. It was easier than ever to think that with the light bright, the water of the ornamental pool glinting like steel, the smell of dusty flowers and the air hot in his nostrils. A loser. He could leave him to Buckholz, after he had made his report to 'Franklin'. Gardiner was a man he had never met, just a victim of one of dozens of such betrayal operations.

He strolled under the stunted, emaciated trees on the western edge of the gardens, the noises of children and hot, exasperated mothers and nurses accompanying him as he stepped on the earth beneath the regimented trees. A blonde girl swung from a climbing frame, giggling shrilly as a boy tried to tug her down; another girl hung by the crooks of her knees, her hands trying to keep her inverted skirt modestly in place. He looked, too, at young women, fashionable bright blobs of colour, smooth willowy movement that further increased his sense of well-being. No further thought of his present vulnerability to someone like Gardiner was able to dispel the comfort of the day which extended into the secret areas of his life – his relations with the girl, and his treachery, which he had long ago ceased to consider as such.

Power. He had admitted that long ago, a long time. Years of the post-war period in the emergent CIA, and a brilliant career outlined. Then re-enlistment in US Army Intelligence after Korea, and the same kind of success. There was no reason on earth why he should have become a double for the KGB. Except power – the secret kind, the superb and massive joke that accompanied him like a constant companion or a lover, knowing himself to be completely other than he was presumed even by his closest friends and colleagues. Whenever he contemplated himself in this light, he was aware of the most luxurious sense of self-congratulation, something as fierce and present to him as a woman's aroused body.

Philby's removal from trust had been a severe blow to his masters at the Centre. He had been designed to be an eventual head of British Intelligence. Philby's downfall had precipitated his own recruitment because Philby had also been close to the NATO Intelligence hierarchy. He recalled the meetings with 'Franklin' in Washington, and the classic bluff of pretending to recruit Petrovich while being himself recruited. Then the succession of meetings in which he supplied information to the KGB while receiving disguised low-grade intelligence and the occasional top-level stuff from 'Franklin' to preserve the fiction.

He had deposited the tapes he had made of the last meetings he had attended in the pre-selected drop that morning – early; this meeting was to supply a simple verbal summary, and an instructional briefing by Petrovich; also it was precipitated by Lidbrooke. The SIS and the CIA were both satisfied that he was the traitor inside NATO.

Van Lederer anticipated a period of inactivity on his return to Langley, and until his transfer to Saigon. There, he knew, in that whole new ballgame, he would be of immeasurable value to the KGB. Not that the degree of his usefulness particularly interested him; only the secret power it evinced.

He replaced his sunglasses and walked out from beneath the ranks of trees into the bright sunlight. He saw 'Franklin' carrying the jacket of his suit, and a packet of sandwiches. In unconscious imitation, he patted his own pocket, touching the greaseproof wrapping of his own lunch, hearing it crinkle at his touch.

He watched 'Franklin' sit down at an already occupied bench, and wandered past him. He patrolled the ornamental pool, looking at the leggy, desirable girls – except that it was too hot, he thought, and he had other business.

At twelve-fifteen he sat at the same bench, and opened his lunch, seeming to take no notice of the man who sat near him, steadily munching at his own sandwiches.

It was after three when van Lederer got back to the Embassy. He felt heady and leaden with the sunlight and the talk, and with sitting on after 'Franklin' had left; and then to make some kind of tour out of a stroll round the Sorbonne area before the car picked him up and took him back to the Place de la Concorde. The sports car he had driven to the meeting would be collected later in the day.

He sat in his office, and told his temporary secretary that he wanted no interruptions and would take no calls. Then he filled a paper cup with water and took two aspirin. He closed the blinds and sat at his desk in the premature evening of the room, relaxing.

He had anticipated the meeting, almost entirely. Except for Petrovich's irritating habit of requiring some kind of ideological commitment from his agents. That had always annoyed van Lederer. The Centre demanded no such commitment – often, they were suspicious of it. In Petrovich, it was a cast of mind. Of course, he knew the cause. Petrovich was well aware of the old 'Wolfgroup'; it was a thought to make him smile. He had never possessed an intellectual hatred of Communism. It had been the secrecy of the group,

the enormous power of life and death, that had held him.
The old man, Grantham, long dead, who had persuaded
Churchill and Roosevelt of the necessity of such a group,
had possessed the hatred; but he'd never demanded it from
Constant or himself – only efficiency.

He felt himself relax. His neck muscles unbunched, were
less unyielding to the touch of the thick fingers. He put his
feet up on the bare desk, and clasped his hands behind his
head. He stared at the ceiling.

It was without genuine irritation that he picked up the
telephone when it rang at three forty-five.

'I thought I said no calls, Miss Belding.'

'I'm sorry General. This is code-identified, and I thought
you'd like to take it.' She sounded coolly efficient.

'What identification?'

'NATO-code-name "Goriot", General.'

'Mm. Put him through.' He listened to the clicks, saw in
his mind the strong face that belonged to the code-name, so
inappropriate to the name of the inoffensive, leeched old
man in Balzac's book. 'Yes?' he said when he heard the
voice. 'What's on?'

'It is important that I meet with you today. I have some
information concerning the man Lidbrooke which I find
most suspicious . . .'

'Lidbrooke? What do you mean – suspicious?'

'I think the SIS may have killed the wrong man – that's
how suspicious it is!'

'For the love of Christ, are you sure?'

'No, by no means certain. But definitely suspicious.'

'O.K., O.K. – let me think about this.' He could feel the
muscles tying up once more at the back of his neck, and his
head seemed to throb. Sweat broke out across his back,
sticking his shirt to the back of his chair when he moved.
He concentrated on controlling his voice. 'Why come to me,
"Goriot"? You got your own men, surely? Remember, I'm
retired as Chairman . . .'

'Which makes you an excellent confidant for my purposes.

Look, let me show you what I've turned up, and you ca
judge who to take it to, if anyone. Meet me at the Caf
Chartres in the Madeleine, say at four-thirty? It's jus
around the corner from you.'

'Why not come here?'

'No! I want *you* to see this, first. Then I'll come back wit
you, if that's what you advise. Agreed?'

'O.K. – yes, I'll be there.'

'Good. Au 'voir.'

Van Lederer put down the receiver, and realised that i
was damp with sweat at earpiece and mouthpiece, as if h
had been thoroughly soaked in the last few moments. A hc
shower. He wiped his hand on his trouser leg, leaving
damp stain on the light cotton. He stood up, flexing an
unflexing his hands as if he had been typing or writing with
out pause for a long time. Then he rubbed them on th
buttocks of his trousers, so that he could not see the stain
he made.

'Oh, Christ!' he breathed aloud, and looked at his watch
Three-fifty. Time stretched out before him, forty minute
becoming an endless age, tormenting in prospect.

*It couldn't be – couldn't be! There was no way anyone cou
know.* But the timing of the call from 'Goriot' terrified him
making him incapable of remaining still. The time passe
with terrifying slowness. Even his bladder felt overloade
and his heavy body wholly uncomfortable and no longe
under his control. He was a man normally incapable of fea
Now, some façade that hid the worm had collapsed.

He left the Embassy at four-twenty and strolled, i
changed casual shirt and clean slacks, up the Rue Roya
towards the soft-edged bulk of the Madeleine, its massive
ness made lighter, more airy and Grecian than usual by th
heat-haze.

The fashionable Rue Royale was crowded with tourist
and Parisians returning from work, heading for the cafés
He brushed uncomfortably against bodies, sensing obscurely
as if hearing a distant, shouted warning, the vulnerabilit

of his position in the crowd. He tried to dismiss the idea, and to concentrate on the meeting ahead. He tried not to anticipate the worst, but the sense of his discovery was close like the people round him, against whom he seemed to push ineffectually; oppressive like his headache or a nightmare.

He shook his head, as if to clear it.

It was at that moment that the silencer of the Browning pushed against the space between his shoulder-blades, and Gardiner shot him. The bullet passed through the heart and emerged through the chest wall. The dying van Lederer staggered against a passer-by, clasping at her dress and tearing it – she was stunned by the grossness of the assault until she felt the warm sticky blood, and saw the dead face sliding over her breast, down to the pavement. She began to scream.

Van Lederer had felt the slight pressure of the gun, but little more than that. The gun slid down his frame, tickling him, like a drop of sweat rolling down his back. Then the tearing pain, and the blackness so immediate that the pain was only the briefest of moments.

Gardiner slowed, stepped to one side, and looked into a shop window. The gun was unobtrusive in his pocket again. Then, as the crowd began to hover, bottleneck the pavement, he crossed the Rue Royale and headed for his car. He intended driving out of the city before catching the train to Calais and the channel ferry.

CHAPTER TWELVE

TETHERED GOAT

As Constant looked at him, as if for the solution to some thing, Aubrey said, shaking his head, 'I'm afraid you're right Deputy – you're next.'

Constant stared at the smaller man, as closely shaven a ever, the slight smell of his aftershave seeming to increas Aubrey's self-contained assurance. He was dressed in hi habitual dark jacket and striped trousers. He smiled dis armingly, and Constant was once more irritated by hi perception of a deeper and sharper mind than his own behind the round, child-like face.

'Your confidence is most comforting, Aubrey. The fact is however, that General van Lederer is dead and I am alive I intend remaining in that condition. I do *not* intend tha Richard Gardiner should do so. Do I make myself clear?'

He ignored Aubrey, and looked across his room a Latymer. The man's eyes were dull, almost closed. He ha shaved that morning, but carelessly, and his general appear ance, usually so groomed, had an unkemptness about it The tie was carelessly knotted, and the jacket sleeves were creased, as if Latymer had been wearing the lovat suit fo a long time without removing it.

He nodded in answer, but without real understanding Constant, irritated, checked himself by remembering th death of Latymer's wife. It would not do to challenge th man, there and then. Aubrey could talk to him later in hi unctuous, dutch-uncle style.

'We understand you, Deputy,' Aubrey said in a ton designed to soothe, take unawares. Constant had heard Aubrey managing committees and interrogating defectors and felt he could not trust any of the man's voices.

'Good. That is most gratifying, Aubrey.'

'What do you suggest? The airports and ports are being watched and every policeman in France and England must have his picture by now. What else do you suggest, Deputy?'

'Mm.' Constant steepled his fingers and looked over the thin tower. 'I have given this matter the most urgent consideration. It would appear likely that Gardiner will effect an entry into this country extremely soon. Van Lederer was murdered yesterday afternoon. Gardiner could have caught the night ferry – he could already be here.'

Aubrey realised that Constant was making a display of his unruffled nerves.

'I agree, Deputy. He could have made slight changes in his appearance, and if he's travelling on a simple *carte d'identité* as a French citizen, then we might well not pick him up. Assuming that, what is our next move?'

'First – do you agree that Gardiner must be being operated by an enemy of this country?'

'Is that important?'

'I think it is.' Constant's white skin took on the faintest pink tinge at the neck. 'I think it's important that we not only stop Gardiner, but find out what is happening here.' Aubrey, unsure how much of what he heard was disguised self-interest, merely nodded. 'Good. That means taking him alive – at least temporarily.' There was a sudden light in his eyes, a new urgency in his voice. 'We *must* know what is going on here, Aubrey. From what I gather from the Resident at the US Embassy, there was a telephone call, properly code-identified, that led van Lederer to make that foolish last walk. One thing, therefore, is clear. Either Gardiner knows current NATO code practice, or he was fed the information.'

'You're assuming he made the telephone call?'

'Not necessarily. But it's likely. If so, then he learned that code-name from someone. Any name would do, from someone high up.'

'French code-name – from Balzac?'

'Yes – "Goriot", in fact.'

'That's . . . ?'

'Haussman – SDECE. I've spoken to him, and he made no such call.'

'You believe him?' Latymer asked suddenly from his chair in the corner of the office, placed so that he gave the appearance of being half-wedged against a tall grey filing cabinet.

'I have no reason not to.' Constant replied coldly. 'Have you?'

Latymer looked at him, and there seemed a light of interest for a moment then the dullness returned to his eyes and he observed the edge of the patterned Persian carpet intently. Either that, or the absent stirring of his left shoe.

'He's assisting in some kind of trace, I take it?' Aubrey asked, disturbed by the sight of Latymer and trying to distract Constant's disdainful attention.

'Naturally. He has promised to make as full an investigation as possible. Of course, there won't be time to come up with a satisfactory answer before Gardiner is in a position to make an attempt on my life – to finish this bizarre task. He smiled without humour. 'I wish, in a way, it was as simple as Latymer has always tried to suggest – an old wound reopened. God knows, we did some pretty rotten things in the old group, but I can still believe them necessities of war at the same time as I can sympathise with Gardiner . . .' Aubrey, disbelieving every word, controlled his expression with great care. 'But this is nasty. It's Lidbrooke's ghost come back to haunt us. Can you understand, Aubrey? This is the Centre having a last fling to get even with people like us.'

Aubrey was silent for a long time, then he said, 'I – can just about see that, Deputy. In a strange way, it makes sense. But, how did they get wind of Gardiner in the first place? The NATO code-names I can understand. They're not important. But the whole – *unlikelihood* of this business!' He raised his hands, palms outwards, in defeat of intellect

'But, having done so, it is just too *arcane* to be ignored, wouldn't you think so, Aubrey?' The voice was almost seductive.

Aubrey, looking into Constant's face, nodded. 'I agree. So – what do we do?'

'It is, gentlemen, the time of the tethered goat,' Constant said.

Once more, Aubrey was rubbed uncomfortably by the sense of the man's delight in his own cleverness. Aubrey despised Constant's intellect from his own sense of pride; he was a man of natural humility until forced to deal with intellectual inferiors who paraded their assumed superiority before him.

'Tethered goat?' he said bemusedly, playing his own secret game; amused at the way his pretended ignorance could inflate Constant's ego.

'Yes. A trap for our Mr. Gardiner. I signpost my whereabouts, and we draw him to us. Then we take him, and find out what he has to say for himself.'

Aubrey leapt on the flaw. 'And frighten away his masters, who remain unknown to him in all probability.' He smiled helpfully.

'I had considered that,' Constant observed acidly. 'Perhaps, if we could persuade him he has succeeded, then he will go away again. Then, from the shadows will undoubtedly step the people who have been operating him. Even if only to stop him themselves, and remove the evidence.'

Aubrey looked at Latymer as he considered the idea. He seemed to have adopted the envious passivity of the man at the roulette table without money, intently watching other people win and lose.

'Mm. It all sounds reasonable, Deputy.' He knew Constant didn't give a damn as long as Gardiner didn't kill him. He knew he was being offered a tempting worm on the end of a line, but he swallowed the proffered bait. He *wanted* to know who might be making this strike against

the SIS and the NATO Intelligence Committee. Even if only
to point out to 'C' that the death of Lidbrooke was premature and ill-advised.

He said, 'Very well. That means a place where you're safe
and where he has a chance of getting to you – not London
It means a device whereby he can be duped, and a means of
tailing him secretly when he goes away. Either that, or we
talk to Gardiner and try to get him to help?'

Constant shook his head slightly. 'I don't foresee that
approach being very successful, do you?'

'Perhaps not,' Aubrey consented reluctantly. 'Where do
you suggest we place you as a tempting target, Deputy?'

'I considered my place in the Peak District – what have
you to say to that?'

Aubrey nodded his head after a moment. He could
visualise the country house, its grey façade somehow without
lightness and grace, or good humour; like its owner. It was
set in its own grounds, which could be successfully patrolled.
Yes, it was perhaps a good location.

'Why not one of our own country places?'

'Too specialised. Too safe from intrusion, wouldn't you
say? We do want Gardiner to come into the web, after all.'

Aubrey, seeing a far glow behind the pupils of Constant's
eyes, realised how well the choice had been made of head
of the 'Wolfgroup'. In Aubrey's experience, only long-dead
Grantham had the perception and the cold amorality in
achieving his designs to admire and promote Constant in
that way.

'Agreed,' he said. 'How do we inveigle him there?'

'Something in the newspapers, I think, referring to me in
my civil service capacity. An accident, even the overture of
a mild heart attack, which would lead to my having to
spend some time recuperating ...' He was smiling again,
preening himself before Aubrey.

Aubrey swallowed a sudden vile taste at the back of his
throat. 'That would seem to fit the bill, Deputy. When?'

'No time like the present. I'm due to attend a Foreign

Office reception at lunchtime – perhaps I should fall down, gasping for breath, in the middle of it.'

'Yes – that would make the evening editions, and to-morrow morning's nationals. Do you think he's already in England?'

'Don't you?'

Aubrey nodded.

'What men will you use?'

'I thought the same Beaters, armed of course, who were drafted into Paris for your Lidbrooke operation. Plus some of the SO-1 personnel, under Napier's command. You know, by the way, that he's been appointed temporary second-in-Command of that department?'

'Nice for him,' Aubrey remarked acidly.

' "C" confirmed the temporary appointment yesterday. They will, naturally, have orders to take Gardiner alive, if at all possible.'

'Quite.'

'I'd like you to get up there today, and make the dispositions – the men are already on their way.'

'Naturally.' Aubrey forebore to raise his eyebrows.

'You know the way?'

'I can find it, Deputy.'

'Take Latymer with you,' Constant added darkly.

Latymer, hearing his name, looked up, and said as if to himself, 'It's a bloody messy business, Deputy, wouldn't you say?'

'Gardiner's mess, not ours.'

Latymer looked away from the man's eyes, and stood up. Aubrey went to the door, and took Latymer almost unconsciously by the elbow, as if to guide a blind man, or some ancient. He said to Constant, 'We can expect you this evening, then?'

'I shall be there.'

Constant watched the door close behind his subordinates, and sat back in his chair. His body, though inclined at a new angle, looked no more relaxed than when he had been bolt upright. He placed his fingertips in the same thin tower, and regarded the door of his office over them. His face, narrow and bloodless, seemed less formed somehow, the skin less stretched across fine and prominent bones.

He could not guess who was running Gardiner. Naturally Moscow Centre, as he had suggested, was the obvious choice. Except that *he* was Moscow Centre's man.

He sighed aloud, but for no specific emotion or precise thought. He looked briefly at the ceiling, then focused again on the door.

He was Moscow Centre's man.

Strangely, he had never known the same to be true of Philby, though they must have been working for the same long period, since the old NKVD days. Unlike Philby, he had not been recruited at university. He had dabbled with Marxism, had known one or two of the lesser lights in the circle that gathered about Auden and Isherwood and the others. But little *political* activity. In those days he had still believed in the system he considered would amply reward his brilliance.

With clarity of introspection, he corrected himself. He had begun to believe, even during the war, that the system to which he had given a temporary allegiance was about to fail him in some important way. Even at what he might have considered the height of his secret power, as co-leader of the 'Wolfgroup', he sensed that he had been appointed because of some *lack* within himself – it was a *dirty* job, and they had given it to him and van Lederer, because the job suited them.

Constant stared at his fingernails, as if he saw dried mud beneath them. Yes – his head nodded in confirmation – though he had revelled coldly in the power, the laughter behind the mask, he had known that it was their assessment of his nature, and usefulness, that had given him the appointment. They thought him fit for the dirty jobs – for the night-soil work, for the secret murder, the bureaucracy of death.

It had shown in the last months of 1945. Instead of promotion to a senior position in London, he had been posted to the intelligence side of the Control Commission – the interrogation of refugees from the Russian zone, the questioning of suspected Nazis – an office-boy, little more, under the ineffectual, topering command of a man called Naismith, whom he despised and who laughed at him, showing him the disrespect and contempt of London over the rim of his glass.

Just months after being 'Wolf' – only *months* ... !

In Berlin in 1946, had come his recruitment. After six months or more of being disowned by London, being looked down upon by people who wished to believe that the war had been won by methods learned on the playing fields of their schools and not in the cellars of the Avenue Foch – *that sort of thing was only done by the Germans, surely, old man* – Naismith had said that, or something like it, when Constant, for once drunk in Naismith's company, had blurted out a little of the devalued secret currency of the 'Wolfgroup'. Naismith had called him a liar, laughed at his drunken persistence ...

He remembered suddenly, finding his mind jumpy, and perhaps as an antidote to Naismith's leering contempt, Plekhanov, a huge, hairy man, bearded and with shovel-like hands, their backs covered with black hair. And broken fingernails. He was everything that Constant despised – coarse, vulgar, arrogant, ruthless. He remembered with such vividness that he looked down at his trouser leg, as if he could still feel the weight of Plekhanov's hand on his thigh; he could smell the spicy meal still on his breath, and see the red lips moving in the beard; see the hard dark eyes staring into him, seeming to know him utterly.

The operation had gone wrong – his team, sent into the Russian zone to lift two high-ranking SS officers recently captured who were possible leads to the whereabouts of Eichmann, perhaps even Bormann. His team was captured, after being shot up, and interrogated by the NKVD. He was missing from the Allied sector for two weeks. When he got back, suitably wounded and exhausted, he was Moscow's man.

Why?

The reasons came fresh out of the dark at the back of his head, as if new. There had been no enquiries about his team or himself, from the Allies. He had been written off – it had been the final contempt. *Expendable*. Men who had flattered who had congratulated; the secret meetings, the chains of command he ascended with the ease of a counter in a game of snakes-and-ladders . . .

He smiled to himself, a bitter opening of his lips like a wound in the face – snakes-and-ladders. While he was going up the snakes, he was always regarded as one. And when he went into the Russian zone, he was going down their ladder, the one they had prepared for him.

They wanted him dead and buried and forgotten – a reminder to them all of the kind of unspeakableness they had willingly sanctioned in wartime – *the exigencies of war*, Grantham had told him, *desperate remedies*. Unctuous clown, dead by 1944 when a not-so-secret V bomb fell on his home in Surrey. But Grantham might not have abandoned him to those who inherited the offices in Whitehall and Queen Anne's Gate . . .

He would have done. Constant nodded his head again.

He had been written off.

He had learned to irrevocably hate the people who had abandoned him, in that tiny, damp, icy cell, with the bucket of urine and vomit and faeces in one corner stinking like the corruption of the entire planet. His hands had been *dirty*, his body covered with the lice from the previous occupant that had waited in the rotten straw of the mattress for him – he had woken screaming, beating at his cold body, trying to wipe and slap them from him.

A system too vile to reward his brilliance.

He abandoned it – it was washed from him with the lice – disinfectant, carbolic soap, hot water, clean clothes, a cigarette, a meal, vodka.

Was it as easy as that?

Yes, it had been as easy as that. Plekhanov, when he came, had known all about him, even about the 'Wolfgroup'. He had told them more. It was not held against him; rather, it seemed to guarantee something. And they promised him that he *was* appreciated, always would be. A hero. *Wealthy – he already was. Never mind, more money, paid anywhere, in any currency.* But always the heroism, the respect of a few people, the leaders of the Soviet people, the new Soviet state. They would know of him, respect him.

They had selected him even at Oxford, but had bided their time. Didn't he ever suspect?

He had done nothing, declared himself in no way, when he returned. He was designed to penetrate as deep, climb as high, as he could before he was activated.

There had been no material reason for his bartering with the NKVD. He had money from his mother's family. But he had been powerless. The years of the war, his sense always of being a despised *implement* of others, had crystallised in that filthy, stinking, tiny cell in Berlin when he knew his masters had abandoned him. Plekhanov had held up a mirror for him to regard his brilliance, and he had been dazzled.

He had used the slight patina of heroism that clung to him in the months after his return to assist his posting back to England, and there had set about the task of climbing the snakes and avoiding the ladders ...

And the hugeness, the cosmic size of the joke. People began to forget his wartime activities, respond to his efficiency, his quick mind, his natural aptitude for the clandestine, even the ruthless.

He began to climb – rehabilitated, respected, admired, envied. He watched each stage of his climb as a sequence of more flattering emotions wrung from people he despised. And revelled.

Quite, quite ridiculous. There were times when he had to bite his thumb until it bled to choke back the laughter that threatened after listening to someone who now had to bury a contempt he had once felt secure in showing and come up with a pretence of deference.

And there were other times when he considered he might be betrayed, exchanged and exposed – though he survived the disgrace of Beria, the death of Stalin, the rise and regime of Kruschev. From NKVD to MGB to KGB. Under each regime, he had remained on the most secret files of the Chairman and his Deputies. Plekhanov had been swept away, an old and impotent man, in a show-trial staged by Kruschev as part of his liberalisation of the Russian image abroad. During those years in the late Fifties, he had feared often that he might be traded as some gesture of goodwill towards the British.

But he had held on, and his name had never been known, and the files that referred to him remained locked away. 'Wolf', the old code-name, meant nothing to most of the Centre's people. Only on a handful of occasions since 1946 had the Russians so much as contacted him.

He sighed again, and there was a more distinct pressure on his breathing, around his heart. It was as if he were on the point of suffering the heart attack he had discussed with Aubrey. He stretched his arms above his head, and then slipped his fingers into the pockets of his waistcoat. He tried to be at ease.

Someone knew about him – may have known about him for years. That was frightening, unnerving. Someone was using Gardiner, a concept he was forced to admire, to finish off both the 'Wolverine' and the 'Wolf'. A wolfsbane. A poison, to be administered to the 'Wolf'.

He had never, himself, leaked stuff from inside the NATO Intelligence network. When the Centre had wanted someone to do that, they had come to a meeting place in Helsinki – a KGB Deputy Chairman, no less – and asked for his help. He had to find an agent. They wanted to know about relations inside NATO, especially about the French. They were determined, since the collapse of their network inside the

SDECE, to penetrate the whole Western alliance at its most
fecund point – NATO.

Van Lederer had been his choice. The American had
tumbled greedily for the prize of secret power offered him.
As Constant had known he would.

The pressure to find the source of the leaks inside NATO,
especially the setting-up of SO-4 under Aubrey, had had to
be countered by the dummy use of 'Franklin', van Lederer's
Russian control. So the rumours of reports reaching the
Centre from the Senior Committee had been confirmed by
'Franklin' in his dummy role as a CIA agent; it had had to
be done to protect 'Franklin' and his credibility as a double.
But they had needed a scapegoat quickly, and they had set
up Lidbrooke with Catherine Rollin.

Which should have been the closing of the matter, and
the guarantee of safety for van Lederer, and even for himself.

Who could have known?

He did not, could not, guess. Instead, he wanted to
destroy Gardiner – irrationally, he wanted to wipe him from
the face of the earth. Even if he never found out who was
running him. He had to control that – *wildness*. He was
being threatened from some organisation – CIA, SDECE,
BND, SIS ... It might even be Aubrey. *Someone, someone
knew about him*!

Danes, Turks, Norwegians, Italians ... ?

Insoluble, unless he caught Gardiner, persuaded him to
talk, or that he had done his job, and then waited for his
puppet-master to come out into the light. Then he might see
the hands dangling the strings and recognise the whorls and
loops of the finger prints.

But he had to risk Aubrey finding out about himself.

There was only one alternative to knowledge – and that
was to run, and run now. *Hero of the Soviet Union*, bobbing
up like a cork in Moscow. He would not do that. It was not
heroism, or loyalty to a system he had never completely
embraced in all the post-war years – rather it was the counsel

of inadmissible despair. There was nowhere to run. He could not entertain the *uselessness* of living on a pension in Moscow, in some unholy alliance with Philby and Burgess and MacLean and Blake and others whose names had never been made public. Never that kind of folly – like an old, old man sitting in a windy park in a raincoat, wearing a tarnished medal. He had seen that once, and never understood the significance of the sight – vision?

Since he could not entertain the concept of despair, he functioned practically. It was practical to eliminate the opposition, overt or secret, and impractical to run from it.

He got up and went to the window. From his window in Whitehall, he had a grander vista than this quiet pavement, the few parked cars and pedestrians. No. Overt power was within his grasp, the succession all but assured. He *would* have his revenge on them, those who had left him to rot in Berlin, in the hands of the NKVD. The SIS could, and would, be made to pay for that, inordinately – with a Russian agent as 'C', Head of British Intelligence. He could dupe, finally and absolutely, the system and the class he had learned to hate and despise.

He shook himself like a wet hound, and went back to his chair. It was time to have his heart murmur, and to set up the medical team which would be needed for authenticity.

He thought of Rawlings, his house in the Peaks, just within the Yorkshire county boundary. The killing ground. For Gardiner.

Gardiner lay on the narrow bed, the bedspread pulled back exposing the one thin blanket and the white sheet, reading the *Evening Standard*. He was tired, but his mind would not rest; the body too, as if recipient of that nervous disease, was restless, and he moved his legs and feet spasmodically as if to compensate for an absence of more complete physical activity.

He had remained awake throughout the night, spent on

the train then the night ferry from Calais to Dover. Then
the train journey to Victoria, and the watchful habitation
of a compartment of strangers; and a sharp awareness of
those figures glimpsed only as they passed the corridor
window, categorising their clothes, their appearance, so that
he could check their movements for anything suspicious or
threatening.

To emerge from the station concourse and walk to a bus
stop had been an effort where relief of the mind came to the
assistance of weary limbs. He had spent some hours walking
the streets, having left his suitcase at Euston, an unexpected
station for anyone looking for him. When he had settled on
his obscure and cheap hotel in Bayswater, he collected the
suitcase and booked in. The single room allocated to him
as a man with an assumed Northern accent, down on a
minor business trip, was narrow and sparse. He hardly
noticed it; it was no more than a staging-post

He discovered the item in the newspaper concerning
Constant while his mind was still revolving the difficulties
of making the kill. Constant, forewarned and dangerous
and heavily protected by people like Latymer and even
Aubrey, perhaps. He liked that, adopting his former friends
as opponents in his new war; a pleasing sense of the complete reversal of the past, one which identified himself to
himself more strongly. It gave the hungry ego a loneliness
that it craved, and a sense of being the underdog.

At first, it seemed just the opportunity, but as he sought
the mind which had arranged the information rather than
simply the facts of the report, he understood that it was a
trap. Even the address was given, of the country home.
Vaguely, to be sure, but with sufficient clarity to help him
find it. With nothing but the aid of an OS map.

His momentary disappointment was fierce and deep. It
was a trap, and he was meant to understand it as such. It
was a cry from the battlements, even a vulgar gesture in his
direction. And he *did* feel challenged.

He wished he had a rifle. Thought came down to that,

emotion coalesced around that one object. With a long gun, he could overcome the odds against him.

It was as if he could picture the house. Grounds patrolled, dogs perhaps, certainly marksmen – and Constant at the centre of the sudden web, woven in an afternoon.

Hurry. That was the thing. *Pressure*. He saw the house and its grounds not as a landscape but as a grid, criss-crossed by the burning, wire-like patterns of patrolling men. A time-and-motion study of a trap.

He needed a car, then. The train would be slow, and inexact. He had to be there as soon as possible. By the following morning. They might guess he was already in England, but they would expect some passage of time, some caution. He had changed his foreign currency on the boat, for sterling.

A hire car. And a rifle?

The imponderable. It required a piece of luck. In the long gun he sensed safety, a potency that gratified his sense of being one against many. He needed it, but he could not obtain one – yet. He swung his feet off the bed. He glanced around the room, as if seeing it for the first time and leave-taking in that same moment.

Papers. The only English ones he had were his own – they left a trail, but not a quick, rank one, perhaps. *Money*. He picked up his wallet from the bedside cabinet. *Watch*. Time still for car-hire firms to be doing business. *Clothes*.

Swiftly, he changed his crumpled lightweight suit for slacks and a sweater. Then he put on the stoutest pair of shoes he possessed. Bending to lace them, the sweater was already too warm. But he would need it; it stayed. He pulled on an anorak, finally, and transferred his English papers and his wallet to one pocket. The last *carte d'identité* had already been disposed of, in a waste-basket fixed to a lamp post with looped wire.

And there was nothing else. The suitcase sat, open-mouthed, as if reminding him of something. *Nothing else*.

A faltering moment, a sense of nothingness; the loss of

identity, the certainty of who he was. Then, moving to the door, he gripped the doorknob, and there was release in the movement, the use of limbs suddenly fresher, the creeping fidgety tiredness dismissed. He closed the door behind him, tracking the line of a stained strip of carpet down the corridor. The clerk in the pinched and dim foyer took little notice of him when he deposited his room key on the desk, the plastic slapping against the wood veneer.

Inside the house, it was growing dark, the sunset streaming more thinly into the westward-facing library, the room that Constant had assigned to Latymer and Aubrey as an operation headquarters. The two men sat around an old, long table, maps and sketches scattered on its polished surface. The light of a single desk lamp spread a white, arctic sheen on the papers and the wood. An enlarged photostat of a section of the relevant OS map was receiving attention from Aubrey, who was working in his shirt-sleeves and attempting the double task of concentrating on the operation and of drawing Latymer out of the moody silence in which he had made the journey to Yorkshire, through the crowded minor roads of the Peak District and the holiday traffic and the magnificent scenery.

It was difficult. Latymer was inside his own head, locked up there with God knew what dark thoughts, and the floating, detached image of the dead wife. Aubrey considered he was taking Victoria's death far harder than he had anticipated. He had become almost impatient with this retreated, sullen display of grief and loss.

'All the patrols are on now – the relief teams housed and asleep. To take over at midnight, until six. Then the present teams back on again. Five acres to cover, and we haven't a man to spare. The two of us will have to take a turn later.'

He looked up into Latymer's face, the drawn pallor suddenly sharp to him in the edge of the lamp's whiteness; a shocked awareness of what the man had suffered and was still suffering.

'Yes,' Latymer said.

'You have been listening, Hilary?'

'Yes,' Latymer replied, resentfully. It was as if Aubrey were trying to drag him away from a favourite place, or wake him from a dream. Yet the unrelieved misery of the hours – how many had passed? – that had followed her death were something that he had wanted to escape. If he could do it without betrayal.

Then Aubrey said, 'Do you believe this business of Richard being used by a foreign power?' There was a waspish attempt to denigrate Constant in the tone. 'Or do you think Mr. Constant doesn't trust us to do our best without appealing to national security?'

'What do you mean?' Latymer was struggling with a foreign tongue.

'I mean – is it real?'

After a silence, Latymer said, 'It could be real. Richard has been very lucky, and very efficient. And the telephone call . . .'

'Mm. That is a stumbling-block to be sure. Anyway, it will keep Gardiner alive. Unless Mr. Constant has other plans.'

Latymer appeared startled, or afraid they had been overheard. 'You think he'll have Richard killed, then?'

'I don't know. He may do. Do you want that to happen?'

'Why not? He killed van Lederer. Normal procedure would be to eliminate him as a priority danger . . .' There was something mechanical about the voice.

Aubrey, exasperated, said, 'What the devil's the matter with you?' He stood up, pushed away the heavy chair, and walked across to the drinks tray on the heavy sideboard, near the window that was a dull ochre square in the dark room. The landscape outside was sinking into two dimensions, total shadow. And though he knew that Gardiner was probably not yet out there, he shivered. He did not know for whom.

He poured two Scotches, and took them back to the table.

Latymer, who had heard the gurgle of the bottle and the splash of soda into Aubrey's drink, looked up, took the tumbler, and swallowed at the drink. He coughed, as if unused to it.

'Well?' he said, indicating the drinks with his eyes, and knowing that Aubrey intended being confidential – and probably unorthodox. There was not the habitual smile or tense moment of pleasure as he realised the fact.

'Listen to me, Hilary – and if you've ever listened to anything in your life, listen now.' He allowed a moment in which to gain Latymer's reluctant attention, then he said, 'Constant wanted van Lederer to kill Richard – wipe him out in some CIA heavy-activity operation. But he said he suspected, even then, that Richard was being operated by some third party ...' Aubrey's pale blue eyes were alight. Latymer knew he was worrying at the problem he had set himself. He tried to attend; it seemed that, reluctantly, thoughts of Victoria crowding his awareness now slipped further into his consciousness, occupying the dark corners where they would eventually take up their habitation. He shook his head, and Aubrey misunderstood the gesture.

'What's wrong with my thesis?' he asked in irritation.

'No, nothing. It was something else,' Latymer replied, pressing down the rising idea of betrayal. He refocused his gaze, and Aubrey thankfully saw it sharpen, come to terms with the immediate.

'Right. Constant will kill Gardiner to save his skin – just as he killed Lidbrooke as soon as there was a shred of proof against him!' The fact still rankled. 'So – what are we going to do about it?'

'Do?'

'Do you want Richard to die?'

'I suppose not – but ...'

'No buts. None at all. I'm not letting the chance of a sight of Richard's mysterious operator get away from us, just because Mr. Constant can't take the first whiff of grapeshot – that is not how I see my duty.' He frowned at the suspicion

of pomposity in what he had just said, then went on: 'We
have to stop Constant, get to Richard before he does, or
someone like that little snake Napier. And keep him safe
until *we* can find out what's going on!'

'You realise what you're doing, of course?'

'Of course I damn well do, Hilary! I know what's at stake
here!' He bit back his temper, and added with a sigh,
'Heavens, why can't it remain as simple as it was twenty
years ago – eh? Naughty Nazis, and good brave Englishmen
and Frenchmen and Poles and even Russians. All sweetness
and light, even in our peculiarly dirty game. Betrayals, of
course, duff gen, bad ops going sour on those we sent out . . .
But even then there was Constant, spinning a web, a spider
pretending to be a wolf!' Aubrey's face was twisted in dislike. 'He wasn't fit to tie Richard Gardiner's bootlaces,
Hilary – you know that as well as I do!'

Latymer looked round, again as if for some observer,
some floating ear that might come out of the dark to eaves-
drop. Then he said, 'Take it easy, Aubrey. I know exactly
how you feel, but it won't do any good to let off so much
steam – not here, anyway.'

'Oh, I feel so damned *old*, that's the trouble!' He swallowed
a mouthful of whisky. 'So damned old . . . While that
spiderish individual goes on for ever.' He laughed suddenly
and harshly. 'He's the sort of chap one thinks of as belonging to the other side, not at Queen Anne's Gate with the
rest of we British!'

'I entirely agree, Aubrey. But there he is, and there he will
remain.'

Aubrey waved a dismissive hand. 'Permanent like arctic
frost – eternal, like acne.'

'What's the matter, Aubrey – *you*, the politico, unable to
hide your feelings? What is it?'

'I don't know – something nasty waiting round the corner,
I suppose. Caesar's dreams, or was it Calpurnia's – I forget?
And the dear, ineffectual Prince talking to Horatio – "how
ill all's here about my heart", or something like that. Pre-

monitions. It must be old age!' He tried to shake off the mood by sitting up. Then he relapsed in his seat. 'No, I can't shake it off, and I can't stand by and let *Napier* or one of Constant's "Black Hand Gang" finish off "Achilles". We have to find him!'

Latymer, at last temporarily released from the spell exercised by his wife's memory, said, 'All right. What do we do?'

'Ah!' Aubrey swallowed the last of the whisky, and put down the tumbler – a prop he no longer required, having learned to move his intellectual limbs freely again.

'What have you in mind?'

'Tell me – when will he come?'

'Dawn, of course. When the guard is about to change, and men are tired and bored and off their guard.'

'When else, indeed?' Aubrey was almost jolly. 'Now, let's look at the map, my boy. Where?' His finger tapped the photostat which showed the stretch of country round the estate, the reservoir, and Broomhead Moor to the west and south. The narrow Ewden Beck wound from west to east across the map, towards the two reservoirs and the village of Ewden. As for the estate itself, it comprised spacious gardens, open grounds, and a bordering conifer plantation. Only one north-south road, a minor one, passed the edge of the estate, perhaps half-a-mile from the house.

'Which way will he come?' Latymer asked.

'And how?' Aubrey replied, pursing his lips and gripping them between his fingertips. The two men crouched over the map in the white, dead light.

'Car, that's easy,' Latymer replied, as if playing a game. 'Ease of movement.'

'Right. Up the motorway, and then through Sheffield, perhaps? Mm. It would seem likely, wouldn't it?' Latymer nodded. 'Right. Then he'll have a look at the place before first light. What action will he decide upon?'

'Kill a man and obtain a rifle, if he hasn't already got one.'

Aubrey looked at Latymer as if reminded, amid a romantic speculation, of an unpalatable reality. 'You're right, of course. We mustn't pretend we're saving Sir Galahad from the Dragon, must we? Where will he hide the car?'

Latymer tapped at the map. 'Here. Wigtwizzle. Deep in the plantation, I should think.'

'Mm. What about ... ? No, you're right. Good, good. Mm. That road there?' He pointed to a minor road running northwards into the stretch of woodland on the southern side of Broomhead Reservoir.

'Any one of three roads there.'

'But all bring him to the eastern edge of this estate. In which case, we ought perhaps to tentatively assume that he will take a man out down in this corner?' He pointed, and glanced into Latymer's face, seeking confirmation.

'Useless to speculate, really, since he knows *we'll* be the ones waiting for him, and that we will be carrying out just this kind of exercise ... However, for want of a better suggestion – yes. I agree. There.'

Aubrey was silent for a time, then he stared into Latymer's eyes, and said without inflection, 'Then we'd better be down in that corner ourselves, at first light.' He smiled acidly, and for a moment Latymer was forcibly reminded of Constant. 'And you know who I'm going to post there? No? Our little friend Napier!'

Jean-Jacques Haussman of the SDECE, NATO code-name 'Goriot', arrived at Gatwick soon after midnight in a small aircraft leased to his intelligence service. He was alone, except for the pilot. His ostensible mission was to inspect security staff at the French Embassy. He did not, however, go to the Embassy. Instead, the driver who met him at the airport headed the car across London, and within an hour of landing Haussman was on the M1, heading north.

It was perhaps the first day of autumn, coming early in September; there was a chill, damp, enveloping mist across the folds and open spaces of the estate, and it clung heavily to the dark, stick-like boles of the conifers of the plantation and Wigtwizzle wood that lay beyond it.

Aubrey and Latymer were both in heavy overcoats, dark unmoving figures perched on shooting-sticks, concealed in a brake of rhododendron bushes whose glossy dark leaves hid them from the fence that bordered Constant's property, and which, since the brake assailed one of the slight rises of the land, allowed them to keep watch on it and the man who patrolled that south-eastern corner of the estate.

The visibility was bad, and both men were extremely cold. Each of them sat like a statue, field-glasses to eyes, faces compressed into lines of cold and concentration. Latymer could see the road, like the dim stain of a racecourse beyond the white palings. Except for unseen birds, it was totally silent.

He knew that Gardiner would not use the road. He would have to cross it, but he would never use it to make his approach. The car would be hidden deep within Wigtwizzle. He focused on Napier, head down and face tired as the glasses held him; only by watching Napier would he ever catch sight of their real quarry ...

His mind played with the word, its implications. In what sense was Richard Gardiner their quarry? Aubrey's decisions had made a certain quarry of Napier, the man who was yawning, face half-turned to his glasses at that moment. He was the theatrical tethered goat that Constant had supposedly made of himself. Aubrey, in exposing Napier, was making himself think in channels too much like the oiled grooves of Constant's mind. He still did not know whether Aubrey and he would surprise Gardiner before or after his attack on Napier.

What would they do with Gardiner when they had him? How could they conceal him, or use him to flush out the unsuspecting operator? It was ludicrous to imagine spiriting him to some isolated pub in the Peaks where over a pint of beer they would calmly discuss the next move.

Yet what else was there?

And Gardiner ought to pay . . .

Etienne, Dupuy, Perrier, even Janvier, the professiona
assassin – the moral rectitude deep in Latymer's nature fel
that the man ought not to be able, by complying witl
Aubrey's scheme, to avoid retribution.

'There?' Aubrey breathed, a question not a confirmation
'Over in the trees on the other side of the road. Is that
shadow, or a man?'

Latymer swung the glasses up slightly, so that onl
Napier's head remained in view, and adjusted the focus
Napier's features blurred. Under the conifers, the edge o
Wigtwizzle, damply dark and wreathed in the grey mist, h
saw something move, cautiously. He felt a surging in hi
empty stomach, as at the infusion of alcohol or fear. H
refined the focus still further, even as he heard Aubrey say
'I'm afraid it is . . .' He did not sound genuinely sorry, bu
rather pleased that his prognostication had been prover
correct.

'Are you sure?' he asked, knowing the answer. A glimps
of a white face, an anorak, the purposeful movement from
trunk to trunk. It was a hunting animal. He swung th
glasses so that he focused on Napier's features again. B
his still posture, the tired slope of the shoulders, it wa
evident that he was unaware of Gardiner's proximity. Les
than fifty yards separated them. Only feet of that completel
open, the road and the frail white fence that would separat
the two men for much too short a time. He had a sudde
fear that Aubrey was enjoying the spectacle in a detache
imperial manner. He took the glasses from his eyes for
moment, and saw Aubrey's features settled in grim satisfac
tion; he felt himself a party to what Aubrey intended, a
ineffectual spectator of the drama.

He pressed his glasses back to his eyes. Something in hin
wished for Napier's death as a kind of justice on the crud
implement of Constant's will . . .

He ought to stop it, warn Napier. And he realised that i
he did, Gardiner was a dead man. He was now only yards

from the road, still moving like a stalking animal through the last outliers before the strip of road and the fence.

'What are you going to do?' he breathed urgently.

'Nothing,' was the calm reply.

'What?'

'Be ready to move as soon as ...' He left the sentence unfinished.

'You can't do that!'

'I am doing it,' Aubrey retorted, his tone warning that discussion was at an end. 'Be ready to move when I give the word – it's a hundred yards or more. Let's hope he doesn't shoot the little worm from the other side of the road.'

Latymer concentrated on the scene, as if by staring in dawning horror at the unfolding scene he was contributing something, avoiding the uselessness that seemed to invade him. For a moment, he despised himself as he despised Aubrey and Constant.

Richard Gardiner had taken advantage of Napier's lighting a cigarette. The man should not have done so, but he had previously glanced at his watch and decided that he was on the point of being relieved. He had his shoulder half-turned towards the road as he bent to his cupped hand and the lighter flame that Latymer could see flickering.

Gardiner was over the road swiftly, soundlessly – then he vaulted the white fence that no longer marked Constant's inviolable territory. And Napier, head coming up, suddenly warned by some professional instinct, the rifle turning in his hands, coming level to a bead. Then the splayed arms like a man drowning, and the head flung almost off its delicate perch on the shoulders; and the slow collapse in which tragedy became farce as the body subsided into the long wet grass near the fence.

Latymer could not say at what point Aubrey began running, nor at what point he stopped observing events through the glasses and saw the suddenly removed figures with the naked eye. He only understood that his wellington boots were slopping through the wet restraints of grass, and

Aubrey's dumpy little figure was ahead of him, moving with
surprising speed along the fold where the brake had hidden
them, which would take them towards Gardiner's right; an
accident of the ground which Aubrey had decided to exploit
as soon as he had seen it.

Gardiner had only just moved, only just lowered the stiff
arms, released the Browning from the two-handed grip so
that it hung more innocently in his right hand. He had
taken perhaps two, three steps towards the prone Napier,
towards the rifle concealed by the long grass.

'Stay where you are, Richard!'

Aubrey's voice was ridiculously high and his articulation
damaged by his laboured breathing. Yet the gun was
extended in the posture of challenge, knees slightly bent –
then Latymer, too, was atop the slight remaining rise, and
looking down at Gardiner, and his own gun was held stiffly
and pointed slightly down at the centre of the woollen
shirt – dark olive-green – and Gardiner's navel:

'Don't make us kill you, Richard!' he shouted, but his
voice sounded, even to him, inadequate and quite unthreatening.

CHAPTER THIRTEEN

AT THE KILL

It was patently ridiculous; he understood that. Ridiculous to move, to exercise even an eyelid. Ridiculous, too, the tableau of three middle-aged men, two of them in dark, formal coats, and wellington boots, and himself in slacks and anorak, the slacks stained by his passage through the wet grass and clinging to his legs; some foolish return to the arena of ageing boxers with tired legs and fuddled minds.

The image was incredibly clear to him, so that he forgot to move, to make the attempt. Latymer and Aubrey might have hesitated a fraction had he done so, but they would have killed him. He knew that. Something out of the past, the athletes of a former time with thickened waistlines and minds that carried too much fat ... Ridiculous.

Aubrey walked slowly and somewhat uncertainly down the slope, gun still held out in stiff arms. Latymer moved to one side, and came at him from a different direction. He looked down at the long gun in the grass, and then held out the Browning to Aubrey, butt first, who took it and dropped it into his pocket.

Then he said, 'How are you, Richard? Welcome back.'

'Back? To where, Aubrey?'

'It's been a long journey, Richard.'

Gardiner swivelled his gaze to watch Latymer post himself ten yards away, to his left. The Smith & Wesson dropped to waist level, and remained pointed at his middle. There was no way, he accepted, that he could turn the situation to his advantage.

Strangely, he did not consider the frustration of his hopes, and the closing of the cage upon him; there was something

ultimately unthreatening about the guns held by two ol
acquaintances. As if they were empty, or some nor
aggression pact had been sealed between them.

He said, 'Marked by bodies, Aubrey.' His face seeme
momentarily to crumple. 'But – I had to kill them. I wa
meant to kill them.' Aubrey's gaze was unwinking, and di
not move from his face. The round features, still so schoo
boyish, were bereft of emotion. 'They tried to kill m
Aubrey. After all this time. All of them. It was – fair ... '
The slightest question in the voice.

He seemed to loathe himself suddenly – a spurt of feelin
as if an artery had been severed. A spasm of ugliness, directe
upon himself, flickered across his face. He wanted to te
them, to find some kind of comprehension in them; in th
same moment, he despised the weakness that made hi
want to babble to them.

He went on, 'I – I don't want your sympathy – anyone'
sympathy! Yet I need you to understand. You do under
stand that I *had* to kill them?' He waved his arms weakly
as if signalling for help. He felt that they condemned hin
and he hated their contempt, but was pierced by it. 'You see
it's as if all the rest of it – the time between – didn't exist an
more. It was still 1944 – Christ, you'd have given me
bloody medal if it *was* 1944!' The words ejaculated hatred
He felt he had betrayed something, but he could not under
stand what it was.

'And Constant was behind it all the time – mm?' Aubre
said. Gardiner nodded, and Aubrey almost flinched at th
emotion in the blazing eyes. The prone corpse seemed t
obtrude on their conversation. 'It's over, Richard. I migh
even say I'm sorry for you. But, Constant is too importan
for you to be allowed to remove him – whatever the ..
He left the sentence incomplete. 'Too important.'

'What do we do?' Latymer asked, and then, as if fascinate
by some strange illness, asked, 'Why did you do it? Afte
all this *time*, Richard?'

Gardiner looked at him sharply, and shrugged hi

shoulders as if reaching for some answer hard to articulate. Then the shrug was one of incomprehension, sullen silence.

'We're not taking him back to the house, if that's what you mean,' Aubrey said. 'Not until I've spoken to him, that is. We'll take him to the shooting lodge, up on Broomhead Moor. There's a track from the house, but I don't want to use that ... Too many eyes.' He saw on Gardiner's features the livid growth of hope, like a hectic breaking under the surface of the skin.

'How, then?'

'Where's your car?'

'About a mile and a half into the woods.'

'Good. We'll take that. We can reach the lodge by taking another track, south of here. Drive almost up to the lodge on the blind side from the house. There's no watchman placed up there.' Aubrey smiled. 'I was careful to avoid that.'

Gardiner watched the slight smile on Latymer's face, and the self-satisfaction of Aubrey. He felt a sudden resentment, but let the feeling slide away, unconsidered. He wanted his brain to be empty, to receive impressions as they came, to prepare itself. Yet he also wanted to go on talking to these two men, who belonged to the past that was now his only possession, and they made that past less chill and alone than it had been. Despite the guns, they were not his enemies.

'We'd better get on, then,' Latymer said.

'Quite. Richard – Napier's not a very heavy gentleman, even in death. Put him across one of your broad shoulders, would you? We can deposit him at some distance from here, and under cover. Then you can lead the way.'

The walk through the empty wood, the thinning mist still obstinately clinging to the dark trees and the wet grass, was conducted in silence, like a search or a solemn procession. Latymer and Aubrey kept a respectful distance from Gardiner's back.

Latymer was unable, however, not to concentrate, until the sight caused him an acute physical revulsion, on the

bobbing, dead head of Napier as Gardiner effortlessly
carried him. He noted the neat squaring-off of the hair at
the nape of the neck, the flopping forelock against Gardiner's
anorak, the white cheeks and pinched, sharp nose when the
head swung into profile from time to time. There was something nightmarish about the image – because Napier was
being carried like a sack because of Aubrey's sense of justice,
or revenge, or even callousness.

When Aubrey ordered Gardiner to dump the body in
some bushes, peremptorily, then ordered him to move ahead
again, it was done without pause almost – certainly without
feeling or chagrin. Quite horrible.

The car journey, with Latymer driving, was conducted in
the same silence in the warmth of the Ford's interior.
Aubrey rested the gun on his folded arms, but pressed it
into Gardiner's side. He seemed pleased with the progress
of the car or events, and Gardiner, tired as he suddenly was,
slumped against the passenger window, his head pressed
against the cold glass.

They left the car half-a-mile from the shooting lodge, in
a dell of brown heather, the mist still thick there; though
as they walked out of it, the sun was diffusedly attempting
to breach the grey, cold blanket. This edge of the moor,
which climbed slowly towards Middle Moss and Howden
Moors, was a gradual slope down towards the Ewden –
towards the woods they had just left, and the house.
Rawlings was still lost in the mist, but the lodge itself lay
in a slight hollow, and was invisible to the house.

Gardiner halted before the closed door, as if reluctant to
enter. He turned to Aubrey, who remained where he was.
Latymer passed them to open up the squat, solid wooden
building, low and flat-roofed; something from a frontier
time.

Latymer said, 'Is it kept locked?'

Aubrey was about to reply when Latymer's hand pushed
at the door and it swung silently open. Latymer stepped in,
and Gardiner was immediately behind him, Aubrey bringing

up the rear. Aubrey had passed through the door behind
Gardiner when the occupant of the lodge spoke.

'Bonjour, gentlemen – welcome to my humble abode. Do
please come in. And, M'sieur Aubrey, please do not use
your own people as a shield from behind which to shoot me.'

Aubrey stood to one side, the gun pointing uselessly at the
floor, and said: 'Not my sort of game, that, hiding behind
somebody else. Though it is yours, I gather, "Goriot".'
Aubrey made an effort to smile, to keep shock from his
voice.

'Ah – the price of fame,' Haussman acknowledged, his
gun still pointing at Aubrey. He calculated that there was
no immediate danger from any of the three; but if there
should be, he assumed that Latymer would not move and
endanger Aubrey. His big, square face was smiling, but
there was no trace of humour in his flinty eyes. The shock
of wiry grey hair was smoothed down, and he looked alert
and untired. It was as if he was at the end of a long quest,
or a race in which the prize had proved to his satisfaction.

'You are Gardiner's operator, I take it?' Aubrey said.
Haussman nodded theatrically.

'Operator?' Gardiner whispered, as if emerging from a
trance. 'The photographs – you?' Again, Haussman nodded.
The gun flickered to cover Gardiner, then back to Aubrey
again. Gardiner turned to Aubrey. 'What the hell is going
on?'

'Shall I explain?'

'As you wish,' Haussman said indifferently. His eyes
watched Gardiner for movement, even though he knew he
was the only one of them unarmed.

'This man is a senior officer in the SDECE, French
Intelligence, Richard. He has been using you – as you appear
to know – as his field-agent. Van Lederer was one of his
targets, the other is obviously Constant. Am I correct?'

Haussman nodded again. He watched Gardiner's hands
bunch into fists, and the face work in hatred. He said quickly,
'I think it better, gentlemen, if we all sit down. There will

be less encouragement to sudden moves if you are all
seated ...' He pointed with his free hand at the wooden
chairs gathered round the table.

For a moment, the three men seemed reluctant, even
frozen – then Aubrey sat down and Latymer followed.
Gardiner seemed to hesitate, then took his place at the table.
All three of them now faced Haussman, whose chair was
pushed back from the table, for safety. The gun remained
steady on Aubrey. Gardiner appeared to have slumped in
the chair like a runner whose legs have given out. He
evinced little interest in the man who had operated him. A
creeping sense of being the creature of another will overtook
him, a subtle paralysis. Haussman sensed his helplessness,
as he saw the growing alertness in Aubrey and Latymer.

'Now, we're gathered here,' Aubrey said, 'what do you
have to say to us, housemaster?'

Haussman appeared puzzled, then said, 'A quaint English
joke I presume? There was much the same cryptic nonsense
when I worked on de Gaulle's staff in London.'

'You don't hear so many now that you work with the staff
of Moscow Centre, I suppose.'

Haussman shook his head.

'I shall explain. But, first of all, you must rid yourselves
of the misconception that I am Moscow's man.'

'Surely not Peking?' Latymer asked. 'It must be one of the
satellites, then. Do you distinguish between Moscow and
Prague or Budapest?'

'Please, you will listen. You may come to understand
something other than your silly jokes by the time I have
finished.'

Aubrey raised his hands, palms outward, to signify
acceptance.

'Please go ahead,' he said, placing his gun on the table,
its butt towards Haussman. Then he looked sharply at
Latymer, who disgorged his own gun and laid it on the
rough surface of the table. Haussman nodded in satisfaction.

'On my part, gentlemen, I shall be similarly frank – and

I shall allow whichever of you has M. Gardiner's gun to keep it, for the moment ...' He smiled and Aubrey's face, without betraying any emotion, smiled back. 'I have no men here apart from my driver, who is obtaining some coffee and breakfast in Ewden village. He will return soon. I did not expect you, and so there will not be sufficient food – however, there will be coffee.'

'Many thanks. It wasn't a pleasant night. Rather damp for yesterday's spies, wouldn't you say, "Goriot"?'

Haussman seemed to warm to the code-name and the good-humoured irony of Aubrey's tone.

'We are assuming, I notice, that no one is going to get killed here? There is no place for violent death in this little reunion – mm?'

'Good.'

'What's your story?' Gardiner asked abruptly, his voice sunken into sullenness.

' "Achilles", I apologise to you. You were being used by me, and I understand, I think, what that has meant to you. I have robbed you of your pride – is that not so?' Gardiner was silent, and after a moment Haussman looked away from his eyes, and said to Aubrey and Latymer, 'You are ready to listen?'

'We are at your disposal, Jean-Jacques. Indeed, I might say you have a captive audience. Please to proceed.'

'Very well. I will begin by telling you that your Mr. Constant is Moscow's man – not myself. So was General van Lederer ...' He paused, and though Latymer was about to protest, he was silenced by the unchanging stoniness of Aubrey's features. Haussman continued, perhaps disappointed by the lack of reaction, 'Very well. There is proof, and in the case of van Lederer it can be checked with a reasonable degree of certainty. If the CIA can be persuaded to make the checks ...'

Again, Aubrey was silent, and his silence affected Latymer, whose features were far more mobile.

'But ...' he began, and fell silent.

'I see. A conspiracy of silence. I obviously do not surprise you. Van Lederer was Moscow's man on the NATO Committee, not Lidbrooke. Constant devised and ordered the framing and death of Lidbrooke to prevent the enquiries proceeding any further. I'm sure that you considered the murder of Lidbrooke ill-advised and hasty?' Aubrey's left eyelid flickered twice, but still he said nothing. The silence, every time Haussman stopped speaking, was more strained and tense than before. It did not seem to emanate from Gardiner, the rogue piece in the chess-game, but from Latymer and the robotically-stiff Aubrey.

'Naturally,' Haussman continued, 'you are too professional for the matter not to have caused you concern, however. Van Lederer was being operated by the man the CIA calls "Franklin", their newest and brightest source at Moscow Centre. He is in fact a bona fide agent of the KGB, and not a double.'

'You can prove all this, of course!' Latymer snapped in the moment of silence.

'With difficulty, and with co-operation – but yes, I can. You may discover that my superiors in the Quai d'Orsay, however reluctant, will confirm that I have been engaged on this operation with their knowledge and approval, which would make it more difficult to believe in me as Moscow's man. To discover van Lederer's culpability, you would need to go back to the very beginning of his supposed persuasion of "Franklin" to work for the Americans – there were unscheduled meetings, then, and some rather strange contacts . . .' He paused, then: 'But, in the matter of Constant – he is a "mole", and has been for a very long time.'

'You realise what you're saying?' Latymer asked again. His mind seemed, to Aubrey, suddenly slow and dull and conventional. He was tracing well-signposted paths, trying to avoid the information that was being supplied. Aubrey glared at him.

'I do. I did not expect to have to inform anyone of this.' Haussman shrugged. 'But you caught "Achilles" before he could complete his task, and brought him here, to me. Now you have to be told.'

'What *task*?' Gardiner asked, his lips twisted lividly into a scowl. 'What do you want with me?'

'Ah. You, given the information I possessed, were the answer to my problems, M'sieur. A survivor of the operations of the "Wolfgroup". I learned of you from Etienne de Vaugrigard, who betrayed you to the Gestapo.' He watched the slight shudder run through Gardiner's frame, then continued: 'I was investigating his links with the OAS, and he told me this strange story about the "Wolfgroup", to ensure his loyalty. That was before he confessed, when confronted with facts, figures and photographs. And he mentioned the names of the men who headed the group – Constant and van Lederer. It was almost too wonderful, too convenient, to believe. I promised to protect him against you, as long as you could be led to him. I must admit that, when I checked on you, I assumed you had tried to make yourself forget the war, and escaped into the skin of a civilised man. I brought Dupuy to you, a passive trigger for the kind of man you once were – I gambled that you had not changed too much.'

In the sudden silence, Gardiner's breathing could be heard, mounting to some kind of climax. Haussman steadied the gun on his stomach, and glared warningly.

Aubrey, sensing desperation, laid his hand firmly on Gardiner's arm, restrainingly. He said, 'Richard – it's not worth it. You'll get yourself killed.'

Gardiner turned on him as Aubrey had hoped, his rage transmuted into words rather than imminent action. 'Do I give a – *fuck* whether I get killed or not?' he seemed to scream. 'This – *shit* knew me inside out. Knew me so well that he could *count* on me doing what he wanted!'

Aubrey's eyes widened. 'It doesn't . . .'

'Yes, it does. I knew someone was helping me – I didn't care who, or why. I still don't. I'd have killed them anyway. It's the being so *sure*!'

'I apologise, M'sieur. Had I gone to the CIA or the SIS, I and my organisation would have been immediately suspect. We are not the golden children of NATO at the moment, you understand . . .' He smiled ironically. 'The General who governs France is a great man, but he does not like the British or the Americans, and they mistrust him. This would have been seen as a ploy of his, to cause trouble, even an excuse to leave NATO. So, when you were introduced to the board, by accident – I had to use you.' He stared at Gardiner, his eyes gleaming. 'And, for all your protest, M'sieur – you have lived as never before during the past weeks. You have *enjoyed* yourself!'

Gardiner winced at the glint of knowledge in Haussman's eye, and at the weight of truth the statement carried. He seemed about to speak, then lapsed into silence. Haussman turned his attention to Aubrey and Latymer, as if Gardiner had become relegated in importance.

'I, and my masters, were working for the future. France has no future outside NATO, whatever may be said to the contrary. And we were increasingly concerned at the leakages from inside the Intelligence Committee. We went to work, and we discovered the source of the leaks to be van Lederer. It was a long and difficult business, the process of elimination. At almost the same time, we received word that Constant had been turned by the old NKVD, way back in '46. A man called Plekhanov, long since dead.'

'How do you know that?' Latymer asked in the same waspish, insulted tone. Aubrey sighed with irritation, but maintained his concentration on Haussman.

'A long time ago, Constant was Operations Director of Berlin Station – almost from the day the war ended. He disappeared for two weeks – missing, presumed dead or captured. Old cold-war stuff. Then he turned up, beaten and ill and wounded, but alive and escaped from custody. Welcome home, hero of the hour!' Haussman snorted. 'We learned about it only when a low-grade defector, a Pole sold to us by the Italians after he defected from their Rome embassy staff, came into our possession. We paid over the odds for him because he once worked in the French sector of Berlin.' Aubrey nodded, doll-like and stiff, so that Haussman was surprised by the movement. 'He was on Plekhanov's staff when Constant was taken – and turned. When we learned that, and saw how high Constant had climbed, we knew he was more dangerous to you and to us than Philby would ever have been. But what to do? He was already a Deputy in SIS, and above suspicion.' He paused, then added finally, ' "Achilles" fell from Heaven into our hands, gentlemen. We used him.'

There was a long silence, strained and echoing, in which the lives of the four men seemed to sound hollowly, like their breathing. Latymer looked at Aubrey to break the intolerable quiet, but Aubrey seemed removed from speech by some huge impediment or paralysis. Gardiner, he saw, had retreated into profound melancholy. He was reviewing his life, and there was nothing Latymer could find to say to him. He hated Haussman and his ingenious and violent scheme.

They heard in their separate silences the faint noise of a car, at some distance, and then an interminable time passed before a big man with a heavy moustache pushed open the door, paused, then spoke to Haussman in French.

Then the driver made coffee, and the creeping aroma seemed to unfreeze each mind; steam easing a postage stamp from an envelope, encouraging speculation once more. There was a sense of unity, strange and ephemeral, yet present.

The driver served the coffee, and then left without a word from Haussman, presumably to patrol the area around the lodge. Each man, hands cupped around the mugs taken from the cupboard in the tiny, primitive kitchen, drank gratefully. Latymer sensed it was some kind of pledge, as if he and Aubrey had admitted the truth of what they had been told.

Suddenly, Gardiner said, 'You're all bastards – the lot of you!' There was the same fierce light in his eyes, but, as if he

were no more than a recalcitrant child, he seemed quelled by
Haussman's stare, and relapsed into his former mood, so
much lumpy baggage thrown on the chair. 'Bastards ...'
As if he wished to share the complicity of the moment, he
drank.

'You still say nothing, Aubrey?' Haussman said directly,
lighting a cigarette and offering the packet. Aubrey shook
his head; Latymer accepted. The acrid tobacco stung his
throat, but the rich smell of the French cigarettes filled the
lodge's main room.

'Mm,' Aubrey murmured. 'It does seem incumbent upon
me to say a few words – I realise that.'

'You disbelieve me?'

'Not absolutely. Disappointed in your methods, that goes
without saying. But not entirely disbelieving. I would need
proof of course. Where is this mysterious Pole now?'

'Still in France. Retired to the country. He grows flowers,
I believe.'

'Then I would wish to start with him.'

Latymer sighed, and saw Haussman deliberately relax.
A moment of supreme importance had passed, although
there had seemed an inadequate preparation for it. But
Aubrey had accepted the thesis as a thesis, and was prepared
to test its worth.

'Good. That is very good.'

Aubrey turned his attention to Gardiner, and after a long
moment, he said quietly, 'What do you feel now, Richard?
You've heard everything.'

Gardiner stirred in his hard chair, stared at Aubrey, and
seemed about to defy the whole moment, the whole atmosphere, then said, 'What is there for me to say? It's all sewn
up, isn't it? I don't matter a damn any more, do I?' He seemed
to wish to return to an enforced isolation, as if it comforted
him more than conversation.

Latymer looked at him, unable to guess what might be
going through his mind. He said, 'Of course, Richard
Gardiner would be your accredited agent in this – a member

of SDECE, for the purposes of crimes that might have been committed by him in France?'

'Naturally.'

There was a smile about Gardiner's mouth, as if he was contemptuous of the offer.

Aubrey added, 'Either that, Richard – or we make it an operation of ours, and you work for us.'

'I'm not part of your plans, or your world. And I won't be.'

Aubrey appeared exasperated by the rejection of his offer. 'You don't want to be arrested by the French for murder – nor do you want to be taken out by the CIA. They're very hot on that, making people disappear.'

'Balls.'

'Stop behaving like a sulking schoolboy, Richard! Haussman was right when he chose you. You did it because of what *you* are, not because of what he is or did. Try to consider things a little more rationally than of late, and come to a sensible decision.'

'Sensible – in your world?' There was a coruscating scorn in Gardiner's voice.

'In our world,' Aubrey explained patiently, 'grotesque and ruthless and nightmarish as it sometimes is – there is all the more need for good sense and rationality. Unfortunately, that is what you forgot, M. Haussman, in setting this rogue element loose.' Haussman appeared unabashed. 'I accept some of your reservations concerning the SIS and CIA, and I understand the acute attractions of de Vaugrigard's story ...' He paused, then: 'But, the affair is now in our hands. If you can convince me, then I am prepared to go into the whole thing thoroughly. If you trust me to do that?'

Haussman nodded. He got up from his chair, laid his own gun on the table, butt towards Aubrey, and held out a huge hand. Aubrey shook it with delicate fingers, and smiled briefly.

'I agree. But – what is to be done for M. Gardiner?'

Aubrey looked down at the sullen, petulant face. Yes, he

thought, it *is* petulant now. He is merely sulking, and no longer dangerous. He said, 'He, too, becomes our concern. I don't think you need worry about him, since he is already beginning to realise that the very things which made him "Achilles" are the qualities you desired in your hit man. He will feel complimented, eventually.'

Gardiner looked up at him, his eyes cold. But he said nothing. Perhaps there was the faintest hint of agreement, however grudging, about the mouth.

The door opened suddenly, and the driver came in. Each of them turned to him as to an intruder.

'Men coming,' he said, addressing Haussman. Latymer watched the petulance on Gardiner's face slowly drain away, and suspicion, cunning, seep back to take its place. He felt incapable of reaction himself, as if the news robbed him of motive power, or that the power around that table resided only in talk, words.

Then Aubrey rose in his chair. 'Tell me,' he snapped in French, 'how many, and from which direction?'

Haussman nodded, and the driver replied.

'Four in the main party – coming from the direction of the house. But I saw others, circling to come from the other way ...'

'Then he knows we're here.' Haussman seemed, to Latymer, suddenly crumpled. Even words were paltry. Strangely, he felt no sense of immediate danger, imminent discovery. Some placidity had emerged from somewhere, the comfort of watching a performance only as a spectator. He shook his head as if to clear it.

'He knows *we're* here, I suspect,' Aubrey observed, indicating himself, Latymer and Gardiner. 'They've probably found Napier's body.'

'What will you do?' Haussman asked. He, too, seemed to acquiesce in the situation, resigning all power of decision to Aubrey.

Aubrey's face was compressed with thought for a moment, then he said, 'Are they between here and your car?'

The driver shook his head, shrugged. 'Not at the moment . . .'

'Then it is time for you to go!' He looked directly at Haussman, then at the round-shouldered, slumped form of Gardiner, as if by a premonition. Gardiner appeared indifferent once more. 'This is now a legitimate intelligence operation, Haussman. You will go back to the Embassy, and wait for me to contact you there. Agreed?'

Haussman stood up slowly, and looked at Gardiner as if reluctant to part with some possession of his, prized and effective. Only then did he pick up his gun from the table; he looked at it, then slid it inside his coat.

'Very well, Aubrey. When will you arrive in London?'

'Soon – today, tomorrow. Now – please go!'

Haussman nodded once. 'Very well. I leave matters in ur – capable hands, then.' He motioned to the driver, who went out, then called back, 'All clear.'

Then Haussman, too, was gone. Latymer stood up, and looked at Aubrey, who gathered up the cups of coffee and carried them into the kitchen. Ignoring Gardiner, Latymer followed him.

'What do you intend?'

Aubrey swilled the mugs under the cold tap, then stacked them in the cupboard below the sink. When he looked round at Latymer, his face was mobile with ideas.

'We have captured a very dangerous man, Hilary. Deputy will be delighted, I'm quite sure. We have to ensure that he has *no* suspicion whatsoever that we have talked to anyone, that we know anything.'

He wiped his hands on his coat, and went back into the main room of the lodge. Gardiner sat with his hands loosely on his lap, as if they had no power of sensation now that they no longer held the coffee mug.

'Richard – Hilary, watch the window, there's a good chap – Richard, listen to me. Just play dumb. Understand?'

Gardiner looked slowly up at him, a resentment blazing in his eyes for a moment.

'Oh, dear – I do hope you're not going to be difficult about this.'

'No. I won't be *difficult*!' he replied contemptuously, mimicking Aubrey.

'Good. We followed you up here, and caught you resting. Don't worry. You'll be safe, as long as Constant thinks you're neutralised as a threat ...'

'But I am, aren't I?'

'Perhaps.'

'It's Deputy,' Latymer said from the window.

'Who else?'

'Two of Napier's men – Laker and Monro, one either side of the big white chief.'

'Check the other windows.'

A pause, then: 'Evans is at the rear of the house. Wooller's there, but I can't see any others of our team.'

'What?'

'They're not there. What does it mean?'

'Were it not for young Evans, I'd say it was the execution squad. But, perhaps not ... Constant can't be certain of who is in here, or what might have gone on. I just hope Haussman and his driver haven't been spotted. I think it's time for a word with Deputy, don't you?'

Aubrey went to the door, opened it cautiously, and stepped out. The air was less chill now, and only the last fingers of grey mist wreathed the place. Constant smiled sardonically when he saw the short figure in overcoat and wellingtons. He had dressed himself in a shooting-jacket and knee-breeches.

'Ah, Aubrey. We were just coming to find you. We found Napier. Have you found Gardiner?'

'Yes, Deputy. He gave us quite a chase, but we followed him here. He's inside, disarmed and harmless.'

'Well done.'

'Thank you, Deputy.'

'Wooller reported a car on the road from Ewden – dark-looking chap driving. Seen anything of it?' Aubrey looked at the shotgun broken across the crook of Constant's arm.

He was careful to control his voice. 'No one called. He may be around.'

Constant smiled and said: 'Quite. Well, should we not have a word with Gardiner? Has he told you anything yet?'

Aubrey looked at Laker and Monro and shook his head. There was only one thing to be done. He said, 'I'll get him out.' He turned his back on Constant, and shouted, waving his arm as he did so, 'Hilary, bring out the prisoner, will you?'

The door opened, and Gardiner emerged, followed closely by Latymer, who ostentatiously pointed his gun at Gardiner's back. Gardiner looked suitably truculent and defeated. Latymer closed the door of the lodge behind him.

'Ah,' Constant said as Aubrey turned to face him.

'Good morning, Deputy,' Latymer said briskly. 'We have him, as you see.'

'Indeed. How did you manage it, Latymer? Excellent work, and with such a desperate character.' Aubrey noticed that after a moment's initial inspection, Constant avoided looking into Gardiner's face. Perhaps he was unnerved by the pure and unqualified hate he saw there. Evil eye.

'When we found Napier, the trail led here. Gardiner was sleeping, Deputy. Easy, I'm afraid,' Aubrey remarked conversationally.

'Mm. And he didn't take Napier's rifle. I find that very strange, don't you?'

'Perhaps so, Deputy. But you can ask him about that later.'

'Quite so. Yes, perhaps we should be getting back – lots to do, eh?'

Aubrey held his breath, and avoided looking at Latymer. Then he said, 'Will you lead the way, Deputy?'

'Yes.' Constant seemed undecided, then he said, 'Laker, Monro – we're taking Mr. Gardiner back to the house. You two had better stay up here, and scout about for that foreign-

looking chap that Wooller says he saw. I don't suppose
there's anything to it, but just in case.' He turned to Aubrey
and smiled. Aubrey, turning his gaze from the expressionless
faces of Laker and Monro, detected no sense of irony in
Constant's face. Yet he could not rid himself of the feeling
that he had failed to convince the man, that Constant knew
Haussman had been in the area.

If he knew that, then Aubrey might have consigned
Haussman and his driver to death. Constant would not take
the slightest chance. Aubrey, suddenly out of his moral
depth, choked on the bitter water he swallowed. He could
only, faintly, hope that the Frenchmen had already got away.

'Shall we ... ?' he asked with a forced lightness of tone.

'Of course. You lead the way, Aubrey. I'll bring up the
rear. Both of you keep a good watch on our friend.' This
he addressed to Latymer, who nodded.

They walked down the edge of the moor towards Rawlings,
nestling amid trees, the road a thin ribbon bordered by the
white fence, in a silent procession. Latymer watched
Gardiner carefully – Constant's shotgun was still broken
over his arm, but it was loaded and the work of a moment
to close it, aim, and blow Gardiner's spine through his ribcage, supposing he made a run for it. Thankfully, Gardiner
appeared dulled and spent again, rather than secretive and
tense with plans.

Aubrey listened behind him for distant shots, or voices,
as they dropped away from the lodge. He was very afraid,
but he heard nothing. Evans and Wooller, and others of
the original Beaters – two more that Latymer had not seen
from the lodge windows – followed at a respectful distance.

The sun climbed in the sky, and the mist dispersed so that
the cloudless expanse above them was palely blue, already
bright with heat. Aubrey shed his overcoat, and began to
wipe at his neck and forehead with his silk handkerchief.
Insects hummed noisily in the long, drying grass on the
lower slope near the road.

All the way to the house, Aubrey surreptitiously looked

around him, for Laker and Monro. He saw no sign of either of them.

Aubrey sat in the library, watching Latymer over a tumbler, his mind clogging on the directions he might take, the actions he might consider. Gardiner was being questioned in the wine-cellar by Constant – Aubrey wondered why people like Constant always chose the cellar – but he had no fears that Gardiner would betray the existence of Haussman, or the information he had imparted. He had sent Evans along as an extra guard – the interrogation might be painful, gratuitously violent to satisfy Constant's relieved fear, but it would not be fatal. And nothing like those days in the Avenue Foch must have been . . .

No, he had no fears on Gardiner's part. Only on his own; and beyond the self, fears for the service itself. He was unable to perceive Constant's next moves, and his blindness disturbed him.

Eventually Latymer spoke, disturbing the silence of the sunlit room. 'What sort of danger are we in, Aubrey? I enquire from mixed motives, naturally.'

Aubrey looked at him, and his mind closed on a momentary irritation at Latymer's habitually languid way of speaking.

'I don't know, Hilary. I just don't know, and it *irritates* me that I don't. I want to know where Laker and Monro are. They haven't come back yet, and that worries me. Haussman's car must have left tracks – they may even . . . No, I don't think I want to say that, just at the moment.' He shivered theatrically, and swallowed some of the whisky.

'You think Constant knows – suspects?'

'Oh, yes. He's suspicious, all right. I suspect he's ordered Laker and Monro to kill on sight. There's something about the easy way we took Richard, something about the whole thing that would appear wrong to him – false. His senses are those of a threatened animal. He'll have got wind of something.'

'Well – what do we do?'

'About what we know? I'll have to talk to "C", naturally. He'll have to talk to Haussman, Haussman's superiors, anyone and everyone.'

'The whole thing – it's fantastic, Aubrey!'

'Yes. Very theatrical. Bloody clever. I want desperately to believe it, because I can't stand the sight of Constant! I don't like his methods, his men, or his personality. And it all fits! That's the beauty of it, Hilary. Such a pattern to it all, and going on over all those years. God, the man is next in line of succession, until and unless he makes a prize pratfall!' He shuddered, for effect. 'Think of it – being run directly by Moscow Centre!' He laughed. 'As Arthur Bullen might say – enough to put tits on yer!'

'Stop clowning, Aubrey. Can we take Richard back to London with us – without arousing opposition?'

'Mm. I should think so. After all, I'm officer in charge for the moment. Constant can't not show up with Gardiner, after all. No, I see no difficulty there.'

He got up, and went to the window. By the set of his shoulders, the pugnacious stance, Latymer understood that Aubrey, having talked out his problem, had solved it. The depression was lifting. Aubrey's hand tilted the tumbler to his lips, and he drained the last of the Scotch. Then he turned to Latymer.

'Fill them up, Hilary, would you?'

Latymer took Aubrey's tumbler and his own, and then joined Aubrey at the window with generous measures in both glasses.

'Everything is going to be all right, then?'

'Oh, I should think so, Hilary. Silly to worry, really. Constant should soon tire of roughing up Richard, and then we can all get down to pretending that the operation has drawn to a satisfactory conclusion.'

'You believe Haussman, then?'

'Oh, yes. I believe him. At least, I'm prepared to believe him, which is the same thing. I just have to get "C" to

ircumvent Constant for a while, until we have checked the
hole thing out. Not that he'll get up to too much harm
ith van Lederer out of the way.'

He stopped. Latymer, seeing his intent gaze, looked out
f the window. 'Laker – and Monro,' he breathed.

'Quickly – get your field-glasses.'

Latymer crossed to the table, and then returned to the
indow, handing Aubrey the glasses, taking his whisky.
ubrey fiddled the leather strap free, then raised the glasses
᠎ his eyes. Aubrey looked out at Laker and Monro ap-
roaching the house from the direction of the shooting-
᠎dge, their shotguns broken over their arms – no, Laker had
rifle, Monro the shotgun.

'Well?' he said impatiently. Aubrey handed him the
asses.

'What do you take that to be that Monro is carrying in
s left hand?'

Latymer refocused the glasses. Sky, then down to Laker's
ce, set and expressionless as the two men came across the
ounds towards Rawlings. Monro was partly hidden.
atymer was about to exclaim against his being obscured, as
he might thereby get Laker to move, when he saw what
ubrey wished him to see.

'A briefcase?'

'Do you think, in all honesty, Hilary, that Monro is
oonlighting from the service as a part-time executive or
hoolmaster? Would that be a reasonable assumption on
ır part?'

Latymer concentrated on the idly swinging case in Monro's
ınd. Unbelievable. Frightening. He had noticed the catch
᠎ Aubrey's voice which the languid words could not
sguise.

'No. They've found it, somewhere ...'

'Exactly my thought. And it doesn't take a seer to tell you
here. Or does it?'

'Then they've – ?'

'They may indeed have.'

'Oh my God – two SDECE men, just like that!' Latyn
couldn't make his fingers click audibly, as if they were co

'Just like that – quick and perhaps even silent.' There v
a wintry smile on Aubrey's face, which appeared drawn, a
much thinner and older.

Latymer saw Laker and Monro pass out of his field
vision, towards the front of the house.

'I – we have to make sure, Aubrey – have to ...'

'Yes, I suppose so.' A pause, then: 'You'd better be
your way, hadn't you?' Latymer nodded, but did not mo
'I'll wait for you here. And don't be too long. It might ma
Deputy suspicious!'

Latymer did not find the bodies. Only the car, obviou
and innocently empty. No damage – it appeared. He ma
it out, hidden as it was by thick bushes, and moved cautiou
towards it down the slope of a dell no more than a quar
of a mile from the lodge. He could see tyre tracks lead
into the bushes – and then a set of tyre prints deeper in
soft ground, as if the car had stood there for some time

It seemed at first as if the sunlight dappling down throu
the trees was reflecting off dew in the grass. When he
closer, still perhaps thirty yards from the car in the bush
he saw that the sunlight was reflecting off shards a
splinters of glass. His boots crunched on them – many
them.

Windscreen. He knew it, casting about, kicking at
grass, treading on the deep tyre impression – looking rou
so that he saw the way the car had been heading, presuma
from the point where it had been parked.

Flattened grass, a swathe, as if something had been dr
ged from this spot ...

He hurried to the car, then, and pulled away the mask
twigs and branches, the noise seeming amplified, as if
movements were suddenly those of outrage, frenzy.

The car was empty, as he had known it would be. Th

was no windscreen – shotgun blast at close range? He wrenched open the driver's door. Glass on the seat, in the padding of the roof-lining, in the dash ...

Flies buzzed – but only a few, because there was no body, and only a little blood which was quickly drying. The bodies must have been dead almost at once. No blood on the back seat. Perhaps Haussman had –

Had only got out, to be shot or bludgeoned. It didn't matter, and they had not heard the shots, not here down in this dell on the far side of the lodge.

Latymer was sick with understanding. The procession of bodies. Sick, too, because of his own danger, the danger that discovery brought. Sick for Aubrey, too ...

The car had been left for collection. He scouted round hurriedly, but saw no sign of the bodies. He reluctantly, yet urgently, climbed the dell again, looking back only once. The events down there were part of the past already – what he had to do now was warn Aubrey.

'Getting rid of a couple of SDECE men is serious, if it ever comes out – but *us*?'

Latymer felt Aubrey watching him closely from the window. As for himself, he sat and stared at a painting above the library fireplace – a landscape that seemed to need a stag or a maiden. Something anyway – even an empty car, and a small bloodstain.

To Aubrey, looking from the window, Latymer's fine features were haloed with light, the grey hair made golden again. He looked remarkably young, the features softened by the light behind them. There seemed a confidence about the man that he could not share, a sense of invincibility given him by his club tie and sober suiting.

'I don't know – but I shouldn't count on coming out of this unscratched. You've heard of the Bushido-Endgame, after all ...'

Latymer looked quizzically at him. 'You mean that he might kill us, and Gardiner, and do whatever damage he

can before anyone catches up with him?' His voice was un
certain. 'I don't believe it.'

'What about Stolze, that East German in the BfV in '57
He was the case who gave rise to the term Bushido-Endgam
– maximisation of destruction by a double on the point o
being exposed. He wiped out two networks singlehanded
rolled up a ciphers department, and leaked two dozen o
more new names to the Abteilung before he got himself sho
And there have been others – our man in Prague, Dempster
killed the head of his section, gelignited the records o
Czech Intelligence for Africa and Western Europe, the
threw himself under a train as the police were chasing hi
along the platform of the station . . .'

'All right – I believe you! He may do that. What do w
do, then, to prevent it?'

'I'd call "C" direct, but I'm certain that would seal ou
fate, as the romantic writers have it. Of course, it's possib
that Constant, having been a "mole" for so long, and, I'
certain, never having been activated as a double, might n
feel obliged to blow himself to the heavens to damage us .
In which case, he'll simply pack his bags and disappear.'

'You think so? I confess I don't understand the man
can't feel the way his mind works.' Latymer was langui
again, as if the more sordid aspects of his fate had vanishe
replaced by something more comfortable and gentlemanl
'How do we stop him?'

There was a long silence, and then Latymer heard Aubre
say, 'We have the weapon here to hand. The thing is, oug
we to use it?'

'What do you mean?'

'*Who*. His name is Richard Gardiner. We might ju
complete Haussman's design for him. A fitting epitaph.'

'You're serious, Aubrey?'

'Deadly serious.' He stood up, crossed the room to t
bottle of Scotch on top of the cabinet. 'Just like Consta
to offer a man blended instead of malt. He probably bu
it in a supermarket. I suppose that should have warned m

years ago . . .' He poured himself a drink, turned to Latymer, who held out his glass to be replenished, and said, 'I am serious, Hilary. We must get rid of Constant. We can't afford another scandal, and we can't have him going over, under or behind the Curtain and making us all look fools – imagine the restructuring, the blown networks, the names . . . No, we can't have that. Philby was bad enough, but Constant is privy to the whole picture! And he won't stay here, not now, unless he can get rid of us, bluff the French, and be certain that no one will ever ask questions. And he can't be certain of that.' Aubrey was punctuating his sentences by pointing with the hand that held the glass. The liquid slopped in the tumbler, catching at Latymer's attention as he tried to find opposing arguments.

There were none.

'I accept – most of what you say. But – how can we?' It was almost a plea, as if he were now being asked to bloody his hands, having retained some moral aloofness up to that point. He seemed to resent his position.

'I know what you feel, Hilary – systems, routines, all tell you not to kill your superior. But, you do believe that he has killed Haussman and his driver on *suspicion*, no more than that? Well, do you?'

After a long and strained silence that became artificial and evasive, Latymer said, 'Yes, I do believe it. And that makes the rest of it true.'

Aubrey touched him on the shoulder. 'Thank you, Hilary. I'm glad you're with me.' He moved away, as if embarrassed at the nakedness of Latymer's eyes as they looked at him, and the sense of lost innocence they seemed to express. He sat down heavily.

'Right. Where shall we begin?'

'Do you think Constant will run?'

'Yes, I do. On balance, he will come to consider that to be the wisest course. However much he would like to get back at Gardiner and us. He'll settle for having paid off Haussman, and be blowed to the rest. Let us assume that he arrives in this room before very long, and tells us that he has to go back to London, or some such – then what do we do? And what about Gardiner?'

'Do we have to use Richard?' There was the same plea in the voice, as if Latymer remained uncommitted.

'Yes, we do.' Aubrey's face was grave. 'If we kill Constant, then we ourselves may be considered agents of a foreign power ...' His lips twisted round the euphemism. 'Only a rogue element – that was what Haussman intended when he used Gardiner – and he was right.'

'Right? What *right* is there in the matter?'

'Very well. Lie down and let the Constant steamroller drive straight over you! Or let him get away with this, and make his peace with his Moscow control!' Aubrey was angry, scything in his sharpest voice at the hedge of moral intractables that Latymer had erected around himself. 'You want to do *nothing*, Hilary? It is not in our power to do nothing, to let things carry on as they are. Can't you see that?'

Latymer's face acquired a sullen scowl, then, after a silence, he nodded his head. 'Yes, I see that. It's just that ...'

'I don't want him to be used, either. But he has to be. Constant has to die in his identity as the "Wolf", not as a Russian "mole". He will do that, if we release Gardiner.'

'*If* Constant decides to leave,' Latymer warned.

Constant did not stay for lunch. A little after twelve, he entered the library, and was at his most affable and untrustworthy. Aubrey, conscious of the game the Deputy was playing, acted as if he suspected nothing. Constant stood in front of the fireplace and looked at each of them.

'I'm afraid I've been summoned back to London – immediate from "C".' He let the words sink in. 'A small aircraft will be at my disposal this afternoon – a field near Sheffield. I'm sorry there won't be room for the two of you and your captive ...' He smiled. 'However, I would wish you to return to London as quickly as possible. There is sufficient transport here for the purpose.'

'What is our destination, Deputy?'

'Ah. I don't think we've finished with Mr. Gardiner yet. It had better be the country house for the moment. Hand him over to the staff there, and we can wrap this thing up with your reports.' He added: 'It only remains for me to thank you both, sincerely. I am most grateful for your help ...' He nodded to each of them, then said, 'Well, I must be on my way. Good-day, gentlemen.'

As soon as the door snapped shut behind him, Aubrey said, 'I'll delay him – get Gardiner out of the cellar, and make sure he's armed!' Latymer seemed charmed by Constant's smooth, normal tones. Aubrey barked, 'Do it! Gardiner has to be free before Constant leaves. When he's gone is time enough to get through to "C" and try to explain this thing. Get on with it!'

Then he was through the door, and calling after Constant. Latymer did not hear what he was saying as he and Constant went into another room and he crossed the hall, heading for the cellar door.

He flicked on the light, and walked gingerly down the stairs. There had been no one on guard at the door, and he wondered for a moment if Constant had killed Gardiner. There was a strip of light coming from beneath another door, and the coolness of the cellar struck him. The smell of mustiness, but not damp. Something unused, like the house itself. He pushed open the door, and Evans looked up from his chair where he was reading a newspaper, and avoiding looking at Gardiner, who was slumped in another chair, his head on his chest.

'Hello, Mr. Latymer, can I help you?' Though he completed the words, he did not complete the sense. Latymer had the revolver in his hand, and it was pointed at Evans.

'Untie him!' he snapped.

'What the hell ... ?'

'Do it!' It was an echo of Aubrey's bark, and it seemed to retain its force, urging Latymer to action, cleansing the sullen body of lethargy and reluctance.

Evans looked into Latymer's eyes, and then did as he was told. Latymer looked into Gardiner's face, which revealed the gratuitous bruising of his interrogation. The grey eyes were sharp with concentration, but puzzled also. And the beginnings of a sense of hope. Latymer recoiled almost physically from the killing thing he saw in the face.

Beyond the single naked bulb and its hard circle of light, the racks of bottles retreated into shadow. Yet the nature of the place as a wine-cellar could not mask its naked function at that moment. The eyes focused only on the lit area, the whitewashed bare walls and the chair placed in the middle of the flagged floor; and the form of the man in the chair and the guard.

'Who did this to him?' he snapped at Evans, fumbling with the last knots behind Gardiner's back.

'Simons, mostly.'

Gardiner stood up, and rubbed his wrists, then chafed the discoloured ankles where he rolled down his socks. The cords had been tied very tightly. Then he looked at Latymer. 'Time to go, is it?'

'For you, yes. Constant is leaving.' He glanced at Evans. 'Tie him up.' Evans appeared affronted, and Gardiner surprised. 'Don't waste time – just do it!'

Evans sat meekly in the chair, events having outpaced his optimism, his essential lack of gravity with regard to his work. Gardiner tied him swiftly and expertly.

Latymer, realising that Evans had to overhear, wasted no time.

'Constant is leaving. He has to be stopped. For all sorts of reasons, you're the man to do it. You know why. He's killed the Frenchman and now he's on his way out.'

'You *want* me to kill him?'

'Yes, damn it!' He watched Gardiner pick up Evans's gun from the chair where it had been meekly laid, and looked at Evans's wide face, still shocked. 'Evans, this is Mr. Aubrey's operation, as from now. Be sensible and sit where you are. I'll release you before very long – understand?'

'Yes.'

'Now, Richard. Upstairs. Constant is heading for Sheffield, and that means the road through Wigtwizzle, and then alongside the Broomhead Reservoir to Ewden. It will be one chance, and only one. Understand?'

'Give me a long gun.' Gardiner said simply. Latymer watched the face set in a pattern he had only glimpsed before in the car opposite Notre Dame when Perrier was deliberately released by Haussman; in briefings in Baker Street a world ago. Now it seemed his natural and habitual expression.

'There isn't one –'

'Bloody incompetent!' Gardiner snapped. It was grotesque, the most unexpected of remarks, but in the narrow tunnel of Gardiner's view the only one applicable. He grimaced and turned to the door. 'What about him?' he said of Evans.

'Leave him!' Latymer snapped in sudden unease.

Gardiner smiled contemptuously, and then went through the door and up the stairs. Latymer saw the situation outpacing him now: Gardiner was in control of his own destiny, crude and violent as it obviously was – and as he wished it.

Wooller was crossing the hall, a rifle slung over his shoulder. It was chance, and Latymer, had he seen him before Gardiner, might have cursed it. Gardiner, seeing only the gun clearly and the bulk of the man out of focus and muzzily dark, fired from the waist, twice. The explosions rocked Latymer, echoing off the panelling of the hall, the dark, closed doors. When he saw Wooller, he was lying on the chequered tiles, sprawled untidily on their clean pattern. Gardiner bent over him and picked up the Armalite rifle, checking it expertly.

'Which way out – the back way?' he snapped. Latymer's brain was still clogged by the noise and the dying.

'This one . . .' Latymer said slowly, opening the door to a sitting-room he remembered overlooked the rear lawns which sloped gently to a line of trees and the rest of the grounds. 'Make your way down towards . . .'

Gardiner heaved up the window.

'I'll make my own way,' he said softly. Then, as if he remembered something forgotten for a long time, said: 'I'll kill him for you – sometime, if not now.' Then, as if in valediction for the whole of his past, he asked, 'Wish me luck?' It was something from the door in an aircraft fuselage, or over a wartime dinner at the officers' club.

He lifted his leg over the window sill, the rifle slung over his shoulder, and then he dropped onto the gravel path separating the house from the grounds. Latymer watched him running, swiftly and warily, and it was as if he was watching a conscious performance of arts he had either forgotten or never used.

The door banged back on its hinges, and Constant entered the cool airy room behind him, his face suffused with anger, a pale tinge to the dead skin; Aubrey was just behind him, and then Laker, a gun in his hand.

'Kill him – kill him now!' Constant ordered, his mouth working as if the words were filling it. 'Kill him, Latymer!'

Laker, as if sensing something hidden in the situation, elbowed Constant and Latymer out of the way.

'I'll do it!'

He raised the .357 Magnum to his eyes, arms stiff, and carefully squeezed off three shots. Gardiner did not turn, but broke the course he had been taking, beginning to weave erratically towards the trees, a stiff line of markers ahead of him. It was evident he was unhit.

'Get a rifleman!' Constant snapped. Laker left the room. 'Get men after him – everyone!' Constant called after him. 'I want him taken or killed!'

He turned to Latymer, still at the window. Gardiner was beyond the trees now, and spotted only with difficulty, a shadow dwindling across the grounds.

Latymer said, 'I'm sorry, Deputy . . .'

'Sorry?' Constant asked in his most austerely mocking

tone. His eyes were bleak. 'Why, what have you to be sorry for, Latymer?'

'I – should have shot him when I saw him coming into this room. I don't know why I hesitated.'

'Yes, you should have. How could he have managed to escape?'

Aubrey saw a furious activity behind the unreflecting surfaces of Constant's eyes, as if a sequence of images through the wrong end of the telescope. Constant was beginning to panic. He knew why they had released Gardiner.

'Sorry, Deputy – but we'll have him again before night, I can assure you of that.' Aubrey was brisk, officious. He saw Constant's eyes gleam, as if he guessed the whole strategy in one moment of insight.

'Quite. It will, of course, mean a serious reprimand, if not worse.' He nodded as if he had seen the challenge, his mind stooping to the cast gage. Aubrey saw that the last fragment of the puzzle fitted. He had read Constant correctly. But Constant, he saw, still believed he could win.

'I am leaving now!' he snapped. 'Get things organised.' He left the room, and Latymer looked at his watch. Then he looked out of the window. A figure ran towards the trees, but there was no sign of Gardiner.

'Has he time?' Latymer asked.

'I hope so. He's all that's left to us. Without him, the cupboard is bare.' His face became grim. 'He has to get him! I'm willing to bet the telephone is out of order.'

Aubrey turned to the window, and the lawns down to the trees were empty. Gardiner was well ahead of the pursuit. He heard a car engine fire, and the screech of tyres on the gravel of the front drive. Constant was on his way, and suddenly Aubrey felt helpless. It required an act of faith to believe that Constant was driving to his death. He looked at Latymer's features, and found no such faith there.

He wanted to look at a map, suddenly – a failure of nerve.

Gardiner's chest heaved with the effort. The Armalite

rifle, held in one hand, banged painfully against his thigh with each stride. He was in Wigtwizzle now, converging on the road that Constant's car would have to take. He was heading for the reservoir, praying that he would be there in time and that the doubts tumbling in his mind would leave him. He wanted, with a choking desire, to be in time. His blood pounded in his brain, and his body ached from the beating they had given him.

As he ran, there was a sudden fusion of memory's circuits, prompted by pain, and it was as if his whole person jolted in him, and screamed at the perspective that was his life. He was running through the woods, from the train towards the river, and the SS were firing behind him. 1944. Without checking his stride, he squashed the memories bubbling through. In a moment, no more, he was calm, and he thought about nothing then. One nightmarish moment, and it was over, that tunnel of pain down which something horrid and misshapen made its way, and he afraid to look at its face, which was only a mirror. Now, there was nothing but the path through the trees, and the ears straining to pick up the first sounds of a car.

There was nothing to think about, except the hatred of Constant, which made his grip on the rifle sweaty with fearful anticipations; that was enough to substitute for the flashing imagery of the past, the bright fish beneath the surface of the blood, winking in and out of shadows.

He had to repay. The past had become a formula, a slim package of blood and bone and nerves and brain, with a name and an identity, and a life that could be let out ...

The trees opened, and the stream of the Ewden, flowing into the reservoir, was just below him. He paused, breathing suddenly loud in the silence of the racing blood, and then crossed the last yards to the minor road which crossed the stream by a narrow bridge which humped over the water.

He was on the bridge when he heard the car. On one side of the bridge was the reservoir, a sheet of dark water under the cloudless hot sky, and on the other the trees and the stream. And then the car, heading out of Wigtwizzle, two faces in the front seats, a driver's and the cadaverous patch of white that was Constant's.

It took no more than a second. He regretted, clearly and distinctly, not having reached the bank of the reservoir and the overlooking trees on the other side of the bridge, from which Olympian height he had designed the end of the drama. He regretted his suddenly turning body, the noise of the car, the untidiness and unfitness of it . . .

He switched the rifle to automatic, and squeezed the trigger. The windscreen dissolved in a frosty gleam, then emptied back into the car under the awesome pressure and firing speed of the rifle. Then the car swerved into the side of the bridge, halting itself abruptly – with sufficient force to eject one of the occupants through the shattered windscreen and onto the bonnet.

Then the car toppled, and the body slid onto the road as the car eased itself down the bank towards the stream, where it slid with a drowning gurgle into the Ewden.

The magazine was empty, and the deafening din silence again before the body popped comic and doll-like through the shattered windscreen. Gardiner's hearing came back, and he could apprehend the drowning of the car, distantly. Then he walked over to the body, and looked down at it. He turned it over with his foot.

The head had been lying in a pool of muddy water, and the white shirt and neat collar had become soaked and stained. One manicured hand was outflung, and the nails were dirty. The head flopped stupidly in a way its owner would not have allowed in life as the body turned onto its back.

There were four holes in the thin, dead face, and lacerations, more vivid in places than the small blue holes, from the flying glass of the windscreen. There were tears in the cloth of the jacket, and a red patch, beginning but stemmed, on the shirt, near the breastbone.

The man had been wiped out, swept aside.

Gardiner stood there for a little time, as if paying some final valediction to the crumpled thing that was growing cold, and which now, even to him, was less than nothing.

And he was satisfied. Pleased with the complete reduction of the living Constant to this nameless, breathless, stained thing on a narrow bridge, riddled and erased. His satisfaction was complete.

Tiger Hunt!
JADE TIGER
Craig Thomas

The bait: a defecting Chinese agent selling secrets.
The trail: every bolt-hole and hide-out from Hong
Kong to Berlin.
The quarry: JADE TIGER
JADE TIGER, the thrilling new masterpiece from
Craig Thomas, finds espionage veteran Kenneth
Aubrey facing his toughest assignment yet. In six
months he could crack the Chinese defector. But he
doesn't have months, he has weeks. Two weeks
before the Berlin Wall is bulldozed into history. Two
weeks to discover the truth behind the network of
misinformation coming his way . . .
JADE TIGER is the story of a race against time, a
chase across three continents. Ranging from the
heart of Communist China to the Australian
Outback. JADE TIGER is classic thriller writing of
the highest order.

ADVENTURE/THRILLER   0 7221 8451 4   £2.25

Don't miss Craig Thomas' other bestsellers:
FIREFOX
SNOW FALCON
RAT TRAP
WOLFSBANE
SEA LEOPARD
also available in Sphere books.

Pick up the pulse-pounding action where
FIREFOX left off . . .

FIREFOX DOWN

Craig Thomas

Bestselling author of FIREFOX

FIREFOX IS MISSING . . .
EVERYONE WANTS IT BACK . . .
THE RACE IS *ON* TO RECOVER THE FIREFOX!

FIREFOX: the NATO codename for a supersonic Soviet warplane so
deadly it can wipe the West out of the skies.

Stolen for the West by ace U.S. pilot Mitchell Gant, the Firefox is shot
down in a hair-raising dogfight. Now the plane lies submerged
beneath the icy waters of a frozen Finnish lake, waiting to be salvaged
by British Intelligence. And Mitchell Gant is running for his life, from
the tracker dogs and helicopter patrols of the KGB border guard. As
international tension mounts, East and West wage a desperate
offstage battle – a frantic race to FIND THE FIREFOX!

ADVENTURE/THRILLER   0 7221 8449 2   £2.25

"A remarkable tour de force".
THE TIMES

DUNN'S
CONUNDRUM
STAN LEE

Harry Dunn seemed to have out-spied the masters when he set up the library. Twelve people worked there, and they had access to absolutely everything. All the strategic information, all the secrets big and small – on tape, on film and on paper, they had the lot.

But one of the Librarians had somehow beaten the system, and had clandestinely leaked their biggest secret of all. And with East–West relations reaching countdown level, that left Harry with one hell of a headache . . .

"Tough, funny, quirky, bawdy, suspenseful".
JOHN D. MACDONALD

"The mind-bending fantasy is conducted with earthy relish".
SUNDAY TIMES

0 7221 5455 2   ADVENTURE THRILLER   £2.95

A SELECTION OF BESTSELLERS FROM SPHERE

FICTION

DUNN'S CONUNDRUM	Stan Lee	£2.95 ☐
GOLDEN TALLY	Pamela Oldfield	£2.95 ☐
HUSBANDS AND LOVERS	Ruth Harris	£2.95 ☐
SWITCH	William Bayer	£2.25 ☐

FILM & TV TIE-IN

BOON	Anthony Masters	£2.50 ☐
LADY JANE	Anthony Smith	£1.95 ☐

NON-FICTION

THE FALL OF SAIGON	David Butler	£3.95 ☐
THE AMBRIDGE YEARS	Dan Archer	£2.50 ☐
THE SUNDAY EXPRESS DIET BOOK	Marina Andrews	£2.50 ☐
THE PRICE OF TRUTH	John Lawrenson and Lionel Barber	£3.50 ☐

All Sphere books are available at your local bookshop or newsagent, or can be ordered direct from the publisher. Just tick the titles you want and fill in the form below.

Name _____

Address _____

_____

Write to Sphere Books, Cash Sales Department, P.O. Box 11, Falmouth Cornwall TR10 9EN

Please enclose a cheque or postal order to the value of the cover price plus

UK: 45p for the first book, 20p for the second book and 14p for each additional book ordered to a maximum charge of £1.63.

OVERSEAS: 75p for the first book plus 21p per copy for each additional book.

BFPO & EIRE: 45p for the first book, 20p for the second book plus 14p per copy for the next 7 books, thereafter 8p per book.

Sphere Books reserve the right to show new retail prices on covers which may differ from those previously advertised in the text or elsewhere, and to increase postal rates in accordance with the PO.

TRIGGER OF VENGEANCE

For almost half a lifetime ex-agent Richard Gardiner has
buried his searing memories of treachery and torture, of
that nightmare time in the bloody cellars of the Gestapo
and the hideous sick double-cross that followed when
freedom appeared to be within his grasp. The killing-
ground is among old friends and enemies. The search is for
the man who always betrayed and murdered by proxy. The
man known as WOLF . . .

'Classic espionage . . . fiercely told' THE TIMES

Craig Thomas' other bestsellers
RAT TRAP   SEA LEOPARD
FIREFOX   JADE TIGER
SNOW FALCON
are also available in Sphere Books

0 7221 8452 2   ADVENTURE/THRILLER

UNITED KINGDOM £2.95

ISBN 0-7221-8452-2

00295

9 780722 184523